He could sense that she did not want him to leave, and he found that his feet would not take him to the door behind her.

"Vashti," he whispered.

"Yes?"

"You know I've wanted you a long time."

She started, her hand flying to her throat as she gazed at him through the deep pools of her dark eyes. "You . . . want . . ."

"—For a long time," he continued.

A deep flush rose from her throat to her brow. She swayed unsteadily on her feet for a moment, and when he noticed, he rushed to her, taking her in his arms, her skirts swinging against his legs. Pressing her tightly against him, he took a long draught from her lips, parting them to reach the soft places beyond. She shuddered, her hands clutching his shoulders until her fingers dug into his flesh. "Oh, Jared," she cried. "Me too."

THIS SHINING SPLENDOR

by Janet Louise Roberts
writing as Louisa Bronte

Also by Louisa Bronte
from Jove

THE VALLETTE HERITAGE
THE VAN RHYNE HERITAGE
THE GUNTHER HERITAGE

THIS SHINING SPLENDOR

JANET LOUISE ROBERTS
WRITING AS LOUISA BRONTE

A JOVE BOOK

THIS SHINING SPLENDOR

A Jove Book / published by arrangement with
Series International, Inc.

PRINTING HISTORY
Jove edition / March 1984

ISBN: 0-515-07610-4

Jove books are published by The Berkley Publishing Group,
200 Madison Avenue, New York, N.Y. 10016. The words
"A JOVE BOOK" and the "J" with sunburst are
trademarks belonging to Jove Publications, Inc.

PRINTED IN THE UNITED STATES OF AMERICA

*To the industrial families
that helped make America great...*

LEMUEL LANDAU
b. 1804–d. 1866
(1) m. Esther Marks
b. 1809–d. 1846
(1829)

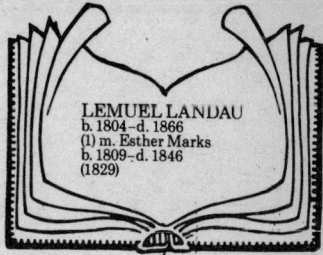

Vashti Roth
b. 1828
m. Hermann
Cohen (d. 1855)
(1844)

Jared
b. 1830
m. Miriam Ginzberg
(1854)

Malachi
b. 1832

Sapphira
b. 1859

Amaris
b. 1847
m. Peter Malchus
(1863)

Eden
b. 1850
m. Asher
Landau
(1868)

Gideon
b. 1855
m. Rachel Dallmeyer, b. 1860
(1880)

Rosemary
b. 1857

Peter
b.
1864

Andrew
b.
1866

Esther
b.
1867

Judith
b.
1869

Simon
b. 1881

Franklin
b. 1884

Thaddeus
b. 1888

Miriam
b. 1890

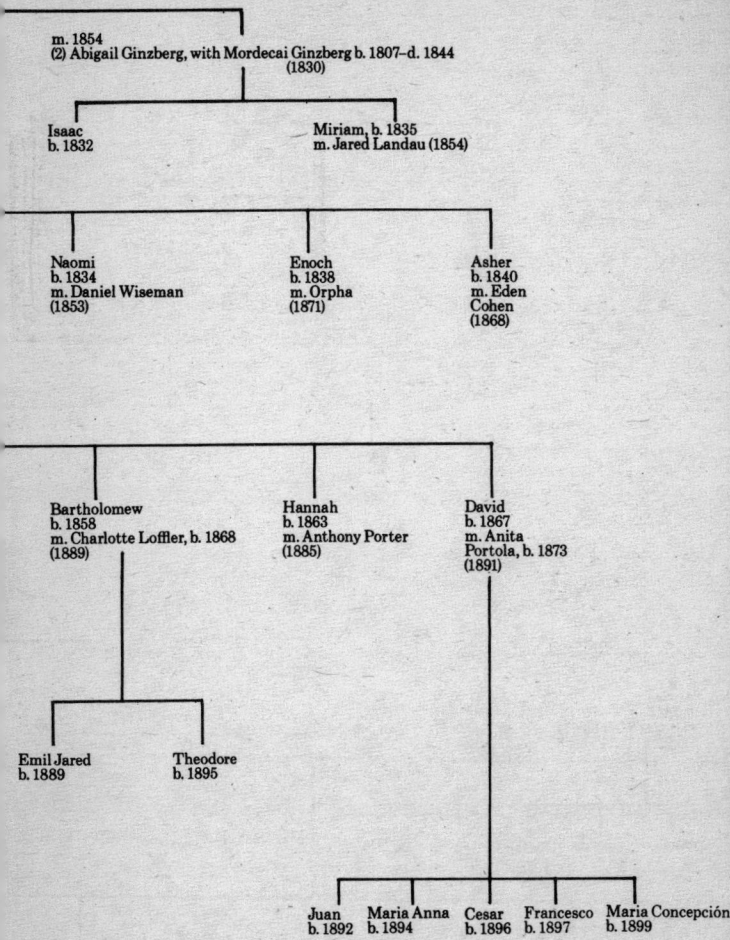

m. 1854
(2) Abigail Ginzberg, with Mordecai Ginzberg b. 1807–d. 1844
(1830)

Isaac
b. 1832

Miriam, b. 1835
m. Jared Landau (1854)

Naomi
b. 1834
m. Daniel Wiseman
(1853)

Enoch
b. 1838
m. Orpha
(1871)

Asher
b. 1840
m. Eden
Cohen
(1868)

Bartholomew
b. 1858
m. Charlotte Loffler, b. 1868
(1889)

Hannah
b. 1863
m. Anthony Porter
(1885)

David
b. 1867
m. Anita
Portola, b. 1873
(1891)

Emil Jared
b. 1889

Theodore
b. 1895

Juan
b. 1892

Maria Anna
b. 1894

Cesar
b. 1896

Francesco
b. 1897

Maria Concepción
b. 1899

PART I

1850–1875

Chapter 1

Bent by the weight of his backpack, Jared Landau's body ached with weariness caused by hiking deep into the river valleys of Germany for a month. As a traveling peddlar, he sold his stock of lace, scissors, thread, watches, and nails to eager housewives who relished the finer things of life. And now for the first time in a month he was nearing his Swiss homeland.

Crossing the velvety meadows watered by Switzerland's and Germany's wide rivers, Jared paused to let his pack slip to the mossy earth and wipe away the perspiration that clung to his face. He gazed at the vineyards set in neat rows on the hillsides, and beyond to the distant village, looking doll-like in the distance.

Switzerland, he mused, was so different from Germany. His people, for instance, had a passion for clocks, which they fixed in every village church tower. Jared, putting a hand to his brow and squinting his eyes, could just make out one that read five minutes to three. He half smiled. The clocks were in steeples that towered to the heavens as if to underscore his people's preoccupation with the Calvinist religion—forever gently chiding them that time was slipping away and every moment must be employed to obtain their lifelong goal, salvation.

Yet his people also appreciated beauty, not just the rigors

of the spirit. Every house in the village, every outlying farm-house, was covered with ornate frescoes featuring scenes of Christian saints, passages from the New Testament, flowers and meadows and the mountains that loomed protectively all around them.

Jared raised his gaze still higher to those majestic peaks so beautiful to behold, yet so dangerous. Many a traveler had died trying to cross the peaks to freedom. Knowing the least risky routes, Jared had been thinking of traveling farther than he had ever dared travel before. He wanted to go to America. He'd heard it was the land of the free. In his travels, he'd heard that the Germans who had gone to America—allowed to do so freely by authorities—did not return to their homelands, they were so satisfied. Could even a Jew go and be free?

Shaking his head, Jared lifted the pack, settled it on his broad shoulders, and strode on through the meadows of blue alpine flowers and white and gold daisies. He spotted a yellow flower with a brown stamen, the color immediately reminding him of the deep brown eyes of Miriam Ginzberg. He reveled in her memory, her long brown hair that flowed loosely down her back, her shy way of gazing at him, her slim, energetic body, her eager willingness to help others.

The memory pained him. How could they ever be happy? There were few ways to escape the straitened circumstances that every day threatened to engulf them. They were Jews, and every action was made under the censoring eye of Jew-hating authorities who dictated where Jews slept, where they lived, and when they could marry.

Home was a white-painted house nestled in the Jewish section of Lengnau, Switzerland. Jared thought about it with a deepening longing as the driving spring rains showered down on him. Soaked, exhausted, with only a little money left from selling his wares, he was weary of more than just the long, hard journey. He had paid so many Jew tolls on his way home—and would have to pay one more to reenter the Jewish ghetto of Lengnau—that the month's trip would show little profit.

But he entered the town, paid the Jew toll without flicking an eye, and strode down the narrow cobblestoned street to the door he knew was the entryway to peace. Even as he approached, the door was opened. He bowed his head as he stepped over the threshold. It was late on a Friday afternoon in May 1850, and everyone would be preparing for dinner.

"Peace to all within," Jared said in his deep voice.

A gentle girlish voice answered, "Peace be with you."

Jared slid his pack to the floor and bent over to unfasten the straps allowing time for his eyes to adjust to the different light. Then he straightened up to gaze into the greeter's dark brown eyes: it was Miriam Ginzberg. He smiled, his smile slowly fading as he noted the look of concern on her lovely face; something was wrong.

It was then that he heard the voices raised in the parlor. "It is not right, it is not just!" Someone was crying. "How can they deny us the right to marry? Tell me!" Jared recognized the angry voice of Miriam's mother—Abigail.

Jared's father—Lemuel Landau—answered, "It is God's will that we should suffer." But his voice was bitter.

Jared raised his eyebrows at Miriam, whose pretty oval face was pinched with pain. "The authorities have refused to let them marry," he stated, no question in his tone.

She nodded. "Yes. They said my mother and your father do not have enough money to marry. Yet if they were to report all the property they owned, they'd have it all taxed away."

"So is it always," Jared said.

He rubbed his shoulders and revolved them slowly to relieve the ache. Miriam looked at him in concern. "Come, rest—I will bring some hot soup," she murmured.

He nodded as she disappeared down the dark hall into the kitchen. Removing his heavy soaked coat and shapeless brimmed hat and setting his round skullcap on the top of his curly black head, he strode into the parlor. The argument immediately ceased.

"Jared," his father cried in surprise. He crossed the room with his arms outspread and hugged him deeply, then blessed him for his safe return. The Landau and Ginzberg children looked on in wonder, only hanging back long enough until their parents had finished their greetings. Then they raced forward to kiss Jared's cheeks and amid their cries of excitement, they fanned around him on the floor or on the few chairs in the room to heatedly exchange the latest news.

Their excitement at his return was palpable, though Jared knew they were distressed about this latest collision with Swiss authorities. They passionately wished him to do something; after all, their hard-working father and the lovely Abigail Ginz-

5

berg deserved to marry. And a combined family would survive the difficult ghetto life better than a single one, alone. It was only common sense.

Miriam entered the room quietly and set a bowl of soup in front of Jared. He thanked her warmly and lifted the bowl in his reddened hands, sipping the hot soup and letting it course through his chilled body, relaxing his tired limbs. Miriam had also brought bread, from which he tore off bits, then ate ravenously.

As the others relayed news, Jared observed the others more than listened to them. They hadn't changed. His sister, Naomi, sixteen—a year older than lovely Miriam—physically resembled her. Both had dark and serious eyes framed by dark hair. They were both good looking girls, and someday they would make such wonderful mothers, he thought fondly.

Isaac Ginzberg, Miriam's brother, stayed a little apart from the others, commanding a corner wingback chair instead of huddling near the fire with the others. He listened quietly, having little to say. Since his father had died, he had been the man of the Ginzberg family and the responsibility had weighed heavily on him. Two years younger than Jared, he was now eighteen.

Jared glanced at his own three brothers. They all shared the dark handsome features of the Landau family, though in different proportions. Malachi was shorter than the others, with brawny shoulders. He was eighteen, Isaac's age, but he seemed much less responsible in his belief that the world owed him something and that he deserved to sit in comfort as riches poured into his lap. He envied Jared because he felt Jared's job was adventurous, gave him the freedom that Malachi hungered for. Jared's soft mouth twisted. How would Malachi take the insults, the suspicious glares, the dogs set on "the Jew peddler," the bargaining and the haggling as shrewd housewives tried to drive down the price that was already low? Only patience and a placid face against their hostility enabled Jared to earn anything at all.

The other two were Enoch, twelve, and Asher, ten—too young to participate but old enough to listen intently to all that unfolded. Asher was also old enough to be held responsible for his often selfish and sly behavior, a trait to which their father was blind. Jared for instance knew that Asher had stolen some objects from several Christian stores—nails, an apple,

6

a raffia bottle with a candle still intact. When he had confronted Asher, the boy had lied at first, then claimed he'd found the objects in a trashbin.

"Do you know what trouble father could have if you're caught, you young fool?" Jared had asked angrily. "Jews are always suspect. What if this were discovered? You would make much misery for us all!"

"They won't catch me," Asher had scoffed, his dark eyes brightly burning over his latest treasure—a cigar box. "I'll sell these and have money!"

The memory of their confrontation still pained Jared.

Miriam and Naomi disappeared into the kitchen; they had to finish preparing supper, but it wasn't before long that Miriam appeared in the doorway inviting the families to the freshly set table. Jared stood up wearily, holding his hand to his tired aching back. He caught Miriam's sympathetic gaze and smiled back. She blushed at first and then quickly slipped into the kitchen. She was a sweet, kind child, he thought as he straightened with an effort and followed the others. They circled a large wooden table that Jared and his father had constructed by hand and sat on rude chairs or boxes. The cheerful clatter of tin spoons and pewter plates, along with their laughter, soon rang out in the air. Life almost seemed normal.

Jared noticed that his father and Abigail Ginzberg exchanged glances often during the course of the meal. She was a brisk, competent woman with a gentle round face framed in dark brown hair so like her daughter's, though now hers was streaked with gray. She would be a good wife to his father, Lemuel. The authorities were fools for refusing this marriage. No one should be allowed to interfere in other's lives, he mused.

But for Jews in Lengnau interference was a daily occurrence. They could do nothing without permission, and they were heavily taxed in all matters.

It was so cruelly unfair. If the real amount of money they owned was revealed to the authorities, the family would have nothing left to live on. And they had labored too long for that to happen. Any Christian Swiss would have been praised for the Landaus' enterprise. And they needed the money for dowries and for their futures.

Jared sighed. Something had to be done. There must be an answer. He scanned the faces of his family. All of them struggled to appear happy, yet he sensed an underlying despair. And this latest blow by the authorities particularly had them downcast.

They had few choices. "Trust no one but the family," was their motto. Lemuel had voiced it often, and Jared firmly believed in it. He had learned early that he could trust nobody outside the family; it had always been so. And yet the family now could barely support its members.

His father drooped over his bowl of soup.

Abigail bent anxiously toward him. "Eat, Lemuel, eat. You cannot go without food."

Naomi's sweet, anxious face turned from one parent to the other. Jared had always felt closest to her, though now he could see that her face had become motherly, concerned, over the last few months. She had grown up rapidly. Since their mother's death, she had fed and clothed the rest and, in Jared's absence, kept the house going. The demands on her were too much for a young girl.

Was the time ripe to bring up what was on his mind? Should he pose again the notion of their departing this safe but freedomless town for a possibly dangerous but freedom-bound place like the New World?

Yet the New World would mean a whole new beginning, a new start, renewed hope. America. His family had scoffed at him the last time he'd brought it up, his father had shaken his head, yet Jared was convinced it was their only hope. He would try to thrust aside the thought, yet the notion beckoned him again and again, crying out the name that reverberated through his mind, America!

Later that evening the families attended the synagogue together; they'd muffled themselves against the driving rain in scarves and cloaks and coats, and while Jared and the other men spread out in the pews on one side of the temple, the women sat in those on the other side. He watched Miriam and her mother protect Naomi by flanking her. He nodded. Naomi needed this marriage of her father and Miriam's mother, Jared thought, largely because she had struggled along for so long by herself. Enoch was supposed to help her, but he sometimes got caught up in his own amusements or in Asher's mischief. They were two young scamps, Jared mused, with too much time on their hands. Time would no doubt take care of them, but until then—

8

He bowed his head in prayer and tried to lose himself in the timeworn Scripture, finding comfort in its words, while his mind veered back to their troubles, scanning them for a solution. If only the authorities would leave them more free—

"God, help me guide my family," Jared whispered, holding his head in his hands. "Help me to help them—there must be some way—"

He ought to resign himself to their lot, he thought. It had been theirs for centuries. Their ancestors in Central Europe had been driven from one town to another, from one country to another, in ceaseless turmoil, as scapegoats for one ill after another. If the crops failed, it was because the Jews had cast a spell on them. If a cow died, it was because a Jew lived nearby. Worse yet, when wars erupted and disease spread, the Jews were blamed. And most ominous of all, if Christians had borrowed money from the Jews and could not repay, they reviled his people as cursed moneylenders, the cause of all economic tragedies. "Kill them," they would cry. Then all debts would be wiped out! A simple solution. One the generations had resorted to, resulting in his people being hounded from pillar to post, hated, suspect—why, why, why, God? What solution is there? Where can we go where we are not hounded to death?

"America!" an inner voice seemed to cry.

Jared sat tensely, his back stiff, his unseeing gaze on the white-haired man at the altar who was reading the Torah to them. The voice that recited the sacred words was drowned out by his own piercing whisper: "America!"

On his journeys into Germany he had encountered women talking excitedly, or men who had gathered in the village squares to discuss in breathless eager words: "America—my son writes—my cousin says his uncle wrote—I have heard—I had a letter from America—there is work, work, work! There is land to take! Homesteading! The economy is good! The pay is good! America!"

And Jared and his family had received letters from distant relatives, as well as from friends who had dared to make the fearsome journey. "In America there is no Jew toll! Christians and Jews pay the same taxes! A Jew can own a house and land without bribery. He can do business in metals, not like in Europe! He can loan money and the law says it must be repaid. He can marry whomever he chooses!"

They had not believed such freedom existed. "Dreams, idle foolishness," Lemuel had scoffed. "Listen to them. They believe gold is in the streets for them to pick up!"

"America," the voice in Jared's mind whispered. "Freedom. I can be free. Free! Free! To live as other men, to stand upright! Freedom. America!"

Jared scarcely heard the remainder of the service. His father thought he was weary and needed sleep. His understanding smile touched his eldest son. Such a fine boy, his smile said, such a fine hard working son.

That night Jared lay awake in the dark because his aching body refused to relax into sleep and his mind ranged over everything, like a dog searching for a place to hide his bone. He turned his ideas around and around. Perhaps the men he'd spoken to had been bragging. Perhaps they felt compelled to conceal a misjudgement in leaving Switzerland for some magical fabled life in America, and found the reality hardly half the truth! Or perhaps they exaggerated—

Yet the fact remained—he consoled himself—they had stayed, not returned! They said they owned homes. They worked in stores or on farms. Their letters were cheerful and hopeful. Before he knew it, Jared drifted off into a deep sleep.

The next morning he awakened slowly. It was apparently late in the morning. The sunlight beamed in through the narrow windows, streamed across the bed, warming him. Is it an omen? he wondered, stretching on the bed to his full height. He felt good. The sun shines, and I waken thinking about America and freedom!

He heard his father scolding his brothers gently. "Let him alone, he is weary, he works hard!"

Enoch said in a whining voice, "But I have to do his work also! Why can't he get up and help?"

Asher chimed in, "He has fun all month, has adventures and goes about the world, then when he comes home he lies abed all the morning while we sweep and mend the cart!"

Jared grimaced and swung his long legs off the mattress. Let the boys learn the hard way what it was to work and peddle! To walk from early morning to late at night, to lie in a meadow on both warm and cold nights because nobody would let him sleep in their barn. To endure scorn, even fear, because nobody knew what those Jew peddlers would do next! To have dogs set loose on him— He must ask Naomi to mend his trousers.

He had cobbled only the leg after that one dog attack on his way home.

Lemuel remonstrated sternly, "Let him be, let him be!"

And Naomi chided more softly, "It is the Sabbath! None of us works today, you know that. Asher, Enoch! Peace!"

"But he should not sleep late!" they continued to grumble, and then the voices died away. Lemuel must have taken them by their ears to the parlor for Scripture reading.

Jared washed and dressed in his best clothes, which Naomi had cleaned and pressed for him. He went down and joined the prayers, reading aloud in his turn, while all the time he was thinking of the New World.

The Ginzbergs came over later, and the two families shared their noonday meal. Already they felt like one family, not two, though their houses were separated by two streets. Abigail helped get the dinner, and Miriam and Naomi were like sisters, helping each other silently, as if they didn't need to exchange words.

Conversation at dinner was spare. All of them were thinking of the future and what it might bring. The girls washed the dishes, then joined the others in the parlor. Jared had built up the fire, bringing in more wood and arranging the logs in the hearth skillfully. Now he stood at the mantel, gazing down into the red heart of the fire. Could they do it, could they risk the journey? What if they only met disaster at the end of the tunnel? How he would blame himself—

"What are you thinking, my son?" Lemuel asked from his seat on the sofa beside Abigail. Already they seemed to belong together, Jared thought as he gazed into his father's anxious face.

Jared straightened his shoulders, bracing himself for a renewed flood of objections and doubts. "I have been thinking, Father, that our solution is—America."

"America!" Lemuel cried. "What madness is this? It is too far away! We have discussed this before. It is impossible!"

Abigail was silent, gazing up at Jared. Her eyes had begun to brighten.

"Yes, America," Jared said firmly. "Yes, it is far away. Far from troubles, from the prejudice we deal with constantly. I have heard talk in Germany. Men speak of America as a land of many freedoms. Even Jews can walk about without paying tolls. No passport from one area to another. And our taxes

11

would be no more than what's imposed on the Christians."

"That is not believable," disagreed Lemuel. "I know what the letters say—but how can there be such a place? Everybody taxes Jews, for marrying, burying, for coming and going—"

"Not in America. And we could go, Father," Jared said slowly, carefully. "We could sell the two houses—"

"We could marry!" Abigail breathed. "We could combine our families—we could work and not be terrified all the time—"

Jared happened to glance at Miriam's face as she sat beside Naomi. Her face was uplifted to him, her hands clasped together, and her eyes glowed. Hers was a look of worship toward him. She seemed to say with her eyes, It is a miracle!

He smiled at her. "It would be good, a good life," he said as though just to her, though he spoke to them all. "We would work hard, yes. It will be expensive to obtain permits to leave here, and we will have little money left after the long journey. But after we arrive—our work will be for us!"

Miriam's steady rapturous gaze uplifted him, and he persisted in calm arguments, meeting all their fears and doubts with self-assured and steady answers.

And so it was finally agreed. They would seek permission to leave.

Jared did not depart on Sunday afternoon to travel north to peddle once more. His pack remained in the corner of the kitchen. Lemuel and Abigail consulted the other Jewish families, especially the elders. They agreed to do all they could to help the two families leave, though they were dubious about the wisdom in even trying.

Then Lemuel, Abigail, Jared, and Isaac went to the Christian authorities. Despite their steady arguments, they experienced humiliation and insults. Finally they offered bribes, slipped in an envelope to each man.

Jared had decided on their main "reasons" for leaving. "We wish to join some of our relatives in America," he said.

"They will support you?" The authorities asked. They wondered why nine Jews wished to leave the fertile valley of the river Surb. Why should anybody want to leave? They must have dark and devious motives.

"No, we will work hard," Jared said meekly. "We wish only the opportunity to live near our relatives."

When one hard man wished to refuse them, Jared gathered

12

all his patience. "And it will mean nine less Jews in Lengnau, Your Honor."

The man scowled, thought, and finally accepted some gold coins before stamping their papers. Jared watched the stamping on the inked cloth and the handwritten papers, holding his breath all the while. Would this be the final permission?

It was, and that night the families rejoiced together, some with happiness and others with doubts. But it was exciting to plan what they could take with them, what they must leave behind, what route they would travel.

"Let us go to Philadelphia," Jared urged. "The letters from Pennsylvania indicate that Jews live in peace beside their Quaker neighbors, who trouble nobody."

"I cannot believe there is such a place," Lemuel muttered, but he allowed himself to be persuaded by gentle Abigail.

They left their houses in the care of one Jewish elder who would handle the sales. The houses must be offered three times to Christians and refused before any Jews were allowed to buy them. That could take a long time. The Jew secretly paid the Landaus and Ginzbergs for the houses ahead of time, so they had increased their coffers even more before leaving. No one could forecast what would happen along the way, much less after they arrived.

A cart was packed with their possessions—Abigail's bedstead, which had been in her family many generations; several paintings of ancestors in hardwood frames; three folding rockers which would be useful on their trip as well as in their home later; and sacks of food, clothes, shoes, cloaks, some books, sewing boxes, and the peddler pack.

They walked to the banks of the Rhine near their home, then purchased passage north on a riverboat, to Coblenz, where they changed boats to another heading west, to Rotterdam, in the Low Countries. For the first time in most of their lives, they were traveling to new and strange places, and the experience was frightening.

Lemuel prayed day and night, muttering the words at times, saying them aloud at other times. "Lord God, forgive me if I have gone astray! Forgive me and help me, in my misery. Do not lead me wrongly, oh Lord. I have my two families to care for. Do not allow me to give them more misery!"

Jared felt even more grief than his father, for it was he who had suggested the journey. But Miriam, concerned about his

13

worried visage, cast him a smile and whispered, "I know it is right! We shall be free and happy in the new land! America! It will be good to us, you will see!"

And he squeezed her hand gratefully, made more cheerful by her trust and the glow in her eyes.

The youngest boys grumbled when meals were not on time or when they ate cold food or if they had to help draw or push the cart out of mud. They whined almost constantly, unable to raise up their eyes to the hills and see the beauty that lay beyond them. When Abigail scolded them, they were insolent and Lemuel had to be stern with them.

"But she is not our mother!" Asher would protest.

"She will be soon, though she may no longer wish it, seeing your stupid and ungracious behavior!" Lemuel would say sternly.

Finally they came to Rotterdam. Jared, Lemuel, and Isaac tramped the docks searching for the right ship. In German they asked for a ship bound directly for Philadelphia, and finally, after much anxious waiting, one slipped into port.

Eagerly the Landaus booked passage, but to their consternation they had to wait three days while the ship unloaded and took on fresh water and provisions.

It was a fine day in midsummer that their ship finally sailed out of port. Their spaces were in the rat-infested steerage, the women separate from the men, though both families slept on uncomfortable board planks called bunks. They cooked in small buckets over a common fire, taking their turns.

The weather was fine for a time, until their ship started plying the Atlantic and they encountered storms, which made the sailing vessel veer from side to side sickeningly.

"But it isn't as bad as in the spring and autumn," Jared encouraged them all. He had been talking to several friendly sailors, learning English as quickly as he could. It would be useful in the New World.

Abigail smiled faintly and pressed her handkerchief to her lips. Lemuel urged her to walk on deck with him and held her arm anxiously as they staggered about.

Jared took the arms of Miriam and his sister, to walk them around deck, where the sea breeze would refresh them. Isaac urged Malachi to come with him. The other two boys amused each other, getting into mischief as they raced about. Jared let them go, knowing the sailors would give them a prompt rebuke if they went too far.

14

Jared and Miriam leaned against the railing. Naomi had drifted away, to lean over the back railing and gaze at the ship's blue-white wake.

"You are not afraid of this new world," Jared said in a low voice.

Miriam smiled and shook her head. "It could not be so bad as in Lengnau," she replied with quiet confidence. "And I have prayed much. I prayed before you came home. All were so gloomy and in despair. I prayed that when you returned, you would have a solution for us. And you did!"

They were so close, he could feel her against his warm body, and he studied her beautiful oval face, the soft pink mouth. If he were to kiss that mouth . . . he was startled by his own wish.

"You prayed—for me," he said soberly.

"Yes," she said, her sweet breath against his cheek. Then she added, "And for us all. And when you said the word *America*, you said it like a message from heaven."

"It was that, a message from heaven," he dared to tell her. His father might have scolded him for letting his mind drift during prayers. He might have said he was presumptuous, thinking he heard the voice of God. "I was praying that night in the synagogue, desperately asking for help. And I heard a voice say America to me. Clearly. Do not say this to Father or your mother, please. They may think me mad or wicked. But I did hear that voice."

Miriam nodded, her lovely straight brown hair caught in a pink ribbon at her neck. The hood of the cloak had fallen back, and Jared wished he could stroke that soft delicate hair, so full of light and life. "I believe you, Jared, and I shall not tell of it. I think it must have been the Lord speaking to you. And He will be with us and comfort us. He is a good God, and our people have suffered much. Surely He will help us in the New World."

"I hope so. I mean to work hard—"

"You always do, Jared," she said gently.

"Thank you." They leaned together on the railing and were silent, his arm linked in hers to brace her against the bucking ship tossed by the huge waves. It was good to hold her, to be near to her, to hear her sweet soft voice.

On the voyage, that long three-month journey, they grew closer. Lemuel and Abigail were absorbed with each other.

Isaac and Malachi talked together about what they might do on landing in America, how they might find work. Naomi was absorbed with her thoughts and tactfully left Miriam and Jared together often. The younger boys thought of nothing but their play and their stomachs.

So Jared and Miriam talked frequently, strolling along the deck. When they grew tired, they sat on boxes and gazed at the sea, or at nights they studied the stars and talked of the future. Anything was possible in the new land, and there was cause for much jubilant, if cautious, speculation.

The ship encountered storms several days in a row, but the foul weather never lasted long. July and August was a good time of year, said one older sailor, pausing in making rope to speak to Jared and Miriam; she was quiet at his side.

"Yes, yes, good days, these are. Now in the winter, you'll see ice on the ropes, me lad! Yes, ice, and the winds howling, and us blown miles out of our path, and foundering maybe. Lucky you are to have come this time of year!"

"Luck—or God's will," Miriam said as they strolled on. "You came from Germany in the spring, and we left in early summer. God's hand must be leading us."

Jared closed his hand over hers, which was resting in the crook of his arm. "I hope so, I pray so," he said. He had never felt so happy, so hopeful. How rosy life seemed!

Only a few months ago he had been struggling from one village to another, stopping at isolated farmhouses, urging housewives to buy his goods. He had endured snows, rains, thunderstorms, lightning, dogs, bulls in the pastures, hostile farmers and townsmen. Now he was here, a man of leisure for a time, strolling with a pretty girl on his arm! And facing the future with hope, not despair.

"It is a miracle," he said.

And Miriam nodded. "Yes, a miracle," she said softly.

One evening Jared dared to draw Miriam into the shelter of his cloak as they stood on deck in the wind. "Are you warm enough, or shall we go below?" he asked.

"Oh no, let us remain just a little longer," she whispered.

Her face shone bright in the moonlight, and stars seemed to gleam in her eyes as she gazed up at him. He bent and touched his lips very softly to hers. What a jolt he felt, what pleasure at the sweet touch!

He felt her catch her breath. Straightening, he said nothing, holding his breath in the hope that she would not object or reprimand him. She simply leaned her cheek into his shoulder, saying nothing. They stood motionless on the deck that way, then gazed up at the bright stars in the west. And both of them thought that those stars also shone on the land where they would one day live.

Chapter 2

"Philadelphia is like the Promised Land!" Miriam cried shortly after they arrived in the American city and began looking for a hostel in which to stay until they found a home. "The beautiful lawns, the fine houses, and no one spits at us!"

The young boys laughed and jeered at her. But Jared set his strong jaw. "She is right. It is like the Promised Land. We have such freedom here—such freedom I have never dreamed of in my entire life!" he scolded.

Jared felt intoxicated sometimes by the deep draughts of freedom he could feel in the very air and on the streets through which they walked. He had no Jew tolls to pay as he crossed from one neighborhood to another, and marveled at the tentative smiles of children when he peddled his wares up into the Pennsylvania Dutch countryside—smiles instead of frowns and fear. And after he had been peddling for a year, the housewives and farmers were beginning to welcome him and his goods!

"Ah, Mr. Landau," one farmer called out early in the spring as Jared trudged along the road. When the man pulled up his wagon, Jared had moved to the side of the road fearfully, for the man was carrying a whip in one hand. But he made no motion to hit Jared with it. "You will be sure to stop at my farm? It is just down the road a mile, that white house with the red barn," he said, as he pointed with the whip. "The good wife, she complains she has no sharp scissors and no threads!"

Jared had gaped at him in amazement, then managed to nod. "Yes, sir, I shall be sure to stop there!"

He had trudged on as the farmer turned his team of horses around and drove off in the opposite direction. At the white house, the man's wife had greeted Jared happily, had given him a glass of cold water before eagerly buying from his stock of goods.

What a difference between this land and Switzerland! he thought.

Jared's pack was stocked with threads, small lengths of cloth, scissors, and nails, as always. But he had added blacking polish for the newfangled iron cooking ranges that had replaced the kitchen fireplace in most farmhouses. The ranges burned coal and made a mess, the housewives complained, but the polish helped. If only it did not leave a residue of blacking on the housewives' hands, which was hard to remove from their fingers. But they bought it from Jared nonetheless.

On the long journeys, Jared had plenty of time to think. He always brought a good book to read with him, and at night, as he lay in the fields ready to sleep, he would read for a time. He was also learning English. Miriam helped him there. She was taking courses with Naomi and the boys, and when he came home on weekends, she taught him what she had learned during the week. All of them were eager to learn in the New World, and to their surprise they were allowed to attend public schools! They would never stop marveling at the opportunities here.

Jared's pack was as heavy as ever, but his heart was much lighter. He now looked to the future with hope and resolved that when he was settled, earning a little more money, and when Miriam was older and had finished school, they would marry. It was understood between them.

And how Miriam had bloomed! She seemed prettier by the week. Her cheeks were pink, her hair glossy, and she was no longer too lean, now that she dined on that good hearty German food. She sang as she worked, and nobody was around who would scold her as they did in Switzerland.

Lemuel had married Abigail as soon as they had arrived in Philadelphia. Their families had joined the synagogue, and they attended regularly.

They even managed to buy a house, a small one and in a

19

muddy section on the outskirts of Philadelphia. It was run-down, small, and cramped, but it was their own! And they had not been forced to purchase permits.

Lemuel had taken a job in a grocery store owned by a Gentile. Everybody had wondered why a Christian would hire a Jew, but not after they met the owner, Mr. Harold White. The man had two daughters, who had married and left him alone. The Landaus were shocked that daughters would do such a terrible thing. Not only did they marry and leave his home and him unprovided—for his wife was dead—but they left Philadelphia as well, moving to another state! And they rarely came to visit! The poor, dear man, the Landaus thought. The old man defended his progeny, of course, and said he was pleased that they had gone to live in Florida, where the fishing was so excellent.

Mr. White was frail and white-haired, though not much older than Lemuel. How he rejoiced to have such a fine scholarly man to work with, he told Lemuel. When business was slow, they rearranged the shelves, and Lemuel would shift forward the goods that looked good from the windows and attract customers. And they would talk of books and travel and ancient wisdom. "A good man, for all his religion," Lemuel would say to the family.

Mr. White lived over the store and moved about slowly at night, gazing in a lonely way through the windows to the lamplit streets below. Lemuel, having returned late at night because he'd forgotten to do something that day, had caught glimpses of him several times.

"Our family shall remain together," Lemuel swore to the assembled members. "What a shame it is. That decent man goes to church every Sunday, and his daughters have no thought of him!"

Lemuel vowed that the family would work together, would plan together. They would cling to each other, help each other, and all would be good. The world outside mattered less than the world within their home.

Lemuel urged his sons to come to the grocery store and work after school. They came, both for the pennies they could earn and for the fun they could have. Malachi enjoyed driving the grocery wagon and its amiable white horse to deliver goods. The boys swept out the store, opened boxes, set goods on the shelves, and cleaned the small stable in the back. They often grumbled, but when they were paid, spent the money eagerly enough.

One week of spring storms, Jared dared to remain home instead of peddling in the countryside. Taking a week off was an unaccustomed luxury. He used the time to help paint the house—and was awed by the fact they did not have to get permission to do so! Other wonders abounded, too. They could nurture their property openly and were encouraged to do so. In Lengnau, a Jew who wished to make improvements on his house was held in suspicion, if not impounded to undergo severe questioning by authorities.

In the early evening, Jared washed up, donned his coat, and took the small carriage to the hardware store where Isaac worked for two wealthy men—a father and son named Jerome and Herman Cohen. He liked the men, finding them kindly, scholarly, and devout the few times he dropped by to see his brother.

Jared discovered the store still open, with customers dashing in from the heavy steaming rains to purchase nails or paint or carpenter's tools. Isaac had often said that as long as the customers came, the Cohens would remain open. They were keen businessmen, and this was how they had become wealthy. Jared watched them work.

Jerome was small, bearded, and slight. He owned three stores in Philadelphia and went from one to the other to supervise them. His son, Herman, was frail and ill much of the time, his spectacled narrow face beaming vaguely on all who spoke to him.

Jerome Cohen was the first to look up and see Jared. He smiled kindly at him. "Peace be with you," he said in Yiddish.

"And with you." Jared bowed his head to him, then entered the back part of the store to wait. He liked to watch the bustle and to listen to the rounds of bargaining.

Herman was working patiently with a fretful woman who had been sent to the store by her husband. "But he wants a particular kind of hammer. See, he drew this picture of it," she said, then showed the older man the drawing.

Herman adjusted his spectacles and studied the picture. "Ah, I see how it is," he murmured, and poked about in a drawer, taking out one hammer after another until he found the right one. "This is it, you see?" he explained, comparing it to the drawing.

Finally satisfied, she paid him and departed.

21

As she left, a woman entered the store holding two small girls by the hands. Herman's face immediately brightened, then he strode forward to grasp the hand of one of the girls. "My dear Vashti, out in this terrible weather?" he scolded the woman gently.

She laughed at him kindly, her red lips enlivened. Taller than her husband, she was voluptuous, her round figure beautifully set off in a yellow silk dress and darker silk cloak. "We shall not melt!" she cried. "The girls were impatient for you to come home, so I said we would take a walk and meet Papa!"

Herman's face softened at this display of devotion. His glasses steamed up, and he had to wipe them vigorously. The older girl clung to his hand when he had finished, and he gazed down at her and then at the younger one adoringly. What pretty children, Jared thought. Both girls were lovely, the older one slim and dark and small like her father, the younger one with shining black curls, a beautiful face, and black sparkling eyes.

And the mother! Jared could not keep from staring at her. She attracted all gazes in the dusky store. Vashti Cohen's figure was so full and glorious! She had glossy black curls, which enhanced the purity of her magnolia-white face. Yet there was fire and passion in her, a sparkle in her black eyes, so huge and intelligent. Her black eyebrows shadowed her eyes, giving them emphasis, and her forehead was broad. Jared knew that Vashti was a woman of beauty and magnificent vitality, and he felt deeply disquieted.

Herman almost forgot his work as he stared at her adoringly. Jerome gently called for him to wait on a customer. Herman flushed, then returned quickly to his duties. Vashti retreated to the back of the room, where Jared was sitting. He nearly bolted from his seat to give her the one rocking chair in the room. She smiled broadly and greeted him.

"Peace be with you," she said, her voice rich and deep.

"Peace be with you," he murmured, and stood back as she sat down gracefully. The older girl came to her and leaned against her knee. The woman's slim white hand caressed the child's straight dark hair. "What beautiful children you have, madam!" Jared exclaimed.

She smiled up at him, her red mouth full and sensuous. Her dark eyes met his straight on, then glanced away with no hint of flirtation intended. He sensed a well of sensual feeling that had never been tapped. He drew a deep breath, chiding himself. She was a married woman after all!

"You are most kind. I am a fortunate woman," she said, her full voice like a bowl of plums, he thought.

They waited in silence, he uncomfortably. She finally murmured, "My name is Mrs. Cohen. And you are—?"

"Forgive my ill manners." He stepped toward her and bowed. All decorum had flown from his head! "I am Jared Landau. Isaac's mother married my father, as you may know."

She smiled quickly, deliciously, her face lighting up in newfound friendliness. "Ah, you are of that family! Of course. What a fine woman is Abigail Landau. Your house is blessed."

"You are very kind."

"I have seen you in synagogue with your wonderful father. Isaac speaks of him as of a mentor."

"We are a close family."

"Good, good." She smiled, her gaze resting on her husband as he fussed about a counter of yard goods; his lank hair had fallen across his narrow forehead. "My parents died when I was young," she confided unexpectedly. "I have missed having a family. The Cohens have been so good to me."

Jared thought it was an odd way to speak of her husband and father-in-law. But as he watched her, he suddenly saw that there was affection in the way she looked at her husband, without there being deep, passionate feelings. Jared drew a deep breath. He felt as though a door had been unlatched and he had peered inside, without having a right to be there.

It was a way of his, this ability to understand people with only a few words, a keen observer, his father would boast! Yet it was a curse. He was a good salesman, he knew when a housewife longed for a particular article. But he also understood people's unexpressed suffering and longings and he felt uncomfortable with the intimacies they had never meant to expose.

The rain poured down outside, and the hour grew late. Still the Cohens stood patiently and listened to their customers, trying to please them. Yet Jared knew people had drifted in because the lamps were lit and it was a warm place to stand for a time.

Jared shifted his feet and dared to speak again. "May I know the names of your lovely young girls?"

23

Vashti Cohen stirred, and the smooth skirts over her knees slid sensuously over them, as though they loved to touch her. Jared could not keep from staring at the shape of her legs, the silk hugging them daringly. "My older girl here is Amaris, and my younger one is Eden."

"Lovely names, and fine girls," he murmured, though he had observed how Amaris stood still and the younger one, Eden, darted about mischievously through the store, grabbing whatever objects she could reach. Her grandfather also watched her worriedly, distracted from his selling as she grabbed a rag doll or a broom or a length of cloth dangling from the counter. Her laugh would ring out as the object was rescued from her, or she would pout and speak shrilly in anger.

"You have no children of your own?" she asked politely.

"I am not married yet, madam."

Her smooth red lips parted in a generous smile. "You have not then experienced the joy of having children of your own. I wish you that joy one day, sir. There is no pleasure to equal having children of one's own, watching them grow and develop." Her voice was tender and sweet.

Eden tugged crossly at her father's hand. "Papa, I want to go home. I am hungry. I want my supper!" Her childish voice echoed as she raised it shrilly again.

"Yes, yes, my angel!" he reassured her, and glanced hopefully toward his father.

Vashti Cohen, hearing this exchange, spoke firmly. "Eden, come here, and stop bothering your father in his work!"

"No! I want to go home!" the girl pouted, and dashed about the store when her father tried to hold her beside him.

Jerome Cohen sighed and shook his head. "It is time to stop," he said reluctantly. "We will go home now." He crossed to the door and pulled down the shade, then did the same on the windows next to the door.

Herman obediently nodded and began to put dustcloths over the counters. Isaac held the door open for the last customers, who regretfully departed the warmth. Vashti sat in silence until they were ready. Jared felt she wanted to rush out, but held herself firmly in check. She had much self-discipline, yet something in her longed to run and cry out even as her little Eden did. She had acquired patience, yet he sensed it was not natural to her.

Finally they parted, saying good night to each other. Jared

drove the small carriage, while Isaac sat at his side, saying little.

Jared was full of curiosity, yet he did not know how to satisfy it. He hungered to know more about Vashti and her husband and what seemed to him to be a difficult marriage. "He must be much older than she is," he finally said.

"Oh yes." Isaac nodded. "Some fourteen years."

"The marriage was arranged by the rabbi?"

"No, by her father." Isaac bestirred himself to say more. "She was sixteen when her father lay dying. Her mother had departed this life some five years before that. They had money and only one child. Her father worried that she might be married for his money. So he turned to his old friend Jerome Cohen, and they arranged the marriage to his son, Herman, who was very pleased and proud. He loves her still very much as you can see. They have the two girls and hope for a son one day—naturally."

"Naturally," Jared murmured, frowning into the darkness and rain. The water poured off his shapeless hat as he stepped down from the carriage, which had come to a stop at the small stable behind the house.

"Now Jerome and his son have three stores," Isaac added suddenly and matter-of-factly.

Then Jared understood. The girl had been married for her money, after all. She'd been paired with a docile, scholarly man, all her passion bottled up inside her since she was sixteen. She'd had a child probably a year later, and had her money taken from her and managed by her father-in-law. Still, all would come to her one day. Her husband was much older and frail. But Jared had to wonder uneasily. Was it right that a woman should be married for her money, married against her wishes, her will? It was the law, it was the custom—but when did the woman's feelings enter the picture?

Isaac's voice intruded into his thoughts. "She has a maid and a cleaning woman," he added. "Still, she cleans and does the laundry herself much of the time and insists that the scrubbing be done well. I dined once in their home. She is a very good cook, everything was prepared by her own hands. Mr. Herman explained it so."

"A fine woman, God's blessing on her," Jared murmured. But as they marched into the house, Jared was upset he could not forget Vashti's red lips.

*   *   *

Time flew by, too quickly. Jared was always on the road,
but what time he lost with his family, he gained in creating a
network of customers who burst into smiles whenever he appeared on their doorsteps. In two years' time he had so many
orders for his stove polish, he needed to find a chemist through
a South Street dye factory to help him improve his formula.
"Which ingredients leave the residue on the housewives' hands?"
he asked of the chemist—an older one—in the Sixteenth Street
townhouse.

The chemist shrugged, the question posing no problem for
him. After thanking him, and insisting he accept a fat fee—
against his objections—Jared went home thoughtfully, rumi-
nating over what he'd learned.

He labored some weeks in his spare time, cooking up messes
on the stove at home and working in the stable with various
compounds. Finally he came up with a polish that cleaned
without leaving behind the awful black residue on the cleaners'
hand. In excitement, he and his father ordered cans made, and
brewed the mixture weekly. Then during the week Jared sold
the cans to customers who glowed with pleasure and satisfaction. The family marveled that they could keep their profit
instead of turning it over to another maker, or a government
agency.

Now the money flowed in. Abigail would gasp excitedly
over the weekly accounts. "More for the bank, dear Lemuel!"
she would cry.

Lemuel's wages at the store had increased, and they saved
carefully for their dream of starting a business of their own.
Then one afternoon in 1854, Jared returned home from peddling
to find them very excited. He slipped the pack to the floor,
murmured his greetings, and listened to their news.

"Mr. White's daughter came home!"

"She wishes him to live with her!"

"He was so excited, he cried!"

"She wishes him to move to Florida with her!"

"She worries about him, is it not fine? Our poor, dear man,
how good he is! How he deserves a dutiful daughter!"

Jared finally managed to get a word in edgewise. He turned
to Miriam. "But what about Father's job?" he asked. "What
about the grocery?"

Miriam sighed deeply, her eyes sparkling. "He is selling

the grocery to Father! That is why we are all so excited! Father will own a store! Imagine that! Only four years in Philadelphia, four years in America, and Father owns a store!"

It was indeed an occasion of great joy. They had a celebration dinner, and the next day their neighbors came and rejoiced with them. Mr. White, along with his daughter, arrived later in the day to discuss the deal.

The men sat in the living room deciding on the terms of the agreement and how they would go to the bank and sign the necessary papers. Business would have long ago been resolved except the two older men would often stop and speak of other matters—about old Mrs. Smith and how her deliveries must be made regularly, about Mr. Templeton and his finicky appetite, about the apartment over the store, and about the good times they had had working together.

Mrs. White's daughter Mary smiled at them all. "I am so happy Father is going to live with us," she confided. "My children should know their grandfather!"

Abigail agreed and added impulsively, "The hour grows late, yet the men are not done talking. Will you remain for dinner?"

As soon as she said it, her hand flew to her mouth. The talking stopped as Lemuel gazed at his wife in horror. To insult these nice people, to treat them like Jews, to invite them to the Landau table with them! Surely the Whites and the others would rise up in shock and shake the dust of the house from their shoes! They would reject the deal completely. They would—

"How kind of you!" Mary said, beaming. "Do you have enough for us all? It is an imposition—"

Abigail almost fainted on the spot. Miriam hurried to the kitchen, fussing about the table service, and the seat arrangements. She finally arranged for the three youngest boys to dine at a Jewish neighbor's house, so the rest would have enough food and seats at the Landau table. And besides, Miriam reflected, Asher would have been sure to make some foolish remark and ruin everything. He had no tact, and a mischievous sense of humor.

Within half an hour, they all sat down together, and then froze. A prayer? Could the Landaus say a prayer before Christians? Miriam looked from Jared to his father, her eyes showing confusion.

"Grace before meals?" murmured Mr. White, saving the

27

moment, his silvery hair standing up where he had run his fingers through it again and again. "One of the grand Old Testament prayers?"

Lemuel swallowed, nodded, and bent his head. He prayed solemnly, and blessed them all at the end.

"Thank you, how very lovely," murmured Mary, and shook out her napkin briskly. She was a practical woman, with a sharp eye for the comfort of her menfolk. She turned to Abigail. "I have three sons, and how they torment me. Yet I miss them, now we are away for the week," she said.

While they talked, Miriam and Naomi served the food, then slipped back into their seats to eat. Jared could hardly swallow, he was so excited. Truly this America was a wonderful place! Imagine Christians and Jews sitting at table eating together and talking naturally! Silent with wonder, he caught Miriam's bright eyes, and they smiled at each other. Each knew the other's thoughts, as so often happened between them of late.

They forced themselves to turn their attention to the conversation at the dinner table.

"I helped build that grocery store with my own hands," Harold White rambled on mistily, blinking his eyes. "Never did I think to leave it while I was alive! I pounded nails into the sideboards, I built the shelves—"

"And I watched you and begged for little logs to make a store of my own." Mary said, smiling.

He patted her hand. "Yes, you did. We made a little store for you, and you put your smallest dolls into it. My, how short a time ago that was, and now your mother is gone and you are a mother yourself—"

"You plan to remain in Florida now?" Abigail asked.

"Yes, yes, my husband is happy in his new job," Mary said. "He works on the boat docks and can be outdoors all the time. The fishing in Florida is that good! His health is good—"

"God be thanked," Miriam murmured automatically. Her eyes glowed at the story. All of them knew that her husband had been ill, his lungs bad from factory work.

"Thank you, yes, God be thanked. He fishes much of the time and brings home everything left after the store has what it needs. I have a little garden and grow all our vegetables, and we have a peach tree and one of limes—"

"Limes? What are they?" Jared asked. He marveled at the things she told him, finally absorbing the fact that Florida was quite a different place from Philadelphia. Not only were there warm sunny days and cool nights, but it was very warm in winter, hot in the summer, and boasted beaches where strollers could walk in bare feet. And the men swam in the ocean! Amazing.

The conversation continued late into the evening, the families parting reluctantly. The next day they met at the bank to complete the transaction. Jared went with his father, stood by to witness signatures, and all the time he felt a sense of elation.

What an amazing world was this America! Who would have thought four years ago that such prosperity would come to them, not to mention such friendliness between Christians and Jews! To think that they could sit together at table and speak of their families and work and play in intimate terms, as friends.

Jared was possessed by such a delirium of excitement that he could scarcely breathe. He raised his dazzled eyes to the ceiling of the bank and noted the fine workmanship in the plaster, the beautiful bronze lamps. He returned to the present scene and noted the courtesy of the Gentile bankers. Jerome Cohen had an account here and had one day told Lemuel, "You should open an account and put your money in here. Let it gather interest. What? You still have it in socks in the mattress! Shameful. What if a thief should break in?"

Lemuel now turned to one of the bankers. "I have been considering opening an account here. I have money to put in," he said hesitantly, watching their expressions.

The two bankers beamed at each other and rubbed their hands. "Naturally! Naturally. And ours is one of the safest banks in the country," they assured him. They brought him forms to fill out and explained how checks worked. They told how he could send a paper to Mr. White monthly in payment for the grocery, instead of sending paper money. Yes they swore, the check was as good as money, as good as coins. Mr. White would deposit the check in his bank account in Florida. How amazing!

Finally the transaction was done. Lemuel Landau, Jew of Lengnau who had had to pay a Jew toll in order to enter the street where his house stood, was bowed out of the Philadelphia bank by two Gentile bankers, as the proud owner of a grocery store, a bank account, and a fine new checkbook.

Chapter 3

"You can't tell me what to do! You ain't my mother!" Asher cried in a rage and stormed out of the house.

Miriam's pained gaze met her mother's. They shook their heads. "How difficult he is, even more so now that Naomi has married," her mother murmured. Her hands shook as she folded clothes just brought in from the backyard line.

Miriam remained silent, feeling both angry and hurt for her mother. Asher was so rude and difficult. And she herself felt lonely for Naomi. Of course she was happy for her new sister, who had married a fine man. Daniel Wiseman had been shy and silent, bulky, and easily embarrassed when spoken to. But one could tell from Naomi's glowing face that she was a happy woman. They had married last fall and had a room in a boarding house. One day they would have a house! Daniel worked long hours in a bank.

"Friday. Jared comes home soon," Abigail sighed. "Perhaps I can speak to him. He is firm with the boys and will stand for no nonsense. Lemuel—he is too gentle with them, I fear. Such a good man, how lucky I am," she added automatically, her expression troubled.

But she was right. Lemuel was too soft with the children. Unlike Jared, Miriam thought proudly. Jared stood for no nonsense! Such a fine man he was, strong and proud, his head always held high.

As she thought of Jared, she smiled dreamily down at her ironing. She pressed the linen carefully. Jared's shirt, his dear shirt, had to be pressed neatly and lovingly. If her mother had not been there, Miriam would have raised it to her lips reverently.

She adored Jared. And in the four years they had been in America, he had gained even more in stature. How respected he was, how men listened to him, even the older and wise ones! He read a lot, especially the newspapers, and learned more all the time. He had quickly learned English, even though he had had no time to go to school.

And he understood the politics of America—he could talk with anyone about the candidates and the issues, since he pored constantly over the information in the papers. He worked so hard all week, and when he came home he read and studied, in addition to helping in the stable and at the grocery. How did he have the energy? He was powerful, that was it!

And now he was so much more hopeful than he was in Switzerland. Miriam shuddered at the memory of those bad times. They all had hope now. No longer did they cringe at the sight of a policeman or a deputy sheriff. They could hold their heads as high as anybody, and they bowed only when they felt respect. What a difference! What freedom they had, as Jared had often promised.

Miriam set the iron back on the stove and neatly folded Jared's shirt. So lost in thought was she that she started when a hand touched her arm.

"Peace be with you!" said a strong familiar voice.

She whirled about and gazed into Jared's bronzed, smiling face. "Jared! You are home early!" she cried in surprise.

"Yes. I have business to attend to," he told her mysteriously, and his handsome black eyes twinkled.

"Business?" she asked blankly. "About the grocery?"

"Hum, it might involve the grocery, yes, it might. Yet that is incidental," he added, and laughed. He put his arms about her boldly. And he bent his head and kissed her lips gently yet firmly, in the way that sent her heart beating rapidly.

She closed her eyes in rapture. How wonderful he was, so strong, so sure, so intelligent. And he loved her! He said so with his words and with his eyes and in his manner to her. What a fortunate girl she was! And one day they would marry—if he wished it.

"I must go and speak with Father, Miriam," he said gently as he released her. She picked up the hot iron and pressed it firmly to another shirt. He had set down his pack in the hallway, and she was thinking that she must start some hot water and wash his clothes for him quickly. She could be done by six o'clock, when they could enjoy the Sabbath services together.

He saw her pick up the bucket then, to go for water. "No, do not go now, Miriam."

"I would but heat water for the laundry—shall you empty your pack now?" she asked shyly.

"No. I shall not go out this week, as all is going well," he said, that mysterious smile creasing his handsome face.

Curious, she set down everything and turned to face him, her hands on her hips. "And what do you plan, Jared Landau?" she asked with mock sternness. "Do you plan to tell me, eh?"

His big bronzed hand cupped her round chin and gently stroked her cheek. "I plan to marry you," he said softly. "Miriam, will you marry me this week?"

She gasped, her heart beating wildly, and she gazed up at him in bewilderment. "Marry—this week—oh, Jared!"

"We have been pledged for this long time," he said. "And there is the apartment over the store, empty all month. I will ask Father if we may have the apartment for our home. Will that please you, Miriam?"

She gasped again, unable to believe his words. She felt a warm glow burning inside her. Marriage, not just in some distant future—but *now?*

She could not be coy and fluttery. Her feelings ran too deep. She gazed up at him, her loyal brown eyes wide and joyful. "Oh, whenever you wish, Jared. You know—I do—love you."

His long arms wrapped about her, and he lifted her off her feet and kissed her. "Dearest Miriam! I am so happy. I shall ask Father now. I shall go find him."

When he left her, her mind was in a dither. She could scarcely finish the ironing for her distraction. Marriage! So soon!

And when her mother was told a little later, Abigail too balked. "No, not this next week!"

But Jared insisted.

"Why wait?" he asked. They had money. Lemuel, financially well off, had offered the couple the apartment over the store, free of charge. And Jared was making enough to support

Miriam and himself. Isaac brought in money, and Naomi had offered to help Miriam and Abigail arrange for the wedding clothes and prepare the apartment.

So it happened. The rabbi was notified, some friends invited to the ceremony, and more appeared who were not invited, but who, because the Landaus were well known and respected, came to witness the synagogue wedding and wish the young couple well.

Miriam wore a new dress, hastily purchased from a dressmaker who kept back stock dresses. Her pale blue morning gown had a close-fitting jacket bodice. The long, full skirt gathered at her slim waist, then fell in full pleats to her shoes. A ruched silk bonnet of matching blue framed her round, pretty face, and she wore a deep red rose at her throat. Her dark brown straight hair had been heated and curled with tongs, forming demure ringlets about her face and below her bonnet.

Jared wore a dark blue frockcoat edged with narrow black braid, new shoes, and a white linen shirt with ruffles. His father had given him as a wedding gift a new waistcoat of splendid yellow hue, and his trousers were pale cream with a narrow blue stripe. He had never looked so grand, Miriam thought with great pride.

If only she might make him happy all her life! That would be her one aim and ambition, she thought. If God permitted, if God willed it, she would make him the happiest man in the world—or at least in Philadelphia!

The wedding, though hastily arranged, was a fine one, to Abigail's relief. She felt so happy to have this wedding between her dear daughter and Jared, who was like a son to her, she could burst with pride. She knew he was an ambitious and hard-working man and that he would take good care of Miriam. And her daughter loved him, and had loved him for years. What a fine marriage they would have! Now she could turn her attention to her son, Isaac, who woefully showed no inclination toward marriage. A wrongful choice! But one which could be changed. Abigail glanced about through the wedding guests for a likely candidate. A man like Isaac did not know he needed a wife until his mother showed him he did. She would plan it all.

After the reception, at which everyone drank and ate too much, Miriam and Jared drove back to the grocery store. They stepped up the outdoor flight of stairs that rose to the apartment.

The place was dark, and Jared paused to light a candle.

He found the oil lamp and lit it. Miriam stood silently, frozen by a sudden fear. Abigail had told her what to expect—but that was different from knowing how to act, from being confident—from not being afraid.

Jared was moving about, taking off his fine blue frockcoat, his waistcoat, carefully setting them on hangers which he hung in the closet. He finally turned back to Miriam, gazing at her and smiling warmly.

"Well, my dear, would you like a hot cup of tea?" he said finally, and went to the iron sink to fill the kettle from the water pump.

He was being so calm, so matter-of-fact. She swallowed and reached up to untie her bonnet strings. She managed to remove the bonnet and set it on the side table. Her pretty ruched bonnet! Her unaccustomed curly hair. Everything was so strange—

"It seemed odd—" She managed to say after clearing her throat. "Coming back—here—to the apartment..."

Jared smiled at her, after he had lit the stove. "Yes, I thought the horse would turn back to the old house! I'm sure he thinks it odd to be in our stable."

She finished fixing the tea, and they sat down at the table and drank it. "Next week, I'll make the curtains," she said. "Would you like blue or yellow?"

He considered it seriously. "I think yellow would be bright and cheerful. Yet I like blue," he said.

She laughed. "That is not very helpful!"

He smiled. "You must do as you wish, my dear. It is your home, and this is your domain."

Miriam turned serious again.

"Oh—yes, it is, isn't it?"

She had never had her own place before, a place where she made the decisions. Her mother had ruled in everything. And now it was up to her to choose the material for curtains! How odd, yet how nice.

Jared finished his tea and reached for the gazette sitting beside his teacup. "I think I'll read the newspaper," he said. "I haven't read one in two days."

She was startled, before she realized that he was being considerate. He was letting her undress for bed alone in the

bedroom. She blushed vividly and mumbled, "Then I think . . . I
think . . ."

"Yes," he said, not looking up from the paper. His face
was also flushed, she thought, though the room was not all
that warm.

She went to the bedroom and managed to unhook her dress,
though she felt all thumbs. She took off the many undergar-
ments and the hoop that held out her skirts, then donned a
long, voluminous cotton nightdress with a lace collar and cuffs.
Would he like it? Would he think she looked nice? And then
she felt hot all over that he would see her like this.

She washed herself in the little basin of cool water, not
wishing to go out and get more hot water from the kettle. And
when she felt refreshed enough, she slid into bed and blew out
the lamp. She immediately regretted her action for how would
Jared get to bed?

But he had apparently undressed in the parlor, for shortly
he came into the bedroom, in his nightshirt, leaving the door
open. The room was dim, with only light from the purple sky
coming into it from the opened windows.

He came to the bed and slipped under the sheet. They did
not need a blanket tonight, and she had folded it back neatly
at the end of the bed. The candlewick bedspread had looked
so nice, too—she felt a moment's regret that he had not seen
it. All white and tufted and pretty, a gift from Vashti Cohen. . . .
How kind everybody had been, how generous . . .

"What are you thinking about?" Jared asked, lying down
beside her. "You seem far away!"

"How kind everybody is to me, to us," she said softly.
"What a fortunate woman I am!"

"It is I who am fortunate—didn't you hear everyone con-
gratulate me?" he protested in a whisper.

But Miriam knew who was the fortunate one. It was she.
Jared could have had any girl in Philadelphia, in all of Pennsylvania. He was handsome, strong, and smart. It was easy to
see he would rise in the world. And he had chosen her for his
partner in life! she marveled.

He draped his arm across her gently. She gasped a little,
stiffening in spite of her resolve to lie quietly and let him do
what he wanted. Abigail had explained that all Miriam had to
do was lie still and endure what was going to happen. Naomi

35

had added, in her ear, that later on she would enjoy it. It takes time, she had said. At first there would be pain—

Pain? From Jared? Miriam could scarcely believe it—

Jared kissed her gently and then more strongly, his mouth moving over hers, biting and nibbling. "How lovely you are, how soft and smooth—" he murmured.

Miriam could only lie still. His hand caressed her shoulders, then gently pulled on the cotton that covered her full breasts. She bit back a gasp of shock. Was he going to touch her— like that?

She was deeply shocked at the intimacy of his touch. Nothing anyone had said had prepared her for this. Jared had kissed her before, he had held her, but then it had been gentle and more inhibited.

Now—now he touched her everywhere, running his hands over her rounded body. Uninhibitedly. He pushed up her cotton nightdress and massaged her thighs with his hand. She gulped to keep from protesting.

And despite her feelings of resistance there was something in his touch that thrilled her, excited her. Warmth ran through her body, from her thighs to her heart, making her heart beat faster and faster. He bent over her, and kissed her mouth again and again, the kiss growing deeper each time. She felt she was sinking deeply into an unknown abyss, into dark, mysterious depths where anything could happen.

He moved over her—and suddenly she realized he was naked! She felt his strong hard legs pressing against hers, his hands stroking her body. And something hard, urgent, warm against her thighs.

He probed, and she thought his hand was between her legs, touching her secret places. He murmured, "Let me, Miriam— do not be afraid—I must do this—"

With renewed resolve she tried to lie still and not squirm, but suddenly she felt a sharp pain. She cried out involuntarily, twisting from him as she felt the pain again.

"Just a—minute—" he gasped. "Only a—minute—" And he thrust again, more strongly. This time it felt as though he'd torn her flesh, and her thighs ached from the pressure. She bit her lips until the blood came into her mouth, fighting against the protests that threatened to erupt from her throat.

Then something burst in him, and he was suddenly relieved. It puzzled her deeply. She could not remember what Naomi had said—had she told her about this? Her head moved blindly on the pillow, her eyes squeezed shut against the ache.

Finally it was over. Jared lay back, breathing hard. "How sweet you are, Miriam," he said, gasping. "How adorable, lovely, sweet—"

She felt numb. He was so grateful. For what? Letting him do this to her? How strange was marriage—would she often feel pain, and would he always be grateful afterward? Was this the woman's part in marriage? She knew childbirth would hurt, but this as well?

Was it a woman's place to feel pain and a man's to inflict it? Why was a woman supposed to be so glad when a man chose her for his marriage partner? For a moment deep resentment filled her. Then she lay back, passive.

Jared slept deeply, snoring occasionally beside her. Miriam lay still, unable to sleep for the pain in her thighs and the bewilderment of her thoughts. Finally, when she was sure he slept hard, she rose and went to the kitchen. She dared not light the lamp. In the dimness from the night-dark window, she washed her legs and thighs. She found blood on the towel and rinsed it again.

She went back to bed and composed herself for sleep, though it did not come for a long time.

The following nights were better. Jared was tender and considerate until passion overcame him, and then he went driving on her like a stallion on a mare. She had seen horses in a field, had felt curious and embarrassed yet forced to watch from wonder. And he was like that, so strong, so forceful—

When her thighs ached no more, she felt better. And when he was gone for a week, peddling in the Pennsylvania countryside, she relaxed, used medications, and slept blissfully alone. It was a relief to her when he was gone—something she admitted only to herself.

"You miss Jared," Abigail said brightly, and Miriam smiled and nodded, not in deception, but because she did miss his presence, and knew later on it would be better. This she promised to herself.

And when he returned she welcomed him home gladly. She had scrubbed out the little apartment, bought lengths of yellow fabric for curtains, and finished making two shirts for him. Later she would make herself a summer dress. He had urged her to buy the fabric for it. It was always sweet to hear his

37

concern for her. "You have been well and busy? You have not worked too hard? Naomi came over on Tuesday as she promised, to help measure the curtains?"

"Yes, yes, all went well. See what I bought." She held up the fabrics.

He approved of her choices warmly, sat her down to regale her with little incidents from his journeys. Later they went to synagogue together, and on the way home she leaned against him in the little carriage. It was good to belong with him, and everybody surely envied her such a fine, strong, handsome husband!

The next week, while he was gone again, she made the curtains. Her brother, Isaac, came over from the hardware store to help her hang them.

"I am tired of living at home. I would like to live in a boarding house like Naomi and Daniel," he confided.

Miriam was shocked but tried to hide her reaction. Isaac had confided in her at times, and to keep his confidence she had always tried to understand and help him. He had worked hard for them, maturing into adulthood early because of the difficult years before his mother's remarriage.

"Why do you wish that, Isaac?" she asked, standing on a chair to adjust the valances but concentrating on his words.

"Oh, Mother is after me to marry. I don't want to marry. Maybe never! A family is a big responsibility. And I have had enough of responsibility. A man likes to be free—at least for a time," he added hastily. "I never had a chance to roam about, like Jared does."

She tried to comprehend his feelings. "Do you wish to peddle? Do you want to travel out with a pack? It is a hard life. Jared, strong as he is, often comes home bone weary, especially in bad weather."

"Goodness, no! I have no wish to work harder than I do already! The Cohens work from morning to night, and they think I must too! No wonder they are wealthy. No, I don't want to work harder, and I know that if I had a wife and children, I'd have to. Miriam, what I want—what I want is to be free! To enjoy life!"

Enjoy life. Her brother's words echoed in her mind. Was a person not put into the world to work, to suffer, to create new life, before going to heaven? Wasn't that what the Bible taught? On impulse, after her brother had left, Miriam lit the oil lamps and sat reading the Bible all evening—wasting time, as her mother would have said. But Miriam wanted to know where it said life should not be enjoyed.

She found nothing. Thoughtfully she closed the large volume. Jared had brought the Bible to their new home with him and leafed through it often. Miriam had not read much of it; it always struck her as men's reading. But now she resolved to do it more often—when Jared wasn't home. It had some strange words, some strange thoughts, most of which were addressed to men, sternly. "Man is born unto trouble, as the sparks fly upward," it said in the Book of Job.

And in Proverbs, so many of the messages seemed cryptic, others were clear enough. It admonished men to work hard, to keep the Lord's words, to be righteous. She blushed when she found the part about staying away from "strange women."

The words went on: "Let thy fountain be blessed; and rejoice with the wife of thy youth. Let her be as the loving hind and pleasant roe; let her breasts satisfy thee at all times, and be thou ravished always with her love."

There, she thought. That seems to mean a man should enjoy his wife. And she began to understand that Jared did enjoy her, touching and loving her.

She read the Song of Solomon and blushed deeply, though she found the song fascinating. She, too, would try to enjoy her husband's lovemaking, which had become less painful. She was beginning to relax and lie in his arms and answer his kisses with her own.

When Jared came home, he was better pleased with her and lay longer with her. He liked to caress her breasts, and for the first time, she thought she knew why. It had something to do with the elemental nature of man, which the Bible spoke of often. She wished she could enjoy the final act more, yet it seemed too closely aligned with what animals did. Jared seemed to expect more from her, some expression of joy and rapture that he himself felt. But she could not return the same height of passion, however much she tried.

Jared was shocked when he came home one Friday to find Miriam helping Lemuel in the grocery store.

"What is this? Where is Malachi? Where are the boys?" he asked sternly in front of the customers.

Miriam glanced up with a happy smile to see him, but it faded on finding him so cross.

"Peace be with you," she murmured, but he brushed away her words, demanding to know where the boys were.

"Late, my son," Lemuel said, embarrassed before the glares of his curious customers.

Jared's lips were pressed together in a grim line. Tired as he was, he started to help in the store and stayed until closing. Then he urged Lemuel to come upstairs to rest. Miriam felt guilty when she saw the weariness in her husband's face, his wet and muddy clothes. The autumn's business had been heavy.

Upstairs, Lemuel sank down into the couch, and Miriam hastily prepared hot tea. As the men drank, she shook out Jared's coat and hung it out to dry near the window. She would brush it down in the morning. Glancing over his discarded clothing, she spotted his boots—how worn and muddy they'd become! She shook her head over them sadly and set them tenderly on the sill to dry, first stuffing them with newspapers.

"Malachi and Isaac have left home," Miriam could hear Lemuel confess, his hair all ruffled under his skullcap. "I could not persuade them to remain."

Jared nearly jumped from his chair. "What? *Persuade?* What is this? They are your sons, and their duty is to obey you!" he thundered.

"I have talked with them, I have questioned them, I have pleaded—" Lemuel cried.

"Pleaded! You should order them!"

"They are of age," Lemuel said in a low, troubled voice. He shook his white head, and his shoulders seemed more stooped tonight in the black frockcoat. "I cannot prevent them. And Abigail has been scolding them both that they do not interest themselves in women. She says they are of age to marry."

"Ah," Jared said, frowning. "And do they not like women?"

Miriam was puzzled at his tone. Lemuel said quickly, as though horrified, "Yes, yes, of course! They are but young and wish to be free."

"Free," Jared said. "Free, is it? They are too restless. Freedom means responsibility. They have a duty to you and to their mother."

"We fret over the younger boys also," Lemuel sighed. "Enoch is not so bad, but Asher can be very mischievous, and he leads his older brother into trouble. Then there is scolding and noise, and Isaac says he cannot bear it."

"Asher should be whipped more often!" Jared cried.

40

"I wanted to keep the family together," his father said, his hands flat on the table, as though he had emptied them of responsibility. "They should all stay together. A man is nothing if he has not his sons."

Jared compressed his lips. Miriam saw that he was very angry. He worked hard and had little patience for those who neglected their responsibilities. He was a hard man at times, she thought, thinking everybody should be as strong.

"But that does not explain why nobody works in the store today," Jared said flatly.

Lemuel hung his head. "Malachi has obtained a job in the pharmacy down the street," he admitted. "He says he likes chemistry better and soon will start his own shop!"

"His own shop!" Jared cried. "What madness is this? He has not saved a penny!"

He glared at his father suspiciously. Miriam, sensing the mounting tension, began to bustle about preparing supper. She knew what would follow, since Lemuel in his despair had confided in her that morning.

"I have—I promised—" he stumbled.

"What have you promised, Father?" Jared asked in an ominously quiet tone.

"To pay for the shop—he will repay me someday. He likes the work. If he learns well, in six months I will buy the shop for him. The owner wishes to retire."

Jared sat in angry silence, his mouth set, his eyes blazing. He would not reproach his father, but he could scarcely contain his fury. When Lemuel had left, almost creeping out, Miriam braced herself for the storm.

Jared hit his fist on the table, just as she expected. "To pay for the shop!" he said furiously. "It is not enough that Malachi should leave home and deprive them of his earnings, little enough though he gives them! No, he will set himself up as a chemist, though he knows nothing about the field! How can my father be so foolish! He should command them, not let them tug him about by the ear!"

Miriam held her silence, letting him rave on as she prepared the supper and set it before him. Finally spent, he ate quietly. She was troubled that Jared was so angry.

They went to synagogue and sat apart, then came home together. He had scarcely spoken a word to his family. Asher had made a face at him, impudently. Enoch had giggled. And

41

his father had not had the courage to reprove them! Malachi and Isaac had sat apart in another section of the synagogue, not even with the family!

"Impudence and disloyalty," Jared fumed on reaching home. "It is not to be borne! Yet what can I do? My father deserves my loyalty. I cannot reproach him."

"One must honor one's father and mother," Miriam murmured.

"Yes, yes, of course," he said, scarcely hearing her. "It is the Lord's will. But I shall not rule my own family so! They shall not mock me and run away from work!"

"Your father is a good man and a gentle man. The boys take advantage of his goodness," Miriam said carefully. She had wanted to tell him her news, but this was scarcely the time.

"It shall not be so with our family," Jared repeated. "No, no, never. I shall teach our children from infancy that their loyalty is to the family! One can trust nobody but one's own family in this world, you know this. You know how it was in Switzerland, you were old enough."

Miriam nodded, her eyes full of pain. "I remember it well, Jared. Every whisper might be repeated, the authorities were always listening. The family only was to be trusted. Even another Jew might betray, out of fear."

"Yes, it was ever so. Only the family could be trusted. And if the family splinters, what good is it? It is like a tree struck by lightning, hollow within."

He was silent for a time, then sighed. "Miriam, when we have children—".

Sitting in her rocking chair, she started violently, nearly dropping the sewing in her hands. "Yes, Jared?"

He was pacing the floor, moving to the window then back to the table where the gazettes of the week lay forgotten. "We shall train them," he said. "Their first loyalty shall always be to the family! If one instills it early enough, they will remember it. We must do this, Miriam."

She gazed up at him, her eyes bright with admiration. He was so strong, so firm. His father was good, but weaker. From somewhere Jared had gained wisdom and strength. He would hold firm, he would hold them together, their own family!

"Yes, Jared, you are right," she cried. "You will be the head of our family, you will train our children to grow upright.

They shall respect you and listen always to your words. For you are wise, and they shall know it."

He dropped beside her unexpectedly and put his arm on her lap, moving aside the sewing. "Miriam, you are the best wife in the world. How do I deserve you? No, no, God has been better to me than I deserve!"

His unusually humble words made her eyes mist up. Impulsively she bent and pressed her cheek to his thick dark curly hair. "It is I who am grateful to the Lord," she whispered. "How good He has been to me, that I am your wife! And better yet—" she hesitated. "There is news, Jared."

"News, my love?" He gazed up at her. "What news?"

She blushed and smiled, trembling as she said sweetly, "That family you spoke of—it will begin before long, my husband!"

He gazed at her, absorbing her words, comprehending more from her smile and blush than from what she said. "Oh, Miriam—a child? We are to have a child?"

"Yes, Jared. If God wills, it will come in May of next year."

He got up, tenderly gathering her in his arms, and sitting down with her in his lap. Hugging her, he asked, "It is true, this joy is ours?"

"It is true—are you happy?"

"I am the happiest man in the world," he cried. "No, the happiest man in America! That is even better!" He laughed, then kissed her tenderly, as though afraid she might break. "Oh, what a joy! Does Father know, and Mother?"

"No," she said simply. "Only Naomi and the doctor. I wanted you to be the first in the family to know, but Naomi guessed and insisted on taking me to her doctor. I fainted last Wednesday."

"Fainted!" he said anxiously. "And you worked in the store? My darling, never again! You must take care from now on."

Jared was so tender and gentle with her that night that she willingly agreed to whatever he advised. She adored him; he was so good, so wise, so smart. And she thanked heaven above for her excellent fortune!

43

Chapter 4

Extremes of deep joy and deep sorrow washed over the Jewish community of Philadelphia in the next few months. A spell of rainy, freezing weather brought on a wave of colds and pneumonia. Several elderly citizens died in the foul weather's wake, among them Jerome Cohen. The date was December 12, 1854.

Herman Cohen grieved deeply for his wizened old father. He tried to keep the hardware stores going, running from one store to the other, braving all kinds of weather. By February 1855, Herman, always a frail man himself, was gravely ill. Vashti nursed him. Other women came to help. But all to no avail. Herman Cohen died within days.

The grieving widow was sorely beset. She had so much money that men began to court her with scandalous promptness. She sent them away with sharp angry words and turned to others for advice. Among them, Lemuel Landau and his son Jared were asked for help and counsel.

Jared gladly pitched in. He set his sharp brain to Vashti's financial matters, studying banking and interest rates, bonds and stocks as never before. All had advised Mrs. Cohen to sell the hardware stores and invest the money.

Isaac had been upset over that decision. He had worked very hard in the stores, and now his job might be lost, for he worried that the new owners would hire their own relatives and friends.

Yet Vashti astonished them all by selling only two of the stores, keeping the main one. And she asked Isaac to remain and manage it after a fine raise in salary. He accepted promptly, and strutted about with a swelled chest for a time—until hard work and anxieties made him more realistic.

"And she comes to the store to observe only when I ask what she wishes done about a matter!" he said proudly. "She is no woman to nag at a man!"

Miriam congratulated him warmly. "You are doing so well, and she trusts you, that's what is so fine."

She had gotten about more and more awkwardly as winter advanced. When it was icy, Jared forbade her to go out, for the outside steps were slippery and the inner stairs were dark. He set lamps at the bottom and the top of the stairs, but she seldom used them, just in case. Lemuel would bring home the groceries she wanted, and Isaac came every evening when Jared was gone, to make sure she lacked for nothing, and sometimes to share her evening meal and talk freely of his day.

"Mother still is after me to marry," he said angrily one evening in April. "She invites me home to Sunday dinner, and every time there is a different girl to meet! I shall from now on refuse to go!"

Miriam sighed thoughtfully. "Tell her you are too busy with your new duties, you cannot take time for courting now. Your work must come first, you have great responsibilities."

Isaac glanced at her, then began to grin. "You are very smart, my sister!" he said more cheerfully. "Of course, I am very busy. I must prove myself in the work or lose my job! I shall tell her that!"

Isaac was working hard but happily, and Miriam did not want him to feel distress. He was young still—not yet twenty-three. Why should he consider marriage so soon? Jared wasn't much older, but he seemed more mature than her brother, who was more the standard for men his age than the exception.

Miriam went into labor in the middle of May 1855. Jared was home, having remained there that week because it was time for the baby to come. And little Gideon arrived on time. He was always very prompt, his mother would tease later in his life. He was a long baby, with long sturdy feet, and Abigail, leaning over him critically, predicted he would be tall.

"What a fine, handsome baby!" she cooed delightedly. "And such strong lungs!"

The baby was a miracle and a delight. Miriam held him constantly, which the infant boy delighted in, blinking up at her vaguely and casting to all his admirers the same gummy blissful smile. His fine, curly hair was a dark fuzz on his well-shaped head. His features reflected his father's, the same strong jaw would thrust out when he wailed for his milk.

Jared could not stop admiring him and reluctantly had to depart each Sunday afternoon to return to his peddling in the countryside. He could scarcely bear to leave his blossoming wife and handsome son, considering seriously relinquishing his peddling job for some type of work that offered greater income in town.

When Enoch expressed a wish to go out adventuring—as he coined Jared's trade—Jared grimly let his younger brother accompany him for a week. To his surprise, Enoch took well to the job. He had a shy charm and determination. The housewives liked the curly-haired boy and bought from his stock of wares enthusiastically.

Jared turned over the work to his younger brother, relieved that Enoch would be out from under the strong, malicious influence of mischievous Asher, who was still in school. When Enoch got the job, Asher also wanted to drop out. "Enoch has! Why should I stay?" he wailed to Jared.

"Because you are only fifteen," replied Jared firmly. Their father, Lemuel, said little and looked troubled. "You will stay until you are at least sixteen! And study harder! Do you want to be a village idiot?"

Asher was stung. But from then on he worked harder at his studies, if sulkily.

Jared had done himself out of a job but it gave him an opportunity to look for something that could feed on and expand his experiences. He had a feeling he wanted to spread his wings and fly like an eagle! This was America, anything could happen. A banker offered to take him in and train him, but the pay was too low and the office confining.

Then one Sunday afternoon Vashti Cohen appeared at the door of their small apartment. Miriam greeted her with a smile of welcome, feeling more acquainted with the wealthy woman now that she had helped when the Cohen men had died; she had cooked and minded the children during the funerals and memorial services.

Miriam had since then gone about the neighborhood—like a gentle angel—administering to the sick and poor. She was such a fine woman, Jared thought. So generous of impulse. He would not think of stopping her unless she became worn down. She would prepare chicken soup for a sick woman or scrub floors for a family when the mother was ill. She had nursed several small children with such skill, she was much in demand. And she never accepted pay.

"The Lord has been good to me and to mine," she said. "How can I repay His kindness? Only by giving of myself."

And Jared was startled sometimes by the extent of her charitable works. Any neighbor was apt to receive her gifts of food, clothing, a small sum of money, gifts of labor. Jew or Gentile, Quaker or Catholic, all were her neighbors and the recipients of her generosity.

In her happiness she thought only to give richly of what she had already received. How kind the good Lord had been to her, she thought, to rescue her from the ghettoes of Switzerland, to carry her safely to the New World of America, to grant her the love of a fine, strong man and now the joy of a small son! Truly she was blessed.

She worked from morning to night, singing as she toiled. Neighbors Jared scarcely knew would smile at him and say, "What a wonderful wife you have, Mr. Landau! Your home is truly praiseworthy."

He would thank them gravely, wondering at Miriam's stamina. She seemed so small and frail, yet she found strength for these charitable works while keeping her house scrubbed and beautiful, her son happy, her husband comfortable. She never denied him her bed, even in weariness she received him with a smile. He wished her to be more passionate, but it did not seem to be in her nature, and he scolded himself for the wish. She was always gentle and sweet to him.

Jared never wearied of the sight of his wife with the baby after a feeding. She would come from the bedroom, her dress neatly buttoned up the baby at her shoulder burping contentedly. She would rock him to sleep, crooning to him, her round pretty face shining with pleasure. She had become a little more plump from the birth, but he found the additional weight attractive.

The baby was now almost two months old, and was trying to hold up his head. His eyes were turning darker, and his dark hair was more full and curly. Jared forgot to read his gazette in the pleasure of watching them. Miriam smiled across at him.

"What time does Mrs. Cohen come?"

He glanced at the grandfather clock, which had belonged to Jerome Cohen. Vashti had kept two in her home, urging the Landaus to take one in memory of Jerome. She had generously given his clothes to the poor, his watch to Isaac, and other possessions to his friends and to the synagogue.

"She comes soon," he said. He frowned. "She seemed very troubled when she spoke to me after synagogue on Friday."

"I know. I saw her face," Miriam said, sighing. "She seems thinner and more nervous. What a grief to happen to her, both father-in-law and dear husband gone in a few months. No wonder she is upset."

"Perhaps she will marry again," Jared said, and felt a pang at the thought. A new husband would take over everything, as would be his right. A woman needed a man to take charge of her life, her children, her money. Still, Jared had enjoyed her confidence, giving her advice, helping her manage her business affairs.

"She is very beautiful," Miriam was saying. "And still so young. And her children need a father. But then who could adore them as much as Herman Cohen? Truly he thought the world of his lovely daughters and wife."

"Yes, it is a shame he was taken so soon."

Miriam rocked in silence, her expression vaguely troubled. They both heard steps on the outside stairs, and Jared rose at once to open the door.

"Peace to all within this house!"

Miriam and Jared responded with a smile to the full, rich voice of Vashti Cohen as she swept inside. With her entrance the small dark apartment seemed even smaller and darker. Her black full skirts were so thick she had to turn sideways to slip through the door. She wore a jet pin and dangling earrings, and her magnolia-white face shone beautifully against the black ruched bonnet.

"Peace be with you!" Miriam stood to greet her, and little Gideon at her shoulder murmured something sleepily.

Vashti's lovely face softened. "Oh, the lovely babe! What a precious jewel! How fortunate you are, Mrs. Landau!"

"Thank you, Mrs. Cohen! Pray sit, and be at home!" Miriam smiled her sweet smile and seated herself in the rocker after her guest had settled herself in a chair with a flourish of silk skirts.

Jared sat down on the straight chair at the table. Vashti Cohen carried not only a small jet beaded bag, but a folder of papers and a thick envelope. Jared realized it was business that troubled her, and his heart swelled in pride to think she trusted him.

After the first formalities, he asked bluntly, "I think you are much upset about business, Mrs. Cohen."

"Please, call me Vashti, and let me call you Jared and Miriam," she said, an appealing smile on her full, ripe lips.

"Please do, Vashti," he said, and Miriam nodded, her cheek pressed to the baby's soft head.

Vashti paused a moment, as if to gather her thoughts. Her gaze absently fell on the little boy in Miriam's arms. "As you know," she said gravely, "I am now rather wealthy—and very worried. The rabbi came to me not a month after Herman's death—my dear Herman scarcely cold in his grave—and approached me on the subject of remarrying! I cried out at him, 'How can you say this? I have been numb with grief, I have scarcely begun to believe my dear husband is gone from me! Give me time, give me time.'" Her eyes filled with tears.

"Everybody knew what a kind husband you had," Miriam said quietly. "Everybody admired the good Mr. Cohen and his fine father."

Vashti nodded and dabbed her eyes with her handkerchief. Jared was embarrassed, mostly because all he could keep thinking was how lovely she was, even in her grief.

"Forgive me, I did not come to weep on your shoulders, generous though you are in your attentions," Vashti said, recovering with an effort. "I mean to say, to tell you that I am not convinced I should marry again."

Jared stared at her, a little shocked. "Not marry again?" he echoed. How could such a woman manage by herself?

"You will understand," she said. "The rabbi comes, he tells me again and again that such a man is asking to court me. One man after another. And one is a widower with four children, four sons! I ask you, Mr. Landau—Jared," she corrected herself with an appealing smile, and an outstretched hand. "What would happen to my daughters?"

Jared could not think for a minute. Miriam was quicker. "You mean he would put his sons first, and your daughters might have to beg for a dowry," she said softly.

Vashti turned to her. "Exactly! How could I be sure that after I put Mr. Cohen's money into his trust, he would not betray that trust? A man thinks first of his sons, is that not so? I must think of Herman's children, what is best for them. It is not that I would be selfish with the children of another husband, but what if—"

She paused, and her pearly white skin took on a deep pink blush. Her eyes, so large and dark, so beautiful, were modestly lowered, revealing her dark silky lashes.

"What if he put his children first?" Jared finally nodded. He knew in the same circumstances he would put his sons first. So he understood. "Yes, it is not wise to trust anybody, not at present. Perhaps one day you could meet a man you trust, and marry him."

"Yes, yes, that is what I mean," Vashti agreed soberly. "Now, I am going to tell you something that goes against what I have said. I am going to trust both of you with some information and trust you to tell nobody else."

Miriam's eyes opened wide. Jared felt excitement pulsing inside him. This beautiful intelligent woman trusted him! She needed serious confidential advice, and she had turned to him. "You have our word," he said, glancing at Miriam, who nodded but rose to put the baby down in the bedroom.

Vashti stood up also and moved to the table with her papers. She spread them out on the table, then seated herself in a straight chair across from Jared. She waited until Miriam returned, then gestured to another chair. "Please sit—listen to what I say."

Miriam seated herself and glanced in bewilderment at the pages, charts and maps with red lines on them. The other woman seemed to be freshly excited, yet she had a firm control, which amazed Jared. What was she planning?

"Last winter, when Jerome fell very ill, he called my husband and myself to his bedside. He wished to give us these papers concerning his business interests. I thought they dealt only with the three stores, his stocks, and so on—but they also contained a lot more. He also told us about a mine he had helped finance."

"A mine!" Jared said blankly. "A coal mine?"

"No, no. A friend of his was a wanderer. Jerome was fond

of him and gave him money for supplies to go west and prospect. The man—Jeremiah Jones—would return from time to time with glowing stories of his adventures, though he never really found anything. Then one year he came back with stories of a mine he had found and laid claim to."

"Gold?" Miriam whispered, her eyes growing huge with excitement.

Vashti shook her head, an understanding smile on her lips. "No. If he had, I don't think I would've believed it. No, what he found is something that could be precious someday. Copper."

Jared had to search his memory to remember what copper was. He recalled it was a metal, useful in some iron forges and for coins. He did not know what else.

Vashti was spreading out an old map, much creased and marked. "Mr. Jones said one must go to St. Louis, then west, out to Bent's Fort and beyond. A wagon follows the settler trails, past Indian settlements that can be dangerous," she was saying with immense practicality and coolness, "and to the Rocky Mountains. There are some forts—"

Jared was appalled. He stared at the map, and at another she unfolded. Was this madness?

Vashti's dark eyes were glowing. She traced the trails lovingly, as though they were rivers gorging with life. "Mr. Jones said a traveler stops at these forts to obtain help from the army before going deeper into the frontier, near what they call the Rocky Mountains. On reaching the mine area, there are small settlements of miners who mine the copper, fill wagonloads, and drive east. At St. Louis, they turn over the wagons to drivers, who take them back here, to Philadelphia and New York. The railroads carry the cargo to the various mills on the east coast where the metal is processed."

Jared was stunned. Miriam looked incredulous. The only stories they had heard of the West were about its wildness and its hostile, murderous Indians. Nothing of mines, and only vague rumors of gold, except in California, of course.

Vashti sat gazing at the maps with a vague smile on her lips, dreaming. Jared finally roused himself from his stupor and asked, "But what can you do with this mine? Is it now yours?"

"Oh yes. Mr. Jones died and left all to Jerome, who left it to Herman and me. It is my biggest problem," she sighed. "I could forget it until later. But other miners might take it in the meantime and steal the copper. The mine is so far from anywhere else, except for a small mining camp, that stealing could easily be done."

"You need someone to go and investigate and hire a miner you can trust," Jared said slowly.

"Yes, that is it," she said. "I do not wish to give away the mine or to sell my rights in it. I think it could mean much money one day. Certainly Jerome wished us to find out what could be done with it."

"Hum. Maybe there is someone we could hire to go out—"

Vashti was shaking her head. "No. I want to go." The words were spoken so calmly they did not soak in for a moment.

"You! Go west! To those uncivilized lands—" Jared was aghast. She was so gentle, such a lady—the idea was unthinkable. But he himself had already started to think about the possibilities.

"Mr. Jones said there are decent, respectable women in the West—army wives and their daughters, and the Spanish ladies married to owners of the haciendas, the ranches there. He says they are fine people, and that the territory in general is usually safe. The Indians live away on the ranges, or back in the mountains near the Rio Grande. I'm thinking I'd like to take my daughters and live there for a time."

"Live there!" Miriam burst out. "How can you think of that? It is so—so primitive. It is sure to be dangerous—"

Vashti nodded her head slowly. "Yes, but you know, I have always longed to have some adventure in my life. I listened to the stories Jeremiah Jones told, and longed to see the places he described so vividly. And in Philadelphia I will be hounded until I marry. They will not accept me, and I think my best alternative is to go west. My problem, though, is to find someone trustworthy enough to guide me there. I also need someone to help me build or purchase a small but comfortable house and possibly help me get started with the mine."

She sat back calmly, as though she had not suggested the outlandish. Only a little smile curled her red lips, and an excited passion flashed in her black eyes.

The three talked for a long time that afternoon. Vashti finally had to remain for supper, so they could talk a little longer. It was not until ten o'clock that Jared drove her home, where a woman who shared the large house had baby-sat Vashti's children.

"You will think about this and help me?" she asked as he handed her down from the carriage.

Jared nodded. "I can think of nothing else, I am so excited about it." He smiled, though gravely.

"Good. Be assured I am resolved about the project." She spoke with care in front of the other woman, standing on the steps, waiting. "It is most important to me and to the children."

Over the next few days, Jared thought and thought about it. He kept his own counsel. What he had been thinking was so overwhelming that he scarcely dared consider it, much less talk to someone else about it.

Finally he discussed his plan with Miriam. She listened seriously, trying to comprehend his excitement. "You would go west with her?" she asked slowly. "You would—stay?"

"No, no, no," he said impatiently, scarcely seeing her shock. "I would accompany her west, see her settled, put someone in to manage the mine, then return home. It would take perhaps six months at the most."

"You would go alone?" she asked again.

"No, I think I would hire two drivers. We would need supplies—perhaps a large barouche, if that is practical. Perhaps we could take two of the Conestoga wagons and hire more drivers and hunters to go with us from St. Louis."

He frowned over maps and charts and in the interim talked frequently to Vashti. He met her at the hardware store, and they would go into the back office, discussing the issue for hours. Isaac was very curious, as was Lemuel.

But when they learned of his plans, what an explosion! He had to explain to them why he was going away for such a long time. "To leave your good wife!" Abigail reproached him one day.

Jared shrugged his shoulders and set his handsome jaw, in that thrusting way he used when he was fixed on a decision. It brought back memories of Switzerland. "She will be over the grocery," he said. "Father can watch over her, and I beg you to call often."

Abigail was hushed.

His plans progressed. He explained them to Vashti, then said that to be fair, he would have to be rewarded. And the best payment was a percentage of the mine.

To his relief, she did not refute him. "I was thinking about that. I did not know what to pay you for hire. I was going to pay for the supplies, your wages, but I didn't know what else. An interest in the mine is just perfect. How's twenty-five percent?"

It was more than he had dreamed. She was too generous. But he realized she was very determined and willing to give much to see her dream become reality.

They told nobody about the mines. The community knew only that Vashti had inherited some land out west near the Rockies and planned to live there for a time, until she decided whether or not to sell it.

The rabbi and the women were horrified by the notion, and tried to dissuade her. But the more the rabbi urged Vashti to marry and settle down, the more determined she was to leave Philadelphia and proclaim her independence.

Jared thought, They are driving her away! And he began to realize that for Vashti this journey would be as much an escape from civilization's demands on her as a wealthy widow as it was an adventure to a new land. She wanted to see new places, mountains, deserts, even wild Indians! But more, she wanted to escape from those who would rule her.

And Jared realized also, from talking with her and observing her, that she had been trammeled so long, all her life, that freedom excited her. She felt as if intoxicated by a rare vintage wine. The recent events in her life were unlocking an infinite number of doors to her, and she could never bear to walk into a cage again.

And Jared, too, felt as though he'd once been in a cage—his life in Switzerland and in Germany, the life of a Jewish peddler who was hated and despised, and hedged in by rules and tolls.

For Vashti, the cage had been her life as a woman. Marriage had been her cage, obedience to men who dominated her, took her money, and did with it what they wanted.

He realized that her nature mirrored his own—the reason he found her so appealing. And that she was even stronger, more willful, more passionately devoted to life in all its turmoil than he was. A remarkable feat for any being.

He could only admire her for it. And he resolved to help her all he could, and to learn a little by her example.

Chapter 5

Jared felt such a surge of excitement, he could barely restrain himself. They had been driving in their small wagon train for nearly six weeks and had penetrated well into the western territory—having crossed the Missouri River days ago. They were bound for a post along the Platte River, beyond which, all they would have to do, is keep their eyes fixed on the horizon and the great peaks of the Rockies to indicate their way to their destination.

They had been fortunate along the route. As Jared had prepared to go, he had been introduced to an army captain, Nicholas Frazer, who'd been assigned to the Platte River post and was taking his wife, Anna, and daughter, Rebecca, twelve years old, with him.

Jared had talked long with the stiff, formal captain who wanted company on the trip, but who was dubious about taking on greenhorns—and Jews at that. But several talks with Jared had finally convinced him, and Vashti's determination and practical advice about the trip, had swayed him completely.

In Philadelphia, Jared had hired two drivers not only to man the two wagons but to care for their oxen teams. Vashti had decided to take some household goods with her, as well as some items to start a hardware store in the mining camp. If the money did not flow in regularly from the mine, she figured, she could still earn enough for herself and the children with the store. So one wagon was filled with household items, another with the beds she and her children would sleep in along the route, as well as once they found a home in their new town.

Unwieldy but practical, smiled Jared. He slept in a narrow bed fitted into another wagon, sharing space with a cargo of knives, hatchets, nails, hammers, saws, and mining tools. Vashti would be ready to start soon after they arrived. All she would need would be a house with an upstairs apartment and a number of shelves nailed together for a downstairs store.

He could see that Vashti felt the electricity too. Her eyes glowed and her face had come alive. She had acquired a tan in the sunshine, despite the fact she wore a sunbonnet during the day. She had discarded black, saying it was too hot for traveling, but Jared believed that she was also discarding the trammels of her widowhood and sorrow.

They talked and laughed together at nights around the campfire, as Captain Frazer and Anna became slowly thawed. Traveling together promoted comradeship.

One night, well into their journey, Captain Frazer finished his chores and came back to the fire. He left the corporal behind as guard, and the two privates nearby sleeping; later, they would join one of the team's drivers to walk guard while the other's slept. The captain believed in strict military procedure, to Jared's relief.

"Mr. Landau, how well can you shoot that thing?" Captain Frazer nodded toward Jared's ancient musket.

"Not well," Jared said simply. "I have two of the new rifles with me and some pistols and ammunition. However, as we leave St. Louis, I am more and more aware it is not enough to leave all our defense to you."

The captain's look softened. "You are wise. We must all be armed and ready and skilled in weapons. I have told Anna she must learn to shoot."

The blue-eyed army wife smiled faintly. A very quiet and self-controlled woman, she had blond hair bleached to an ashen color by the sun. "I am willing to learn, dear," she said with resignation.

"And I also," Vashti said, her black eyes gleaming. "I think it would be well for me, since I will be living in the West."

She no longer spoke in terms of returning, and Jared suspected she previously had done so to satisfy the rabbi and her neighbors. She had sold the house, saying merely that it was too big for her small family, and quietly gave Isaac instructions to bank the profits from the hardware store. Jared felt she had thought for some time of not returning. She wanted adventure, freedom, and her own self-created world.

With his usual punctilious care, the captain proceeded to demonstrate the revolver to them all. He had each member of the wagon train load and unload it, aim it while empty, and he explained all its parts. The next day he instructed Jared in aiming the revolver, and finally had him shoot at rabbits.

Jared seemed to have a natural aptitude for shooting, with his keen eyesight and his steady hand.

That evening the captain covered the same ground, only with a rifle. And over the next few days he taught Vashti and Anna and his daughter, Rebecca. Amaris, at eight, seemed young for this, but Vashti insisted she should learn how to shoot too. The young girl surprisingly took to the unwieldy weapon calmly. Eden, at five, was too small, though she sulked at being left out of their "games."

By the time they had been on the more dangerous trail a month, they were all skilled in handling the revolver and Jared had particularly mastered the rifle. Constant aiming, without expending the ammunition, sharpened his eyesight. They had plenty of supplies. The captain's wagon was freighted with arms and ammunition that he was carrying to the fort, so they were well prepared. Jared sometimes had the feeling that the captain longed for military action. He kept scanning the horizon as if hoping to sight hostile Indians on the ridges.

Jared was not so wistful for that kind of adventure. He did become accustomed to seeing small bands of Indians riding at a distance, watching their wagon train. Vashti helped drive the wagons, a rifle at her side, the sunbonnet scarcely concealing her beautiful face and flashing eyes.

She was courteous as ever, but she seemed more distant. Jared caught her smiling to herself, humming a little song.

"You are happy?" he asked as they stopped at a stream to fill their water bottles and barrels.

She flashed a smile at him. "So happy," she said simply. "I feel so—so free. I cannot express to you—I felt so imprisoned—not that my husband was not everything good and kind," she added hastily, a shadow darkening her face.

"Of course," he said automatically. "All admired the Cohens. They were kind and hard-working folk."

"Yes," she said briefly, and turned away as though weary of the subject.

They came to Bent's Fort, the men openly admiring the two beautiful women, one so blond, the other so dark. "I don't like this," growled Captain Frazer to Jared. "We'll rest up a day, and go on. We need no supplies from them."

"Only meat and fresh vegetables," Jared agreed, and rolled up in a blanket outside of the room where Vashti slept with her two small girls.

As they approached the mining district, Vashti and Jared talked more. She chattered away about her dream of having a sturdy house, preferably made of stone, so as to be less of a fire hazard. The store would be in the front room downstairs. In the back would be the kitchen and parlor. And another room would be used for conducting business. The desk and a metal safe she had brought with her would go there.

She drew a picture of the house she wanted made, surprising Jared at her close attention to detail. Captain Frazer asked to look at her design, and he studied it carefully.

"Madam, you are a true architect!" he exclaimed. "This is a fine house, just right for an uncivilized town. I cannot approve of your living without a man to protect you however. I suggest you find a strong man to marry as soon as possible."

"You are most kind, Captain Frazer," she said sweetly, and he nodded at her, pleased that she accepted his advice so readily.

Jared concealed a smile. The captain did not know Vashti as well as he did.

"I would suggest also, madam, that you construct shutters of heavy wood that can be barred on the inside of the windows, so that you can close off the house and protect it from any invasion. There may be a miners revolt, such as I have heard about. Or thieves tempted by the money in your safe."

She laughed a moment, thrilled by his concern, then questioned him about the shutters. He obligingly explained them and drew a picture of one, based on some of the architectural features of a fort. She listened carefully, then altered her drawing a little to take into account her new knowledge. The basement would be shallow, she explained to the men, for keeping fruits and vegetables. But there would be no entrance from the outside, only from a plank door in the kitchen floor. The kitchen door would be as thick as the front door, and barred from inside.

The captain drew a picture of the sturdiest door he'd ever seen. Made of four-inch-thick wood, it was doubly reinforced by a heavy X of wood nailed across the face of the door. "This is how the eastern forts were made at the time of the Indian uprisings," he explained. "It is very difficult for Indians to crash through it with their tomahawks. And even a battering ram would have trouble."

It wasn't before long that a small detachment of cavalry reached them and escorted them on to their fort. There, Jared and Vashti and their drivers rested for a week.

The fort commander assigned a small patrol to accompany them to the Rockies, where the mining town nestled. He was troubled when he learned Mrs. Cohen would live in the Colorado town with two pretty daughters. He had daughters of his own. "Life in a fort for them is bad enough, but in a mining town—" He shook his head.

Vashti smiled, her sensuous features soft and relaxed. "It is what I wish to do, and I have known miners, sir. They can be rough looking, but their hearts are pure as gold."

Now calm and confident, she had blossomed on the journey, developing into another woman from the one Jared had known in Philadelphia. She laughed more readily, she spoke up with more decisiveness. Jared, too, felt happier. A new ambition burned in him brightly. He had been stunned at the vastness of the wilderness, the magnificence of the plains and the mountains. Why, here there was so much beautiful land for the taking, it caught a man's breath! Seeing a thick copse of trees and grasslands with wild ponies grazing on it, he longed to claim it for his own.

Yet he was no farmer, he knew. A sadness filled him. And a lambent hope: perhaps the mining life would be enough.

When the time came for them to resume their journey, they shook hands with Captain Frazer and his wife, sorry to leave them, but promising to visit should they come that way again.

Then Jared left to see to the horses. They had recently sold the oxen and bought sturdy Indian ponies to pull their wagons over the mountain trails. What a place was this western land, he thought, that a distance of a few hundred miles meant nothing!

59

*   *   *

The army patrol kept brisk order on the remainder of their journey. The lieutenant was making maps of the area as he went, and he was busy day and night. Jared and Vashti often talked alone at the campfire, comfortably.

"I have so longed to get away and thought I never would," she confided dreamily one night, raising her face to the stars. "I was so young when I married, I had such dreams—" she halted abruptly.

"And then—" Jared prompted.

She gave a sharp sigh. The girls were sound asleep in the wagon behind her. "Then—I found my life full of routine. Cooking. Scrubbing. Visiting the sick. Waiting for my husband to come home. Waiting on my father-in-law, a good man," she added hastily. "I asked about money, accounts. They replied that they would take care of it all. I wanted to go back to school and complete my education in history and science and mathematics. I did not need such knowledge, they said." A little smile curled her lips.

"So you studied in secret?"

Her black eyes flashed in surprise at Jared. She nodded. Her sunbonnet had come off, and it dangled by the strings about her neck. The firelight flamed on her thick black glossy hair, and it was all Jared could do to keep his hands from caressing it.

"Yes. I could learn as quickly as any man!" she admitted. "My knowledge of math was always better than the boys in school! I could read more rapidly than they, yet because I was a girl—" she hesitated. "Of course, my husband was very intelligent," she said quickly.

"Do not pretend with me, Vashti." Jared spoke quietly. He had been reading her face for the past several weeks. "Let there be truth between us. You have resented being a woman, being forced to conceal your mind. You know you're capable of managing a hardware store as well as your father-in-law and your husband." He laughed a moment. "Probably *better* than your husband, because he was in such frail health."

She bent her head. "Yes," she said in a muffled voice. "I am ashamed of my thoughts. How often I went for a walk, and walked faster and faster to burn out my bitterness. I tried to help, but they only told me to take care of the house. I

60

wanted to take university courses, but they were horrified. My children should be enough, though of course if I could but produce a boy it would be splendid! My girls, so beautiful and so bright, they were not enough. All they saw was that I'd failed to produce a son!"

Jared was silent, half in sympathy, half in surprise at her outspoken anger. After all, a man did want a son. He groped to understand her feelings. A woman was always repressed, he admitted.

"You are unusual, Vashti," he tried to explain. "Most women are content to be wives and mothers. Most women do not wish to learn much. Most women do not care about reading and being skillful in mathematics."

An odd little smile pulled at her sulky full lips. "Of course you are right, Jared," she said obediently.

Jared looked at her sharply and was silent for a time.

"Do you believe many women wish for these things?" he asked.

Her round shoulders lifted in a shrug, and he was sharply aware of her beauty, of her large breasts, the narrow waist, the curve of her hips under the thick blue cotton dress.

"As you say, Jared," she said calmly.

"No. Tell me. I want to hear your views. I know that my own wife, Miriam, is fully content to remain home and take care of our son," he said.

She hesitated, and unwillingly he remembered Miriam's many trips to neighbors, in need of nursing, assuaging, a few coins. She was such a good Jewish woman, he thought, grateful to God for His goodness to her.

"I suppose most women are content," Vashti finally sighed. "I suppose I am—different. I want to strike out, to live in a different place, to test myself against the world. I want to see if I can make a living for myself and the children—"

"There is no real need for that," Jared said, worried by the difficulty of her task. "Your husband, God rest him, left you well off."

"Yes, he did," she said quietly, remotely. There were no more words to say.

They turned in early, he on the ground wrapped in a blanket, thinking for a time before sleeping, she in her wagon, not making a sound.

* * *

They reached the mining camp in late October. Jared realized uneasily he would not be home as soon as he had thought. It was something he could not help, for the trip was long, the land new. He would make it up to his family somehow. Meanwhile he forgot any time schedule and reveled in the crude outdoor life. How far away seemed the ghetto in Switzerland, Germany, and cross housewives! Even Philadelphia seemed a touch stifling in comparison to this wide, open land.

Here in the mountains a man could be away from every human being for a time if he wished. The winds howled across the snowy peaks, and on the ground the snow blanketed any unsightly feature. The woods teamed with deer, bears, panthers, and eagles, as well as a wealth of huge rabbits, chipmunks, squirrels, and a multitude of birds. The wildlife seemed to live in a world so vast and untamed that his own spirits expanded to fill the terrain they occupied.

Vashti immediately put her plans for the house into effect, supervising the work force, which was composed of miners and the two drivers who had conducted them west. The men cut the stone, having quarried it from the mountains, and made the walls fast and secure by setting them with a mixture of small pebbles and clay, which dried quickly between the quarried stones.

In the meantime, Jared surveyed the mine and its operations. He concealed his ignorance by quietly studying the men at work until he understood the operation fully. Within a month they had extracted so much ore, four wagons were loaded and sent east for marketing.

Jared pored over the books every night. Vashti wanted him to understand all the mine's operations and to update the ledgers. She herself worked long hours eagerly, amazing Jared at both her endurance and her comprehension of the business. He came to respect her shrewdness, her knowledge of human nature, her quick decisions. And she settled into the rough life as though she'd been born into it yesterday.

Her daughter Amaris loved it too. She often accompanied Jared to the mine, where she watched the men intently and waited patiently. Finally she grew bold enough to climb into the shaft's loading wagon and ride it to the bottom of the short

62

tunnel, her laugh ringing out all the way. At the bottom, the roughened miners, amused, would lift her out and carry her back to the surface. For all her lack of fear, the mine was no place for a child.

Vashti was on target in her feelings about the miners. They were big, tough men—powerful and silent until they went on a drinking spree. But in the interim, with Vashti and her small daughters they were blushing eager gentlemen, willing to do anything she asked of them. They recognized the Cohens as ladies, and they accorded them every courtesy. The only other woman in the camp was an Indian squaw who did their laundry.

Jared finally concluded reluctantly he would have to return east. He had his family to think of; Miriam would be worried.

So he embarked on the long overland journey in early February, when there was a letup in the snow. He arrived in Philadelphia within two months, in early April.

Miriam greeted him with relief and amazement. He had grown a heavy black beard and moustache and was so tanned that she didn't recognize him when the tall muscular figure strode into the grocery store.

She had been sitting in the back room, knitting, with her small son playing on the floor at her feet. Jared stepped up to her, wearing the familiar thick black overcoat and boots and beamed at her from behind the beard. When she didn't respond, he drew her into his arms. Miriam shrieked, and Isaac in the other room started, stunned at the affront to his sister.

"Don't you know me?" Jared cried indignantly.

Miriam drew back, startled. "Jared!" She laughed and cried and scolded him, hugging him. Gideon, at her feet, began to laugh also, and Jared, seeing him for the first time, tenderly reached down and picked up the infant.

"My fine strong boy! How big you are!" Indeed, the boy had grown amazingly.

When the greetings were over, they told him the store had been doing very well and that Miriam had been keeping the books. Isaac was so busy, he had fallen far behind.

Jared frowned at the news. He wanted his wife to have her leisure, to attend to their family. "No more," he cried firmly. "I will do them."

Over the next few weeks, he put the mine-managing experience to use, updating not only the grocery's ledgers but the hardware's. His father had been very ill, he learned, and his brothers had been trying to run both businesses. The books were in a tangle.

Jared and Miriam sat up late at night. She wanted to hear all about the wonders of the West. She had missed him terribly. She told him that Isaac had matured; he was now very reliable. And Enoch was progressing too—enjoying the traveling, but in need of more of the family's formula for stove polish. He didn't know how to mix it. Jared laughed aloud. He promised to show his brother all the most "intimate" details, and indeed, the next day, Jared led his younger brother to the garage where he'd first mixed the unique blend, and together they made a supply to last a year.

But Jared had returned east for another reason, and now he could set himself to face the task. He found a few books in the library and local bookstores and sat down to absorb all he could on mines and the mining industry, no easy endeavor.

Then he traveled around the eastern seaboard, looked, listened, learned from engineers, miners, smelters, and forgers. He learned everything he could, not only about copper, but about any kind of mining.

In his travels he stumbled on a real gold mine—a smelter who would do a better job and pay top prices for Landau-Cohen copper than any other. Jared broke the first contract he'd already signed, in order to seal this new agreement. Vashti Cohen, as he told his wife, had empowered him in writing to conduct and forge what new deals he could find.

After a painful but necessary parting the summer of 1857, Jared headed west again. He rode out on the last leg of the journey, this time with an army lieutenant and a retiring major.

When he arrived in Copper Creek, he found Vashti thriving on the cold mountain air, enjoying her labors and eager to buy more hardware supplies. She listened intently to his reports, thanking him sincerely for his efforts in their behalf.

"Together we can do very well Jared," she cried excitedly, dreamily. "I am grateful you are the one who manages all for me."

Jared's handsome face reddened. "I think you would do well no matter who worked with you," he replied, though pleased with her words of praise.

Jared poked about in the mine, firing one troublemaker, raising the wages of the others, appointing a foreman. They had discovered another copper vein, even thicker and richer than the first, so Jared split the work force to mine both.

"It will not do, just to work the rich veins," he said to Vashti. "We need to exploit both the poorer quality and the purer ore."

She agreed to that. She had become tanned, healthy, quite content in her new life. It seemed to him that she had grown even taller—but that could not be. It was just that she now held her head erect, proudly, rarely wearing a bonnet or hat. Her glossy black hair shone like a blackbird in the sunshine, and she was more beautiful than ever. The men would have courted her, but were not encouraged.

"My life is my children," she told Jared.

Meanwhile she taught the girls herself, as well as English and writing to the Indian squaw.

"Why do you do that?" Jared had asked, amazed.

Vashti had smiled. "She is a woman. It interests me. And besides, it is nice to have another woman to talk with."

Jared felt baffled. Why did she do that when she had so much other work to do? There must be some other motive, but he could not fathom it.

He returned home this time in October. Miriam was by now expecting his second child. For some reason, the child was not acting right in the womb, and Miriam gave birth prematurely. Abigail came and stayed with them for weeks.

The baby girl survived and grew lovely. Her name was Rosemary. She had been born near Chanukah in 1857, and the last of the snow had melted before—to their relief—the baby smiled and began to cry and become active like a normal child.

"What a beautiful family we have," mused Jared one evening in April, gazing contentedly about the apartment. He saw Gideon drawing with a black pencil on a big sheet of butcher paper as the baby cooed in Miriam's arms.

Miriam smiled tenderly at her little daughter. The birth had been hard, and perhaps because of that the baby was all the more precious to her. "Yes, beautiful," she agreed softly.

"We shall keep our family together," Jared said, puffing on his pipe. He had newly taken up smoking, and claimed it soothed and calmed him in the evening.

"Yes, Jared. We shall be always together."

"Father is worrying all the time. It is too late for worry. He is too lenient with his sons."

"He was very hurt when Malachi insulted him last Sunday." Miriam shook her head, her gentle face reflecting her sorrow.

"I know. I could have spanked him, but it is too late for that. He owes father much money from the store and makes no attempt to pay him back. No wonder the business founders! One cannot profit with such poor business methods. And in the grocery—the accounts show too many people owing money."

"Father remembers the old days in Switzerland, the way everybody had to help everyone else," Miriam said.

"Yes, but charity is one thing, poor business is another. But that is beyond my aid. He must do as he thinks best. I was thinking about something else, Miriam. Two other matters."

"Yes, Jared? You go west again?"

He stared, amazed always when Miriam could read his thoughts. "Yes, I must go again this summer. The mine needs supervision. However, I was thinking—I should like to build a house for us."

Her face lit up and her brown eyes glowed like dark jewels. How lovely she was! he thought. "Oh, Jared, do you mean it? A house—for us?"

"Yes. We are outgrowing the apartment," he smiled. He rose and drew her and the baby up into his strong arms. "Does that please you, eh?"

"Of course, but—can we afford it?" she added quickly.

He nodded. "Yes, I have been looking at houses. However, they do not please me. I want ours to be larger and grander. Miriam—I not only mean to leave poverty far behind us, I mean for us to be rich one day."

Miriam gazed up at him, then nodded solemnly. "You can do it, Jared. If God wills," she added.

"You know we must not talk about the mine to others, however my share of it is bringing such money!" He shook his head in disbelief and happiness. "Twenty-five percent—it adds up quickly! And the new smelter pays us much more. Father will wonder where the money comes from. But this is not his business."

"No, Jared," she said obediently.

"One day I shall be a millionaire," he said.

And she believed him.

When he rode west in June, he left Miriam the pleasant and exciting task of planning a house. She had looked at sketches with him, and they had traveled around looking at houses for sale. Before long they both spotted what they wanted.

Jared had drawn a rough outline, and Miriam filled it in beautifully, and with an eye for spaciousness—a major reason the west drew him. She would make sure it was a feature of her home—not to chain him there. Jared needed his freedom. But to make sure he always returned.

They also talked about colors, and decided to furnish it traditionally.

"And when I return I shall hire a builder," he said, giving her a swift hug and kiss to the forehead. "I want a big, lovely house for my wonderful wife and growing family!" He touched her body, not yet swollen with the child she would bear in December. "What will it be, Miriam—boy or girl?"

Miriam laughed and kissed her husband's cheek. "It doesn't matter to me, husband. As long as you're the father."

Jared smiled, and held her to him tenderly. "You are the finest wife in the world," he whispered. "The most loyal, the most devoted. And you have given me a fine son and lovely daughter, what more could I ask?"

Miriam flushed, embarrassed. She gazed into her husband's eyes, her own twinkling with humor. "It is *my* pleasure of course, husband," she said. "And you can always ask for more."

They laughed, and he kissed her more fervently. In bed that night, she still did not show much passion; rather, she endured his lovemaking. But he knew she loved him deeply, devotedly, and his love for her warmed and satisfied his spirit. His body was not so satisfied, but he upbraided himself for this. A good woman did not take pleasure in sex as a man did. If anything, it showed how virtuous she was, he decided.

He wouldn't worry about the baby. Miriam would have plenty of help with Abigail, Naomi and the others nearby to lessen her load. And when he returned—in time for the birth—he'd be a proud father again, a thought that gave a man deep contentment, a heritage he could hold on to, a flaming tree that marked a man's course through life and signaled the world he had lived and his blood had nourished their generations.

Chapter 6

When Jared set out this time, deeply contented, he could also barely contain the excitement that surged through his veins. He always felt this way—a keen sense of anticipation—just before starting out on the trip westward. He knew what was before him—the wide-open spaces, the glimpses of wild and free Indians riding the ridges on their ponies, like chosen keepers of the sacred sanctuary of the West. There were the sturdy pioneers, the grave, valiant army soldiers, the forts strung out over intervals of hundreds of miles. Such a vast country, blessed by the hand of eternity. It stirred his imagination.

He rode again with army men who would tell him when some of their officers were due to set out. He would meet them on the trail, sometimes leaving Philadelphia with his drivers and Conestoga wagons, sometimes meeting them at St. Louis, across the Mississippi River.

St. Louis was where his wild spirit of freedom began to stir. Herds of buffalo roamed over the plains. Mud huts or wooden cabins could be glimpsed in the distance. Wild horses ran free, their tails held high and their manes streaming in the wind.

There were the nights of sitting around campfires in the rough, honest companionship of hard men. Days of traveling with eyes alert to danger, sometimes walking at the same pace as the wagons, rumbling over the rough terrain, and sometimes spelling the drivers from their difficult task. Sunrises blazed red and gold, gilding the deserts with beauty, making the morning on a river camp a green delight of shade and coolness. Sunsets of stretching, weary muscles, the pleasure of calculating the number of miles traveled over, pausing to admire the orange streaking the skies.

Jared brought this time a heavy load of hardware and mining supplies, since Vashti was doing well with the store. Every time he returned, he had the satisfaction of taking a heavy store of gold nuggets and coins to bank for her. Her bank accounts and stocks were piling up beyond belief. She trusted him completely, and he did all the banking and planning for her children's future.

His face shadowed as he thought of his own family. Lemuel was often ill, and when he was not, he was worrying over his debts. His irresponsible brother Malachi went his own way merrily, spending the family's hard-earned money, with no thought of repaying his father. It was incredible that Lemuel did not insist on being repaid. "It is his heritage," the old man always replied sadly.

Jared bit back angry words, resolving his business dealings with his own children would be strict, though fair. And they should not wander off to do as they pleased! He would keep them together in the same business—whatever that business would be. *Trust no one but the family.* And keep that family together. Hadn't that been the Landau creed?

At the fort, he paused a few days while a patrol was organized to accompany him and his drivers to Copper Creek. Already he could see a change. More settlers had come west, creating more small towns, more mining settlements. There were also more forts, though fewer Indians could be seen. The battles were being fought out on the plains.

"The Indians know they are losing the battles," said the captain with satisfaction when the caravan stopped for a midday break. "This land belongs to the white people. They're civilized and can manage it all properly. The Indians wasted it all!"

This puzzled Jared, for the Indians occupied the territory first. But Captain Frazer was probably right; he had been educated at Harvard.

Someday Gideon would go to school at some big school like Harvard, Jared vowed. His sons would do even better than their father! That was the law of the land—the next generations must be better off than the previous ones. Ever higher, ever more important, ever wealthier, if it could be managed.

He arrived at Copper Creek in mid-August. Vashti flew out of the fine stone building to greet him, her face shining in welcome. She raised her arms as though she would hug him, then dropped them to her side. "Jared, how good to see you!"

"You have been lonely?" he asked quickly.

She flung back her head and laughed. "Lonely? I have never been less lonely, less solitary! Come, come—let me help you unpack!"

She was full of energy, bursting with life and health and happiness. Her girls had grown taller. Amaris was a quietly lovely girl, and Eden was startlingly pretty. Both girls would be heart breakers, Jared thought.

Some of the miners helped the drivers carry the goods into a thick stone shed Vashti had had built. They locked it up, and Jared came into the house, leaving the drivers to take care of the wagons and Indian ponies.

"Winona will have dinner ready," Vashti said.

"Winona?" He had forgotten the name of the Indian squaw. She was standing at the wood fire, and turned at the sound of her name to flash him a shy smile. She was large, bulky with a placid face.

"Good day, Mr. Landau," she said carefully.

"Ah, you speak English well now!" he exclaimed in surprise.

She bowed her dark head. "Thank you."

Vashti stood by, pleased. "She learned very quickly. We talk all the time now. She is my friend."

Jared was a little shocked that she spoke of an Indian woman as her friend. The woman did serve a good dinner, of thick juicy steaks, corn, beans, fruit. She washed up afterward and then went home to her husband and children.

"She works for you now?" Jared asked.

"Yes, although she also takes in laundry. I have insisted that the miners pay her more," Vashti said calmly. "Her husband was a miner, but he was injured in a cave-in. Now she earns enough to take care of him and her children."

"And her husband accepts that?" Jared asked, puzzled. He drank the tea Vashti had prepared and studied her over the rim of the fine china cup.

Vashti had changed so much since their first meeting in the Cohen's store. He remembered her quiet patience as she waited in the back room for the men to finish their work. She had reminded him of a repressed spinster, though she was married and had children. Yet he had sensed such vibrant life pulsing through her, he had found his own pulse quickening. Now she was blossoming. Her face glowed with golden health, her hair was thick and black and curly, glossy in the sunlight. She was like a big goddess of fertility, he mused, and was embarrassed by his feelings.

Vashti, oblivious to his preoccupation, was saying, "No, he was ashamed, and he used to beat her. But I stopped that. I told him I would have him arrested and thrown in jail in a town far away and he would never see his wife and children again." She drained her tea and smiled up at Jared, who was clearly surprised.

"And he stopped beating her?"

"He tried it once again, but I went to him and said I was serious. If it happened one more time, I would send for an officer. So he finally believes me. He sulks, but he does not beat her."

In the next days, Jared found that Vashti had influenced the town in more than one way. She was respected and admired; men tipped their hats to her. They made eyes at her, and more than one man spoke to Jared about courting her. They seemed to feel he was her guardian, and they sought his permission to do so.

He was angered about that. He felt protective toward her—but her guardian, an elder counselor? No!

They usually spent the evening together, going over the books, discussing plans for the future. The work had grown heavy; more miners were hired to handle the load and now eight wagons were sent to St. Louis and on east to sell the copper. Someone talked of building a smelter near to them, which was an exciting idea. It would save the long journey and its expenses.

She really needed a manager here, Jared thought. The work in the hardware store plus her work with the children took up too much time. He began looking about and talking to men to see if he could find a man who would have the right leadership qualities.

"I think perhaps Ben Moran will be the right man," he finally said reluctantly to Vashti. "I do not like the man, he is too—too facile. But he knows the work, and he is a hard worker and a natural leader. And he is more educated than the others."

"Ben Moran would probably be good," Vashti agreed. "He is Irish and has studied mining in the east. He came west to work and found he could only mine copper here. There were no management positions available. The only fault I find is that he has drifted from place to place, but maybe if he had the right job—"

Jared nodded. "Well, I shall talk to him again tomorrow." He stood up and stretched. They had already talked long into the night.

"When do you leave this time, Jared?" Vashti stood and faced him. The lamp on the table lit up her features and sent glimmering lights over her blue silk dress. She usually wore cotton dresses that she sewed by hand, but in the evening she wore her old dresses from Philadelphia, the blue silk, the gold silk, the light blue faille with the deep bertha collar. The hoops of her crinoline made the skirts bell about her long legs as she moved gracefully.

"As long as it takes," he said, smiling, wondering how deep her concern really was. "Probably I shall leave in September. I should like to be home before Chanukah this year, for the sake of the children." He didn't know why, but he didn't mention the baby Miriam was pregnant with now.

Her face softened, it always did when he mentioned children. "Ah yes, I long to see your children. A handsome boy and a sweet baby girl, judging from the photographs you brought."

There was a brief silence that deepened. Vashti bent over the lamp as though to blow it out, then stopped. The light outlined her figure against the darkness of the wall. The children were quietly sleeping in the back room, the upstairs parlor was in the front, and her bedroom behind it. Downstairs was mostly occupied by the business, the store in the front, the office behind it. The only domestic room was the kitchen, which doubled up as dining room, at the very back of the house.

This was a pleasant room. She had had a pine table built and placed in the center of the room. Hand-built sofas and chairs had been covered with cushions and in bright chintz fabrics. The lamps were colorful, two red and two yellow, set about on a bookcase and a lamp stand. The curtains were of hand-crocheted lace, with draperies of thick creamy linen.

"You have made this look like a home," Jared said, waving his arm to take in the room.

"Thank you. I want the girls to feel comfortable here. Amaris does, but Eden grows restless. I fear she will not be satisfied when she is older," Vashti said, her dark eyes reflecting her worries. "She seems such a dissatisfied girl, unlike her sister. What did I do wrong in raising her? Her father sadly indulged her, she was so pretty," she sighed. "He could not refuse her demands for new dolls, new dresses, new bonnets, toys."

"He was proud of them both, and of you," Jared said uncomfortably.

"Yes. Proud," Vashti said absently. She turned and brushed aside the curtains to gaze out into the pitch dark night. "Yet in Philadelphia I would gaze from the window at the streets outside, at the streetlamps and the people, and feel such loneliness. I felt so—useless. I craved something—I did not know what. At times I felt I could—burst."

"Why?" Jared asked intently. "I do want to know, Vashti."

She kept her back to him, as though she could not speak to his face.

"I felt so—unnecessary. Anybody could do what I did. I could read, write, speak several languages—and there was no one to whom I could speak them. My hands rested in my lap." She raised them and gazed at them. They were rough now, reddened by work and cold water and harsh soap. "So soft and white and useless," she murmured. "My husband came home, fell into his bed, and groaned. Sometimes he could not even get enough energy to speak to me. You know when Amaris was conceived? Herman was very ill one winter; his father was told by the doctors he must not work. We spent much time together. I came to his bed in the next room—that was when."

"You were too much alone," Jared said, finally beginning to understand. "The Cohens thought they worked for the family—I think they worked for themselves. For pride, for building up a fortune—"

"I thought so. I had no need of luxuries, yet they piled them on me. One time—for my birthday—I was given a diamond necklace. I wore it at a party, for about five hours. Then it was taken from me and locked in a safe—in a safe," she cried bitterly. "My toy was too valuable for me to play with! I wore it only twice again, for about six hours each time. I would rather they had given me a cheap locket out of affection and to please me instead of thinking of me—*me*—as an investment in diamonds!"

Jared walked to her impulsively and grasped her shoulders. He felt her quiver, and desire coursed through him. He wanted to comfort her, to console her. "Now you can buy yourself what you wish," he said softly. "A pretty necklace, a pair of earbobs, a lace collar, and so you do. That is why you wear this—" And his tanned finger flicked at the gold hoop earrings she wore. They were big, brazen, defiant—nothing she would have worn in Philadelphia.

"Yes." She nodded and leaned briefly against him. He felt the heat of her upper body, the brush of her full skirts against his legs.

"And here you are not lonely?" he asked, and his hands moved down over her shoulders, rubbing them, soothing her, while heat and passion moved up him from his loins to his heart and down again.

"Oh yes, lonely, alone. But it is not the same. I do not sit and wait patiently for men to come home and bed down. I do not have a schedule suited to anybody else. I rise when I wish, near dawn, so I can see the sunrise against the mountain peaks. Sometimes I sleep in the hot drowsy summer afternoons, often in the meadows where the girls and I gather armloads of flowers. And at night, if I choose, I read for hours in the lamplight and feel the dark stillness close in about me, and I know I can do whatever I wish. Read until morning or sleep on the sofa or sit and dream about nothing."

Her intimate words moved him deeply. He bent and brushed his lips against her cheek. He felt her start and stiffen.

"Vashti, I am happy for you," he said.

"Thank you." She turned, and his arms fell away. Her large dark eyes gazed up at him, straight on. "I think you do understand me, Jared," she said slowly. "I am glad."

He reached to brush her soft cheek with his hand, and she seemed to tremble. "There is much passion in you, Vashti," he said softly. "I thought that from the first. Passion, fiery spirit, and nowhere to spread your wings."

"I felt—in a cage. Conventions—demands on me that were both too much and too little. Too much time, too little depth. I was wasting my life. Now—whatever happens, I shall not be sorry, because I am having the chance to choose what I

74

wish. That is the most a body can have in this world, Jared. The opportunity to choose. Men have it—women do not. But I shall!"

He nodded. She was unusual, he thought. Most women did not want to make decisions for themselves. But Vashti wanted to have the freedom to make her own choices, to make mistakes if she must, and to live with them.

He leaned toward her slowly, giving her the chance to turn away. Softly he brushed his lips against her mouth, and started at the full heated moistness of them. She was so warm, she felt feverish. Yet her cheeks were cool.

He stood erect. "Good night, Vashti. Sleep well—"

She smiled faintly. "You also, Jared. I will see you tomorrow morning. We will speak to Ben Moran."

She held the light for him to the front door, from where he went to his shack to sleep. He lay awake for a time, feeling, pondering. He could not think straight, his loins burned so. He could not stop thinking of Vashti. What a spirit she had, how it blazed. They were much alike in their wants, their needs.

He fell into a half-sleep, haunted by Vashti's beautiful face, but on rising the next day, he couldn't remember exactly how she figured in his dreams.

By mid-morning, as previously agreed, he and Vashti met with Ben Moran and talked much of the day about their plans for the mines, then offered him the job of manager. He accepted it eagerly. He had many good ideas about its operations, and he seemed to be fair of mind. He would treat the men well, Jared thought.

He was Irish, and almost six feet tall. He had light brown straight hair and vivid blue eyes like the sea. He had an easy charm and a lilting voice, and he often sang as he worked— wild Irish airs, happy songs of home and sad songs of exile. The men liked him—he was a hard worker, yet good-tempered, unless someone spoke ill of Ireland. He could drink and fight at night and the next day start to work again, fresh.

He talked long about Ireland's problems—the famine that struck down his people. "No good in Ireland anymore," he said to Jared later over a mug of beer. "Nowhere to work, nothing to do for an honest man but to steal!"

Jared peered at him thoughtfully. "It was bad for us in Switzerland, too," he said. "For us America has been the land of opportunity, the land of the future. There we had no hope.

75

Here we have not only hope, but the chance to dream dreams that can come true."

"I like that! I like that!" Moran cried, and he raised his mug high. "Drink—to dreams that can come true!"

Vashti and Jared discussed it again that evening after dinner. The girls had gone to bed, and the house was quiet. When the curtains were drawn back, they could see a few lamps flickering down the slope of the mountain, around Copper Creek.

"I think he will do well. I shall watch him sharply the first months," Vashti said. "But I think I can trust him. It will give me enough time for other projects. Some of the miners want to learn to read and write."

Jared shook his head, smiling. "You will exhaust yourself, my dear!"

She started and a deep blush came to her cheeks. She avoided his gaze, but did not rebuke him for his words. "No, I think not. When one does enjoyable work, it is not exhaustive. One becomes pleasantly weary and goes to sleep with a happy feeling."

Silence deepened between them. Jared knew he should excuse himself and leave her. Yet he wanted to stay, to watch the lamplight's play on her hair, the changing emotions in her face. How beautiful she was, now more than ever. Her own personality had been allowed to break through its bonds, and blossom to its full beauty.

He stood, which prompted her to do so too. He could sense that she did not want him to leave, and he found that his feet would not take him to the door behind her.

"Vashti," he whispered huskily, overcome by emotion.

"Yes?"

"You know I've wanted you a long time—" he said, hesitantly, uncertain of her reaction.

She started, her hand flying to her throat as she gazed at him through the deep pools of her dark eyes in the shadow beyond the lamp. "You . . . want . . ."

"You. For a long time. I desire you with the profound torment of a man who sees your beautiful face, your beautiful body, and can't help committing adultery in his mind—"

A deep flush rose from her throat to her brow. She swayed unsteadily on her feet a moment, and when he noticed, he rushed to her, taking her in his arms as her skirts swung against his legs. Pressing her tightly against him, he took a long draught

76

from her lips, parting them to reach the soft places beyond. She shuddered, her hands clutched his shoulders until her fingers dug into his flesh. "Oh, Jared," she cried.

He answered with his own shudder, his hunger growing beyond his ability to stop. "Vashti—I must have—"

She did not repel him. Her body leaned against his, all rounded womanhood, warm and scented. He imagined taking her on her wide bed, and the craving grew beyond bounds.

He began to unfasten the little frog clasps of her bodice. She did not stop him as his lips continued to play over hers. She opened her mouth wider, so he could probe her sweet depths. Clasped tightly together, her arms about his neck, they swayed as he unfastened her gown to the waist and slipped his hand inside. He felt her soft large breasts, caressing the nipple under the cotton undergarment, and watched as it hardened sweetly to his touch.

He drew her to the bedroom, and in the darkness she removed her clothes until her round body shone whitely in the gloom. His muscular hands touched and stroked her hungrily, and he could scarcely wait to tear off his own clothes.

He led her to the bed, pushing her down. "Wait," he said hoarsely. "Wait—but a moment—"

She lay across the bed where he had led her. He had been rough, but not a sound or objection rose from her throat. Her dark eyes gazed up at him, burning with desire, as he ripped the clothes from his body, his frock coat, his trousers, his shirt—

Clothes off, he climbed into bed beside her, roughly pressing against her soft body, which seemed to melt under his touch. Her legs came up around him; her arms folded over his back. He thrust at her at once, and she received him—their hunger mutual.

He gave her no mercy, and she wanted none. Passion flared swiftly between them, desire gripped them both in ecstacy. She made only a soft moaning sound when he went deeply into her. He was relentless in his drive to release his passion, in a way he would never have done with Miriam. He'd had Miriam many times and she had always yielded, but she had never relished this moment in the primitive way this woman did. And something primitive in himself was unlocked as he relinquished all rational control. He wanted her, every inch of her flesh, and to kiss her passionate mouth, he wound her thick hair around his large hand so he could hold her head in place. As their lips melded, his hips ground into hers. He was betraying Miriam, his gentle wife, and he flinched from the thought. But Vashti—she was like his other half. Her passionate nature matched his own. He wanted her to cling to him, to be part of him. He needed her like a glass of fiery whisky, not the clean pure water of gentle Miriam.

He managed to hold back the final response for a time, wanting to lie deeply inside her being for a while. She held him, and her hips moved again and again, moving around and around, as though she also wanted more and more. At the final moment, she quivered, her body arching open to him like a desert flower after rain. But hardly skipping a beat, he came to her once more, pounding at her in the sheer agony of desire, trying to make her part of his own body for a time, and he could hear her responding in ecstasy. He adored her, he loved her, in quite a different way than Miriam.

His breath was gone then. He lay back, gasping, and heard her soft moans. He flung his arm across her limp, wet body possessively, and his hand caressed her heavy breasts. She put a weak hand on his arm and acknowledged his possession, clinging to him. He felt wild, lordly, her master!

After that evening, he came to her night after night. He hungered for her during the days, gazing at her when they were supposed to be working. A deep flush covered her face, and she shyly avoided his eyes. Nights she was not shy in the large wide bed, and she lay waiting for him till he finished work. She was wanton in his arms, crying out for him if he lingered too long in his adoration. They were lovers in every sense of the word, and he experimented with her in every caress they could devise.

They satisfied in each other something wild and primitive, something they hungered for. They walked in meadows with the two girls and sat watching the children, touching only with their looks. Yet they were together; he had but to glance at her to know she also wanted him.

They would gaze at the mountains, and talk prosaically about the work of mining. But underneath he was singing to her of his rapture, of his desire.

"The wagons will go east next week—" And how I hunger for your ripe thighs! he wanted to add, anguished at the thought of separation.

"Yes, yes, and yes," she said. She tossed a flower at him that she had held between her lips, and he touched it with his. He stretched out at her feet lazily, and her slipper touched his side. It moved slowly down his hip to his thigh, and he felt the instant response.

"I would like to work deep in the mine—" he murmured.

"You work hard enough," she said innocently, her throat barely catching the laughter at their symbolic intimacy.

"A mill wheel—" he said.

"Yes, I like that—" She nodded. And that night he worked on her, around and around, and lay back for her to ride him with her round beautiful thighs. They could do anything together, and she enjoyed it, and he loved it. How she matched his spirit! He loved her the more deeply all the time.

Jared lingered long into the season, making excuses to stay longer. He built more shelves for the hardware store and planed them to perfection. "Such trouble for a few shelves," Vashti said, her eyes full of laughter.

"Oh, I expect to be repaid," he said. He smoothed the wood, stroked it with his tanned fingers, and looked at her waist.

It was inevitable. By October she was pregnant with his child. He was tight-lipped. He had had too much enjoyment of her—she would have to pay the price, not he. "I feel I should apologize to you. Vashti, I had not planned this!"

"I was not careful," she said. "Neither were you. We will be more careful the next time," she said calmly, forgiveness in her eyes.

"You will do nothing?"

"No, I will have the child. Everybody will know—but it does not matter. I have resolved to live free, to take what richness life could offer. Now I will pay with a smile."

"But the child—"

"Wait until we see what happens," she said evenly. "Out here, it is not so bad. When he or she grows up, well—school in the East, and a new life. I want no one to suffer because of me, nor will I let anyone stop me from doing what I wish!"

He hated to leave her. Desire for her raged in his blood like some wild fever, but most of all he hated to leave her to have the child alone.

"I shall not be alone. Winona will help me, Jared, and Amaris is sensible too, she will help with a baby."

"But the talk—the men—"

"If they do not respect me, they will respect my ability with a rifle!"

So he finally left her in November, riding hard and fast with an officer retiring from the army. He arrived in Philadelphia in December 1858, in time to witness the birth of his third child, Bartholomew.

Bart was a fine, hefty child, just like his brother Gideon had been. He would be a tall sturdy boy one day, and when he cooed in his proud mother's arms, he struggled with much strength.

Despite her obvious pleasure with her new baby, there were shadows under Miriam's eyes, and Jared noted that she was reserved around him. And despite his joy in his new son, Jared felt terrible now that he was back in Philadelphia.

What if Miriam should hear about the child Vashti expected? Fortunately few people from Copper Creek journeyed east— he had a chance of keeping this from Miriam. Dear good Miriam; he did not want her to be hurt. But all the winter he worried about Vashti. He was quiet, abrupt with his family and friends. They thought he worried about the prosperity of the mine and the house he was constructing, to be furnished with fine expensive goods.

It was his guilt that tore him apart. He loved two women! He adored and worshiped his good Miriam. But Vashti was a fiery brand in his blood. He burned for her, wanted her.

To forget, he worked hard on the house and at night he was so tired he could blessedly sleep in the same bed with Miriam. He had approved of Miriam's plans and enlarged on them. The house was huge, three stories plus a deep basement for storing food and other goods. The drawing room was of red plush and mahogany, the hallway wide with mirrors and coat hooks and umbrella stands, like everybody had these days. The dining room seated twenty easily, and potted plants adorned the corners.

The doors were wide enough to accommodate the ladies in their fashionable hoop skirts, and indeed the Landaus entertained many guests in the evenings; they were popular and becoming wealthy. Jared had many acquaintances among bankers, mining engineers, army families.

The front bedroom upstairs, stretched the width of the house, with a corner shut off from the bedroom for a washroom. He had a newfangled tub installed, with running water from pipes, a smart toilet, and a wide dressing table with mirrors and washbowls. Everything worked like a dream!

They had bedrooms for the older children, a nursery for the new baby, and servants' quarters on the third floor. Two guests rooms were often occupied with friends traveling through.

Jared could not wait to ride west again. He needed to know how Vashti was faring. He knew Miriam was doing fine. So he went in June 1859, trembling with eagerness, to find himself the father of a baby girl. Sapphira—for that was what she had named the girl—was a small replica of Vashti. Beautiful, all fuzzy black curls and dazzling deep eyes that flashed blue to black, a large full rosebud mouth. Jared felt shaken when he held the infant.

The work had grown so much, Ben Moran was exultant. He was a little impertinent to Vashti, and Jared spoke sternly to him. He would have no insults hurled at Vashti, though her position in the community had subtly changed on her giving birth to his child. She was a widow woman with a lover, and the community was less than forgiving.

"But I expected it," Vashti said. "I can accept it. Do not worry about me, Jared." She smiled and added, "I have resolved to live life to the fullest, I shall have no regrets. I want what I want and am willing to pay the price."

"I will do what I can for our daughter," Jared said, holding her in his arms in the wide bed. He held her possessively, anxiously. If only he could marry her and remain here! But his duty was to Miriam, his wedded wife. He still loved her, gently, as reverently as he had on their wedding day.

But Vashti had his passion. She was a . . . fulfilling woman. She was earth mother, wife, mistress. He loved her with wild hungry needs.

Jared exulted over his family. He recalled the patriarchs of old—their several wives and their numberless children. How potent he felt—two women and four children! If only he could tell the truth in public! He scolded himself and prayed, but he could not refrain from feeling happy. They were all children of his blood! How passionate Vashti was, how warm his Miriam.

He wished he did not have to be careful. He wished he could have them both openly, wildly, devoted to him, loving and responsive to him in their separate ways.

But he knew that his love would have to remain secret. His

mouth twitched as he thought how shocked the congregation of his synagogue would be if they knew the truth. And worse, from now on he would have to be careful, to spare his fiery Vashti from a host of illegitimate children and the public scorn that would surely be unleashed if the truth were revealed.

Chapter 7

Miriam Landau peeled off her wet, stained apron and straightened her aching back, stretching and rubbing her stiff shoulders briefly.

As she emerged from the hospital's changing room, she smiled at the doctor in the outer room. "I will come again tomorrow at the same time," she said.

"You are a good woman," he said with admiration. He was a Gentile and he was amazed again and again that this lovely, wealthy Jewish woman lent her valuable time to nurse his patients.

"The Lord has been gracious to me." She smiled, glancing into the ward. "It is good the illness is dying down. It has been a bad winter."

"Yes, I'm thankful spring is coming."

The carriage was waiting for her outside, and the coachman handed her carefully into the barouche. She sank into the cushions, closing her eyes briefly. Tonight, she knew, Jared would tell her he was going west again this summer.

Her heart ached. She knew something had happened on that journey two years ago. He had returned a different man, not so open, much more cautious in his speech, often absent in his manner.

She had understood what had happened. On several nights

after his return, Jared had rolled to her in bed, touched her intimately in his sleep, and whispered Vashti's name.

He had been kind to Miriam as always, loving her in bed, treating her respectfully during the day. She had found it difficult to pretend all was well. She had gone down on her knees to pray passionately that she could endure the burden of knowing her husband was unfaithful to her.

Praying had helped some, soothing the jealousy and wild anger she felt at her husband's going again and again to Vashti— so passion-filled, so full of spirit, so luscious and ripe. Her imagination tormented her, visualizing Jared and that woman in bed together.

And Jared's caresses had over the years grown so much more—lascivious. If he had grown more fond of Miriam, had lavished the caresses on her out of a growing passion for her, she would have felt like responding, trying to match the change in his caresses. Yet she felt the caresses were for Vashti, and they made her shrink. She could not help but think of his mistress as Jared made love to her, and she froze inside. When he asked her impatiently for more kisses, it was an effort to satisfy him.

Only the long hours of work that exhausted her helped her sleep at night and not toss in anger. "The Lord has been good to me," she said over and over, and believed it. Did she not have a fine, hard-working husband, three wonderful handsome children, healthy and contented days in a big, splendid house?

"If only he had been faithful—" A bitterness would well in her. She had to stifle it sternly. Anybody had sorrows and griefs; this was her burden. She must endure it.

Perhaps she had been too proud. This might be a punishment for her. The Lord chastised his own. So she bent her back in more work and drove herself to exhaustion.

Perhaps one day the Lord would forgive her for whatever sin she had committed. She must try to pray harder and be serene of spirit and accept Jared as he was.

Yet it made her more quiet and submissive. She did not feel like pitting her strength against Jared, arguing with him, suggesting ideas that countered his own. She had always been quiet and meek, she must continue to be.

While he was gone in the west, she had many lonely nights. Sometimes Isaac came to visit, sometimes Abigail came to stay for the day. Then Miriam was bright and quick of conversation.

But when she was alone again, she read and studied. She had completed several university courses in history, mathematics, and bookkeeping, letter writing, and English for business, to help Jared all the more. She had quietly taken over much of the bookkeeping for her brother Isaac and her father-in-law, growing more feeble by the day. Jared did not realize how much of her handwriting was in the account books. He obviously had other things on his mind.

Most of all, her charity works sustained her. She felt useful, needed, dedicated to the Lord, who might one day forgive her for her many sins of pride and bitterness.

So she went out daily to deliver hot soup to a sick neighbor, or call on friends whose husbands or children had died, or comfort those who were afflicted, or offer her time for nursing in the hospital when they were short of male nurses. Nursing was a strange occupation for a woman, but the doctors seemed grateful to her for her gift of soothing a feverish patient or one in pain. She had a gift for saying the right thing, knowing where the pain ached worst, calming a dying man with her inspired words about the nature of life after death.

The barouche pulled up at her large fine house, and the coachman helped her out before taking the carriage back to the stable. Miriam walked up into the house. It was late; dinner would be ready. She needed to wash thoroughly before she greeted anybody. So she climbed the stairs to her room on the second floor, washed, and changed her dress for the evening.

She slipped into her dark blue silk one, which Jared liked. It had a pretty lace collar and cuffs. Around her neck she wore a silver locket that Jared had given her on the birth of their first son.

Then she went upstairs to the nursery to check in on Bart. He was fine as usual, such a high-spirited laughing boy! Her eldest, Gideon, had been good, but much more quiet. Bart was a lively one. And dear Rosemary—always frail, but so sweet. Miriam held her for a little time, singing to her, before descending the stairs to the drawing room. She heard the deep voices rising from the room before she reached the door. Adjusting her face to a welcoming smile—for whomever it might be—she took a deep breath, for she was almost too weary for company, and stepped into the room.

Jared and his brother Malachi rose to their feet instantly, both faces turned to her. Malachi had such mournful brown eyes, as though begging the world to be kind to him. So selfish he was, she thought, and thrust the thought to the back of her mind. She held out her hand with a welcoming smile. "Malachi, it has been long since you honored us."

"God be with you," he murmured, and touched her hand timidly. He was so shy, she wondered at the stories about her bachelor brother-in-law, involving fast women from the seediest part of town.

Jared smiled at her absently, but made no move to kiss her cheek. She gave him a bright smile and seated herself in the rocker, moving slowly back and forth for comfort.

Often Miriam had wondered what would happen if she confronted Jared with her feeling that he was Vashti's lover. She could picture three possible outcomes. One—he would be repentant and swear never to see Vashti again. She would forgive him, and they would live more happily together. Two—he would be angry and cold to her, and continue to see Vashti. A crevice would open between them, growing wider and wider as the years went on. Three—he would be furious, break off from her, divorce, and go live with Vashti openly, if not marry her.

Miriam thought dispassionately that the third was the likeliest outcome. Vashti was beautiful, desirable—and wealthy. Jared admired her for having much money. And Miriam had none of her own.

Miriam had a practical nature, like her mother. She shrank from letting the world know she was not woman enough to keep her man. To be divorced—shamed—and have her children taken from her, for Jared would not release his sons, of whom he was very proud, not unless he had a fine son from Vashti . . .

The maid called them to dinner. Miriam led the way, and the two men followed. The food was delicious as always. She ate heartily. She was getting plump, but Jared did not seem to mind. The roast beef was delicious, as were the potatoes boiled in their skins, and the pea-carrot side dish. The dessert was a tart made with canned cherries.

The men ate heartily, then retired to the parlor. Miriam hesitated until Jared said, "Come with us. This will concern you also, my love!"

When he smiled like that, behind his black beard, extending his hand to take hers, she would have followed him anywhere.

So kind he could be, so charming. And he did love her, it was so obvious. Could a man love two women? It seemed Jared could.

So she settled herself in the rocker everyone knew was hers, with its padded seat of blue velvet and its low height—to allow her feet to touch the floor as she rocked—and listened.

Malachi began at once, in a burst. "I am tired of the pharmacy, Jared. It is not interesting to me anymore. Day after day, it's the same thing. Mr. Asher's bad throat, Mrs. Ellis's condition—I am sick myself of all their sicknesses!"

"And you want to come into business with me," Jared finished dryly. "Of course you would have to sell the pharmacy—"

"My assistant wants to buy it, that is no problem. His father has money enough."

"And with the money you will repay all you owe Father."

Malachi squirmed in his chair uneasily. "Why—Father does not want it back! He said so! And the money would buy an interest in your mine!"

"Oh no," Jared said evenly. "The mine is my business. Nobody buys it from me. You would work for me with a salary. And follow my orders!"

Malachi's face fell. "But—but Jared—you are rich! I want to be rich also!"

Miriam and Jared exchanged a quick amused look; they could easily read each other's thoughts. The young man thought it was so easy to amass wealth. He thought all he had to do was attach himself to Jared's coattails and ride upward! He did not know or care how hard and long Jared had worked to achieve his present good fortune.

"Those would be my terms," Jared said after a pause. "You would work for me at a salary. And you would have to pledge complete loyalty to me, and be discreet about the family's business dealings. I cannot have everybody knowing about the business. If anybody learns how I work, you see," he explained in child's terms, "then he could do likewise and maybe take the business from me!"

"Oh yes, yes, I see!" Malachi cried. "I promise to be ever loyal." His youthful face glowed.

Jared was amused. "Well, I do need a man I can trust. I want you to learn all about the mining process. We will begin with the operations in the East. You will go to the smelter and learn about the work there. Then you will meet the copper wagons, make sure they get to the smelter intact—with no loads lost or stolen—and you will see to refitting the wagons to go west, buying the hardware stock for Mrs. Cohen—"

"And drive them west?" Malachi asked eagerly.

"Not at present," Jared said. "I shall go myself. There is much to do when I get there. I have to inspect the mine, make sure the manager is making the right decisions, balance the books—"

Malachi's face fell again. He was obviously disappointed. But he brightened when Jared told him to learn how to shoot a revolver, a rifle, and a shotgun. He took his leave, thanking Jared profusely.

Malachi sold the pharmacy and reluctantly returned the money he owed his father. Old Lemuel was ill and languid, and he appreciated receiving the money. Abigail, too, was grateful to Jared for obtaining the repayment. The business was not as profitable as it once had been, since Lemuel could not devote so much time to it. The rest of the family was doing well, except that the profit Isaac was making in Vashti's hardware store was going to Vashti. Enoch was still peddling in the countryside, but he was growing restless. Jared decided to persuade him to give it up and go into the grocery to help their father. He did, and Enoch was obviously more content; soon he moved into the apartment over the grocery. Asher also wanted a project. Jared put him to work helping both his brothers in their separate stores.

"I wish I could remain in Philadelphia and oversee them," he told Miriam one day. "Father is too soft with them all. But I must build our own fortune, and you know the only place to do that is in the west. I am thinking of buying a mine. I have heard a man has made a strike and has not the ambition to follow it up with all the work of hiring men and buying equipment."

Miriam set her jaw. After all, she knew this was coming.

When he went west that summer, she settled into the old routine of doing without her husband. She saw to the children, visited neighbors, found out who needed help and quietly assisted them. She found this satisfying, and while it kept her hands busy, her mind was quiet.

When Jared returned, he was absent of mind for a time, with a faint pleased smile on his lips. Miriam felt tired and bitter and wondered if she should do something definite about leaving him.

Yet she loved him, and he lay with her often and treated her with respect and affection.

Yet she knew—knew he had been with Vashti.

While he had bought a second mine, and while he was home he worried about the overseeing of it. He did not entirely trust Ben Moran, he told her. He frowned over the accounts, then praised her for keeping them so well.

He paid more attention to Gideon. The boy was growing rapidly, and he liked nothing better than following his father from grocery store to bank to hardware store to club to synagogue to business meeting. Jared tolerated him at first, then grew accustomed to the small footsteps pacing behind him, the eager questions.

"The lad is growing up," Jared said. "He is a smart lad." They often went off in the carriage together, Gideon trotting eagerly after his father.

In 1861, the ominous rumblings of war broke out into a real war. In Philadelphia, they were close to the action, and the hospitals spilled over with the wounded. Miriam volunteered to help all the more.

Her days were busy; she had little time for family, yet they came first with her. She rushed here and there, worried over the young dear boys who streamed back from the war, injured in body and mind. She also worried over Jared, furiously busy with his copper.

For some reason obscure to her, copper was important in war. Jared explained the matter to her over and over—something to do with wires and iron. Whatever the reason, Jared bought a third mine and was frantically riding between Philadelphia and Copper Creek. Since rails had been laid west, he was at least able to go part of the way by train.

He would load the hardware supplies, the mining equipment, rifles, and ammunition into a railroad car in Philadelphia bound for Chicago. Once there, the cargo was unloaded into another railroad car and taken to St. Louis. Although over time the railroad crept west, he still had to purchase Conestoga wagons, hire drivers, and go as far as Colorado. Still, the burgeoning rail system made the journey shorter.

The army needed copper, and Jared had a reputation for his reliability. He was supplied with escorts from St. Louis westward, sneaking past most bands of marauding Indians. Though not all.

He returned home thinner, more haggard. His trips were no longer made in a leisurely and pleasurable way. But he continued to make them. There were now three mines to demand his attention.

Miriam did her best to keep everything comfortable for him when he finally reached home. She would not let the children fuss in front of him. They were cautioned to be quiet and good. And further, she would not let his larger family trouble him either. She settled controversies over the stores and money before he arrived home.

She became pregnant on one of his return journeys, though she continued to work at the hospital. But that winter the work became too much for her. The pregnancy and the sad, terrible hospital sights troubled her greatly and sapped her vitality.

Jared came home to find her nearing collapse. He forgot his own cares and stayed home for a time, forbidding her to go out. Her face was nearly ashen, her shoulders sagged, and she broke down in tears too easily.

Jared came home to find her weeping over her sewing. He took the small garment in her hands from her, and pulled her into his arms.

"My dear wife, my dearest dearest Miriam, what troubles you?" he cried tenderly. His anxious face so close to hers, his troubled dark eyes so worried for her, made her cry even more profusely.

He held her tightly and soothed her by stroking her soft hair.

"My darling, my darling, you are exhausted," he murmured, his lips against her forehead. "Come, let me put you to bed, and you shall be cosseted with sugared tea."

She did not want bed and sugared tea, she wanted Jared holding her, thinking only of her. "Oh, darling Jared, do not be troubled," she said, and tried to smile. "I am being a silly woman, worrying over nothing. I am healthy—and the baby will come when it wishes to."

"You have spoiled me, Miriam," he said softly. "Every time you have been so brave and uncomplaining. Now it terrifies me that you weep. Can I do anything at all for you?"

"Only hold me," she said, and he did so, his arms strong

90

around her. He pressed her head to his shoulder as they sat on the sofa, and she felt peace.

He patted her swollen stomach. "This bad baby shall come soon and give you rest."

She smiled as he meant for her to do. "Do not speak of your child so, Jared," she managed with pretended severity. "What if he hears?"

"Just as well. He must mind his papa!"

They laughed together, and she felt much better. Jared took great care of her, spending all his evenings with her and coming home early from his business to make sure all was well. Her condition improved, and she felt more content.

"I just want spoiling," she said to herself, and smiled at her reflection in the mirror. Still, his concern was sweet.

A baby girl was born in March 1863, and they named her Hannah, for Jared's grandmother, who was buried in Switzerland. She had been an indomitable soul, much loved and admired. It was a good name for a strong sturdy baby with serene eyes and fluffy black hair.

"It is interesting," Miriam said to Jared as they peered at the baby in her crib, "how a character shows up so very early! Gideon was quiet and good-natured, yet wanted his way so early. Rosemary—my dear frail girl—" And her face shadowed. "She never fusses, even when I know she feels the pain in her spine. Such a good, gentle girl."

"And Bart, so mischievous and charming—always wanting whatever toys Gideon has!" Jared grimaced. "He stormed at me for leaving him behind when I went to work yesterday."

"He is being naughty," Miriam said. "I will speak severely to him."

"Well, I am flattered he wants to be with his papa," Jared admitted, his arm around her. He gave her a quick squeeze. "How proud I am of my fine family!"

A little later she dared to say casually, as she sat sewing baby clothes in the drawing room, "Speaking of children and their characters—I have often wondered how Vashti's girls turned out."

She felt Jared staring at her. "Well—" he said, slowly, and made a great thing of filling his pipe. "Well—Amaris is a fine young girl. She has married a young miner and they do not have much money, but they are as happy as a couple can be.

She has fitted up a cabin for them both, and sews curtains and linens all the day. He works hard—I thought to put him in charge of one of my mines, but he is very young yet."

"And Eden? She was always a mischief, and she whined so," recalled Miriam. "I should not say so, but I thought she would give Vashti trouble." She dared not look up. She rarely asked after Vashti. She scarcely trusted herself to do so, fearing he would guess her jealousy of the woman. Vashti had so much—such a superb figure, brilliance of wit, and such grace, and so much money—

Yet she did not have a husband, much as she might want Jared.

"You are quite right. Eden is but thirteen, but already she attracts men like a patch of clover attracts bees. Vashti cannot please her with homemade clothes. Eden wants silks and velvets, and Vashti has asked me to bring some the next time I return."

"I see. Yes. I wonder that Vashti keeps her in the West. Are there no relatives to send Eden to?"

Miriam held her breath then. Would Jared suggest that she take in Eden? Had she talked herself into a trap through sheer nervousness? She did not think she could endure to rear a child of Vashti.

"No, she has never mentioned wishing that. She keeps the girls close to her and has educated them herself. All the girls are taught by her and learn quickly. She has also taught them housekeeping, cooking, and sewing—"

Jared had picked up a gazette and now gazed absently at the war news. Miriam's heart felt as though it had stopped a beat before racing on.

All the girls—all the girls— His words echoed in her head. She sewed feverishly and accidentally pricked her finger with the needle. She could not even cry out, but sat and stared blankly at the blood on her finger.

All the girls—

Vashti had taken two girls west with her.

All the girls—how many? At least one more—and she guessed that the girl must be Jared's.

Miriam had felt the same pain before, when she realized Vashti and Jared were lovers. Now she knew it was possible to feel even more pain. A girl—a child—at least one child—

Vashti had had his child—one if not more—

She raised her head, she wanted to lash out at him, accuse him—

Jared wiped his forehead wearily with his handkerchief. He was haggard, had lost weight. So many young men had gone into the army, fighting for the North, that Jared had to help out in both the family's stores, going from one to the other. Also, the army needed food, so he would go to their warehouse and fill their orders in crates and baskets with his own strong arms.

At night he worked on the books, wrote letters, read the gazettes for casualties in worry for their friends' and neighbors' sons. Now he looked up, sighing. "The poor lad of the Murphys—he died last night. I was told today at the store."

"Young Steven Murphy—oh no, Jared. I thought he was recovering..." She forgot her own feelings. How little she felt, next to deaths rising from this tragic war.

"No, they had to operate on his leg again. The gangrene set in. He did not survive."

"I must go to Mrs. Murphy tomorrow. Poor dear soul, her second son gone—" She wondered what she should do for her. A basket of food after the funeral? An offer to help clean the house? They did not have servants. Yes, she would go in old clothes and stay the day and help with the cooking and cleaning. She'd stay in the kitchen while guests came to express their sympathy.

Miriam liked to show sympathy in practical ways. Yes, she would cook and scrub for Mrs. Murphy—poor woman, two sons gone.

"When will it end?" she whispered. "Oh, dear Lord—we must pray hard for the ending of this war..."

The war came near them in Philadelphia, an invasion from the South was threatened. That summer Jared did not go west. He worried that the southern forces would break into Philadelphia and attack their homes.

The wounded streamed into the city, some in crowded and bloody railroad cars. Others in wagons piled on straw, others on foot. All were handled roughly. Miriam took some into their home. The drawing room and parlor and dining room were cleared out, and mattresses were laid down for the injured and dying.

They forgot about everything but the soldiers, and the war. And the war seemed to go on and on.

Young Gideon and Rosemary helped in their way. Gideon became skilled at carrying hot water and bandages for his mother and the other nurses. And sweet little Rosemary would sit beside a soldier, hold his hand, and gaze at him with sweet sympathy. Her eyes were so full of gentle caring that the soldiers liked to have her nearby. "What a dear child—I have a little one of my own," they would confide.

Miriam worried a bit about the effect on the children of seeing all this misery. But the soldiers were soothed by their presence, and the children didn't seem to mind helping. Rosemary confided, "He said I helped him, Mama, just by listening to him talk."

"You are my own good girl," Miriam said, and held her close. "We must pray for the end of the war, and that our soldiers get well again."

Chapter 8

By the time the War Between the States had ended, Jared Landau was a millionaire. He was proud of it. He had come far from their Switzerland days, when they had lived in poverty and dread of an unknown future.

These days his father was often bedridden. Jared and his brothers took care of Lemuel's business, though it was painfully obvious to everyone that his desire for life was slowly ebbing from him.

Jared had not gone west for three years. In 1866 he decided he had to check in on the mining business, despite the heavy work load in Philadelphia and at the East Coast smelters.

He decided to take his restless brother Malachi with him and put him in charge of bookkeeping for the three mines. He wanted to gauge Ben Moran's progress—and of course he hungered for the sight of Vashti and Sapphira.

He had not figured on Gideon. The lad was eleven, unusually strong and intelligent for his age. He now followed Jared everywhere, listening and learning, a superb student even in school. A silent lad, he seemed to absorb everything through his large dark eyes and eager handsome face.

"Let me come with you, Papa!" he would insist night after night when his father came home from work.

"Now, Gideon, you are too young!" Jared would pat his

shoulders. "When you are older—" He was proud of the boy, so precocious and hungry for adventure at such a young age.

Miriam looked concerned and shook her head. However, Gideon continued to beg, cunningly voicing his arguments.

"I mean to learn the work, Papa! One is never too young to start! I want to help you! I have done well in school this year, the master says so, and my mathematics is very good! Do let me come! I won't be in the way, I promise!"

He wore Jared down. Jared was so fond of the boy now and so accustomed to having him at his heels, a silent small shadow, alert and energetic. Jared had even become accustomed to talking to Gideon absently about work problems. Gideon listened and listened, his black eyes shining.

Jared finally decided to take him. Miriam was dismayed, weeping. "Jared, he is too young! What will happen to him? This is sheer madness! He is only eleven!"

"Nonsense, I will keep a stern eye on him, and we will be escorted by an army patrol from St. Louis. We'll be well protected."

"If he is killed," Miriam moaned, her hands at her heart. "Lord help us all. Jared, I beg of you—not my son!"

The more Miriam pleaded and argued, the more Jared became convinced it was time his son cut the apron strings. "No more, my dear. Gideon will be safe with me. He is right, he might as well learn young. He'll grow into a stronger man."

And so one day in late May they set out. They'd ride the railroad train to Chicago, change for St. Louis, and pick up drivers and wagons for the long haul west. A railroad car was loaded with fresh hardware supplies, arms, gunpowder, and dresses and yardgoods; there was also thread and needles and scissors for Vashti and the girls.

Miriam was silent as she watched them depart, her face pinched and sallow. She was against this journey, but she would argue no more. Jared kissed her tenderly, absently. "Now do not worry about us, Miriam! Stay well. Do not work yourself to the bone."

"Safe journey, the Lord be with you," she murmured, and turned to Gideon. She embraced the boy tightly, her cheek on his curly dark hair.

"I'll be fine, Mama, do not worry about me!" Gideon assured her. Her worn hand curved about his young cheek, and she gazed down into his eyes. Her mouth worked, but she could not speak. She kissed his forehead instead, and sent him on his way.

Jared was radiantly happy to be on his way. He had missed the journeys, the wild adventures, the love of Vashti who spiced his otherwise bland existence. This was living! The comradeship of tough reliable men, the empty spaces under the vast sky, the sight of the new railroad crawling westward across the plains. He talked and talked to the silent yet listening Gideon, to the eager Malachi, about life in the West.

In St. Louis they disembarked and hired drivers for the five wagons they needed to buy for their cargo. They met up with their patrol, led by a captain, several privates, and a sergeant who were heading to the forts on the farthest reaches of the untamed West.

Gideon thrived on the life. He learned to ride one of the army horses and to load a long rifle, shooting it on the run. He already knew how to handle a revolver—Jared had given him one of his own. His eager young face turned golden brown from the sun, and the boy seemed to grow taller by the month. He could shoot a rabbit, skin it, and cook it on a spit over the huge roaring campfire. He was afraid of nothing, not the howling wolves, the occasional bear, or the Indians who singly or in clusters followed them at a distance as if to decipher what they were up to.

They were such a large group, well armed, that the Landau party did not fear the Indians, restive though they were reputed to be. Sometimes their group could hear the Indians howling from afar, and Jared would dart up in his blanket roll and listen intently. But he knew the guards remained alert—there was good discipline in their patrol. Gideon was trained by the men and allowed to stand watch with one of the privates. He was proud to learn so much of army life.

Timid Malachi seemed to grow also, though his quiet nature prevented his older brother to tell by how much. Still he listened to the stories of the men, the bragging, the laughter, and entered into the life eagerly. He was weary of the life in the East, he had told Jared. He did not want to marry and be tied down, and his father's wife and the rabbi were always after him, matching him with this or that girl.

They finally reached the army fort and rested for a few days before ambling on to Copper Creek, the soldiers left behind them. As they delved deeper into the mountains, they felt its icy breath drifting over them even in the summer haze and had to don woolen overcoats. Gideon's eyes grew huge, he was so captivated by this whole new unimagined way of life. He couldn't ask his father enough questions about the copper, the mines, the mountains, the wild animals, the miners.

Jared was patient and thrilled to be back in this majestic mountain fairyland.

Before long they arrived, unmolested, in Copper Creek. As their mules ambled into the dusty small town, some miners emerged from the few businesses, the women left the houses, the fast women came from the saloon—and Vashti and her girls ran from their home—all to greet the travelers.

Jared swung down, laughing, dusty, black-bearded, and swept Vashti into his arms. He was so hungry for her, he forgot all caution—he kissed her heartily. She was lovelier than ever, though a streak of white hair swept across her brow.

"Oh, Jared—oh, Jared—I so hoped you would come—" She was half-laughing, half-crying.

Jared became aware of Gideon's stare. He helped the boy down from his mule, but Gideon continued to stare.

Jared had anticipated this moment. He introduced Vashti. "This is Mrs. Cohen, who owns half the town," he said, smiling.

Gideon nodded politely. "How do you do, Mrs. Cohen."

"And these are her girls, Amaris, Eden, and Sapphira."

Amaris was pregnant with her first child; she had matured much since her marriage. Eden was sultry, full-blown, her eyes too knowing. His dear little Sapphira, seven, came timidly to Jared and received his tender kiss. She was lovely, her dark eyes beautiful in a heart-shaped face framed with the dusky curls.

After the welcome, Jared took his son and brother to a boarding house and settled them into rooms. In their suite, he felt the boy's silently accusing eyes on his back.

"Well, you know it now, boy," he said brusquely, turning to face him. He had lived with this for so long, he had become accustomed to it and hated to feel guilty. "She is my daughter," he said softly to the unstated question in Gideon's eyes.

"Sapphira—is my—sister?" the boy asked hesitantly.

"Half-sister," said Jared.

"And Mrs. Cohen...does everybody know—except my mother?"

Jared sitting in a chair, ready for a long explanation, squirmed uncomfortably. "Well—everybody here knows, but no one back East. You must be silent about it, you realize."

Gideon stood there, his hands at his sides, struggling with himself. His eyes made Jared feel so uneasy. "I thought you— you would never—not you, Father," he said in a low voice.

"I am human," Jared cried. "How could I help it? She is so beautiful—and she is so alone, fighting the world! You cannot understand this yet, son, but we also love each other."

"What about—Mother?"

Jared was worried about the boy's feelings. How did you explain these things?

"I respect and love your mother beyond all women," he said carefully. "She is my wife, the mother of my children. A better woman never walked the earth—"

Gideon continued to stare at him. Jared rose, and began to unpack his gear, thinking of how he had stifled the guilt these many years. He had been so proud of his daughter, of the fact that Vashti loved him so passionately. The boy would surely understand someday. Surely.

The next day Jared went to the mines. He had left his brother Malachi to unpack the hardware goods and other supplies. He could not face Vashti this morning, not with Gideon looking on, silently condemning.

At the mine office he found that the bookkeeper, a miner who had lung trouble and could no longer work in the mines, was struggling with the books. The miner watched furtively as Jared pored over them.

And Jared found something definitely wrong. He had kept accounts of the wagon loads sent east to the smelters, so he knew the prices, the gross amounts, the net amounts, the profits. And now he noticed that too many wagon loads of copper ore had not made his ledgers; they'd been diverted elsewhere.

By late afternoon, Jared called a meeting of everyone. Vashti Cohen, Malachi, Jared Landau, and Ben Moran assembled in the bookkeeper's office. The bookkeeper was wringing his hands, afraid to speak.

Jared accused pointblank the manager of cheating.

"You're a liar!" Moran cried, his tanned face flushed. "You've been away for years. How do you expect to understand all that was going on? We were getting poor rates for the ore—"

"The government was paying top dollar!" Jared cried fur-

99

iously. "In the East, I got plenty for the ore; they needed it for the war—"

"Well, out west they didn't paid half that," Moran said sullenly, his face creased by emotion. "It was dangerous to send all those wagons east. Why, our men would have been killed! The ore went where I could get some money for it— of course, the money wasn't great—which is why the accounts show like that. But I did my best!" he ended virtuously, flashing his eyes at Vashti as though to force her to back him up.

"It is true, Jared," she interrupted in her rich voice. "Mr. Moran explained the problem to me. I did not want the men in more danger than was necessary—"

"Why not send a large band of armed men to Chicago as protectors and ship it east by rail?" Jared demanded. "It would have been safer."

"No, it would not have," Moran said self-confidently. "The larger group would have attracted more attention! Why, the Confederates were swarming all over the West! They watched for gold and copper shipments. They would have attacked quickly if they had known we were sending ore east! You don't know what trouble we had during the war. You were safely abiding in Philadelphia!"

His sneer as he said *Philadelphia* was one step too far.

"I dismiss you," Jared said swiftly. "You have shown bad judgment and still don't understand how you lost us a great deal of money! Worse, I am not convinced you did not deliberately cheat us."

"Jared!" Vashti cried, shocked and pale. "You should not say such things!"

"Are you calling me a liar and a cheat?" Moran demanded, his hand pressed to the holstered revolver that hung from his lavishly decorated belt.

Jared swallowed. He was furious with himself for not carrying a weapon on him. He would have to back down or the angry Irishman would let his temper loose, leading to a bloody scene in front of his brother and Vashti.

With forced calm, he said, "I said you had bad judgment. I think you lost me money, and Mrs. Cohen also. You should have sent the wagons east."

"Please, my friends!" Vashti pleaded. Moran's hand continued to hover near his revolver. "Do not let us quarrel! The money is sufficient for our needs. I am sure Mr. Moran acted in our interests."

His hand slowly leaving the holster, Moran said, narrow-eyed, "Well, I'll accept an apology!"

"I'll apologize," Jared said, hating the taste in his mouth. "But I cannot let you run the mines any longer. I am dismissing you."

"You can't do that!" Moran cried furiously. "She owns the mine—not you!"

"We own it together," Jared said. "And I'm firing you! I'm sure a man of your talents can find a good job elsewhere!"

Moran stared at him.

Vashti entered the fray quickly, distress in her voice. "It is not easy to find a good manager, Jared! Let us consider this more carefully, when we are calm. Mr. Moran should stay on. Nobody around here has such experience as he does, and nobody manages the men so well. We have had no strike, while other mines have."

Damn the woman, Jared thought furiously. Why could she not stay out of it? He had had Moran convinced he would have to leave. Now the handsome gamecock was ruffling his feathers again.

"Don't worry, Mrs. Cohen," Moran said, grinning humorlessly. "I'll stay on and look after your affairs real good! Nobody chases Ben Moran away!"

There was a silence in the room. Jared was adamant. But what could he do? He and Vashti owned the mine together. But Vashti had three-fourth's interest.

"We will discuss this in private," Jared said to her coldly, brushing past her out the door.

But when he spoke to Vashti later, he found her determined. "Jared, you must not interfere. You have been gone for three years, you do not know how difficult it is to manage! My one comfort was that Ben Moran managed the mine so well I didn't have to worry about it! I had enough with my girls, the war, thieves—"

"Ben Moran is stealing from us! Doesn't that mean anything to you!" he cried, standing before her, glaring.

She raised her soft round chin and glared back. Her black eyes were harder than he had ever seen them before. "It is your word against his—and it is Ben Moran who has been here these past three years!"

"Vashti, you will have to choose between us! Do you believe him or me?" Jared said finally, madly furious that Vashti would defy him and doubt his judgment.

She was silent for a moment. Turning her back, she gazed from the window of her office at the line of mountains looming in the distance, the snow capping their peaks. On some slopes the landscape was bleak, showing where gaps had been torn in the hills to obtain copper. "I have to live here, Jared, and it has not been easy." She paused, sighing. "I will choose Ben Moran."

He could not believe his ears. A thought came to mind. "Is he your lover?"

She swung around. She did not even try to answer, only stared at him with her fists clenched.

"That is it, then," he said, and strode out. She had taken Ben Moran as her lover, which was why she insisted on supporting him in this feud. Anger fused with anguished pain.

He packed his things after giving Malachi instructions on how to run the two mines he owned. He could do nothing about the one he owned with Vashti—she had more than half interest; her word prevailed.

He had a cruel thought. He could understand why men did not want women to control money and mines. They let their hearts rule their heads. What a stupid thing to do, keeping on a thief and cheater like Ben Moran!

Jared departed with Gideon a week later. He scarcely saw Vashti again, except to take her order for the next cargo of hardware and personal notions.

"When will you return?" Vashti asked in a troubled voice. He thought she regretted their quarrel but was too proud to apologize and ask that they continue where they left off.

He also refused to soften. She had displayed poor judgment, in his opinion, and she could live with the consequences! He would try to handle her affairs from the East as before, but one day she must find another manager. So he answered her curtly. "Another six months, maybe more. I'll send you word."

He kissed Sapphira and held her close for a long moment. He hated to leave her like this. He had wanted to stay the summer and get better acquainted.

But he could not remain with Ben Moran seated in power, acting like some triumphant rooster pacing the barnyard. Jared was certain Vashti had slept with the Irishman. How could she have done that? he rankled again. Setting his daughter back into her mother's arms, he climbed up onto the creaking wagon seat next to Gideon, and nodded to Vashti, looking somberly on. Then on this hot August day, he and Gideon drove out of town, wordlessly, the rest of the train of wagons trailing behind.

Gideon had been very quiet. He had wandered around the mines on their brief stay, poking around the shafts and men, asking questions, watching the mining and the rock exploding, and mostly hanging back, observing with his intent gaze. Now, on the first miles of their journey, he refrained from breaking the silence; he sensed his father's moodiness, and his own at leaving Copper Creek so soon after arriving.

And Jared *was* moody. He was smarting. Every mile that put distance between himself and Vashti made him long for her all the more. He wanted her expression soft and full of love for him. He wanted her sensuous white body pressing against his, soft and full as it ignited the white flame of passion that coursed through his body when he was with her. He had been thinking of her, longing for her...Damn it all! Those years of wanting, those eager miles of the voyage west—all in vain. Damn silly quarrel. Why were women so stupid about business?

The hooves of the sturdy mules, loaded with copper, rang out clearly in the summer air; they were sure-footed mountain animals, and the drivers knew their business. Nights were quiet in the hills. The guards watched and listened, striding slowly back and forth beyond the campfires. Indians were worse now; they were becoming desperate as white men shoved and pushed their way farther into Indian lands.

Gideon seemed to rouse from his absorption and talk more freely. Mostly, he asked questions about the mines, the copper, the processing. What happened when the copper reached the East? How was it smelted? What percentage of the profit did they get? Then he asked about the land, the Indians, the soldiers, and the pioneers. Who owned the land? How did one file on a strike?

Jared found relief in answering his questions and forgetting the dreadful gap between him and Vashti. He talked each day, explaining the business, his plans for future expansion. They must wait and see how much need there was for copper now that the war was over. Prices might drop, unless the new railroads and other businesses increased the need for copper. If prices bottomed out, there was always lead mining, coal, even silver or gold to go into.

They reached the army post where they'd left the soldiers

on their way to Copper Creek. Captain Nicholas Frazer was now in command of the post, and his wife, Anna, made the Landaus feel welcome. They remained for several days.

Gideon went about the post, examining it, talking to the soldiers, especially the ones they had come west with.

Jared smoked his pipe, and talked idly to Frazer about the Indian troubles, the miners who had drifted through, the new prospectors.

"I can see you are troubled, my friend," Frazer said, one day as they returned from a brief patrol. "Can I help you in any way?"

Jared sighed. "I have been making up my mind. I think I must go back to Copper Creek. Unfinished business."

Frazer nodded, his face impassive as always. He shielded his eyes and gazed west across the plains to the mountains. "I thought you came early," he said. "Best to face problems and sort them out at once. An untreated wound festers."

Jared gazed at him thoughtfully. How much did he know or guess? He had spoken briefly of the mine troubles, of Ben Moran. The captain must have worked out the rest for himself.

"Yes, I must go back—and treat the wound," Jared sighed.

"I can give you a patrol as far as the foothills."

Jared thanked him, and planned to leave again in two days. He came to life, he felt, and his vigor returned. He had reached a decision. He could not walk away and leave Ben Moran to do as he wished with the mine. Malachi was not a strong man. And Vashti Cohen—well, she was a woman.

Chapter 9

It felt odd to ride into Copper Creek so quietly, this time mounted on sleek energetic horses. There were no long lines of mules or horses and drivers, no jingle of bells and shrill whoops of drivers to stir the town out of their homes and offices.

Jared and Gideon rode directly to the mine office, stirring up a cloud of dust as they passed on the unpaved street. This time Jared had buckled on his gun belt and made sure his revolver was loaded. Gideon who was watching, slipped a knife into his own belt. His father scarcely noticed. Peering at the door of the mine office, Jared warned, "You stay out here, son."

Gideon's mouth though was pressed into a grim line and he did not reply. He looked older than his years, with all the dark handsome features of the Landau men, but with a tall grace the others in the family were not fortunate enough to possess. Sliding off his horse, he grabbed his father's reigns and tethered it, along with his own, to the hitching post; then he stood back and waited.

Jared had hoped to find the mine bookkeeper alone, or with Malachi. But as he pushed open the screen door and stepped inside, he saw a stranger next to Ben Moran.

The tall Irishman glanced up, then nearly gasped. He was obviously shocked and angered by Jared's appearance. The stranger looked on mildly curious. Wearing a frockcoat and white shirt, Jared guessed he was a businessman.

"What the hell are you doing here?" Moran blurted out, and his hand went to his revolver at the belt.

Jared kept his arms swinging loose. He glanced at the stranger. "Who are you?"

"None of your damn business!" the stranger shot out. "Who is this man, Moran?"

"I'm Jared Landau, part owner of the mine he claims to run," he said. He had stiffened warily, but now he felt a wave of keen excitement blazing through him.

Now the stranger looked uneasy, glancing from one to the other. He backed up. "I'm not in this quarrel—" he said, waving his hands. He stood against the wall, glancing toward the door.

"I asked who you are, stranger!" Jared demanded.

"Just—just from the smelter—doing business—"

"How much are you paying per load of ore?" Jared bluntly asked.

Moran cried out, "None of his business—shut your mouth!" But it was too late. The stranger blurted out the amount.

It was far more than what Moran had claimed the smelter paid.

"So—damn your eyes—you have been cheating!" Jared said.

"No, I can explain everything. I'm not a cheat—let me explain—" Then Moran lost his nerve. Out of fear, he yanked out his revolver and shot at Jared.

Jared felt the bullet hit high in his right shoulder. The arm dropped to his side. He could not pull his own gun, and Moran's blue eyes blazed in triumph as he thumbed back the trigger once more.

Jared jumped at him. He was not as big a man, but he was tough and hard from years of work. He knocked Moran down, spilling the gun out of Moran's hand. The stranger grabbed it up.

Jared had no time to look to see whose side he was on. The man yelled, "I'm not in this—I'm going—" And he ran out the door.

Gideon was suddenly there, watching. His knife came out. Moran had his hands on Jared's throat, and they wrestled over and over on the dirt floor. Jared, on his side, his right arm dangling, tried to keep Moran from killing him by pressing his thumbs into Jared's neck. The pressure increased. With an intense effort Jared rolled over on top of Moran and knocked his head against the dirt floor. Then suddenly Moran was over him again, his face red and flushed, eyes popping with rage. The pain in Jared's throat sent the blood drumming in his head, his vision blurring.

He heard a woman's scream, then the stranger yelling, and the room seemed filled with people.

"Let him go—let him go," Vashti cried. Moran's hands tightened.

Gideon's arm came up from nowhere and descended into Moran's throat. The man groaned, and blood spurted over Jared, blinding him. The man collapsed over him, and Jared could not move.

Someone shoved Moran off Jared, the body flopping aside limply. Malachi bent down, his face strained, and helped Jared up.

"My God—what happened—shot—the boy knifed—saw it all—Moran shot first—"

The voices dimmed in Jared's ears, and he swayed as the pain shot up and down his arm. He caught hold of a small shoulder. It was Gideon, holding him up.

"Lean on me, Papa," the boy said in a shrill tone. His face was greenish-gold. Jared leaned on his son, unable to speak.

"What happened—what happened?" Others were trying to push into the room. Someone bent over Moran.

"The man is dead! Moran is dead!"

"He was cheating my papa!" Gideon said gravely, his voice changing as he spoke. It went from deep to high, then he cleared his throat. "He tried to kill my papa! He shot him. Then he tried to choke him to death!"

"That's right," Malachi said nervously, glancing about the room, his eyes glazed with shock. "Moran tried to kill my brother! I saw it all!"

A brief informal court was held right there. Several drifters and an injured miner had seen most of the incident. They knew about Moran.

Mutters went about:

"Tried to cheat Landau. Tried to take his woman, Mrs. Cohen."

"Bad blood between them."

"Fight—Moran fired—that's his gun."

"The smelter man saw it—fair fight—"

The equally informal verdict, by the court of necessity, held that Jared and his son had killed Ben Moran in a fair fight; Moran had shot first, and Jared had defended himself. Case closed. Bury the loser.

Several men carried Moran off to bury him. The business of the town went on. The excitement was over, though it would be talked about, chewed over with meals, gulped down with drinks for years.

Several women shook their heads over the fact that the boy had done the knifing. Brave lad, but too bad he had had to see such a fight, to do such a deed—so young too! Well, the West was a tough place, best to grow up sooner than later.

Jared and Gideon went off to the boardinghouse where they had stayed before. Gideon's shirt was soaked with blood. Jared insisted he change right away. The Indian woman, Winona, appeared from nowhere and helped the boy, while the woman who ran the boardinghouse brought hot water, a knife, and a bottle of sour whisky. Jared drank until he was nearly insensible while Winona heated the knife.

Vashti appeared ashen-faced, watching. Gideon stood with tight mouth, eyes burning dry, while Winona dug out the bullet from his father's shoulder. Jared still felt enough pain that he blacked out completely, limp on the broken-down sofa.

When he came to, the bandage bound his arm tightly, and he had a fierce headache and hangover. He lay quiet after they moved him to the bedroom.

Gideon hovered over him anxiously. "Papa, can I get you anything? A drink, food?"

"Lots of hot tea," Jared said weakly. "Feel parched as the desert."

Gideon left, to return with a tray and teapot and cups. Vashti came also, pale but composed. They drank in silence.

Jared finally looked at his young son. "Proud of you, Gideon. Hated you had to do it, but you showed lots of courage."

The boy's normal color had not returned. He nodded, his face down. "I got sick to my stomach," he mumbled. "Guess I'm not so tough—not yet."

Vashti, somewhere behind the boy, said tightly, "You didn't have to kill the man! Ben Moran always had a temper, but he cooled down fast."

Jared glanced over and caught sight of Vashti, whose dark eyes were blazing. Her hair, always so beautiful and lustrous, was disheveled. Her face was not quite the right color.

"Did you want me to wait till he killed me?" he asked coldly.

She sighed, shook her head, brushing back the rebellious locks of hair. "I cannot understand violence," she said. "Why, why did you have to come back and pick a fight?"

Jared was silent, too weak to explain to her. If he had not returned, Ben Moran would have gone on cheating, lying, getting more and more powerful, until a showdown would have been inevitable. Better to get it over with before the man swelled too far beyond him.

Vashti, uncomprehending, left.

Gideon said in a quiet voice. "I see why you came back, Papa. You couldn't let him get away with it."

"That's right," Jared sighed wearily. His mouth felt like it was stuffed with cotton, his head hurt so much he wished he could take it off and get some rest. He moved painfully in the sagging bed, rattling the corn husks. "Better now than later. Never does to let a man get away with cheating. Never trust him again. Never turn your back, never walk away. Settle it now."

"I understand, Papa." Gideon said quietly, and left the room to let his father sleep.

Jared recovered quickly, for the cool air in the high altitude seemed to promote healing. He walked out within two days and soon regained his strength.

Jared with his brother and son silently went over the books. The bookkeeper that Moran had hired was fired. Jared wanted nobody who had taken a part in cheating him.

Vashti begged him to return and talk to her. Jared went over to her house one evening, prepared to be stern. She had interfered, and it had almost cost him his life.

They sat down in the office-parlor to talk. Eden had gone to bed early, a smirk on her lips as she let Jared in. Such a knowing, precocious child, he thought with distaste. Vashti had best marry her off well before long; she needed a strict marriage to keep her in line. At sixteen, she looked over a man too closely, she had no modesty.

How different from Amaris, so settled and content and glowing with love for her husband. Some women were born to marriage, loving, a family. Others were troublemakers, fast women from the very cradle! He thought of Miriam, so settled and happy in their marriage, then dismissed the thought quickly. It made him feel so guilty. She was faithful, but it was natural for her.

Vashti looked at Jared's sling, and her lips trembled. "Oh, Jared—your arm..."

"It is healing," he said brusquely.

"But you could have been killed!"

"I thought you were worried about Moran getting killed," he said dryly. Hadn't she slept with the man? Granted, it had been a long three years—

"Killing is terrible, it seems so unnecessary, so uncivilized," she said, glancing away. "I cannot understand why men cannot settle matters peacefully."

"He shot first," Jared said.

She sighed, held out her hands appealingly. "I know, I know. But why did he shoot? He should not have worn guns— I told him that made for trouble. If one does not carry a gun, one is not tempted to shoot."

"I'm sorry you did not succeed in your arguments," Jared said bitterly. "It might have saved me a bullet wound and him a grave."

"Oh, Jared! This is not what I meant to talk about!"

"What, then? The accounts? They are coming along well. Malachi can straighten them out. He has a good head for figures. We will just write off the amount Moran walked off with. I suppose he spent it as fast as he got it."

"I think so... he did have some gold and diamonds—"

"What happened to them?" Jared interrupted.

Vashti was flushed. "The woman who cleaned his body brought them to me. She gave away his clothes to a miner who needed them... he was injured..."

"Where are the gold and diamonds?"

She indicated a cigar box and opened it. He surveyed the contents silently. There was a gold watch, a chain of nuggets, crude diamond rings set in gold, and a bracelet of diamonds set in gold. He sifted through them idly.

"Do you want them?" Vashti asked.

He shook his head. "No. You keep them, unless he has relatives."

"Distant relatives in Ireland, nobody else," he said.

Jared shrugged. "No sense bothering. I doubt if they bothered about him. Why did the woman bring them to you?" He glanced at her suspiciously, trying to veil his jealousy.

Her eyes downcast, Vashti said, "Why, the town knows he cheated me—and you."

"Yes. That's right." Jared wondered again, when Moran had had her. A luscious woman, still desirable in her late thirties. A widow, hungry for a man—but he might be doing her wrong.

He sighed. How to see into the heart of such a woman? She would have sworn she would be faithful to him—yet—

Vashti shut the box and put it away in a drawer. "I'll put this in the safe tomorrow," she said.

"Give something to Amaris, she never asks for anything," Jared said abruptly.

Vashti smiled tenderly. "I know, such a good girl!"

"Eden always gets because she begs and grabs. What are you going to do about her?"

"Eden? She is only sixteen!"

"You married at sixteen."

"I was—was planned for," Vashti said. "They—arranged it. I would not do that to Eden."

"Might be better. She is man-hungry, and this town has twenty times more men than women."

"I won't arrange a marriage for Eden! I hated—I mean, I disliked marrying so early," Vashti said.

"You got a better man for it," he said tightly.

There was a long silence between them as Vashti sat down, head bent demurely, the lamplight shining on her dark glossy curly hair.

"Damnit," Jared blurted out. "Why did you interfere, Vashti? Why did you defend that damn crook? Why didn't you let a man take care of men's business?"

Her hands stirred, then were still. She swallowed, and Jared watched the slight emotion evidenced by the movement of her throat. He felt like striking her for the trouble she had caused. The trouble a beautiful woman could cause! And his loins still ached for her. He wanted to wrestle her to the bed, make her give in, force her. Punish her! She had interfered, caused trouble, and as a result, a man was dead. His own son, Gideon, had been forced to kill. He'd never be a boy again.

To be faced so young with the fact that man was mortal. To know a life could be snuffed out in a moment. Gideon

111

would be facing his own mortality, and Jared could not help him much. Maybe when they got home the rabbi could talk to him and comfort him, teach him. Jared must arrange that. Jared felt helpless in the face of such an enormous task. He himself had learned early that man was mortal, that a Jew could die quickly at the careless, despising hand of a Gentile. He had not wanted his son to know death so close-by, so very early.

He came back to the present, to the bowed head of Vashti. Gazing at her meek, bowed body, Jared wanted her. He got up and went over to her. Vashti, so desirable, sometimes so withdrawn into her own self. He wanted to own her, to hurt her, to know her completely and possess her in every sense of the word.

"I will say good night," he said coldly, his gaze lingering on her bent head.

She jumped up and put her hand on his unhurt arm. She pleaded, "Forgive me! I did not mean to hurt you!" Tears welled up in her large dark eyes and rolled slowly down her tanned face.

"A woman like you must hurt. It is your nature," he said crisply. "Being the way you are, looking as you do, you hurt a man by your very walk, the sway of your hips—"

She flushed deeply. "Jared!"

"It is true," he told her gloomily. "A woman like you is a torch to a dry heap of logs. An untended campfire in a tinder-dry forest. One cannot help the blaze that follows—"

She fell into his arms, clutching at his shoulders. Tears rolled down her face. "Jared, I am so sorry, I am so sorry. It was all my fault—and I hate myself for it. All I wanted was to be independent, to fend for myself. But the world belongs to men . . . I could not help it . . ."

He silenced her with his lips. He kissed her fiercely, holding her in his good arm. She mumbled against him, but he did not care what she said, he only knew he blazed with fire at the touch of her against him.

They went upstairs to the bedroom, and fell across the bed, still clutching, still holding on to each other fiercely. Vashti's mouth trailed across Jared's cheek, his lips, tasting, biting; her fingers clutched at his shoulders, his back. When his shirt was removed, she ran her hands over his firm muscular chest, moaning.

Pushing him away, she removed her clothes hastily, then

showed herself to him in the lamplight that glowed dimly from the table.

Swiftly he removed the rest of his clothes, and then she bent over him on the mussed bed, full-lipped, mysterious of eye, dark shadows across her face. Her luxurious, silky hair hung free, and he tangled his hand in it and brought her head down to his. He kissed her fiercely. "It has been too damn long," he moaned.

"I know, too long, I want—" she sighed, leaning against his long body. Her glorious weight, the rounded thighs, her breasts hanging over him, then pressing on his chest, drove him to new height. He pinched her nipples, and she moaned deep in her throat.

He fondled her, his good hand between their bodies, caressing her rounded stomach, the warm thighs, her most secret places. She shuddered with pleasure. His hand went to her hips, pressing her closer till she sheathed him completely, and they sighed their mutual rapture, her dark eyes glowing with wild pleasure. As they rode to the summits together, he found he couldn't help wondering if she had done this with that Irishman Moran, with his liquid tongue and flattering ways.

He didn't want to think of him, but before he could stop himself he had a flash of memory—the Irishman lying sprawled and covered in red blood in the dust.

He flinched and moved away.

"What is it? Too much?" Vashti whispered, pausing, kissing him.

He pulled her face down to his, his hand gripping a tress of silky hair. "Kiss me, shut up," he growled.

He needed to order her about, needed to give her pain with pleasure, wanted to hurt her for what she had done. She did as he ordered, and when they were almost there, he struck her on the hips, bringing her down with a thud. She cried out, mouth open, head back, arching. He felt her quivering, made her stay there, his fingers pressed into her rich thigh, until he burst with pleasure.

Afterward he lay beside her sleeping, but wakened, uneasy, at the sound of a creaking floorboard. He kept silent, turning his head slowly, his eyes half-opened and senses alert.

He saw the door open slightly, saw bright eyes peering inside. The light from the lantern didn't reach far but he could make out a scarlet mouth, teeth biting lips, a white curious

113

face—Eden, damn her. Watching them. Seeing him with her mother.

He did not speak, let her think he was sleeping. She seemed to study their naked bodies for a time, then slowly withdrew her head. The floorboards creaked as she returned to her room.

Jared could not return to sleep. He thought of the girl's young but lush body, her greedy eyes. Damn. She was ripe for marriage. He wondered if she played with the young men always hanging around her.

Thinking about her made him restless. Vashti stirred, and he bent over her, wakening her with his kisses and his hands on her body. She stirred again, smiled with eyes shut, and murmured, "Jared. Oh, I needed you—"

Her body moved sensuously. He stroked the ripe breasts, then her midriff, then her silken thighs. His fingers learned her over again, and he did not speak as he moved over her. Now it was wildness all over again, but she did not complain, she seemed to enjoy his firmness with her. Her dark eyes shone in the moonlight. Her fingers dug into his back, and her fingernails scraped along his spine, making him groan with lust.

During the following weeks, he came often to her and slept all night with her. The town's gaze followed them about knowingly. And Gideon stayed with Malachi in his crude cabin, learning about the books, the town's doings, the mines, what the miners said, how they worked.

The boy knew, the town knew. Vashti once said, "The new banker wants to marry me."

Her mouth was ripe and somehow sullen. Jared smiled unpleasantly. There was more conflict than love between them now. "Even now? When he knows about us?"

She nodded, lifting her chin. "Mr. Dallmeyer is a good man. He is a widower, his daughter, Rachel, is a sweet little girl. He needs me."

"I thought his sister had come to take care of them."

"Yes. Ruth. A spinster, but a good woman. She has little understanding of children, however. I could be good for him—and his girl."

"So why don't you marry him if he still wants you?"

Jared leaned back in the chair, challenging her.

She shrugged her round shoulders. "I don't know. He wants a son. I probably could not give him a son."

114

"Maybe you could."

She studied him. "Jared, why do you speak so to me?" she asked plaintively. "You know I love you. I cannot marry you, it is impossible, but then why should I not marry another man?"

"I don't think you would be happy, Vashti. He has no passion in him, and you are very passionate. You'd starve without it."

She stared at him, then smiled alluringly. "You know I would, so do I. I am—alive." She stretched her arms above her head sensuously. "Before, when I was married, I was still a child, an innocent. I did not know what it was to be free, to live as I wished. I knew I wanted more—more—"

"And you like to be independent, control your money," he teased.

"Yes, for me and the girls," she said seriously. She brought her arms down and folded them across her chest, contemplating the account books that lay before her on the table. "Yes, money and freedom. It has been worth it all—all—"

He got up abruptly. He hated for her to drift away from him with that dreamy half-smile on her mouth. He stood behind her, his good hand moving down from her shoulders to her breasts. "And you need nobody—" he whispered.

Her hands closed over his, pressing it to her breasts. "Oh, Jared, you know . . . how I feel . . ."

He bent over her and kissed her brow soberly. He could feel the shuddering response in her body as he leaned against her deliberately. "And when I am away from you, I think of you and hunger so badly—"

"Do you? Do you?" She turned her head and pressed her lips against his wrist.

"You will refuse Dallmeyer," he demanded rather than asked.

She nodded, the rich hair shining in the sunlight streaming in through the window. "Of course," she said.

His hand went to her waist and pressed her against him. "You belong to me," he said, and his fingers pressed cruelly against her. She only sighed and lay against him.

He was reluctant to leave her; he lingered long. But finally he and Gideon had to pack up and return east, arriving in Philadelphia by Chanukah.

All responsibilities seemed to descend upon him at once. He found Miriam pregnant and the baby due in February. He found his father had died in his absence and that his brothers had had to contend with the funeral and all its problems by themselves.

They had tried to settle the will in his absence. Jared sighed and settled down to unravel their mismanagement.

He missed his father, that poor frail man who had led them from Switzerland, who had been unable to hold his family together. The grocery had foundered, his children had deceived him, Asher openly defied him, his son Jared had left the business and struck out on his own.

"But I had to, Papa," Jared said silently to the grave, as he visited it daily for a time. He felt guilty. "I had to leave, don't you see? I had to make my way. My own children will remain with me. I have learned my lesson from you—one must keep a strict hand on all."

He felt his father hovering above him, vaguely smiling, vaguely reproachful, as a mist of memory wisping in a cloud. "My son, my eldest son," he thought he could hear his father saying. "What a good boy! How proud I am of you! Do not forget my teachings!"

"I have kept your teachings, Father," Jared muttered. "Except—"

Except he had been set on becoming a millionaire. Except he had lived openly with a woman not his wife and fathered a child by her. Except he had felt contempt for his brothers, and had used them.

"But I must do this—I am strong and must rule them all, Father," he explained to the unanswering grave. "A man has this chance in America, don't you see it?"

A man could be anything he chose to be in America, this land of freedom and vast lands. Thrusting aside his feelings of guilt, Jared realized Lemuel might be proud of all his son had accomplished for the Landaus, for their heritage. And there was much more to do to ensure a strong Landau lineage.

All it took was brains, enterprise, cleverness, and the will to succeed. He had all of that. Success—it would come because he fought for it.

Chapter 10

Miriam went into labor on a cool evening in February 1867 and after a short time delivered her fifth child, a son whom they named David. He was a merry, bright child, with dancing dark eyes and more mischief in him than even his brother Bart.

"David, he is born with music and charm in him," Miriam mused, bending over the child, who laughed much more than he cried. How someday he would have his own way!

Jared decided the house was now too small for them. In vain Miriam protested. "My dear, we have a huge house," she cried out to him. "This huge place—and all our neighbors so very good to us!"

"*You* are good to *them*. You do too much, always going out and helping," he scolded fondly. "Not three weeks from David's birth, and you went to Mrs. Lloyd's to help in her birth."

"The Lord has been good to me," Miriam said. "I am so happy the child is all right, and his mother fine." It had been a difficult first birth for the girl, and she had been in much pain. Miriam had soothed her with gentle motherly words, hot tea, comfort.

Miriam was reluctant to move until Jared had found a splendid, larger house in a finer, wealthier suburb of Philadelphia, farther from the downtown, which was awash with new immigrants. How long it seemed since they had come to these shores. How crowded America was becoming.

They moved into the splendid home in April, and the following month Jared had to depart for the West. Gideon wanted to accompany him, but Jared firmly refused, remembering in horror what had happened the first time, his son caught in the middle of his feud with Moran. Gideon had been sent to the rabbi this winter to work out any longlasting harmful effects, and fortunately the boy seemed so far healthy, if aged.

Miriam was puzzled. "He went last year—"

"He is still too young." Jared's gaze met his son's firmly, warningly. They had not told Miriam what had happened. "Not this year, son. Maybe soon."

"But, Father, you may need—" Gideon halted at Jared's shake of the head and the anger in his eyes.

"Asher comes with me. He will be learning much of the trade—he's coming of age."

Worried about the mines and fearing his studious and easygoing brother Malachi could not handle everything himself, Jared had talked to his other brothers. Enoch had no wish to go west; he lived a calm life running the grocery store, not caring if it thrived spectacularly or not. Mild success was fine. Isaac was busy with the hardware store and his bachelor life.

Jared was suspicious of anybody outside the family, so he had reluctantly turned to his youngest brother, and found Asher tired of his own routine. Ready to go west, ready for adventure, Asher eagerly accepted Jared's offer.

He also wanted shares in the mines, which didn't suit Jared at all. When Gideon was grown, the boy would automatically be a partner. But not his brothers. They would not profit by his cunning and drive and hard work. Only by their own.

Instead, Jared offered Asher a high salary, almost as much as he was paying Malachi, and Asher reluctantly and poutingly accepted, as though doing Jared a favor.

The two Landau men joined an army patrol outside St. Louis, as usual. Meanwhile, Jared worked Asher very hard to see if he could handle rough work. To his surprise, Asher worked willingly day and night, helping load the railroad cars, the wagons, learning to use weapons, jumping in where softer men feared to tread.

Asher's face grew tanned, his beard grew long, his eyes sparkled the farther west they went. "This is a good life!" he exclaimed over and over. "How could I have remained so long in Philadelphia? There is nothing there for a man with ambitions!"

Jared bit his tongue. Asher had never been so ambitious before. He would have to learn that opportunities did not float through the air—they came with hard work and digging, as in the copper mine, yielding results over time. Jared could only hope he would keep interested in hard work.

They arrived in Copper Creek in June 1867. Jared was pleased to see that Malachi was working hard at the books and that they were in good order. He had always had a sharp mathematical mind. The mines were each under the direction of a foreman, who reported directly to Malachi. And Malachi showed every sign of enjoying his position of power. So when Jared offered him a pay raise, Malachi couldn't help but show his disappointment. He had wanted shares in the mines, to be a co-owner.

Jared said no. "That is another matter, Malachi," he said. "Why not save your money and buy a claim?"

"But, Jared, I would not know which claim to buy!" He looked at Jared with helpless, melancholy eyes.

Jared shrugged. "I can help you choose one—"

But Malachi wanted more, he wanted everything handed to him, so he wouldn't have to struggle. Jared hoped Malachi wouldn't make trouble for him in the future.

Vashti Cohen gave a big dinner for them, excited and happy that Jared had returned. The table was crammed, with napkins, red candles, hot dishes of food. Winona cooked and served a huge dish of deer meat. Asher had never eaten venison before and pronounced it delicious. They had corn, beans, greens, and a large two-layer cake.

Amaris came with her husband, contented, shy, silent, and more plump after childbirth. They left early so her husband could get some sleep before the morning shift.

Vashti's other daughter, the wily one, Eden, dressed in a red cotton dress, low cut, was showing her rounded breasts. She wore a long golden chain and the gold bracelet with diamonds. Jared remembered from where the objects came immediately.

He asked Vashti privately later, "Did you give Amaris nothing?"

Vashti looked worried. "She wanted nothing, Jared. She

never liked Ben Moran and wanted no remembrance of him. I told her it was good to have money and jewels—for the future. She wanted nothing."

"Give her some money from the mine, then. It is not right for a family to give one child so much more than another."

"I will do it. You are right, Jared." As promised, Vashti transferred some money to Amaris's account in the bank— despite Amaris's loud protests.

Jared spoke to her kindly. "You do not know what the future holds, Amaris. Someday your mother may need you."

He thought, rightly, that this appeal would work when another might not. Sure enough, she smiled gently. "My mother has only to ask for anything I might have."

The money, some five thousand dollars, was safe with Amaris, and Jared planned with Vashti to open an account for Amaris in Philadelphia, to which he would add money from what they netted from their business. She would never be wanting if she needed to take care of a feeble mother.

Asher had been making eyes at the beautiful Eden ever since meeting her, complimenting her lavishly. She was blooming under his praise. She found him a much more civilized man, she said, than any she'd met in Copper Creek.

He was ten years older than Eden, so Jared thought nothing of it. He was not much taller than she, at five feet four inches, and he was burlier than the other Landau brothers, but with the same comely dark features. He had never seemed one for flattery, though his tongue gained impetus when he talked to Eden. To her, he was attractive and she liked that—black curly hair and a nice beard, and bold black eyes that thought nothing of raking her figure.

Jared warned Vashti. "Asher often visits the madams at home—he is notorious for his bawdy-house visits. Do not let Eden be alone with him, although I think he would respect her."

"He has never married?" Vashti asked, surprised. "I wonder at him. He seems nice and a hard worker."

He had been impressed at Asher's eager learning. Jared had told him on their arrival to the West that Malachi was in charge. Asher was to help his older brother in every way he could. And though Asher seemed to show respect for both his older brothers, Jared would reserve final judgment.

Jared came often to Vashti, and they had more tender relations than the previous year. She welcomed him to her bed, and they made love wildly, with more abandon than before. She pleased him very much—she was mature, sensitive to his wants, and was as passionate as he was. She made Miriam seem cold and impassive, though Miriam had a loving, generous heart. Women were very different, Jared decided.

He had never felt so great. Vashti made him feel he was the most powerful man in the world. They rarely failed to reach the heights of passion together. He would be tired by morning and ready to sleep half the day, but when he finally awoke for work, he hummed and sang to himself as he got ready, feeling more refreshed than if he hadn't been with her.

He shared a house with his brothers, which Malachi had bought for the company. Winona had found an Indian woman to cook and clean for them. When he slept with Vashti, he went to her house, where they could have the peace and quiet they needed.

Through the summer, Asher worked hard on the books, learning all about the accounts. He asked many intelligent questions of Malachi, Jared, Vashti, the miners, the foremen. Jared was pleased, though he was wary about the way his brothers' hunger for more riches grew. He could countenance no greed in his household.

By September he had to return to the Landau concerns in Philadelphia, and while there, he concentrated on investing money into his and Vashti's accounts. Using her letter of authority, he transferred half her accounts to an account under Amaris's name, and then invested the rest for her. He wouldn't tell Amaris about the transfers; it would be a pleasant surprise for her one day. Eden could have money when she came of age.

For Sapphira, he had already set up an account; he had been putting money into it yearly. He felt such a great tenderness for his young black-eyed daughter, so sweet and gentle and timid. He had a feeling Eden bullied her, though Vashti was protective enough to shelter her.

Miriam had made the great new house comfortable. Each child had a separate room, and they had bathrooms all over the second and third floors and four guest rooms.

Miriam had had to hire a butler, footmen, and a number of maids, plus two cooks. She protested against all the expense, but Jared had laughed and hugged her.

"We are now in the wealthy classes, my dear! We shall entertain more! I do not want you to lift a finger to work."

She was thoughtful, resting against him. Finally she straightened and gazed into his eyes. "Jared, I should like to set up a fund with some of that money, if we may."

He frowned. "A fund, my dear?"

"Yes, Jared. To aid the hospitals," she said carefully. "There is so much sickness, you would not believe it. Rosemary told me that she wished to become a nurse, yet I fear she will never have the strength for it. We thought it would be good to set up money to pay girls to train for nursing. And for young men to enter medical school, since it is so expensive."

Jared was quiet, gazing into her anxious dark eyes. "How good you are," he said finally. "How you think of everyone before yourself! Yes, we shall do this. It is a noble thought. The Lord has been very good to us."

Miriam released a great sigh of relief and kissed his cheek. "Thank you, Jared, thank you so very much. I am grateful to you. Can it be set up soon? I want so much to help people more than I do—"

He kissed her cheek and lips tenderly, reverently. "As soon as may be. We shall discuss it further with our lawyers, but meanwhile, do not say you help people too little. You are gone every day on your works of mercy."

"Never enough," she sighed. "Never enough. If I had ten hands, it would not be enough."

He held her soft body against himself, marveling at her.

He enjoyed the big mansion. It was a sign of his hard work, and prosperity. Abigail came to live with them, since she found that the old house she had shared with Lemuel had too many memories. She helped Miriam with the entertaining, but mostly with the young children, loving them with grandmotherly care and brisk discipline.

They entertained quite a bit that winter. Jared invited bankers, lawyers, associates, businessmen from New York City, hard-eyed moneymen and their frivolous hoop-skirted wives. He ordered new elaborate gowns for his wife to compete with them and jewelry to dangle about her, despite all her protests.

"I feel like a doll dangling with chains and bells," she said quaintly, shaking her diamond necklace and the long string of pearls. "Surely it is not right to wear so much all at once!"

122

The jewelry did not look right on her full figure, he decided, surveying her. Vashti with her tall splendid figure, would have looked barbarically magnificent, but he stifled the thought. "It does look a bit overdone," he said. "Perhaps just the pearls tonight. They go well with the black—"

"Yes, just the pearls," Miriam agreed with relief, and she returned the diamonds to him to put in the safe.

She might not have been the smartest dressed or most beautiful woman there, but she was the most admired, he decided proudly. Her sweet disposition, her gracious way of putting them all at ease, her refusal to gossip with malice, her plain speaking all made them comfortable, from whatever walk of life they came.

"Mother is the nicest lady of all," Gideon said, then added, "She never puts on airs!"

He was growing up, and he begged to go west with Jared the following summer. Jared put him off once more, setting off in late April and forcing Gideon, tall for his age and regal in bearing, to remain in school. The lad was very disappointed.

"Remember—next year, Papa!" Gideon cried after his father as he climbed the steps into the train. A pleading look creased the boy's handsome features.

Jared leaned far out the window to watch his wife and son wave, until the train, rumbling down the tracks, turned and they were lost to sight.

Jared felt more complacent as he became caught up in transferring his wares from the railroad cars in Chicago and later in St. Louis. It was 1868, and the West was settling down, in spite of rumors of Indian uprisings. Jared didn't spot a hint of smoke in the sky or dust from Indian ponies following the trains on the ridges.

And before he knew it, he was safely in Copper Creek. It was early June, earlier than he had expected to be there. His brother Malachi opened his mouth wide on seeing him, relief evident in his worried, melancholy face.

"Damnit, it's good you came, Jared!" he cried. Jared smiled in return, and the two brothers clapped each other on the back in greeting.

But when they entered the mine's offices, their youngest brother, Asher, was nowhere to be seen. Jared, sensing trouble, turned serious. "What's up? What is going on?"

Malachi settled into a chair, a sharp eye on his elder brother's features. "That Eden Cohen is a fast piece. She and Asher got together soon after you left, running all about together, making people talk. Anyway, her mother insisted on her stopping, and instead she and Asher went off and got married."

"Married!" Jared cried, trying to digest what he'd just been told. "Well, perhaps for the best—"

"Ain't all," Malachi said, warming up to the story. "Asher, he went to a judge and got hold of all Mrs. Cohen's property. Eden kicked her mother out of the house and hardware store. She says her husband runs everything now. And that judge—he said women couldn't take care of their own affairs, she should be glad she has such a smart son-in-law to take care of her!"

"What?" Jared cried, not believing his ears. He jumped to his feet. "Why, Asher can't do that!"

"He did," Malachi said, his dark eyes flashing. "Did it fast, too, before anybody could stop him. You just ask him—he'll be glad to tell you how smart he is!"

Jared sat in the swivel chair, brooding and angry. Asher hadn't changed at all, after all—he was just as greedy and cunning as ever, his character obviously formed early and for all time. He sighed. "Well, I had better see Vashti," he said.

"You won't find her at Asher's house anymore!" Malachi said, shaking his graying head sadly. "She's over at Amaris's. She's living there now. Eden won't allow her in the store!"

"Damnit," Jared swore. He strode off to the house he and Malachi owned. He needed to wash and change while he thought out a course of action.

That evening he went to Amaris's house and found Peter, her young husband, just returning from work.

"A bad thing," Jared muttered.

"Yes, sir, bad." The man was quiet, good-hearted, solid as his name. "It about broke Mrs. Cohen's heart, sir. Well, she'll always have a home with us. You'll find her changed. Kinda downhearted."

Peter escorted him in and left to call Amaris to come and entertain till her mother descended. They were talking when Vashti sauntered into the parlor.

"Oh, Jared," she said, and flew into his arms. She had lost weight, her looks had faded, and she seemed shockingly older and unsure.

"I am surprised nobody stopped Asher," Jared said tightly, holding her close.

Then, remembering Amaris and Peter, she drew back and wiped her eyes. "Yes, I tried. I went to the judge—it was sixty miles away, and Peter was kind enough to drive me. I asked the judge to look at the books, that I have taken care of my affairs since my husband died. He refused—he said I should have remarried. Since I did not, he said, Asher had the right to handle my affairs. Then I tried to get him to turn over all to Peter—" She shook her head. "He would not, he said Asher had presented the case well and all was legally in Asher's hands."

Peter and Amaris looked troubled, yet nothing could change their basic serenity. Amaris spoke up. "After all, it is just money, Mother. Let Asher have the trouble of handling the mine! Why should you work all your life?"

"But it is my life, my *independence* they have taken from me!" She twisted her lovely hands together, her haunted eyes imploring Jared.

"As for me, Mother, it amuses me to see Eden work," Peter said in an effort to lighten the mood. "She is so greedy, she works in the hardware store from morning to night! I am laughing all the time when I think how she used to refuse to help out! Let her work, Mother!"

"Oh, Peter, how can you say that?" Vashti reproached, though Jared was also grinning at the thought. "Eden was always so delicate—"

The married couple exchanged knowing looks. "As delicate as a mule," Peter murmured under his breath.

Amaris kicked him gently, a smile creasing her lovely face.

"Well, well, perhaps it will not harm Eden to work," Jared joined in. "But I shall see that judge who dealt with you that way! He has no right to take your property from you!"

The next day Jared went to see the judge. He was a stiff-necked, self-righteous old codger who thought no woman should have money of her own—she would just lose it, spend it unwisely. In disgust, Jared gave up.

He found Asher in the Cohen home and attempted to talk him out of the greedy snatch. Asher sneered at him. "Try to get it! We know all your motives, Jared! You want to keep control of it yourself!"

"I'm not sure I did so badly," Jared said mildly, keeping control of himself. "The mine has produced well, and the money's been never better."

"There is not as much in the accounts here as there should

be," Asher said slyly, glancing at his wife. "You must have some money tucked away in Philadelphia or New York City! Get me our fair share, Jared, and I'll give you a commission!"

"The hell with that," Jared cried, happily aware of the amount he had put in Amaris's account.

"I'll find out where the money is!" Asher threatened, his smile quickly fading. He seemed almost reptilian, his beard and hair oiled heavily and glistening. He kept touching Eden possessively, her knee, her thigh, her arms near the breasts. Passion was thick between them; Eden's aura of seductiveness was painfully like her mother's. "I'll get a lawyer and we'll sue you if you hold any funds due us back!"

Jared held his own, disgusted, angry with himself that he had brought Asher west and trusted him. "You always were a cunning bastard," he muttered.

Asher took the comment as a compliment and grinned. "Now you begin to know me," he said earnestly.

"That I do. What about the supplies I brought west? Do you want them for the store?"

"Of course," said Asher, his smugness fleeing. "We have paid for them!"

"No, you have not. I paid for them in the East," Jared said, enjoying this moment. "You'll pay for them, or I'll turn them over to someone else to start a store!"

Asher cursed him. Eden did not even pretend to close her ears against her husband's oaths slung at his own brother. She seemed to enjoy the exchange; her dark eyes glistened with excitement.

"Don't you try to turn anybody against me," Asher warned. "Don't forget, I can always go back to Philadelphia! You try to see that judge again to take the money and stock from me, I'll talk to Miriam!"

"What are you talking about?" Jared asked curtly.

Asher and his wife exchanged a look of amusement. "Eden has seen you with her mama! She knows what is going on! And that Sapphira is—a bastard—your child! Miriam will be plenty shocked at your ways. You're an old devil!" He chuckled, his eyes bright.

Jared sat very still, burning inside. He knew Asher would enjoy telling Miriam the truth, and in fact, no matter what the outcome of this conflict, if Asher ever went east, he would tell that good worthy woman about Jared's affair.

It was then that Jared realized his hands were tied; Asher would have to get away with his money-grubbing scheme. The stakes were too high; Miriam wouldn't be an unwitting victim if Jared could help it.

He rose to leave. "Well, I wish you joy in all your conspiracies," he said dryly. "I'm pulling out of the Cohen mine. From now on it is all yours—as soon as you pay me for my share. You will have nothing to do with my mines. Malachi will take care of all that."

Asher looked startled, rising slowly. "But—but you need me! You hired me—I'm doing a good job—"

"I'm sure you will have more than enough work on your hands with Mrs. Cohen's properties. I would not want to impose," Jared said in a courteously mocking tone.

"But I don't want to buy you out," Asher wailed.

Eden poked him. "Tell him he has to stay in," she said angrily. "Tell him he has to keep you on!"

"Your husband will be too busy with the Cohen mine and the hardware store, Mrs. Landau," Jared said. "After all, women cannot take care of such matters. You will find Asher will have to tend both the store and the accounts, as he told the judge. Women are not capable of managing money!"

He strode out, in his long-legged way, before they caught their breaths enough to curse him.

At the mine office, he and Malachi sorted out the accounts. When Asher came in after him, panting, he tossed the Cohen mine books at Jared and told him to clear out. Later that week, Jared changed the locks on the door and the safe, commanding Malachi to keep Asher out of the office and out of Jared's affairs.

"As of this date, he is not on my payroll. I can't keep him from running the Cohen mine, but I can keep his nose out of my mines!"

Malachi, well warned, didn't have to be forced to obey this edict, as he was intensely jealous of his younger brother.

Jared appointed Amaris's husband, Peter Malchus, manager of the mines, instructing him to bar Asher and Eden from the office, and he stomped over to their family home, where Sapphira, who was sweet of temperament, lived.

Vashti was subdued, grieved by her daughter's turning against her. And more, she was aghast at the flippant way the courts had assigned her property to her son-in-law. She could not pay

127

a share of rent and food for herself and Sapphira. And as for Sapphira—Eden was refusing to contribute money for the girl's upkeep.

"You need not worry about her," Jared said shortly. He had decided not to tell Vashti about the money in the East. She might let the fact slip that there was a secret cache. "There is my money—enough for both of you. I'll pay Peter now for a year, and each time I come, I will pay again. It will go right into his accounts; Asher can't lay a finger on it. And feel free of any responsibility for Eden—that little mercenary bitch will always fall on her feet."

Vashti sighed and shook her head but did not protest about his hard words directed at Eden. She, too, was disillusioned about her daughter.

And so was Jared about his brother Asher. His own flesh and blood—willing to play such a trick on him and enjoy it! He'd never be forgiven. He'd made a mockery of the family creed set by their father long ago: don't trust anyone but the family. Jared had lived by it. But Asher sorely tried it.

Over the following days, the two Landau brothers had another confrontation in the mine offices. Asher had come to refuse paying Jared for the one-fourth share in the Cohen mine. "Then you can send me my share each year in copper," Jared replied brusquely.

"Well—maybe," Asher said, enjoying playing the big businessman. "What commission will you give me for taking care of your mine?"

"None," Jared said flatly.

To his surprise, Asher did send him a few loads of copper ore, as a token yearly payment for his mine. Jared sold the loads and put the money into an account under his name, secretly setting it aside for Vashti and Sapphira. They should not go hungry, though his selfish brother and Vashti's daughter couldn't have cared less.

Jared had learned a bitter lesson—that even one's family could turn on him. He vowed never to forget how Asher had deceived him, how cruel a blow he had dealt Vashti.

PART II

1875–1890

Chapter 11

Gideon Landau graduated early from MIT and was just twenty when he went west once more to take charge of the operations at Copper Creek with his Uncle Malachi. By now, he was a man some five feet eight inches tall, with black curly hair and serious black eyes.

Jared talked at length to him before he left, explaining what he wanted his oldest son to do. Gideon listened carefully, for he knew his father was a shrewd man. Jared was graying, smaller, not impressive looking next to the tall bearded men of the eastern schools and businesses. But at forty-five he was a millionaire several times over, and he never failed at anything to which he applied his clever mind.

And he meant for all his sons to be millionaires one day, too. By 1875 he had expanded the Landau holdings by so much, they were now mining gold, silver, and lead. The rich lodes were mostly in the Copper Creek area, but Jared had ambitions to go farther south and north, and perhaps into Mexico.

Gideon had spent several summers in the West between semesters as a student. But it was never like it was now. Then he had been on hurried trips, a learner, an apprentice. Now he would be in charge of mining operations and bookkeeping, with his Uncle Malachi's help.

Since the conclusion of the War Between the States, the

West had been bursting with activity, which Gideon noted with amazement each time he visited. There were now more immigrant wagons on the trails, many more army posts on the frontier, many more miners who traveled west with picks and shovels and guns, their heads high.

He arrived in Copper Creek in mid-summer and went right to Uncle Malachi's home after leaving the mules at the mine office for unloading. He had brought mining equipment, hardware, cloth—all the usual supplies. They needed to store their own hardware since they no longer did business with Asher and Eden Landau. While Eden ran the store, Asher ran the mine; they were so greedy, their prices were far beyond the goods' worth.

Jared had considered setting up his own store, but dismissed the thought when he considered the upkeep. When his business reached desperate straits, he simply had the much-needed gear shipped in or brought by pack mule, and then sold it to the miners.

Gideon unloaded his packs in the room he considered his own, and Winona, the Indian woman, came in softly to pour hot water into the clawfoot tub for him. He washed away the trail dust and put on a fresh gray suit and shirt. Winona took his dirty clothes away to wash, turning at the door to say, "Food ready soon, Mr. Gideon."

"Thank you, Winona," he muttered. He strode downstairs and sat down at the rough plank table to enjoy a quiet meal by himself. He liked being alone at times; it gave him time to ponder.

He remembered so vividly his first trip west. The scene leading up to and resulting in his father being shot—the way Gideon had been forced to kill a man. He'd had nightmares for months afterward; he'd been unable to grasp the import of what he'd done, it was so large an event. He had killed! He had taken a life! a voice inside screamed. Surely God would strike him dead for such a despicable deed. To this day he trembled at the sight of lightning; it seemed like God would surely try to reach out and strike him dead.

The rabbi had talked to him, explaining that Gideon had saved his father's life in exchange for the life of a dangerous, evil man. He'd had no other choice.

Gideon's terror had subsided, but he still felt a hard to describe sense of dread hanging over him, a feeling he could never be young again, that his own life was forfeit because he owed God a life. And more, he realized he was mortal, he would die one day.

He had observed other boys his age playing and laughing and screaming with mirth, playing pranks, and living whimsical lives. But Gideon never felt right joining in, needing instead to finish school early, to take on the responsibilities others shed so easily. The thread of life could be cut at a moment's notice.

The word went around in an hour that he was in town. His uncle Malachi came home from the office as Gideon was finishing his strong black tea. His shy smile beamed from behind his thick graying beard. He was as tall as Jared, more burly, and dressed in thick gray flannel shirt and trousers.

"So, lad, you are here!"

"Yes, Uncle," said Gideon, rising to grasp his uncle's hand. Malachi was his favorite uncle; he detested Asher, and Enoch he felt contempt for, so idle and lazy. Uncle Enoch had finally married, and with Aunt Orpha with child, he used every excuse to stay away from work. His wife needed him, or he must oversee the household, and he left the work to his assistant, who was too green to do well. Jared's anger and contempt at home in Philadelphia exploded again and again. Jared had no patience with lazy ones, nor did his son Gideon.

"You have all you want? That woman is a pretty good cook, yes?" Uncle Malachi was awkward before Jared's son, who had gone to college and had earned a degree.

"Fine, Uncle. How is everybody?"

His uncle shrugged. "Good as expected, God be praised."

They sat down, his uncle pouring himself some tea, and then eyeing Gideon over the cup's edge. Gideon knew what he thought—that he was as shrewd as his father. Malachi feared having authority wrested from him. It would hurt his pride. Gideon could not reassure him; he had his father's instructions. His father meant for all the mine operations eventually to come into his own sons' hands. And he trusted nobody but his sons, though they had to prove themselves.

But Gideon could save some of Malachi's pride. He would do his best; Malachi was the least selfish brother.

Uncle Malachi brought a message from Amaris. She wanted Gideon and Malachi to come for dinner that evening. Gideon flinched inwardly. He had no wish to see Mrs. Vashti Cohen. He hated her. But he must go. It was a small town; he would see her again and again as the years unfolded.

Dinner went smoothly. Amaris was an easy-going person, calm and plump and gentle, her smile showing her happiness with her husband and children. Mrs. Cohen was visibly older, seeming shrunken, her glossy black hair streaked with silver strands. Her gaze wandered, and her attention was not often on the company; she twisted her hands in her lap.

"Mama helps with the children so much," Amaris said. "She's good with her teaching the miners to read and write, and she helps with the accounts—"

But Vashti only smiled vaguely, preoccupied with other thoughts. Gideon knew she had been hurt badly by Eden's actions. Her purpose in life seemed wrecked, her independence was lost. She lived in Amaris's house and was dependent on her and her husband. It was not the money she needed, it was the work, the pride.

But Gideon felt little sorrow for her. She had taken what was his mother's, the full attentions of her husband, who'd done nothing but betray Miriam. Sapphira was the full evidence of this. Gideon could not hate the small girl, now sixteen years old, beautiful, yet shy. She would never have the bold confidence and sensual beauty of her mother; she was small and slight, her smile sweet and confiding. She had been protected, yet she knew of her birth. Anxiety betrayed itself at times, a flinching away from Gideon's glance, a bowing of her head in company. Gideon saw her as a victim of other people's boundless desires.

The evening went fast, for all Gideon's resistance to liking Mrs. Cohen. He had learned poise, politeness, the niceties of social living. College had polished him well, and so had his father.

As he walked home with his Uncle Malachi, the older man said with a sigh of pleasure, "That was a good evening, a merry evening."

"Yes, fine," Gideon said.

"We shall have many more of them," his uncle said hopefully.

"We shall be very busy," Gideon said shortly. "I do not like to pass the evenings in idleness."

"You are like your father!"

"Thank you, Uncle."

Malachi was silent, depressed, his anticipated enjoyment of a more social existence blighted.

As they entered the house, Gideon said, "Tomorrow I'll come to the office for the day. The next day I'll be at the mines."

"So like your father," Malachi sighed.

The next days were busy. Gideon received an invitation from his ostracised Uncle Asher and Eden to come for dinner. He decided to go out of a sense of curiosity and loyalty to his father's creed, taking Malachi with him, but when they arrived, they found his uncle had not been invited! A place was set very quickly for the uncle who accompanied him. Gideon took pleasure in watching Eden's sultry pout grow.

Eden, at twenty-five, was glorious, in full bloom. She was short, but her bust and hips were full, her hair curly and black and glossy, like her mother's had been. Like her mother, only worse, thought Gideon grimly, concealing his revulsion when Eden brushed against him—almost purposefully—in passing.

Gideon caught his Uncle Asher's look. Asher was proud of his wife, possessive with her, but he had not shown the least bit of displeasure. All Gideon's senses went on the alert.

"The mines go well," Asher said brightly. He was handsome, with bold black eyes. Though Gideon could see Landau features in him, he did not like the nervously twitching eyelid, his ghastly grin. Neither were familiar. "However, young Peter does not know much. If they were our mines, we could manage better."

"Um," Gideon said, refusing to be provoked.

His Uncle Malachi, however, bristled. "He does very well," he cried. "He is a smart young man. Maybe not fast of brain, but the miners respect him as one of their own."

Asher shrugged, his bright black eyes gleamed. "I could do better. My mine produces higher yields of ore."

"You mean Mrs. Cohen's mine?" Gideon asked politely. He meant to provoke and had succeeded.

Mine, barked Asher. "I run it!"

"Do you give Mrs. Cohen her share?" Gideon asked.

Asher's handsome weak face reddened. Eden gave him a slow sultry look from under long curly black lashes. And her hand brushed against his chest as she served him his plate. He dug into the meat, undercooked venison, and ate around the

135

edges. Amaris was a much better cook, and she loved her work—it showed. She cooked for those she loved and offered it as a token of her feelings. Her home, too, shone with the same love; it was clean and sleek. Miriam's somehow mirrored herself, he mused, though she had many servants.

On the way home, Malachi said indignantly, "How rude they are! And Asher always up at the mines telling Peter what to do! He would do better minding his own business."

"Why does Asher come to our mines?" Gideon demanded sharply.

Malachi shrugged. "He sticks his nose into other's business all the time."

"He has no business there," Gideon said, frowning.

The next day, Gideon went to see Peter.

"Yes, Asher comes up to visit," Peter said. "Why? Do you think he makes mischief?"

"Maybe, but we will watch him closely."

And it turned out that Asher *was* making mischief. He was talking to the miners, trying to incite them by claiming the Landau miners were making more money. Gideon issued orders that Asher was not to be permitted on the grounds of Jared Landau's property. The visits soon stopped.

Asher was furious, and Malachi was puzzled. "He is, after all, my brother," he said one day.

"And my uncle, and one who loves mischief and always did," Gideon replied.

Malachi scratched his head. "Aye, he always did," he said finally. "Loved mischief as a lad, always did."

A message came to Gideon late one afternoon as he worked in the mine office. "Please come quickly, I need help," it said. The note was signed, Eden Landau, with a flourish.

Gideon read it again, then motioned to an older miner who hung around doing odd jobs because he had been crippled in a mining accident years before.

"Ace, go down to Mrs. Landau's store and see what she needs," Gideon said.

Ace went down, returning in an hour. "No help, Mr. Gideon," he said, puzzled. "She was sitting in her parlor, with a black lace thing on, and she got mad when I come."

Gideon smiled to himself. "Thanks, Ace. She is okay, then."

He got another message from Eden. "Pray, come, Gideon. I need your advice!"

He wrote a note, then tore his note up. He did not want messages written between him and his aunt. Instead Gideon went to Asher's office and showed him Eden's note.

"Asher," he said abruptly. "Your wife is pestering me. I don't know what is wrong with her, but maybe she needs a doctor. She is a bit young for hysteria, but maybe she should have had children, eh?"

Asher went red, but did not seem surprised by the note. "Now, Gideon, she is too young for hysteria," he said uncomfortably. "She is—well—she likes attention—"

"So give her more, Uncle!" And Gideon returned to work.

Late that night, on his way home, he was strolling along the path of a silvery stream that gleamed in the moonlight when a form rose up in front of him. He stopped abruptly, peering in the dimness.

"Oh, Gideon, it is you! I'm so frightened!" said a high, girlish voice.

"Aunt Eden!" he said mockingly. "What is wrong with you? Walking in your sleep?"

"Now, Gideon, you know better. I went out for a stroll and I lost my way!"

He knew she had lived here most of her life. He had to stifle a laugh. "Your home is that way," he said pointing.

She fell against him, her hands clutching at his chest. He felt such strong revulsion that he shoved her away. She fell to the ground, moaning. He made no move to pick her up, his chivalry nonexistent where she was concerned.

"Gideon, help me up!"

"What is your intention toward me?" he asked curtly, making no move to touch her. "You are my uncle's wife. Speak plainly."

"I—I love you, Gideon," she whimpered. "He is so much older—oh please, Gideon—" She managed to get up and tried to reach for him. He ducked out of her way, and stood several paces away from her. He was tempted to shower on her his contempt, but he decided revenge would take the form of indifference to her passes.

"Aunt Eden, you forget yourself," he said dryly. "Go home now and forget what you said. I think you are hysterical."

He walked away in the darkness, and stopped under a pine to watch her. She shrieked after him, "Gideon, I am lost—help me—" Then finally, "You bastard!" when he didn't return.

She still pretended to be lost, groping around for the path. Finding it, she started toward her house. He watched grimly.

He was not fooled. Eden loved nobody but herself. So what did they want? Asher must be in this; he had not been able to feign surprise when confronted with his wife's missives.

Did they both think Gideon such a green lad that he would fall into a beautiful older woman's sensual traps? They did not know him. Even if Eden had not been his uncle's wife, Gideon would not have fallen prey. He had learned his lessons early, watching his father and Vashti, and a Cohen woman would never move him to take her to bed.

He despised and detested Vashti and all women like her. Sensual, disturbing, with few morals and less sense—his mother, Miriam, was worth a hundred of her kind, a thousand! He had never been tempted by whores in his youth, even when college friends visited bawdy houses on a weekend lark—they reminded him of his father's mistress. Their activities sickened his stomach. He could wait for marriage, and he would wait until he found a woman as like his mother as possible.

So what did they want from him? Sexual excitement. If it were only Eden who was in this little plot, he would think so. Any woman would be bored in this small town; there was little for them to do outside of house chores, and Eden was far from a housefrau. But what of Uncle Asher? He was greedy, money-mad, and full of malicious mischief. But what did he hope to gain by thrusting his wife into Gideon's arms?

That meant the mines. How did they think they'd get the mines from Gideon's father? Through Gideon? Blackmail? It had to be that. He felt nothing but contempt for their meager attempts. Nevertheless, he would remain alert.

He kept himself too busy to visit Amaris's house often, and he refrained from visiting Uncle Asher's at all, pleading work.

He was up at one of the mines, watching the silver operations, on an afternoon in October. The leaves had begun to turn to their autumn colors. When he looked across the gashes in the mountains, he could see the maples were now crimson, the golden ash and oak brown and orange, and in the background the towering evergreens looked almost black against the sky. On the mountains snow had fallen early. It would be a hard, closed-in winter.

He was gazing absently across the mountains when he felt someone's presence behind him. He turned abruptly and met the open gaze of the most beautiful girl he had ever glimpsed.

Having been caught staring, she smiled in embarrassment. "Are they not lovely?" she asked in a low, soft voice.

Staring, he could scarcely take in what she said. The trees? Lovely? "Oh, yes. A beautiful sight," he agreed gravely, still staring at her face.

She was young, perhaps fifteen. Slight of body, with a promise of a fuller bust and hips, she had thick glossy brown hair, dark as a chestnut burr. The sunlight found red in the curls. A sweet, gentle oval-shaped face, with dark brown eyes like velvety pansies that gazed out at him. She was pleased at the sight of him.

"You don't remember me, Mr. Landau," she said.

"I would have remembered you . . . if we had ever met," he blurted out.

Her eyes widened, and a blush rose to her cheeks. "I, I think not. We met when I was very young . . ."

She was very young now, a lovely rose just budding. "When was that? I'm sorry I don't recall—oh, I know." A name shot to him out of the dark. "You are Rachel!"

He was on the mark. Her face creased in a smile of pleasure. She had been a pretty girl, about six, when he had first come to Copper Creek. Her father, he remembered, was the town's banker. She smiled, slowly, a dimple in her cheek.

"Yes, Rachel Dallmeyer." She finally said, extending her hand. "How do you do?"

He took it in his, fascinated, because it was not smooth but worn with work. Yet it was a soft hand, strong, firm. He liked its feel in his.

"Father and I came up to meet you. We looked for you in the office, and your uncle said you had come here."

He looked past her shoulder, which was easy because he was so much taller than she. She had to be about five feet three or four. He saw her father, graying, nattily dressed in a gray banker's suit, with the odd clashing addition of miner's boots, standing near the mine entrance. He was talking casually to one of the men, grave and dignified.

"I'm sorry you had the trouble," Gideon said. He strode with her back to the mine. She walked quickly, neatly, in small boots, with her cotton dress of blue chintz flowing about her legs. He liked the way the wind blew about her, molding the dress to her, making her brown curls float.

"Ah, Mr. Landau," Mr. Dallmeyer greeted him politely. "We have some business to transact, I believe. I waited for you to come to me." He smiled.

"Forgive me. I did not know—"

"About your investments in the bank. Nothing urgent. However, I thought I must also welcome you to Copper Creek. I have always felt great admiration for your father," he added.

"Thank you," Gideon said. He couldn't help but wonder if this man had been here when Gideon had killed the man who had cheated his father, Ben Moran.

"Well, it is good to welcome another Jewish man to our community. One day we might begin a synagogue," Mr. Dallmeyer said.

"We could begin one now, and hope to attract more Jews," Gideon agreed.

Mr. Dallmeyer smiled. "Now you sound like your father! 'Let us do it now, not wait,' he would say."

"Yes, if an idea is good, it should be taken up as soon as possible."

Shaking his head, but smiling, Dallmeyer went on, "Will you come to dinner this evening? We could talk of business first, then eat some of my daughter's fine cooking."

"That sounds very pleasant," Gideon said at once. He glanced toward Rachel. "So you can cook also?"

She looked puzzled. "Also? You mean in addition to working in the bank?"

He was startled. She was so young. "You work there?"

"Yes. Aunt Ruth gives me lessons for two hours, then I work in the bank for two hours, have lunch, work two more hours, then go home and complete my lessons," she said, the smile showing her dimple again. "I think she means to keep me from having idle hands!"

"Rachel is a good girl," her father said fondly. "And so bright, you wouldn't believe!"

"Now, Father," Rachel murmured. Her bright eyes shared a silent laugh with Gideon, as though he too would smile at her father's extravagant praise.

He did not laugh; he did not feel at all like laughing. He was dazed, a man who had sustained a hard blow to the head and heart. He was finding her as sweet and gentle as he had suspected she was from the start.

He learned at dinner that night that she worked hard and

enjoyed it. Her father had put her to work in the bank when she was twelve, because one of his men had gotten drunk and could not come in on a payday. She had worked so well, she was asked to come in occasionally, then more often, until now, at fifteen, she worked four hours a day. She was as quick as any of the men cashiers, and better at figuring up payrolls, and drawing up shipments for the express. She could be trusted absolutely; she was completely honest, and very careful.

Gideon accepted the next invitation to dinner, and the next. Going to their congenial, friendly home made a wonderful difference in his life, and he was eager to spend time there. He could talk of politics and philosophy and banking to Horatio Dallmeyer, of books and art and music and mining to Rachel and her Aunt Ruth.

Miss Ruth, as she was called, was a placid old spinster. Gideon thought her quiet and dull at first, until he found she had a keen sense of humor that made her sparkle in company she liked. In the presence of those for whom she did not care, she was deliberately dull. She was short, plump, graying, a good cook, a smart woman.

Miss Ruth had had a love affair in her early years, with a Gentile miner whom her family wouldn't let her marry. The man had died in a mine accident, and after much private anguish, she had decided never to marry.

When Horatio Dallmeyer asked her to come to Copper Creek and take care of him and his daughter, Rachel, she had come willingly, to get away from pressures at home, and the rabbi's reproaches. She had some money of her own, not much, but enough to be the target of fortune-hunting men.

The mining community suited her, oddly enough. She was brisk, independent, like a fresh wind blowing through the town. She had started a small school for the children, and she and Vashti Cohen, oddly enough, worked well together as they taught children and miners to read and write and do sums.

Rachel went to school with her aunt and kept up her studies at home when banking work kept her from classes. Together they read the classics and discussed history and philosophy. Her father also discussed them with her, pleased that his only child was so bright and quick and eager.

Gideon came as often as they invited him. He would lounge comfortably in the parlor with Mr. Dallmeyer, discussing business and the world, the Indians, the army camps, the mines.

141

All the while he'd listen for sounds from the kitchen. He liked to hear Rachel's low laugh and her aunt's fresh amusing comments. Miss Ruth took a liking to Gideon, considering him a nice young man who knew how to treat a lady with respect.

She learned that Gideon Landau did not visit the Indian women and the whorehouses down the line. Miss Ruth liked to know what was going on, especially where her adored young charge was concerned.

She saw the look in Gideon's eyes when he gazed at Rachel, and she approved. The girl was young; she could not go out walking alone with any young man. But it didn't hurt to have a fine young man hanging about.

So Gideon was permitted to come often. He quietly adored Rachel, the more he came to know her. She cooked well, she knew how to make a man comfortable. On a cold winter day, when he arrived chilled to the bone, she had a hot stone ready for his feet, the fire going in the fireplace, and a hot cup of tea on a tray.

She read a great deal, and when she saw he was hungry for such knowledge, she began to loan him books from her prized collection.

She loaned him some of the works of Thomas Carlyle, Shakespeare, and the fine poet William Cullen Bryant. One night when he came to visit, she was reading a new volume of the essays of Reverend Ralph Waldo Emerson, and she read one essay aloud to him. They read and discussed "Self-Reliance" animatedly, and later, "Compensation."

It was wonderful to him, to speak with her on these matters, to know their minds fused so often. How intelligent she was, to think about these matters, to care about them, even as his mother had thought and cared. He told her about his mother, and she listened gravely, and smiled sympathetically.

"She sounds like a marvelous woman, good, kind, charitable. And such a good mother," Rachel sighed. He remembered suddenly she had lost her mother at a very early age. Her wide dark brown eyes were wistful. How they sparkled, like brown jewels.

"I wish you could know her," he said.

"One day we may meet. Father wishes me to go east to finishing school. But I dislike the idea of leaving him."

"Oh, you should not go now!" he said hastily, dismayed.

Aunt Ruth smiled over her embroidery. She had been listening as they read, talked, and argued with animation.

At Chanukah, Gideon spent most of his time with the Dallmeyers, on their invitation. He had an open invitation to visit Peter and Amaris Malchus, but that meant seeing Vashti and his half-sister, Sapphira. Whenever he was with them, he was painfully reminded of his father's unfaithfulness.

So he celebrated the holidays with Rachel and her family, and was more than happy to be near her. He was content to watch her grow up. She would not change, become corrupt. There was a bright purity inside her that would never dampen.

Chapter 12

Gideon really applied himself those years in the West. He enjoyed work and loved the wild free spirit of life. He learned about the mines by simply working in them, often lending a hand with the shovel and pick, talking to miners, exchanging lore. He wanted to know all there was to know, not just from his books, but from personal experience.

In his own private studying, he learned both chemical and physical laws of mining, and he often turned this mix around in his mind, whether he sat alone before the fire and read or strode alone through the hills and mountains.

He would gaze into the distance, over the valleys to the mountains, dignified and lofty in the distance, their peaks capped with snow. He would stand in the brisk cold winds and think about how many secrets nature held, even from those who eagerly sought them out. He always held nature in awe and respect, even the dangers lurking there, from avalanches to bobcats to snakes to the icy slickness of mountain paths.

He gradually took more charge of the mines, asserting the authority Jared had given to his oldest son, even when his Uncle Malachi objected peevishly. He changed some of the office procedures to make them more clear and efficient. Peter had no objection to his superior position; he was relieved. He was a simple miner, he said, and the office routine was often wearying.

Yet he was good with the miners. They respected him as one of them and were loyal to him, even when other miners would go on strike. Gideon was glad to keep Peter on as the nominal manager, while Gideon quietly took charge behind the scenes and made the vital decisions.

Gideon studied the smelters he visited, both near Copper Creek and in Denver. He thought it might be smart to build their own smelter one day, since the smelters charged so much and kept the ore to sell for themselves. And it was expensive to send the ores east to smelters there; there was the cost of miners' and drivers' wages, the cost of wagons and oxen, and the dangers from ever more desperate Indians were phenomenal.

He talked to old prospectors, buying claims when he had the chance, as security against the future. Sometimes he accompanied them on their rambles into hidden valleys and the mountains. He loved to go on the long rambling journeys, camping out under the stars, and lulled to sleep by the howl of distant wolves. He would waken early to watch the sun rise, in awe and wonder at the majesty of the slow crimsoning of the eastern sky, the blaze of fire on the white snows. And the sunsets! They made one stand and stare; they overwhelmed with fire and glory as the crimson sun sank behind the snow-peaked mountains and outlined the tall pines and cedars.

He loved the smells of nature—the cedar scent as they strode through forests; the pine boughs under his head for a pillow; the fresh, cold wind that blew from the mountains; the fragrant flowers in the spring and summer; bushes of strong pungent odor; the wild smells of skunks and panthers. He had no dislikes in nature; all were part of the outdoors he had grown to love. He paid respect to the ferocious small yellow wildcats, but enjoyed watching them, sniffing the odors when they were aroused and angry.

And the sights and sounds! He wished he could paint and draw, but the talent was not in him. But he could stand and stare for an hour at a gaunt pine against the vivid sapphire sky, a twisted Judas tree on the edge of a wilderness of copper canyon, a tender blue mountain flower in his palm. He was inarticulate about this; he could not talk to anyone, not even Rachel, about how he felt. He could only feel and draw into

145

his soul the sense of freedom and grandeur all about him.

The miners thought him hard; so he was. He could be tough, he stood no insolence or defiance of his orders. His eyes would grow black and cold as ice, glittering like the black lead they mined if a man dared to defy him. He spoke softly, but he did not hesitate to employ a hard fist when he had to. He might be a city man, but his experience in the outdoors had made him hard as iron, and as ruthless. A wildcat gave no quarter; neither did Gideon. Young as he was, they soon realized he was not to be pushed from his chosen path.

Only a few saw any softness in him, his respect for the few women he admired—his mother, Miss Ruth, Amaris, Rachel. He showed them courtesy, a strong desire to please, an appreciation of the good qualities they brought to his rough life.

Two years went by. Rachel grew a little older, more beautiful, blooming in her young maturity. When more men came to court her, Gideon scowled at them, but he could not keep them away. Her father kept his own counsel and would not let her walk out with any man, though she showed no desire to do so. She smiled impartially on all and kept her distance. The combination of her beauty and the comparative wealth that would be hers brought more admirers as the months and years went on. Gideon fumed to himself, but comforted himself with the thought that she treated all alike. Only he had access to her home and her books and her thoughts. She enjoyed his company and showed it.

Rachel had been accustomed to walking home with her father in midafternoon when her work at the bank was finished. Her father walked home with her, then returned to the bank. But a few times, he would be too busy to be disturbed, and modestly she would slip out by herself, not wishing to bother him.

One day, Gideon went out from the mine office just as she was accosted by a drunken miner. He was enraged. He fought the miner, knocked him out, and left him lying unconscious in the dust; his nose bleeding.

He took Rachel home, and before her aunt, he laid down the law. "You will not walk alone on the street, Rachel! It is not safe! Most of the men respect you, but you have grown too beautiful for them to ignore!"

146

"But, Gideon," she said gently, "most of the men would not do this!" She was still pale from the dreadful encounter. The man had grabbed at her arm, torn her sleeve, and said words she cringed to recall.

"Enough will. When you leave work, send me word and I will walk you home. Should I not be there, Ace or Uncle Malachi will escort you. Promise me this!" And he was adamant until she reluctantly agreed.

Her father was distressed and agreed with Gideon. Either a man from the bank or from the mine office would escort Rachel home whenever he or Gideon were not available.

Gideon was pleased when Rachel came to the mine office one day in early spring in 1877. He set down his pen at once and stood up. She was a pretty sight in a blue cotton dress she had made, with lace at the collar and cuffs. Her brown curly hair was tied back in a blue ribbon, and the curls rippled down her back, catching the lazy sunlight of early spring that shone through the window and casting unexpected red glints through the chestnut color.

His eyes ate her up. His voice was polite. "It is good to see you, Rachel. It has been several days."

Her smile was like sunshine also, lighting up her dark brown eyes. "And you, Gideon. You arc very busy!" she teased.

He smiled slowly, walking toward her. "You are ready to walk home?"

"If you please? Or will Ace accompany me? However, I wished to speak with you should you not be too busy!"

"Never too busy for you."

Uncle Malachi grinned behind his beard, but the young people did not even see him, they had eyes only for each other.

Gideon left with Rachel on his arm. His spirits sang high. The winter was almost over, a few blue gentians swayed in the dusty ground near a shack. Soon the spring would burst out fully, the snow would melt. And Rachel was seventeen. When would her father let her have a husband?

Her small sturdy brown hand rested on his coatsleeve. Her gait in the short boots was light and quick. Her blue skirt swayed against his legs.

He waited for her to speak. He did not say much, for he had never been one for lazy, idle talk. He had important things on his mind; they occupied him, and he could not waste time

147

in small talk. Yet he noticed the sunlight on her face, heard the murmur of the mountain stream beside the road, noted the rushing white water from the snows.

"Gideon," Rachel said finally, her expression serious. "I have a large favor to ask of you. It is most important."

"What do you ask?" He was not gallant; he did not promise anything. Even in love, he was too shrewd for that.

Her mouth was compressed, her brown eyes serious. She gazed ahead of them, where the road ended at the mountain abruptly, at the mines.

"Mrs. Cohen has not long to live, we believe," she said. "Aunt Ruth has been talking with her. Mrs. Cohen wishes to see you, Gideon."

He frowned, unconsciously hardened at once. He disliked the woman so much, yet he had noted how his father's mistress had grown gaunt and thin this winter. She spoke slowly now, losing her breath easily.

When Gideon was silent, Rachel urged him softly. "She is old, Gideon. She is weak. Can you not be generous?"

"I have nothing to say to her," he said curtly.

Her hand pressed his sleeve in silent sympathy. They walked on for a time, slowly. He was thinking deeply, remembering. The shock when he saw his father greet Vashti Cohen with a deep kiss still pained him deeply. The man who had fought his father, the blow Gideon had struck him, the gushing blood that haunted his sleep yet.

"She wishes to ask you something, Gideon. It will not come easy. But she needs your help."

His mouth twisted. When Rachel pleaded, he could not resist. "Very well, I will go. Tonight?"

"This afternoon, if you will," she said. "When Peter is not there and the children are not hovering about."

"Very well." He might as well get it over with. No putting off distasteful tasks.

"Thank you, Gideon."

He left her at her house, not going in. He must go and see Mrs. Cohen right away. From the road he could see her on the porch, rocking slowly in the wooden chair.

As he strode onto the porch, his boots sounding on the planks, the rocking stopped. She watched him approach.

He went up and bowed briefly. "Mrs. Cohen. You wished to see me?"

With the cruel curiosity of the young, he noted the lines

and wrinkles on her face and neck. She had grown thin; her dark eyes looked out dully. Her hands were crippled and the knuckles were shiny with arthritis. No longer beautiful, he saw with bitter satisfaction.

She motioned him to a seat. Her voice was a croak. "Please—sit—thank you—for coming."

"Rachel asked me."

She nodded slowly. Her crow-black hair had turned gray in streaks, though the hair glowed with life, at odds with her weary face.

"I would ask—two questions. Does your—father—come west—this year?"

Gideon answered, "No. Jared—my father—has much work to do at *home*," he cruelly emphasized the word. "And he wished me a free hand in the mines, to learn my way. He does not come."

She bent her head and closed her eyes briefly. "Well—well—" she said. "So. It is so. He comes no more."

He felt a brief ungenerous spurt of satisfaction. No, she would see her lover no more! Jared had grown weary of her. He had his work, his faithful wife. He did not need Vashti Cohen.

One gnarled hand had folded over the heavy brown cane that helped her walk. She opened her eyes, gazed at the mountains beyond him, as though drawing serenity from them.

"He was—most helpful—to me. I would not—have had the freedom I had without his aid. I could not have left Philadelphia—people—" she said haltingly.

Gideon thought she would have done better to stay in a civilized place, where she would not have flaunted her sexuality, drawn his father by her subtle guile.

"You do not know how much freedom meant—to me. A woman. Like an eagle, tied," she murmured. She moved restlessly, as though feeling even now the same stirring.

He was silent.

"For a brief time I was free—until Asher—" She did not finish. "I was going to ask you something. I forget—"

He waited. The gaunt face was closed up, as though she slept. "Ah, I remember." The eyes opened briefly flaring to life.

"Yes, Mrs. Cohen?" he asked politely. "You wish something?"

"I shall die soon, I believe," she said. Her hoarse voice

gathered strength, it came and went as though with brief flickers of passion and life. "I worry about Sapphira—"

"Amaris will take care of her. She is a good woman," he said coldly.

"No. Not what I want—"

He waited with ill-concealed impatience for her to finish her thoughts and speak.

She bent over the cane. Her back was crooked now, and she had little left of the glaring beauty she had once possessed.

"Sapphira. Must go east, Jared said. Jared said he would help her go to—school. A good school. Get her out of here, Gideon."

Gideon frowned at the dusty path before the large cabin. Take Sapphira east? To a good school? Pass her off as a good, fine marriage prospect?

"Jared would want you to help Sapphira," Mrs. Cohen said, and began to cough. She coughed hard, held her handkerchief to her mouth. Her voice was weak, but her will strong. "I beg you, Gideon, when I am gone, take Sapphira east to Jared."

Gideon rebelled inwardly. He did not want to do it. He thought reluctantly of his shy half-sister, the frightened dark eyes, the shy bend of her head. No, she could not stay here, where everybody knew about her.

With his usual quick decision, he nodded. "Yes, I will take her east when you—"

"When I am dead," she said firmly. No "passing on," for her, no "leaving this earth." She said, "Dead. Dead," as though impressing it on herself. "Yes, when I am dead. Take her east. A good life. She is a good girl. My dear Sapphira. Deserves good."

"You have my word on it. I will take her to Jared."

The gaunt face relaxed; she was relieved. She nodded. "Good word. Reliable. Like Jared. Promised. Always kept his word. Thank you."

He stood up, anxious to leave her. She smelled of death now, and because he was young, he disliked it, he could not endure it. "You are welcome. I will keep my word." He began to walk away.

He heard her saying, as though to herself, "Jared helped me be free—for a time. Only for a time. But it was good. Good to be free. For a woman. How hard, how hard, how hard—"

She was still muttering to herself when he turned onto the main dirt road back to his house.

He never saw her alive again. She died two weeks later. She was buried in the cemetery in the mountain meadow outside of town, where some miners, women who had died in child-birth, and a number of children lay.

Amaris wept uncontrollably at the funeral. She said to Gideon, "She was such a good mother, she tried so hard. You don't know how hard she tried."

Eden came, dramatic in black, eyes sharp behind the sheer black veil. She sniffed from time to time, yet Gideon knew she had no feeling for anybody but herself.

Sapphira stood in silence, dazed, distraught. Small and full-bodied, she reminded Gideon unpleasantly of her half-sister Eden. But they were different, Amaris said.

Gideon told Sapphira after the funeral, "Your mother asked me to take you east. I'll do that. We'll go in about a week, as soon as I can get ready."

Her eyes came alive. "To my father?" she gulped eagerly.

He felt a bad taste in his mouth. "To him, yes. He wants to put you in a good school, I think."

"Oh. I thought—I thought I might live with him for a while," she faltered.

He thought of Sapphira, child of Vashti, in Miriam's home. Oh no! His mother must never know.

"No, of course not. You must go to school," he said.

She understood, and her gaze dropped to her dusty shoes. She had turned from the graveside. She nodded. "I'll be ready. Should I take everything? I have my clothes and my books—"

"Yes. All."

She was ready when he came to pick her up that day in early May. He hated to take the time out to go east. It would take six months out of his work schedule and involve covering terrain in which he'd have to be constantly alert. But he had promised.

Sapphira was lovely, and the men on the trail wanted her. Gideon watched her constantly, protectively. She was shy and wary of all men, even her half-brother. She kept to herself modestly, under the protection of an army wife returning home. They arrived in Philadelphia in late June.

Gideon took her to a boardinghouse of good repute and then left for his childhood home. Miriam greeted him with delight and warmth. He confided in Jared when they were alone.

His father listened silently to Gideon's story of Vashti's speech, his promise, and her sudden death. "So she is gone . . ."

he said slowly. "I should have gone west sooner."

Gideon fell silent. He wanted no confidences about what had gone on between them.

His father went on a business trip to New York soon afterward, taking Sapphira with him so as to give his mother no cause for suspicion. He entered her in a good Catholic school with a reputation as a good finishing school for young ladies. Sapphira's marriage would be a problem. She was young, had some money from Jared, but her illegitimate status would always be a stumbling block.

The Jewish schools did not then have a good reputation for educating girls. Wealthy Jews put their children in Catholic schools run by nuns, knowing they would receive a better education and a strict upbringing. She would know prejudice, but Jared thought she must learn how to deal with it. She would encounter it in the world.

When Jared returned to Philadelphia, he found Gideon gathering up supplies to take with him. His cargo included miner's tools, picks, shovels, engines to pump out water from the mines during the rainy season. He also bought a half-wagon load of books of all kinds—classics, recent histories, literature, essays, poetry. He wanted gifts for Rachel that she would accept from him. He could not give her jewelry, not yet.

He thought ahead to a house of their own and bought lengths of cloth for curtains, several pieces of furniture, a huge bed, and dresser and mirror. Jared wondered at him.

"I shall set up housekeeping on my own soon," said Gideon. "I grow tired of living with Uncle Malachi, nice as he is. He snores."

Jared gazed at him. "And you have no woman in mind to share this house with you?"

Gideon half smiled. "I might have," he said.

Jared beamed. "Well, well, well!" he exclaimed. "I hope I shall meet the young lady soon!"

"She is Rachel Dallmeyer. Her father thinks her too young to marry, for she is seventeen. But I shall marry her one day," Gideon announced.

Jared's face creased into a frown. The past forever rose in the present. Dallmeyer had been the man he'd refused to let Vashti marry. He looked at his son, wondering if he knew. But he'd been too young. "She is a fine girl, yes?" he asked, curious. "I remember the family well."

"She is very like Mother."

The frown disappeared. "Ah, ah, good, good!"

Gideon returned west in the autumn. He managed to get to Copper Creek before the first snows fell.

It was like coming home. He watched eagerly for the small town nestled in the valley beside the snow-tipped mountains. The crimson maples had turned to scarlet, the oaks were golden yellow, and the pines stood gauntly against the sky. There was no place like Copper Creek, and it held the girl he adored.

He saw the town in the distance, at sunset and he hurried the weary mules, then rode ahead of them into town. He was too dirty to present himself to Rachel right away. He went to his house, stirred the Indian woman away from her housework, to pour him a bath. At dark, he was standing in front of Rachel's door.

As the door opened, the firelight outlined her slim figure. "Gideon! It is Gideon! Oh, you have come home!" she cried. Her hands reached out for his, and he grasped them. And he felt he had come home.

She drew him into the house, blushing at his intent, happy look. "Look who is here, Aunt Ruth!"

Aunt Ruth bustled into the foyer to greet him kindly. He was invited to dinner and no food had tasted so good to Gideon. Nor was any company more welcome. Mr. Dallmeyer came in to dine with them, weary from work. He sat and listened to their banter.

"Well, son, how is the East?" he asked, and Gideon felt indeed one of the family. He talked of the changes in Philadelphia, the politics, a possible economic recession, the gold reserves.

Gideon turned at last to Rachel, who listening and talking with a bright smile on her lips and in her eyes. "I brought something for you that you cannot refuse," he announced gaily.

"A present? You must ask Papa," she said uneasily.

He laughed. "Your father will welcome it also!" he said mysteriously, promising to bring it by the next day.

The following day, he and some men hauled over the massive crates of books, and he enjoyed hearing Rachel cry out over title after title. "How good you are, Gideon! How wonderful a present! It is for all of us here!"

He beamed at her fondly. The jewelry and laces would come later, when he had the right to give them. For now, the books

153

were welcome, and they could read some of them together.

That winter they read together the works of Mark Twain, laughing immoderately over his humorous writings. *The Innocents Abroad,* and the *Adventures of Tom Sawyer,* amused them for weeks. Mr. Jules Verne's book *Around the World in 80 Days* cast them in wonder and amazement. Surely it must be all imaginary, such strange places!

Rachel enjoyed Miss Alcott's book *"Little Women."* Gideon preferred the stories of the western writer Bret Harte. It seemed very real to him, that background and all those characters; he knew men like them.

He had also found the works of Henry Thoreau, more of Emerson, and the poetry of Alfred Lord Tennyson. With other American and British works, he and Rachel reveled in many a happy evening, shut out from the cold and wintry winds, the snow and ice.

Their discussions also provided pleasant diversion from the work of mining, the worries over possible strikes, the playing out of one lead mine, the fight over a silver strike in the next valley. He could relax on these evenings, and he felt at home with them, welcomed and treated as one of the family.

While Rachel read aloud to them, he could enjoy the play of the firelight on her animated face, the sight of the rounded figure in her favorite blue gown, the grace of her small capable hands. He loved the chestnut glow of her dark brown hair, the sparkle in her brown eyes.

One day she would be his wife, and they would be alone in a house of his design. She would be the mother of his children, and he would be faithful to her unto death. Never would he be tempted to stray, as his father had done. How could he have done that horrible thing?

Gideon could not understand. Intolerant, adoring his mother, admiring his father, he could not comprehend how his father could have strayed from the path of love and duty to take as his mistress that woman Vashti Cohen. Uneasily, he remembered his own reluctant admiration of Sapphira's beauty. So must Vashti's looks have been in her younger days. And there had been such passion in her.

He thought of her words about freedom. Could a woman so desire freedom that she refused to marry again? What had Vashti Cohen wanted that she could not find in a fine marriage?

Surely she had had the chance to marry many a fine man—why even Horatio Dallmeyer, who'd been a widower for years! She could have been foster mother to Rachel! How could she have turned that down?

And in a flash one night, as he and Rachel argued laughingly about a passage in a book, he realized that there was much he did not know about women. They had seemed mysterious creatures, good women or bad, mothers or wives or girls. But women were not all good or all bad. They were like the men he knew. Some had more good points than bad, but none was perfect.

He thought of Uncle Malachi, toiling long and hard for his brother, longing for more yet unable to accomplish his dream. He thought of Asher—tricky, malicious, dishonest—yet working hard also. His Uncle Enoch was good and faithful to his adored wife, but he neglected work to spend more time with his children, who had come late in his life.

Good or bad, black or white; no, it was not so. All men were mixtures of many traits, and so was his father. Jared, so shrewd and smart, so loving of his Miriam and his children, had turned to a mistress and fathered a bastard child.

His Rachel, he thought fondly, she was all good. But other women, like Miss Ruth? She was a fine woman, giving and generous. Yet she kept to herself at times, close-mouthed and withdrawn in silence. She had moods, and at those times they left her alone.

Amaris—a good wife and mother, yet not very smart. Such foolish things she did, like forgetting to take in the laundry when a rain came! How Peter laughed at her! But she did not mind, and laughed in response.

His mind came around reluctantly to Vashti Cohen. Her words about freedom haunted him. Had she been a bad woman? She had taken a lover not her husband, had become the mother of an illegitimate child who must now suffer for her mother's sins. In his mind, it was a terrible evil, it sullied her and whoever she touched.

Yet—yet he felt there was something in Vashti he had not comprehended. He struggled with it. She represented something mysterious and strange, a woman who would not keep to her place. A woman who found ecstasy in being herself, owing loyalty to no man, if for a short time only. She had something else in her, something he found in Ruth Dallmeyer. A woman who did not belong, a woman apart. Yet one he must admire for her strength.

His hate died, and he could visit her grave and take flowers to her, at his father's request. He put mountain flowers near her stone; he thought she would have liked that, blue gentians, mountain daisies. And she lay where the mountains would have been in her sight, could she now see. She was high in the mountain meadow.

Chapter 13

"Young man, you have disrupted our camp again and again," Captain Jenkins said sternly. "I have told you, do not waste ammunition! You set a bad example for my young recruits. They now think they can practice with their rifles at any time. And two water bottles have been shot up and made useless now."

"I am sorry, Captain," Bart Landau said. His merry black eyes flashed in his handsome, lively face. He was a charming young man who could always talk himself out of trouble. He was shorter than his regally tall brother Gideon, more muscular in the shoulders, and warmer—much warmer.

The captain interrupted sternly this time. For the sake of his old friend Jared Landau he had been lenient, but young Bartholomew was trying his patience almost beyond endurance.

"I am not finished! You must obey me, you must listen to what I say. Being sorry after the event is useless. Think first! Think, use your head, young Bart, or we shall all be sorry that you came with us!"

The words stang, and Bart tried to calm down. The wild freedom of camping, of the vast deserts and plains, the breaking loose from family and college, had made him feel like yelling and shooting his rifle and making all kinds of commotion.

When he returned to the campfire his friend Steve, whispered, "Did he chew you out bad? You should be more careful. He could still leave you in St. Louis and send you home."

Bart laughed and swaggered. "Captain Jenkins won't do that! He is a friend of my pa! Besides, he knows I'm going out to work with my brother. He won't stop me."

He grimaced a little, thinking of his brother Gideon. For years he had envied him. Gideon had gone west at the age of eleven. Gideon had had adventures. Gideon had learned to use a rifle and shotgun as well as a pistol.

Jared had praised his elder son as an example to Bart and to young David. "Look at your brother, how dependable he is, how serious! How hard he works! Why cannot you be so serious? How much mischief you make for me!" And he did look older and gray and weary, the lines beginning to permanently crease his face.

Bart had been ashamed and sorry for a time, but his love of mischief wouldn't hold still, and he would again play pranks on the schoolmaster, sneak out to drive the school's carriage away and conceal it in a nearby copse of trees, ride a horse recklessly in a race without his father's permission.

"You started to tell me about your brother Gideon. What's he like? Will he give you a good job?"

The young army privates after weeks on the trail, were bored and willing to listen to anyone's story. They gathered around the handsome, rambunctious youth, the firelight gleaming on their rifle barrels as Bart swelled in pride. He loved being the center of attention, and such an admiring attention for the family he came from. He was a Landau, they had heard of his father, and they knew of their wealth. Landaus were fast becoming legends in the region if not the country.

"Gideon finished school at twenty and went out west again. He was always dreaming of it in the summers, you wouldn't believe it!" Bart laughed loudly. "He may have finished college early and graduated with high honors, but I took as many courses and am graduating early too. The only difference is that I didn't study after midnight, and barely passed. But I'll catch up, don't you worry!"

They stared at him gravely. They had not even finished high school, most of them; enlisting in the army meant one less mouth to feed at home. And here was a wealthy young man who'd gone to college, had a wonderful education, and was flippant about it. They didn't know whether to think him a fool or a wizard.

"What kind of work will you do? Just supervise?" asked one man, tongue in cheek.

Bart eyed him suspiciously. Was he being sarcastic? Then he dismissed the thought with a toss of his dark curly head. His black eyes shone, and he jumped up restlessly. "Oh, Gideon is a mine manager, works with copper and lead," he said with unusual caution. Talk gold to someone, Jared had told him, and you rouse his craziness. "It's a lot of tough work, but I can manage it!"

"So you're going to work in a mine?" asked another, puzzled. The others listened on raptly. "I wouldn't think a college fella would work with a pick and shovel!"

"It won't be that alone," Bart said. "We run a hardware store for our own people, and there are accounts to do. I have already worked in a store, and I've learned all the essentials. I suspect that's what I'll eventually be doing."

Before leaving, his father had talked to him for hours about mining, the West, the men. "They are not your eastern businessmen," Jared had told him. "They are a different breed. You must respect them and their individuality. They are men who have worked alone. They are tough, capable of making their own decisions. You must guide them, not whip them. You must earn their respect or they will not listen to you. Watch your own behavior. Ask nobody to do what you yourself cannot do."

Bart had listened keenly; he would do anything to win this assignment! And it was fascinating to him to hear Jared's stories, to watch his dark eyes sparkle, his face grow younger with the memories. If he had to work the mines awhile to claim his heritage, why, he'd do it!

Once beyond St. Louis, they were on guard all the time. Bart stood guard in his turn, but found it difficult to be silent and stealthy. It was not his nature. He liked to sing and laugh and tell jokes on duty.

The sergeant bawled him out vigorously. "Want the Indians to creep up on us?"

Bart made the mistake of answering back. "Aw, Sergeant, there ain't no Injuns out there! They're all on reservations! Don't fun me—"

"Fun you, is it?" The Irish sergeant went red with wrath, his beefy fists clenched as he stood, legs apart, before this slight, handsome, curly-haired young tenderfoot. "Funning, am I? I'll give you funning! You wait till you see your first wild bucks dead set on getting our scalps!"

Bart tried to keep his mouth shut, but he could not help confiding in a young private. "There ain't no Injuns out there. I read the papers. They're all on reservations! The army just needs some reason to maintain those posts!"

"Gee, you mean it?" the private gasped, eyes wide open. "You mean there ain't no Injuns to fight no more?"

"Naw, the West is all tame," Bart said, swaggering. "My brother works there, has for years, and he talks about setting up schools and starting a synagogue—"

The sergeant overheard them and cast them a cynical look. But he kept his counsel. He'd let them learn the hard way. Meanwhile, he kept a strict watch on them and never put them on guard together, always pairing Bart with an experienced corporal.

The vast plains gave way to deserts, and for days they saw nothing but cactus and twisted Judas trees, a few buffalo trails, herds of wild horses. The sergeant watched the sky, noted the veils of white clouds and nodded slowly.

One afternoon Bart spotted the remnants of a buffalo herd. He told his young friend, "Look out there, Steve, a dozen buffalo. My brother says there's nothing so good as buffalo tongue!"

"How do you get it?" Steve asked in all innocence. "You just cut it out?"

Bart laughed. "No, fool! You shoot and skin it. The skin is used as a blanket in winter. And you cook the flesh for food, but the tongue is best of all."

Steve's eyes brightened. "Let's go get us one, then! The captain will be right pleased. He's been complaining about beans and more beans!"

"Me too. Don't see why we can't have a cow killed now and then," Bart said.

The two scamps went off on horseback without telling anyone of their plans. Camp had been set early beside a small spring. Water was so scarce in this part of the country that they roamed from waterhole to waterhole, when they could find them.

They found the buffalo easily, then circled them quietly to

get upwind of the herd. Then they made a mad dash, firing their rifles for all they were worth. Bart fired at a sturdy young wild-eyed buffalo that was shaggy of mane and dusty. To his exultant pleasure the buffalo stumbled, fell to its knees, shook its shaggy head, and fell over.

"Got one, got one!" Bart yelled, and fired again, for sheer exuberance, into the air.

An answering "crack!" made him glance at Steve. He wondered whether Steve had got one also. To his horror, he saw Steve swaying in the saddle, one hand limp on the reins, the other clapped to his shoulder. Blood oozed between his fingers, but instead of stemming the flow, it began to gush out.

"Steve! What in hell—"

Piercing cries broke the air, the most fearful cries Bart had ever heard, and from out of nowhere Indians on shaggy ponies were racing toward him, firing rifles, shooting arrows from long bows. "Oh my God—" he muttered. He raced over to where Steve was trying to control his maddened horse, grabbed the reins, and yelled, "Let's get out of here!"

He crouched in the saddle, feeling horribly vulnerable. The Indians were yelling and the horses were thundering after them. His horse was a tall stallion, thank goodness, for he veritably flew over the uneven terrain toward camp. He anxiously looked at his young friend as he lay across the horse's neck, still bleeding so—

The peaceful scene in the camp shattered as they saw what approached. Men ran in every direction, as fast as their long legs could carry them. Rifles were pulled out, and shots began mixed with the yells and screams. They were on their knees as Bart rode furiously into the center of camp, scattering the fire, sending the other horses skittering nervously away from the loose pole on which they were tethered.

One of the drivers caught at Steve's horse, stopped him, and pulled him down behind a Conestoga wagon. He bent over him, yanked open the bloody shirt, and started treating the wound. Bart grabbed his rifle, let the horse slow down and halt, then tied it hastily to a wagon before running over to the sergeant.

The sergeant spared him a scathing look. "God, I rue the day we brought you, you young hellion!" he spat out.

Bart gulped and crouched down next to the man. "I shot a buffalo," he explained.

"And roused a lot of young bucks, you did!"

The rifleman spat, and Bart kept silent, watching, firing. The Indians circled around, yelling and screaming while leaning over the sides of their horses as protection. They rode with incredible skill as they fired under the horses' necks and set one wagon canvas on fire with a flame-tipped arrow.

The attack lasted for half an hour, but it seemed like a lifetime to Bart. Finally the young Indians rode off, shaking their rifles and bows, yelling and shouting threats in broken English. "Damn your hides!"

"Get you yet!"

"Damn white men!"

"Filthy blue eyes!"

When they had run off, Bart rose.

The sergeant growled, "Where do you think you're going, Landau?"

Bart reddened at the elaborate sarcasm. "I'll see how Steve is," he said awkwardly.

"He's being taken care of. You set here and watch for them Indians, and I'll tell you when to move!"

The sergeant crawled away, leaving Bart on guard, his ears red to the tips. They left him there for hours, and he watched for Indians till his eyes burned. Someone brought him a plate of cold beans and a stinging hot cup of black coffee. He ate and drank meekly, not saying a word.

He was on guard, off and on, all the night. The Indians came back at dawn, and ripped up the camp with bullets and fire arrows for an hour. Then they raced away once more.

Steve was badly wounded. The captain dug the bullet out, tied him up, and stretched him out in a wagon for the rest of the journey. Bart was given his night watches and the discipline that went with it. He took it quietly, deserving much more. He worried over his friend, sat with him, tried to entertain him with stories, but Steve was hurting too much to do more than grin feebly.

The captain waited for a time, then called Bart aside, and chewed him out for an hour. He wiped up the ground with him, told him how irresponsible and stupid he was, and how his father would be very disappointed in him.

"And if you had left Steve out there to die," he concluded grimly, "you'd be left behind on the trail for the Injuns to scalp, so help me God!"

"I wouldn't have left him—I would not!" Bart cried, deeply shocked.

The captain softened just so slightly it was almost imperceptible. "I know that. That's why I haven't killed you with my fist," he said grimly. "You have guts and you have loyalty. But if you don't grow up, you'll be a dead man in a month! And I won't be accountable for you!"

Bart sobered up. He tried to obey the rules, but he was very aware of the whole outfit's disapproval of him. He had gotten himself into trouble and, worse yet, gotten one of their own shot up.

He worked hard to gain their approval during the rest of the journey. He cut firewood for the camp cook, shot game when ordered, stood guard meekly and silently. But it was difficult to crush down his irrepressible spirit. Before they reached the army post, he had gotten into trouble again.

He had been sent out with another private to shoot some rabbits, or whatever game they could find. They had strict orders to return by dark. But when they had not found game, they wandered farther away, unwilling to give up.

"Sure could use some meat," Bart breathed. "I'm so fed up with beans!"

"It would taste good. I know a way to cook rabbit," said the gawky Tennessee private. "What you do is skin the rabbit, put it on a spit, turn it real slowly over the fire until the juice is just busting out."

"Crack!" sounded a gun. The young men fell to the ground. Bart reached out and grabbed the other man's arm.

"You okay?" he breathed, shocked to the core. If he got another man shot he'd be fit to be tied! But the other man merely groaned, saying, "I'm fine. Someone shot at us. Stay down."

"Yah. Where are the bastards?"

They listened intently, but heard nothing. They lay there cursing silently that they were on foot. It would be a good two miles back to camp. Would the shot carry that far, through the still desert air?

Something seemed to slither on the sand in the distance. Bart stiffened. He hated snakes; he had found one curled up next to him one cool morning. The sergeant had killed it with a rock, but Bart had searched his saddle blanket and shook it out every night from then on. It didn't help. They slithered up in the night, seeking warmth—

Slither . . . silence . . . slither . . .

The young Tennessee private laid aside his rifle and pulled

out his skinning knife. Bart imitated him, watching him intently. There were a few stunted trees on the sandy floor of the desert, which meant they were near to the mountains now.

A dark shape loomed before them. The Tennesseean sprang up, his knife searching in the air, hitting something, which let loose before falling heavily over the two men.

Bart fell over and rolled aside, then stared at the limp shape beside him. The Indian who lay there smelled strongly of stale grease.

No sounds. They waited for other movement, but either his comrades had fled or he was alone. Bart got up. A bullet whined past his ear. He fell down again, panting.

They were pinned down till morning, crouching in the little shelter of a stunted tree and a bush. When dawn came, Bart was red-eyed with staring into the darkness. Nothing was there, so they left the young dead Indian, and walked back to camp.

The sergeant said little as he listened to their halting report, beefy hands on his hips. "You again, young Landau? I shoulda expected it from you. No more detail for you," he growled.

Bart was crushed.

"You were supposed to come back before dark," Steve said when Bart tried to complain to him. Steve was healing, but still had to stay pretty quiet. His gaze reproached Bart. "Don't you see? The rules are meant for safety," he added.

A few days later they reached the army post at the foothills of the Rockies. Bart went in to report to the commander. The captain was there already.

The commander shook his hand, his gaze kindly. "So, you're Jared Landau's boy. You can get into trouble fast, can't you?"

Bart went red. "Yes, sir," he mumbled. "I'm sorry, sir. I caused lots of trouble, I guess."

"Well, Captain Jenkins says you have guts, and loyalty. That counts for a lot," the commander said crisply. "You'll learn caution, but I hope you won't learn the hard way. You could die very quickly out here. For God's sake, lad, be careful! A mistake can kill you."

"Yes, sir," gasped Bart, with relief.

There were some attractive daughters of army men on the post, and he lingered for two weeks, entertaining them with his charm, good looks and laughter.

The commander finally asked him, with elaborate politeness, when he would like to move on to Copper Creek. "I have a patrol going out again this week. Would you like to go with them?"

"Yes, sir." His eyes filled with laughter. "Reckon the sergeant's mad at me about his daughter."

The commander shook his head. "He figures she'll marry army, Mr. Landau. You best go on, and we give you our best wishes!"

Bart took the hint, and when the patrol formed later in the week, he departed with it. He was eager now to reach Copper Creek, for he'd heard about it all his life. But the pace was slow. They had to go with the small, sure-footed mules that carried the hardware and ammunition supplies, the dynamite, the yard goods, and the crates of books Jared had sent out to Gideon. Bart wondered what his brother wanted with so many books that had nothing at all to do with mining. He was through with college. It didn't make sense.

They came at last to the small town nestled under the sharp peaks of snow-covered mountains. Bart felt keenly disappointed. *This* was Copper Creek? Source of the Landaus' new wealth? The setting of his father's fabled adventures?

It was just a small dusty sleepy town with one main street, unpaved, a plank sidewalk beside a few stores, a bank, the mine office. This was his new home?

His Uncle Malachi, shorter than his tall father and bent by age, stepped out onto the office's portico, a smile on his face. "So, Bart, you have come also—to follow your good brother!"

His comment stung. Bart grinned and joked anyway. "Where is my good brother going? I don't know whether I'll follow him, unless he's heading for fun!"

Uncle Malachi grinned more easily. "Ah, Bart, you are a man after my own heart! I show you where there is fun! Some good saloons, and in the valley some places—" He gave the lad a wink. Bart felt like laughing. How much fun could this aging gray uncle find, weighted down by a heavy paunch?

Gideon came out, broad and strong and striking. He had changed enormously since Bart had seen him two years ago, in 1877. He greeted his younger brother warmly. "Good of you to come! We have much work to do! Father told you about the accounts, yes? And you have learned much from MIT?"

Must his older brother start talking work the first minute? Bart wondered. But before anything else transpired, Bart insisted on relieving himself of his baggage and cargo. The men and Gideon helped him move in with his Uncle Malachi. He was surprised to learn that Gideon had built a crude house of his own, made of timber and stone. It was a nice-sized home, with three bedrooms, a parlor, a dining room, a kitchen in the back, and a veranda that wrapped around most of the house.

Bart looked it over in amazement. "You live here alone, Gideon?"

"Yes, for now," he said, looking unrecognizable behind the crisp pointed black beard.

There were neat bookcases on either side of the fireplace in the parlor. Gideon was unpacking the books Bart had brought, setting some on shelves, setting others aside. The fine rosewood sofa had silk cushions. The bed in the large bedroom was huge, with brass steads.

"Well, you have it fine here, Gideon!" Bart cried.

His brother simply smiled, looking around his domain.

Bart felt dissatisfied with his room at the other house, for it was so small and too warm. Nor was the bed long enough for his frame. He complained to his brother after the first night.

Gideon frowned. "You will be gone back east before long." Then after a pause, while he studied Bart, he said, "What happened on the trail? I expected you a month ago."

Uncomfortable, Bart squirmed in his wooden chair. "Oh, we were delayed by Indian attacks," he said vaguely.

Gideon's raised eyebrows were evidence of his bewilderment. "What Indians?"

"Apache," Bart said shortly.

But Gideon wouldn't leave off. He continued asking questions until he had all the facts. When Bart finished, Gideon's look was not of anger, but of disappointment. He stood slowly to his full height and sighed. "Let's get going. I'll show you what you'll be doing."

Bart, anxious about his brother's disappointment, got busy in the mine office right away. He learned what he could, working beside his brother and eagerly asking questions. Gideon was patient and described in detail how the Landaus operated their business out west. Everything was very different from what Bart had learned at MIT, but his schooling helped him to learn quickly.

At the end of the first week, Bart went over to the bank to find out about the town's banking facilities. He was prepared to laugh at its crudeness, but instead found it to be as polished as in the East, with large rooms, teller cages, a huge safe, and several men minding the bank officer desks.

And behind one of the cages stood the prettiest girl he had ever seen. She had a beautiful oval face, chestnut-brown curly hair, large brown eyes that seemed to melt when they concentrated on what her customer was saying. He gasped and strode right up to her window.

"Well—well," he said. He boldly smiled into her eyes. "A mirage in the desert! Sweetheart, where did you come from?"

She blinked her dark black lashes in surprise. "I beg your pardon?" Her soft voice was cool, ladylike.

He realized she was no crude miner's girl and swiftly moderated his tone. He leaned against the cage. "I'm Bart Landau, what's your name?"

"I am Rachel Dallmeyer," she said gravely. "May I assist you, Mr. Landau?"

"Later, Rachel," he said, smiling. "When are you done here? How about lunch?"

"No thank you," she said politely, rather taken aback. "I believe you are here to see my father."

And up behind him came a graying portly man. Her gentle brown eyes focused over his shoulder. "Ah, Bart Landau," the man said. "Your brother asked me to explain our banking operations. Please come this way."

Regretfully Bart left the girl. Young, pretty, and the only child of the banker, as he discovered. He decided to court to her eagerly. He had been looking all his life for someone like her, a lovely lady, vaguely reminding him of his mother, Miriam, a gentle sweet person, so different from the women he had met in his boisterous college days.

To his dismay, she would not walk out with him in the evenings. "No, my father does not permit it," she said calmly, eyeing him with cool reserve. Her eyes didn't melt when she looked into his. He would change that.

"Well, why not in the afternoon? My brother Gideon walks you home," he insisted.

"Only because he says it is necessary. When he is not there, Ace does, or your Uncle Malachi."

"Then let me!"

She only smiled and declined his offer again. But he persisted in his attentions until she invited him to dinner one evening. He went home early, washed up, and put on his best black frockcoat, though the summer evening was warm.

Bart was astonished to find his brother Gideon had already arrived, handsome in a dark blue suit and frilled white shirt. Fortunately he was deep in conversation with Horatio Dallmeyer, giving Bart a chance to woo Rachel.

He coaxed her to play cards with him after dinner. They laughed over the cards, and Gideon watched indulgently from the corner, where he and Horatio were discussing the rising conflict over the miners' wage demands.

Bart was invited back on a Sunday evening and again he unexpectedly found his brother there. After dinner, he coaxed Rachel into playing a card game. But she refused.

"Gideon and I are going to read aloud, Bart," she said. He then had to sit back and watch as she and Gideon took turns reading from a dry book of essays. While they did, he studied her pretty face, the dark shining chestnut curls against her white neck.

Why were they so absorbed by their reading? He himself recalled having to force himself to read in college.

In the next weeks, Bart was sometimes invited to the Dallmeyers', and he applied himself more eagerly to his courtship. Rachel was the prettiest girl in Copper Creek, and he had always been popular with the girls. A summer courtship would be pleasant and would help while away the dull evenings. He found her intelligent, good, always helpful to the people in town, smart in the bank. And she was so pretty when she laughed and her eyes shone.

He was jealous when he saw she had other suitors, a bank clerk from her father's bank, a tall tough miner, an attorney from the East who was here for the summer. If he ever spotted any of the men walking into her house, he would feel pangs of jealousy. He refused to admit he might be falling in love.

He applied himself again to the task of wooing her, irritated that such a pretty girl should resist his charms. Rachel would smile over his jokes, laugh when he came to the bank and try to tease her. But she would send him away when she was busy. The work came first.

My, how smart she was, how pretty, a good worker. He became more serious about her. She would make a good wife! He was crazy about her, he told her. He had fallen in love for the first time in his life.

She smiled indulgently on him and shook her head. "Bart,

Bart, you say that to all the girls! You are not ready to settle down, and neither am I! Can't we be friends?"

"Of course! Will my friend walk in the meadows with me today? It is such a beautiful summer day!" He grinned at her and offered her his arm.

"You tease. You know I have the payroll to do, I told you a dozen times." And she retreated to an inner office where he could not follow.

Disappointed, he returned to the mine office, and his own work. Gideon eyed him sharply, but said nothing about his two-hour absence for lunch.

That evening at home, Bart felt overcome by boredom. Uncle Malachi had turned in early, yawning, and was now snoring heavily in his bedroom.

Bart kicked at the furniture and walked restlessly in circles till he could no longer stand it, then strode out into the street. Where did people go for entertainment in the evenings? Deciding to find out, he strolled down the one main street and peered into the saloon. It was empty, eerily still. Did everybody go to bed at nine o'clock? He went on and turned finally onto the plank sidewalk leading to the Dallmeyer house.

He heard laughter as he went up the steps. Miss Ruth came to the door and opened it.

"Why, Mr. Landau. Come in, come in," she said, smiling dourly.

He walked in eagerly but stopped abruptly when he saw that Gideon and Rachel were on the sofa, their heads bent over a book, laughing. Horatio Dallmeyer was rocking in his chair watching them indulgently, a smile on his lips. Miss Ruth gazed enigmatically at Bart. "Come in," she said again. "Have a seat. Have you dined?"

"Yes—thank you—" he faltered. His mind and stomach wrenched as he noted how his older brother was so close to Rachel. He was nearly touching her!

Shock made him stare and go silent. He nodded to their absent greetings and sat down in the nearest chair to listen glumly as they began reading again.

So his brother was his rival!

He saw that Rachel's eyes sparkled eagerly, that her smile was wide and her dimples flickered in the corners of her mouth. How pretty she was, her curls at her throat, the blue silk dress outlining her round figure, her long straight legs, and the pretty

169

shoes on her feet. He could have knocked Gideon out, he was so angry!

How blind he had been. Gideon was courting Rachel! And more subtly too, appealing to the father, flattering the aunt on their meals! Looking into Rachel's eyes as he listened to what she said. Talking to her father about business.

Bart sat as sullen as a boy, sulky at being bested by his own brother. But it would only be for the time being, he vowed. Gideon might be smart, but he was dull as a clot of earth. Rachel was like all girls—she liked to laugh. Deciding to amuse her, Bart interrupted their reading to tell a story he had heard at the army post, then turned to talk of his adventures and the Indian attacks, which he expanded so outrageously out of proportion, he came across as a national hero.

Rachel listened, her eyes widening and her smile fading as he talked. "Oh, Bart," she finally cried out. "You could have been killed!"

Undeterred, he regaled them with more tales, till the hour approached midnight and they had to break it up.

The next day, Bart was emboldened to waylay Rachel as she was going home from the bank. He insisted on walking her home. "Don't disturb poor Gideon, he is deep in some problem in the mines," he told her.

"Oh—of course," Rachel said. "I never meant to disturb him, he is often so busy."

"Well, he is an important man—and he lives for his work!" Bart said.

Rachel looked at him thoughtfully. When they arrived home, she smiled, "Thank you so much, Bart. No, do not come in, do go and help your brother! He works so hard," she said, and graciously closed the door in his face.

Bart stomped off in a huff. But the refusal made him the more anxious to court her. She was so different! So lovely, so intelligent, such a good cook, such a reserved lady! She would be a fine wife for him! He was crazy in love with her, and he had the whole summer to win her, which he would.

Chapter 14

Rachel felt relief when Bart grudgingly returned east in late September to answer his father's summons. The accounts had to be put in order, and Jared was short-handed on trained help. To Rachel, Bart had been a charmer who made her laugh, but he had also disturbed her by continually staring at her or raking her body boldly with his dark flashing eyes in unguarded moments.

She'd been told by her aunt that Bart had visited the Indian women on several occasions with his Uncle Malachi. It didn't seem right to use the native women this way. Besides, a man could not keep control of himself until marriage—she wanted no part of him. Bart might be amusing, even gallant, but she could never trust him.

She felt happiest with striking, tall Gideon. He treated her with respect, courtesy, and thoughtfulness. He obtained books for her, knowing her passion for thought and language, and truly seemed to enjoy reading with her. He listened, too, to her opinions as though they were as significant as his own.

And never did she feel he was less than genuine. He was certainly handsome, and tall and fine looking, with a pointed black beard and black eyes. But these qualities were less important to her than to other women, even when she felt pride to see them look at him admiringly. He particularly was striking in his black frockcoat and ruffled white shirt. And even on days when he returned from the mines, his suit dusty, his face lined with grime, his eyes red-rimmed with weariness, he looked exceedingly handsome to her.

He worked so hard, too. Rachel absently wished she could somehow relieve his busy burdensome life, knowing he often returned home alone at night to a big empty house, heated his own bath and cooked his own meals, unless Winona could spare time to help him.

She never knew how much he meant to her until one afternoon soon after Bart had headed East. Working in the bank, she heard a big dull boom. It echoed all through the mountains, followed by cries in the street. A mine explosion!

Rachel was sitting on her perch on the high clerk's chair when the explosion occurred and the cries rang out. She felt the blood drain from her face.

"Father!" she gasped, jumping off the high chair and looking around frantically.

He was already starting for the door, gesturing for a clerk to remain behind. "Lock up when you leave," he said curtly, and the older man nodded respectfully.

"I'm coming too," Rachel gasped, following him.

He frowned, finally nodded. She ran with him along the street, people pouring out of their homes, the women with children tagging along. Up on the far hillside smoke billowed out and rose featherlike in the air.

"Where is it?" everyone asked. "Which mine—which one?"

No one knew, but they ran in the direction of the smoke. Some carried buckets in case of water flooding. Rachel felt her throat closing till she choked as she made the unaccustomed journey up the hillside. Her mouth was dry. All she could think was that Gideon might have gone up there that afternoon. She prayed he was in his office, but she could not spot him among the faces in the crowd.

"It's the lead mine—the Landau number one mine," someone cried as they came to the tunnel's mouth.

Rachel had realized which mine had exploded when she'd turned the corner. Usually, the rails were neatly laid in front of the lead mine, but now there was a mangled pile of smoking wood, timber, and chunks of lead.

"Who's down there?" someone cried.

"Five men," one of the black-smeared miners at the collapsed entryway explained.

"Who are they?"

There was a pause. One of the men was Gideon Landau, a miner finally said. Malachi Landau had already discovered the fact that his nephew was among the trapped men. He came over to Rachel and her father, his face dark with worry. He rubbed his scarlet kerchief over his face and beard. "God, if he goes—Lord God, I cannot think what will happen—he is so smart, that boy—what will we all do?"

Rachel's slim hands flew to her heart. The blood seemed to have stopped circulating in her body. Malachi Landau was shrewdly taking her in, then he turned away, with a nod of his head. Mr. Dallmeyer put his arm around his shaken daughter's waist.

"They're usually fine, my dear," he said softly.

She nodded numbly. "What can . . . we do?"

"Blankets, food, water, coffee for the men—"

But Rachel froze. She could not leave the sit. Aunt Ruth, sensing the problem, called to several other women and they went for the supplies. Meanwhile several men were climbing down the shaft, following it into the depths. One came out coughing, scarcely able to walk. He was supported by others and taken to a blanket, where he was set down.

"God, horrid down there, it is," he managed to say, choking. "Fire, smoke—"

"What blew up?"

"The dynamite ignited too soon in the new shaft, crashing timbers all about us. We'll have to take them out one by one to keep the roof from collapsing completely—"

Rachel felt as though she were dying inside. She could imagine timbers fallen over Gideon's long, lithe body, crushing him; his dark curly hair powdered gray with ore dust; his black eyes closed—

"Rachel, some coffee or soup?" her aunt offered. Rachel shook her head numbly. She stood there, hands clasped at her breast. She should be helping—there were other women helping out, yet she could not move.

It was then she realized fully that she loved Gideon. She loved him with all her heart and soul and body. If he died, she too would die, just as Aunt Ruth had done when her lover

173

died. Nothing would ever be the same again.

They waited through the long afternoon. Miners stumbled out of the shaft, coughing and cursing. Others replaced them. Many residents of town and outlying regions came to help, despite the fact they were rivals in ordinary times.

When night came, Rachel had no eyes for the deep red sunset, for the blue-purple twilight, for the blackness of the velvety night sky lit by white stars. If Gideon did not live to see those stars again with her, what beauty would they ever hold for her again?

"Rest," her father urged. She shook her head. She poured herself a cup of coffee and drank it black. It burned her mouth, but she did not feel it.

Fresh timbers were carried into the mine shaft, and the gathered crowd could hear the sounds of the men clearing away rock and debris to shore up the weakened walls of the shaft as they made a path to the trapped men. The women waited in silence, bundled in cloaks and blankets on the ground.

Finally, toward dawn, one of the trapped miners was brought out of the shaft on timbers, unconscious. Women bent over him as he was carried away.

Mr. Dallmeyer came to Rachel. "It is not young Landau," he said gravely. "They say he is injured, but we do not know how badly."

She nodded, biting her lips. He no longer insisted that she go home. He knew she could not leave.

Another man followed, on his feet, but resting on the shoulders of two men for support. He sat down limply on some timbers, his head hanging, and Rachel, who was close enough to see his torn clothes, the long red burns on his arms and face, watched as others carried him off to a makeshift hospital that was set up during the night.

Another man followed, then another. Only Gideon was left—

And finally he came out, after fourteen hours in the shaft. He stumbled out on his own, coughing and bent, but on his feet. He gestured to another man to go ahead. A small cheer rose from the crowd. He looked surprised. His face was blackened, but he held himself upright. He gave them a weary wave of one arm.

"Thank you all," he said softly. "How are the men?"

The group closest told him, and he nodded. Rachel noticed

174

that one arm hung limply. Mr. Dallmeyer went to him, though Rachel could not yet move.

Gideon raised his head, his look seeking her out among the sea of faces in the pale gray dawn light. He came over to her. "My dear, you should not have stayed." He turned his head to cough again.

"I could not go. Oh—Gideon!" Her voice faltered.

"You'll come with us," Mr. Dallmeyer said briskly.

Gideon hesitated, then nodded. Rachel saw a trail of blood that ran from his limp arm, a crude bandage over it.

Her father eased off Gideon's coat, and under it the white shirt was soaked in blood. Rachel tore it off at the shoulder, and silently helped wrap the arm in fresh bandages to staunch the bleeding.

They hobbled down the hill, Gideon moving slowly, wearily, Rachel keeping her arm about his body, boldly close to him. At the Dallmeyer house, Aunt Ruth was ready with hot water and bandages. The doctor could not come right away, for the other men were more seriously injured, she told them as they sauntered into the parlor.

Rachel's aunt applied a compress after cleansing the raw open wound on the upper arm.

"The timbers holding up the walls collapsed after the explosion," Gideon explained. "I was lucky, I was farther from the dynamite. But we were all smothered by debris."

"Oh, Gideon, you might have—have died," Rachel choked.

His good arm went about her shoulders as he drew her silently to him and pressed her comfortingly to his body. She felt the lean hard strength of him, and something inside her seemed to give way. She clung to him and began to sob.

Aunt Ruth went on bandaging his arm while Rachel wept against his good shoulder.

"There now, daughter," Mr. Dallmeyer scolded mildly. "You must control yourself! Gideon's already in much pain, don't burden him more."

She looked up at Gideon, tears streaming down her face. He bent down and gently touched her face with his lips. "I am honored and touched by your tears, my dear," he said quietly.

He was gazing down at her keenly, with his weary red-rimmed black eyes, his face still dark with smoke and grime. "I thought about you, in there, Rachel," he said. "I vowed that when I came out, I would ask you to marry me."

There was an abrupt silence in the Dallmeyer parlor. Mr. Dallmeyer stared at Gideon, and Aunt Ruth went on fastening the bandage until it was done. Rachel felt a little faint, though something inside her at the same time was fluttering.

"Ohhh," she breathed, wiping her eyes with a handkerchief her aunt had handed her. She leaned back to look up at him, a mist filming her eyes. He was gazing down at her strangely, hungrily. "How—how do you feel?" was all she could say.

He squeezed her shoulder and smiled, not to be deterred.

"I have loved you since I first saw you," he said.

"Oh! Oh, Gideon—"

In front of the others, she leaned up and pressed her lips to his. The touch burned through her, and her body arched to his much taller one. His muscular arms held her tightly for a moment, then grudgingly released her.

"Really, Rachel," Aunt Ruth said, trying to sound stern. "Where are your manners? The man's asked you to marry him."

Gideon grinned at her.

There was the sound of someone clearing his throat. It was Horatio Dallmeyer, trying to signal Aunt Ruth. Looking up too, she caught the motioning of his eyes. Clearing her own throat, she slapped her knees lightly and said, "Excuse us, I've got to start breakfast and your father has to start cleaning up."

The lovers watched as their elders retreated, Rachel's aunt into the kitchen, her father upstairs for a bath.

Rachel was laughing and tears were in her eyes at the same time. Gideon gazed down at her tenderly, his big hands on her slim shoulders.

"My love, *will* you marry me, and soon?" he asked quietly. "I have loved you. I want to marry you, make you happy, give you everything in the world that I can."

For a moment she resisted, timid as a young girl can be. Then she yielded. She would never be afraid of Gideon, he was so good, so kind—

She nodded her dark head. "Oh, Gideon. Yes, I do . . . love you also." She turned crimson as she spoke.

He gathered her to himself, his black eyes flaring with passion.

That night he asked her father for her hand, and Horatio Dallmeyer gladly gave it. "Be good to her, Gideon. Be faithful always. I ask no more."

176

"You have my word," Gideon said solemnly, clasping hands with the older man.

Rachel insisted on waiting until March 1880 to get married. She wanted to make a new dress for her wedding from a length of pale blue silk Gideon had brought her from a trip east, and it would take weeks for completion.

Gideon gave her other gifts, too, shortly after their wedding was announced—including more lengths of silk, a number of pieces of lace for berthas, a black lace mantilla he had bought from a Mexican trader, and the house, which, he confessed, had been built for her. Of course.

Rachel was stunned. Had he counted on their marrying so long ago?

She leaned over and embraced him.

The time came all too rapidly for the nervous yet eager bride. On a bright Sunday in mid-March, they stood before a rabbi who had traveled to Copper Creek for their wedding and exchanged their vows before a large curious audience in the crude cabin that was the town's synagogue.

Rachel wore her pale blue dress and a white lace veil that covered her beautiful features and was fastened to a gold crown Gideon had bought three years before. She was a radiantly beautiful bride, and looked serene, with a sparkle in her dark eyes and a flushed coloring in her cheeks. Even the blanket of March snow could do nothing to diminish her joyous spirits.

The newlyweds retired to their new home after the wedding luncheon, the gray wintry sky darkening the house at barely three o'clock in the afternoon. Gideon set to light several lamps.

"Would you like to see your new domain?" he said, smiling.

"Please," she said timidly.

He showed her around proudly. He had paid Winona and two of her girls to sweep and scrub the rough but large cabin until it was clean and presentable for his bride. The parlor was bright with freshly washed white curtains, the sofa and chairs were covered with blue cotton and lace lined their backs and arms. The shelves were spilling over with books, and some were piled neatly to the side. To hide her shyness, Rachel began studying the book bindings, her husband watching on with a warm smile.

She went to the kitchen and admired the new iron stove, the copper pots and pans, the huge kettle that swung over the open fireplace. All was neat and trim, the cupboards filled with bottles and boxes of food. Finally she went to the master bedroom upstairs—a huge room at the back of the house facing the mountains instead of the crude town of Copper Creek. When she wakened in the morning, she would see the lofty mountains rather than the dusty streets.

The bed was huge. It had brass steads and was covered by a white candlewick bedspread. A fine white porcelain basin and pitcher stood on the dresser, and there was a tall matching chest of dark wood lit by a lamp decorated with pink roses and green leaves. Gideon had cleared space for her dresses, and they now hung beside his suits in the far corner wardrobe.

"It looks . . . very fine," she said, and blushed deep rose.

He noticed her self consciousness, and said briskly, "Will you be so kind as to prepare my evening meal for me? I am starved, I ate so little at the wedding feast. I talked all the while!"

She smiled at his words, knowing he never talked too much, and retreated to the parlor with him. When he was well settled in a chair reading a gazette, she went back to the bedroom and changed from the fine silk wedding gown to a practical rose cotton dress, tying an apron at her waist.

This was their first meal together and with elation she looked about the well-supplied kitchen. Then she found a cooked side of venison, a pot of potatoes, a side of bacon, all waiting in the icebox on the back porch.

By five-thirty she had finished preparing a full-course meal and had set the serving dishes out on the table in the dining room between the kitchen and parlor. She called Gideon to eat, trying to sound as casual as she had felt in her father's house.

She was proud of her table setting, including the white cloth, on which the venison and steamed potatoes and canned peaches had been set. Gideon ate heartily, and afterward Rachel washed the dishes while he read in the parlor. She rather missed her Aunt Ruth! They had always exchanged town gossip over the dishes.

She returned to the parlor and sat down. Gideon indicated the book he was reading. "Shall I read aloud for a time?" he asked.

"Pray, do," Rachel said, and folded her hands demurely. Few of the words penetrated her nervous mind. She was thinking of the night to come.

It was fully dark outside when they went to bed. He let her go first, to remove her dress and underclothing and put on the fine frilled cotton nightdress that her aunt had made for this very night. Shivering with cold and nerves, Rachel slid into the wide bed. Then she wondered. Was she on the correct side? Where did he sleep? Oh, why did the first night have to come? Why couldn't they skip it and slide into comfortable married bliss right away? She wished she was as settled and happy as her friend Amaris Malchus.

When Gideon came in, one lamp still burned. He blew it out and undressed in the dark. Only a little light reflected off the white snow from outside, making the landscape seem to shine all night.

She was shivering violently now and Gideon lay down beside her, pressing against her. Putting his arm over her, he drew her close.

"My darling, you are afraid of this night," he said quietly.

She nodded against his chest. "It is not . . . not that you . . . you would not . . ." she faltered.

"I would not hurt you, my love. But it may be that I would without wishing it. Let us learn to know each other slowly, shall we?"

His voice was so tender and loving that she lost her fear. He held her quietly, stroking her body, kissing her lips, and soothing her to sleep. In the morning, she wakened to his smile and cheery words. "It is a beautiful day, the snow is melting. Let's go and walk in the meadows and see if the spring flowers are coming up!"

They spent the next few days walking and talking, either in the fields or at home. And each night she lay in his arms, and slept, learning the feel of his body, but no more.

And slowly they came closer together. One night she came willingly to his arms, and they embraced. When heat rose in her and she felt the heat mirrored in him, they came together, her fear dissolved despite some pain.

As Rachel came to know Gideon, she loved him all the more for his thoughtfulness to her—he gave her his time, his understanding, and passion in bed. It was surely the hand of God to be given a husband like that.

And as the weeks and months went by, their passion grew and they loved in a less inhibited way. Gideon confessed to Rachel he had been a virgin when they married; he had not wanted to learn about sex from whores.

"Oh, Gideon, I am so thankful—" she whispered.

"And I also. I would hate for love to be—so unclean. It is something more between man and wife. I vow to remain true to you all my life and beyond."

She cupped his face in her hands. "And I vow it to you, Gideon. You shall have my love, and you alone, all my life."

They kissed slowly and deeply. Their vows were sacred to them, making their relationship all the more precious. It glowed in their faces and the way they looked at each other. Everyone noticed, but it was stern Aunt Ruth who was most satisfied, convinced this was the way she would have been if her lover had not died.

As spring came on, one night he lay with her and gently removed her nightdress. "I want to see you in the moonlight," he whispered.

He slid off the sheet of soft linen and bent over her, gazing at her rounded limbs, at the breasts so young and round and firm, at the hips so wide and pleasing to him. He brushed his lips from her shoulder to her breasts, where he paused over her nipples, kissing them with his lips until they hardened. She caught her breath at his intimate caresses, not shrinking from him, and slipped her hand into his hair, tangling it in the thick locks.

His free hand roamed her body, the other turned her to him. She shivered at the teasing touch of his fingers as they moved from her hips to her thighs and explored in the tangle of thick hair at her softest places. He had learned how to touch her, how to arouse her responses.

"Oh, Gideon," she finally murmured, opening herself to him. "You make me feel so—so—"

"What, darling?"

"I don't know how to say it, I don't know the words," she confessed shyly.

"Tell me, try to say it."

"Loose—soft—wanting—" she whispered.

He smiled behind the black beard, then bent and kissed her throat. She felt the thick hair of his beard on her breast, and she trembled. She closed her eyes, enjoying his kisses and the feel of his hard body against her.

When he came over her, she moved to accommodate him. Her arms came around him, and her fingers moved up and down his spine. His leg came between her thighs, his knee pressing against her as he stroked her warm softness. She felt the heat rise to her breasts.

Then he moved his knee and came completely over her. She opened wider to receive him and felt joyful at his first slow thrust. What a lover he was, how gentle and yet passionate! He brought them together with teasing slowness, and her heart beat faster and faster. Her fingers dug into his hips, and she pulled him impatiently to her.

Before long, the pulsing excitement throbbed through her whole body, making her gasp and toss her head in ecstasy. He tangled his fingers in her hair to keep her face turned toward him, his lips over her mouth, half open from crying out. In mutual love, they came together fully, and her very soul seemed to delight in him, clasping and clasping him to her.

She nearly fainted with the keen ecstasy of it. And soon he throbbed again and again inside her, and she felt their mutual rise to the heights of passion, followed by their gentle slow descent to a warm sweet release. She wanted his baby, his son or his daughter, and soon. With an agony.

She whispered it to him as he lay breathless beside her. He turned to face her on the pillow, and though the moonlight shone in such a way she couldn't see his eyes, he could see her tender face fully.

"My adored wife. How happy that would make us!"

"I am very happy now Gideon. Very happy."

"And I also! But it will—seal our love," he said.

She put her head down on his smooth bare shoulder and rested her cheek against him. She was so happy, she almost feared the feeling. Could anything or anyone take this away from them?

They fell asleep and woke with the daylight. He smiled at her naked body, and she blushed and pulled the sheet up to her shoulders.

"Do not be ashamed of your loveliness," he murmured.

"I am not. Only—"

"I know." He said gently, and she knew he did understand her modesty in the daylight. He held her, the sheet over them both, and let her hide her blushing face against him. How close their minds were, their hearts.

Gideon came home at noon the next day, his face rueful. "My darling, our happiness is too strong for others to bear!"

181

Startled, Rachel gazed across the dining room table at him. "What do you mean, Gideon?"

"My Uncle Malachi has grown restless. Today he told me he wishes to go back east and find himself a bride!"

Her mouth opened with surprise, and her eyes twinkled.

"Oh, Gideon—he is—is—"

"Almost fifty," Gideon said, nodding. He sighed. "We shall miss him. He is determined to go east and spend some of the money he has saved all these years. He says he can buy a fine wife with it!"

Rachel's beautiful face creased in a frown. She felt keen distaste.

Gideon too lost his smile. "My darling, I did not mean to make you feel insulted."

"I know," she sighed. "Only, men seem to think that all women think of is money, comfort—"

Their gazes met, her tender brown eyes, his intense black ones. "I wanted everything for you, as good a house as possible, furniture, books, comfort. But for you, it would not have mattered if it had been in a log cabin."

She nodded and reached out for his hand. "No, so long as you were in the cabin with me."

He lifted her hand to his lips, and his eyes caressed her. "My love," he said.

Gideon carried on alone with the work while his uncle stubbornly pursued his goals in the East. Gideon had to draw up the payroll, supervise the mining, soothe the ruffled miners, who understandably grew upset when another operator nearby raised wages, and by himself. When the miners threatened to strike unless Gideon raised their pay, he had to hold the fort alone, knowing the Landau concern couldn't afford the pay books unless it built its own smelter. And so far his father, the chief owner of the business, refused to build one, believing the venture would prove costly in the end. Gideon suspected this would be a point of contention between himself and his father. And meanwhile he had to bargain as shrewdly as possible to get a fair rate from smelter operators, who probably overcharged the Landaus, knowing they were wealthy. Gideon would have to get together his figures to prove this, and make an argument with his father to build their own smelter.

Overworked, it was on a dusty August day that Gideon came

out onto the street at the welcome shouts and bells of mule harnesses. He grinned in relief as he recognized the handsome features of his brother Bart, covered with dust and his arms waving to the cheers of the crowd. He always was at his best in front of an audience. Near the office, he slid off one of the shaggy ponies in the lead of the caravan, a wide grin on his handsome mobile face. "Here I am—your troubles are over, Gideon. You have help!" He was shouting. "Wait till you hear my news!"

Gideon stood behind the throng, hands on his hips, smiling at his boisterous, rather bold younger brother. He never thought he'd feel so glad to see him. "And wait until you hear mine," he shouted in return over heads and the sounds of backclapping punctuating the party atmosphere.

When Bart reached him on the portico, the two brothers embraced and walked arm-in-arm into the office. Gideon motioned to a clerk to go and supervise the unloading of the supplies outside.

"You have heard from Uncle Malachi?" Bart laughed. "What a jest!"

Gideon was puzzled, shaking his head. He indicated a straightbacked chair in the corner for his brother, but Bart ignored him. He was dusting off his clothes, looking about eagerly.

"Same old place, same old town," he said. "Everybody fine?"

Gideon took his own seat just as a crippled miner stepped inside the office and raised his limp hat to them. "How are you, Mr. Landau? How's the missus?"

"Just fine, thank you. How're things going?"

"Good, thank'ee. Thank the missus for the side of beef she sent over. Good soul, she is. You're a lucky man, Mr. Landau!"

When he'd gone on, Gideon found Bart staring at him, his face gray under the dust and grime. "What did he mean, the missus? Did you get married, Gideon?"

"Yes I did. Rachel Dallmeyer and I were married in March," he said steadily. "You must come to dinner with us tonight—"

"Rachel!" Bart whispered, freezing in his tracks. "God, you don't mean you married *Rachel?*"

"Yes, I did," Gideon said, rather surprised by Bart's horrified look. "And we're quite happy, Bart. You must come to dinner tonight and see—"

"You—married—Rachel!" Bart repeated incredulously. "But I was going to—I love her—you could not—you knew I was crazy about her—"

Gideon's mouth tightened. He kept hold of his temper, though with difficulty. "I have married her, I have long loved her," he said slowly.

"But she would have waited for me! Why the hell did you have to go marry her!" Bart stared at his brother, his hat set squarely on his head, his handsome face creased with hurt. Gideon felt a pang. "You must have been afraid I would cut you out with Rachel! You did not even wait for me to come and attend your wedding! You did not write and tell Father!"

Gideon's eyebrows arched angrily. "Cut me out? I don't know what you're talking about. Rachel loves me, and I love her dearly," he said quietly, holding fast to his patience. "We married before her family and our friends. And I have written to Father and the family. They will know soon enough."

"God, if I had only stayed the winter," Bart muttered. He rubbed his face, and a spurt of trail dust clung to his long eyelashes. He didn't seem aware of his surroundings. "I came as fast as I could this trip, not even waiting for an army patrol. I was so anxious to see Rachel—"

"Bart, she is my wife!" Gideon said sternly. "Do not trouble my wife! I shall have to forget you are my brother. Be warned!"

Bart suddenly became aware of his surroundings, jumping up. "You threaten me?" he cried.

The two paused. People were passing the open doorway, staring at them both. Bart flung himself out of the office in the direction of the mules, Gideon shaking his head, glad the scene was over.

But it wasn't for Bart. He was so stunned, he worked blindly that day. He unpacked at Malachi's old house, not caring that it was dusty and in need of a thorough cleaning. He got one of the Indian women to bring him hot water, dug out his best clothes from his trunk, and steamed his suit into shape.

As he dressed that evening, he kept reminding himself that Rachel was married. Married! He would have to see her at dinner that night. She'd be bustling around Gideon's house, blooming out of love for him. She would be polite, serve as hostess, listen to his stories—all as Gideon's wife. He was galled, hurt. How could she have done this to him? Gideon must have rushed her. Rachel was not old enough to marry.

Bart had meant to wait another year for her. Surely she had understood his intentions. He had courted her in earnest, he had told her he was crazy about her.

Well, he had his pride. He would laugh and joke with them, but by God, he would never forgive Gideon for snatching away Rachel. He would watch and see if Rachel truly loved Gideon, and was happy. If she was not, he'd pay court again, whether his brother liked it or not.

Slowly he removed from the little leather pouch the miniature he had hired a visiting artist to paint of Rachel the previous summer. He'd told the man to go to the bank and look for Rachel, the beautiful one, and paint a small canvas of her face for him. The man had teased Bart, but made a fine little oval painting, setting it in a gold frame.

Bart gazed down at it. The painting had lived with him this long past year. He had worked for her, confided to her, and reveled in those gentle brown eyes that seemed to talk to him in turn. "Rachel, how could you?" he groaned.

The eyes were silent tonight.

He shook his handsome curly head, still numb. He could not believe it. Well, he would soon see for himself. He shoved the miniature back into its leather case, and slipped it carefully into a trouser pocket.

That evening he strode to Gideon's and Rachel's home intent on being as charming as possible. It was Gideon, grim-faced, who answered his knock, but when he saw the smile on Bart's face, he softened and invited his brother in. Bart hailed Rachel, looking lovely in a lacey blouse and cotton skirt as she came into the living room, wiping her hands on a towel, to greet Bart, before ducking back into the kitchen. She was preparing a lamb roast with beans and potatoes, and as they sat around the steaming aromatic fare later, Bart entertained his hosts with news of home.

"You would not know Uncle Malachi!" he cried after they broke into the roast, which Gideon had ceremoniously cut moments before. "He came home in June, all dressed to the nines in a big white sombrero and cowboy boots. He found Philadelphia too strait-laced for him and took off for New York! Father and I went after him when we heard some gossip. And you should have seen where we found him!"

In spite of his grief, Bart was bursting with laughter remembering the scene. Gideon was smiling too, and Rachel's soft brown eyes had gone wide, unbelieving as she listened.

"What happened to him?" urged Gideon. "He said he wanted to marry—did he find a wife?"

"A wife?" laughed Bart. "In brothels?" Rachel flinched. "No, he is hanging out in saloons, Gideon, holding little girls on his knees! He brags he found gold in the West, and even carries a pouch of it with him, handing out nuggets that he says he dug himself! He is going broke fast, but Father cannot persuade him to stop!"

Rachel shook her head, distressed. "Poor Uncle Malachi."

But Bart went on. "He found a showgirl he goes about with, who has dyed her hair bright yellow. He hangs on her arm— she is a foot taller than he!" Bart doubled up with laughter.

The others were not laughing, however. Gideon looked as though he strongly disapproved, and Rachel was clearly distressed. Bart had to restrain himself. Obviously what he found uproarious, they found upsetting. Maybe they weren't aware that Malachi had frequented the saloons here and spent money on the Indian women and the wretched girls who lived above the saloons.

Bart changed the subject. He brought out the presents he had bought for Rachel. Lengths of silk, jewels, he pressed them all on her. Gideon held up his hand grimly.

"Bart, she is my wife now. She cannot accept these. Keep them for your wife, when you marry!"

In his present mood, Bart refused. "Oh, come on, Gideon," he tried to cajole his brother. "The silks are for Rachel, they match her coloring. Look how they set off her hair and eyes!"

But Gideon refused them all firmly. He would allow Bart only to give them the set of dishes he had bought as a wedding gift. They were of white bone china trimmed with gold and decorated with dainty blue flowers. Rachel thanked him effusively, and did not seem to miss the other gifts when he had to take them home with him again. Bart had the dubious pleasure of seeing the china on the table when he came again to dinner.

He swung from anger to hurt. He did not sleep well at night, and lay awake, thinking of the girl he loved in his brother's arms. How possessive Gideon was! Bart could scarcely look at her without Gideon interrupting and trying to distract him with some remark.

And Bart was lonely. There was no girl in Copper Creek

to match Rachel. Recklessly, he started going again to the Indian girls and could sometimes find forgetfulness in their sensuous arms. In the dark, he thought savagely, all cats look the same. But it was not true. None had the softness and perfumed sweetness of Rachel.

He had been thinking of marrying! Now his life felt empty. He could not think of another girl he would be happy to live with, let alone love.

Chapter 15

The winter of 1880–81 brought both great joy and pain for Gideon. Rachel became pregnant and went about with a radiant smile on her lovely face. Gideon was so proud and happy and anxious over her, he could scarcely concentrate on his work.

Then, as if the gods couldn't let too much good fortune shower down on one mortal man, the miners struck. In anger, they demanded higher wages and a share of the profits. Gideon was appalled. He thought he had warded off all strikes, for they had good labor conditions and were always treated fairly.

But the miners were discontented because of stories they had heard from other miners about regular pay hikes, profit-sharing plans, safety insurance.

Gideon struggled to work with the men, talk with them. He feared violence would erupt.

Against her husband's wishes, meanwhile, Rachel began making visits to the miners' wives and families, telling them in her gentle, earnest way what they would lose by striking. "We would pay more if we had the money to pay," she explained, sitting with them in their small parlors. "You know what the smelters pay to the Landau mines. They may be cheating us, but if we sent the ore back east as we used to, the costs would go even higher because we'd have to pay for drivers and wagons."

"How can the other mines afford it?" one wife asked her belligerently.

Rachel replied promptly, "They're paying higher to lure miners to work for them. Then if the Landaus are driven out of business, they will immediately lower the wages."

"How do you know?" the woman challenged.

"Because there are people who work in the other mining operations who respect the Landaus and who have passed along the truth to us."

The other women turned either sulky or speechless. What could they say? That Rachel Landau was lying? Many of them had grown up with her, and knew she was impeccably honest.

Rachel did this without her husband knowing, and the tension over the subsequent days lessened, though it was Gideon who finally capped the situation. He hired some scabs and opened one of the mines. Violence erupted, bringing some of the miners who abhorred it back to their senses. Reluctantly, they returned to work.

Bitterness would have lingered if Gideon hadn't promised the strike leaders to search for ways to improve conditions. He thought about it all winter, and worried about how dependent the Landaus were on their Copper Creek holdings. The family still owned the grocery store in Philadelphia, which Jared was taking care of, but the income wouldn't support their growing family.

Unless they found other mines—

Gideon poked around that winter, asking questions and learning about abandoned claims in the area. He quietly and quickly bought them up. Then he heard that Mexico hid a fortune in lead, iron, and silver, if only efficient methods could be found to mine the rich lodes—and avoid the desolate mountains and deserts, where bandits abounded.

Before Gideon could make a move, his son was born. It was March of 1881. Rachel had an easy first birth, everybody said. Gideon shuddered, remembering the hours of waiting and her cries coming from their upstairs room. After waiting with her, pacing the floor, clenching his fists over the screaming, he swore he would never take birth for granted again.

The Indian woman Winona and her daughters helped, as well as Amaris, who moved in for a week, caring first for Rachel, then for the baby, young Simon. Gideon was very grateful to the loving gentle woman and to her husband, Peter, who had let her go for the week.

Peter had warned Gideon quietly that it was Asher and Eden who were behind the miner's strike. Asher had joined with a couple other mine operators to raise wages, and they started gossip about how much profit they gave to their men.

"He grows more greedy all the time," Gideon sighed. "I had hoped he would remain in Denver."

Peter grimaced. "I heard that his wife spent so much money, he was in danger of going broke. She nags him all the time," he added, with a long shudder. "My wife's sister—but what a contrast! She should have had children to keep her busy. Then she would not have time to meddle in Landau business."

Even Amaris shunned her sister, but Eden did not seem to mind. She invited men to dinner—supposedly to talk business with Asher, but actually to stroke her vanity by their praises of her, their staring at her. Whether she actually carried on affairs Gideon did not know. But she caused such scandal—which seemed to delight her—the effect was the same.

Rachel ignored both Eden and the stories about her. The company she kept was with those who shared her interests—music, books, religion and, now, her child. She rocked Simon constantly, fed him when he cried, and brought him shyly down to company to show him off. "Is he not a fine child?" she would ask, glowing at the sturdy boy.

In April, when Gideon was more sure that the boy and his mother would be all right, he told Rachel about his plans. "I need to go to Mexico, Rachel. I will be gone as short a time as possible." He explained about the mines there and how the Landaus needed to broaden their base of capital to survive.

She was troubled, upset, but tried to hide it. She put her head on his shoulder as they sat on the sofa. "If you must go, Gideon," she said, her voice shaking, "I will understand."

"I fear I must. One day our mines will be played out and we'll need additional sources of support."

"Played out? Our mines? So deep in the earth?" she gasped.

Gideon nodded. "Say nothing of this, darling, it is between us. But I think Asher's mine—that is, Vashti Cohen's—will be played out in another five or ten years."

She contemplated it, her dismay evident. "It seems impossible! There is so much copper there—"

"There was. Asher has stripped it dry."

"And ours?"

Gideon shrugged. "All mines must play out one day. And the war burned up so much copper, not to mention the railroads today. The one good thing is that the rails joined in eighteen sixty-nine are bringing the railroad close to us. It makes the trip east much easier now, you know," and he coaxed her to smile. "Perhaps Father will come out this year. He can ride most of the way by rail."

Rachel fell silent.

The baby was opening his eyes, blinking with interest, and seeming to recognize his black-bearded father. Gideon sighed to himself. The sooner he left, the sooner he would return.

Responsibility for the mines fell to Bart Landau, while the care of Gideon's wife and baby went to Peter and Amaris Malchus, who moved in with Rachel immediately on his request. Though Gideon felt somewhat reassured, he still did not entirely trust the vagrants, the drunks, or his brother Bart, who through Rachel's pregnancy had hung about when he could, staring hungrily after her.

Less than easy about the situation, Gideon rode the rails south as far as he could. Near the Texas border he bought a good stallion and rode on, carrying a rifle, wearing a two-pistol holster, and keeping a Colt tucked in his saddlebags. He had been warned about traveling alone. But Gideon worried another man would draw attention to them. It was safer with only himself to worry about.

He kept to main trails and passed through one small town after another. Everywhere he found that despite the hunger, poverty, and shabbiness, the Mexican people were gentle and friendly. The women were often beautiful. They had dignity, and for all their poverty, many a family shared their beans and fresh well water with him.

Gideon reached Mexico City in June and began to inquire around. He was soon directed to the chief himself, the dictator Porfirio Díaz, who was part Spanish and part Indian, a plump well-dressed man of immense power. He had helped others overthrow the Emperor Maximilian in the revolution that had shattered Mexico, and in 1867 the Mexicans had taken charge of their own future.

Gideon learned that Díaz was anxious to meet him, having heard of the Landaus' engineering skill and prowess in mining, which would be of great help to his own people.

A formal meeting was arranged. Díaz listened to Gideon and then turned him over to his mining engineer, Colonel Martinez. "You will talk together and report to me," he said.

Gideon knew some Spanish but had trouble with the vocabulary of mining. He finally reverted to English, speaking slowly, interspersing his words with his knowledge of the other language. Privately he resolved to learn Mexican Spanish before he returned. Some of the Mexicans knew French, but hated to speak it because it was the language of the conqueror. Spanish had been also, but the Spaniards had been there in the more distant past.

The two discussed at length Mexico's lead mines, iron mines, and silver mines, some buried deep in the mountains, some in inhospitable deserts in the far northwest. A much larger problem was the Mexicans' smelters, which had been built in the times of the Spanish.

"We need smelters with more recent and efficient methods of working," Colonel Martinez said. "I do not like your idea, to build a railroad to the north and carry the ore to a smelter up north. They will charge us very high, and we cannot afford this expense. Besides, we wish to be self-sufficient one day. How can we do this if the ores go always out of the country?"

Gideon saw his point, but he wondered if his father would. They returned to Porfirio Díaz to report. The dictator was visibly disappointed.

"If you cannot build smelters in our land, we cannot allow you to dig in our mines," he said firmly.

Gideon returned to Copper Creek. To his relief, Jared had arrived to spend the summer and had taken up residence with Bart in Uncle Malachi's old home.

He had been stunned on arriving to find Gideon gone to Mexico. "What were you doing there, my son?" he asked sternly. "Did I give you permission to prospect?"

Jared was angry. "No, Father, but one day soon our mines will play out," he explained, studying his father's weary face anxiously. He looked so much older, with streaks of iron gray, in his hair and lines in his face and throat. "The Landaus must prepare for the future. We cannot depend forever on the mines here. Already the best ore has been taken from them."

Jared studied his son as his son studied him. He saw a young, mature, handsome man with a shrewd look about him—a shrewdness very much his own. He had to smile in pride. Bart, in comparison, was so youthful and charming—but immature. Gideon seemed not a lovable man, though his wife obviously adored him. He was strict, ramrod straight, like an Old Testament prophet.

Jared sighed a little and began again. "I have no wish at this time to go to Mexico, my son. Who would run the mines? I depend on you for the Copper Creek enterprises. Bart cannot run them yet. In another five years, who knows? But not now."

Gideon considered this thoughtfully. They were in the parlor of the large cabin, and Gideon reached down into his five-month-old son's crib and cradled the boy in his arms. The little boy seemed content as Gideon bent to him and gently brushed his lips against the fluff of black fuzz on his head.

Jared mused that Gideon, though severe a few moments ago, had relaxed completely. His son seemed more approachable.

"We do need a smelter *here*, at least, Father," he was saying.

"But we have nobody to build a smelter for us and run it," Jared said. "Until we do, I cannot permit you to try such an enterprise. I know you're familiar with the design and operation of one, but it is not enough to have theoretical knowledge."

Gideon mused a moment, then nodded. "All right, Father. Until the day we can find the right man, I yield. But one day we must build our own so we can control the entire operation— from prospecting to mining to smelting to selling our copper at the market. It's the only way we'll ever be free of competition."

They closed the conversation. But when Bart heard the fruit of the conversation, he was bitterly disappointed.

Jared shook his head firmly. "Your brother and I have discussed it at length already, and we will have to wait on the smelters."

He did not add that Bart was too young to take over the Copper Creek operations. He still liked to play practical jokes, fool around, sleep late, and take time off. Someday he'd mature, though it seemed that Gideon had always been that way. Jared shook his head. It was probably a matter of temperament, probably a matter of experience. Both shaped a man.

That night Jared went to have dinner with his brother Asher and sister-in-law Eden. He had been shocked to find that Gideon and Rachel never visited them and that they had never had them into their home. "But he is your uncle, he is my brother!" Jared gasped. "You mean—never? Not even on holy days?"

"Never," Gideon said, frowning. "I have nothing in common with them. And I don't want Rachel to have anything to do with them."

Jared had contemplated his son in awe. Such strict principles! Such rigid morals! Such determination! Had he trained the lad to be that way? He felt uneasy around his own son.

So later, alone, he went to Asher and Eden's, and to his surprise they greeted him eagerly and with much courtesy. They led him into their spacious home, where they'd set a fine table. "You don't know how Gideon has hurt us," Eden said, tears brimming in her beautiful black eyes during the course of the meal. She reminded him so much of her lovely mother, Vashti— so full-bodied, vigorous, vibrant—he had to catch himself from staring. "We have begged him to come over, haven't we, Asher my love?"

She seemed genuinely fond of Asher, and he returned the feeling. The marriage had worked, Jared thought, and he softened to them, in spite of what they had done to Vashti. After all, they had only tried to get what was due them. And Asher, who was naturally lazy, had worked hard in the store and mine office. He deserved a better life.

They lived in the house Vashti had built for herself. Eden ran the store, Asher ran the mine, and together they did the bookkeeping.

Tonight, Eden wore a becoming lilac print dress of silk, Asher was handsome in a black frockcoat and ruffled shirt. They looked prosperous, but modest. And though they had not added on to the house, they had added a fine piano, lace curtains, blue silk draperies, and several lovely rugs.

If only they had had children, it might have settled Eden, Jared thought. She seemed restless, her eyes roving with vague discontent over the dining table, the living room furniture, through the pictures in a fashion magazine that Jared had brought her.

It was an echo of the early Vashti, before she'd grown old and shrunken with age. Even Miriam was aging better then Vashti had.

Asher finally said, "Jared, you could do me good if you chose." His eyes glittered, and in this light, they appeared fiendish.

Jared couldn't help but flinch. "What is it?" he asked. He wondered if his brother would ask for Gideon's friendship—which was not Jared's to give.

"I have not enough work to do," Asher said. Jared gaped at him. "If I had another mine to work, it would be better. You know, we have but ten miners. I could put another ten to work and supervise them. Gideon has bought up all the claims he can find, and holds them with no intention of working them for a while!"

Jared frowned. He could never take from his own son to give to Asher—not because of the injustice of it, but because Gideon had expanded the Landau business with his own money.

"What do you want me to do for you? You have to be direct, Asher. Are all the claims bought up?"

"I don't know, but when I hear about a claim, Gideon has already bought it," Asher said plaintively. His wife nodded vigorously.

"Yes, Gideon snaps them up like a turtle snapping up flies," she joined in, and laughed charmingly, her deep dimples reminding Jared of how much she looked like her mother. His gaze lingered on her.

He couldn't help but think how different was his own Sapphira. She was as beautiful but was shy, gentle, timid. The finishing school had succeeded in giving her an excellent education and a polish that rivaled New York's best. New York society was not like Philadelphia, but she could slip into it one day. All it took was money and dazzle. And she was already betrothed to a fine young man, with prospects of being a banker on Wall Street, who knew of her past and still accepted her fully.

Jared was pleased that Asher wanted more work. It showed the Landau blood coursed through his veins. Not like Enoch, who neglected the grocery store for his family. Jared had waited until irresponsible brother Malachi had run out of money, then brought him back to Philadelphia and put him to work in the grocery store. He'd thought scornfully that the two lazy roustabouts could then do the work of one man and stay out of trouble. And Jared had bought the hardware store where Isaac still worked, from Asher, and from Vashti's estate, as Asher could not work it from Copper Creek. So he really did owe him a favor, he reasoned.

"Well, well, I'll see what I can do," he promised. Eden

flung her arms about his neck and kissed him with moist lips. It was like touching Vashti, and he hugged her and returned the kiss warmly.

Within the week Jared found out about a mine as soon as Gideon did, and hastily bought the claim from the grizzled prospector who'd put it up for sale.

Gideon complained to him, "What are you going to do with it, Father? Do you mean me to work it one day? Does it go into the Landau holdings in reserve?"

Jared grimaced. He might have known Gideon would ask him directly. No shilly-shallying around with him.

"No, I gave it to your Uncle Asher," he said. "He wants more work to do, and it's best to keep him busy. The devil has work for idle hands to do."

He thought he carried it off well. But Gideon stared at him, outraged, horrified.

"You gave the good claim to Asher—to Eden? To those two conniving, scheming—"

"Now, Gideon!" Jared said sternly, feeling a bit ashamed of himself. "I owed him a favor—"

"For what? Taking Vashti Cohen's property from her? How often have you complained that they cheated her and possibly caused her early death!"

Before his son's steady gaze, Jared glanced away. He bit his lips and steadied his voice. "He is my brother. And he has worked hard these years. He took what was his by right of marriage."

"He took what had been Vashti's property. He did not offer anything to Amaris."

Jared regretted telling his eldest son so much. But he defended himself with as much spirit as possible. "If Asher is busy, he will have less time to think up mischief! You said you suspected the mine strike was partly his conniving. Well, let his hands be busy and his brain occupied with managing. Think—he will stay off your back forever!"

"I don't think it wise to give him anything," Gideon said slowly. "He will expect more. However, it is your business. You bought the claim, you gave it to him. It is done."

But Jared was conscious of Gideon's displeasure. When Bart heard, he simply looked on indifferently. As far as he was concerned, his family had plenty already. If Uncle Asher was so foolish and greedy to want more, why, let him. And that

Eden—she was a piece! She amused him.

Jared was pleased with Asher and Eden Landau's gratitude. Before he returned east, he had dinner with them often and enjoyed their gratitude and flattery. There was no way he'd ever alienate his own brother, no matter what had happened in the past, no matter how foolish their compliments.

Eden reminded him more and more of Vashti, though she wasn't as brilliant, nor were her spirits or courage as high. She didn't dream of another world in which women had limitless, unfettered opportunities—a world that made Jared uneasy.

He dreamed at nights of Vashti, of her remote smile, the flights of imagination, the glow in her face as she spoke of her ambitions. He remembered how happy she had been when she first crossed the plains into the mountains. He visited her grave, sat beside it, studied the blue flowers her daughter Amaris had planted and kept watered.

"Ah, Vashti, how it has turned out," he said aloud. "I felt guilty, but you brought me joy and gave me my lovely daughter Sapphira. Yes, she is happy. I am already attending her wedding this winter. If only you could be there! You would be so proud of her, she's so pretty, so good!"

He found he could not confide to Vashti's grave about the silver mine he had given to Asher. Quietly, he rose and reluctantly took his farewell of her grave. Later that week, he was even more reluctant to leave his little grandson. He sat with the boy in his arms for the last several evenings, though Simon would yawn and finally fall asleep against his shoulder—not the most engaging companion.

"You must bring him east," he said finally. "One day— one day his grandmother must see him. How she longs to meet your lovely wife, Rachel!"

Rachel smiled down at him and bent to take Simon from him. "We shall come east one day. I long to meet Mother Miriam. I've heard so much about all those works of charity."

"Yes, yes, you must come," Jared sighed, but one did not expect they would come east. They would go where Gideon's work took them, just as Jared's family had always followed him. It was a condition he approved of. Work was a man's life, his salvation, and his son would stand in line to achieve, to build even more. That was a man's purpose in life—to create a wonderful life his children would surpass.

Chapter 16

Early in 1884 Rachel went into labor, and before the night was over, she gave birth to another son, whom she named Franklin. It had turned out to be another easy birth.

Gideon was much relieved and happy. He brought three-year-old Simon to the crib, and they bent over to admire the new baby together.

"See his hands, see his hands," Simon said, laughing. He touched a little waving fist gently, a look of wonder in his face. "When will he play with me?"

"A little time yet, my son," Gideon said, smiling. "He must eat much and grow some first."

Not long after Rachel one day found the crib lined with boxes of cereal and sugar. There was a bundle of dirty rooted vegetables from the garden in a corner.

"What is this?" she cried in amazement.

"I did," Simon said with satisfaction from his position on the floor in front of wood soldiers. "He will eat much and pretty soon play with me!"

It was with difficulty that she persuaded him that the baby must have milk first before solid foods. She then coaxed him to eat his cookies instead of playing with them. He was already showing too inventive an imagination, and a Landau trait— generosity.

Gideon would laugh over these incidents. And he took great pride in feeding Simon's growing curiosity about life by letting him tag along after him on Saturdays when he went to the mine office. The boy's eyes were always wide with wonder. He was smart and learned quickly.

Gideon felt so contented, hardly anything could disturb his calm.

Except for Bart. He hovered over Rachel all the time. Though Gideon did not doubt his wife, he did not fully trust his brother. Bart seemed sometimes to lose himself in gazing at Rachel, praising her when she wore a new dress, noticing when she changed her hairstyle. It could be most distressing.

"You are a lucky man, Gideon," Bart sighed from time to time, and Gideon would nod, smiling, but say nothing more.

Rachel always said she felt sorry for the bachelor, which was why she often invited him to dinner. Gideon would simply press his lips together and shake his head. With Bart's over-attention to Rachel, Gideon sometimes was hard pressed to bite down the feelings of jealousy it sometimes stirred. But the dinners always went well. They laughed as they listened to Bart's stories about his adventures. After dinner, they would discuss business while Rachel washed the dishes and cleaned up the kitchen. Then she would ascend the stairs to see to the children, while Bart fully concentrated on the Landau enterprises.

Gideon had to admit that Bart was maturing; his perceptions were more keen. He loved adventure and often went down into the mines to gauge the work's progress, talking and joking with the men, who also enjoyed him. And he would go anywhere Gideon sent him in an effort to find new mining prospects. Bart had no sense of fear. He was a good rider, a fine shot, an excellent hunter, and he displayed an unusual courage in the proximity of hostile Indians. He liked to foil Indian hunters and would come back, laughing uproariously about some episode or another, to Gideon's amusement and Rachel's horror.

Gideon had no complaints about Bart's work. He would work as hard as Gideon, longer hours, never thinking about taking time off. His life was his work, and he made suggestions eagerly about various aspects of it. He showed no signs of wishing to be married; he visited the brothels and the Indian women, who seemed to satisfy him.

"We need a smelter, Gideon," he said one evening, leaning forward with clasped hands, his black eyes sparkling. "No matter what Father says. We should start a smelter right away. Those dealers are robbing us!"

"I know it," Gideon said with a sigh. "But Father thinks there is nobody to build one, nobody to run it, and the change would be too inefficient and costly for a while."

"Nobody here to build one," Bart said gloomily. Suddenly Rachel's steps falling lightly on the stairs sounded. Bart immediately stood up when she entered the room, offering her a chair. His eyes played over her rounded form, but she did not seem to notice, though Gideon, who did, was frowning.

"Thank you, Bart. Do not let me interrupt your conversation," Rachel said, smiling, and picked up her sewing. She was making some small garment for Simon, and her fingers worked busily.

"We were discussing the possibility of building a smelter," Gideon said to distract Bart's attention.

"Maybe we could find someone back east," Bart said.

They thought about it in silence. Gideon knew many of the smelter men back east, but they had no interest in moving West. He needed to find someone who genuinely appreciated the freedom of the West.

Freedom. The word clanged in his mind. Freedom. Who would come west—who would love the wild freedom and open spaces?

A Jew in Europe. The solution came to him swiftly, as if spoken by another in his mind. A Jew, frustrated, feeling the prejudice of his neighbors. But did any European Jew know about smelters? They were not permitted to operate many businesses, much less mine for precious ore. Still, some had good educations—Or there might be a Gentile eager to find a new opportunity and life in America.

"I wonder," he mused aloud.

Bart said alertly, "Someone fresh out of college? Someone young and ambitious—"

"No. I thought . . . someone in Europe, eager to make a change. Someone older, yet willing to make a clean break to toss away a lifetime of restrictions for a new life with few—"

"As your parents came, Gideon," Rachel said eagerly.

"Yes, as they came. Father would understand."

It was April. If he departed now, he could return by late autumn. But it meant leaving Rachel alone with the children—and with a restless Bart.

He thought about it, musing. Bart rambled on to Rachel about some adventure of his, making her laugh and shake her shining dark head.

"So I hid out behind a rock and waited for him to come out—some Injun off the reservation, hungry and dying for that rabbit I shot. I waited him out, and when he come out, I took a shot at his head. He shot back like he was hit! I made him wait all night, then before dawn, I snuck off down the dry creek bed, laughing all the way."

"Oh, Bart, it will be your head if you're not careful!"

"I shall go to Europe," Gideon said suddenly in the midst of their laughter.

They stared at him.

"Gideon! To Europe!" Rachel gasped.

"Yes, I shall find someone to build and work a smelter for us. They have good engineers. I shall go to Germany, where they've worked mines for hundreds of years."

"But to find someone like that and persuade him to leave his work—"

"I shall arrange it," Gideon said, his Landau blood warming at the idea. "I shall offer a high salary. We shall build a house for him—Bart! While I am gone, build a house. Make a fine two-story structure, with sturdy furniture, a good kitchen for his wife, and a garden for vegetables and flowers. I shall say to such and such a man: Come!—you will have everything in this land of boundless opportunity!"

Bart and Rachel were both staring at him, not quite believing their ears. He grinned at them, feeling boyishly delighted. He would make such an offer that the right man could not refuse!

"Rachel, you and Amaris help my brother plan the house and oversee its building. Make it as good as a housekeeper would wish it to be."

"Gideon!" Rachel cried, her whole face lighting up with their new prospects. If her husband could be so bold, so could she. After all, it would mean freedom from the tyranny of smelter owners who didn't care about the Landau enterprises. It would mean prosperity for Copper Creek and, ultimately, a

201

better life for their children. "I can already see what such a house would need—if I draw up a list, will you buy what is needed in the East?"

With Bart quietly looking on, as if not entirely sure of what was transpiring, Gideon jumped to his feet. "Of course, my love, whatever your heart desires!"

Gideon set out for Europe. He had persuaded the Malchus family to move in with Rachel to protect her and his children while he was gone. The house would be a bit crowded, but it would be better than leaving Rachel to fend for herself and the children, with a dashing bachelor brother nearby.

To keep Bart out of trouble, Gideon left him enough work to keep three men busy. Now he had not only his own and Gideon's work, but the task of building the new house. Satisfied, Gideon headed east, not planning to stop in Philadelphia to argue with his father. He would present Jared with the accomplished fact.

Gideon went first to Munich, then to Frankfort, talking with men who knew smelter work, but who were mostly acquainted with old-fashioned methods. They wanted nothing to do with starting a smelter, they were timid or unwilling to make the drastic move to a new world, he thought contemptuously.

Gideon continued to follow leads, roaming from Germany to Austria, more and more anxiously. Perhaps he was too particular. Perhaps he wanted too much. But he needed a knowlegeable man willing to make the change to the New World, one who was innovative enough to work with the problems of mountain life.

By August, he had reached the Bavarian Alps, where, against brilliant blue skies, the mountains reared their sharply spired heads into the crystalline air. Mountain streams flowed down heavily, the mountains, watering the lush meadows of alpine flowers—blue gentian, small red poppies, white and yellow daisies, and tall red salvia.

He admired the Swiss chalets. Their coloring of rich chocolate brown, their balconies, and their window boxes reminded him of the waterfalls flowing around him.

Meanwhile he patiently followed each lead, either dismissing the young ones on meeting them, or finding the elderly reluctant to leave home and grandchildren.

He crossed the Alps to Italy, then circled around again in September to Bavaria and Austria. It wasn't until he arrived in Salzburg that he found a strong lead. He was directed through the twisting and cobblestoned streets to an address. The third floor of the house was lined with window boxes filled with geraniums. The residents lived above the ground-floor jewelry shop run by a Jew.

Gideon rang the iron bell. A girl's head popped out of an opened window, over the window box of scarlet geraniums, blooming in the single band of sunlight that reached like a finger into the narrow dark street below. Her eyes were vivid blue, contrasting with the bright yellow braids of hair that framed her pink cheeks.

She looked very German and Gentile. Gideon felt keen disappointment. He was certain she belonged to a family who would be prejudiced against Jews. Most Jews had fled from Salzburg hundreds of years before; hated and persecuted, they had scattered to the far corners of Europe and to England.

"Who is it? What do you wish?" She was young and plump and pretty, her voice sharp.

"I am Gideon Landau from America," he said politely. He was already thinking where he could go next. "I am seeking the chemist Theodoric Loffler."

The blue eyes widened at him from over the geraniums. "Papa comes home in one hour. You will come up, yes?"

Surprised, Gideon heard the click that meant the latch was being sprung free from upstairs, and he pushed open the heavy wooden door. He stood in a dark hallway. As his eyes adjusted, he could see a flight of stairs in front of him. Ascending it, he came to an open door on the second flight.

The girl stood there, seeming shy but composed. "You will come in?"

She held the door open, and Gideon entered the apartment. Though dark, it was well scrubbed and clean. The windows were open to the air and sunlight, the walls were painted white, and the ceiling had some fine stucco work of intricate design.

The girl was looking at him with wary curiosity. "You are . . . Gentile?" she asked hesitantly.

He shook his head. "No, Jewish." He figured her reaction would be one of disgust, that she would send him away.

Instead, she smiled with relief. "So are we. I am Charlotte

Loffler. My father is Theodoric Loffler, the neighborhood chemist!"

She raised her chin and her eyes shone. Gideon bowed to her solemnly, and suddenly he knew her father was the man he sought.

Charlotte curtseyed to him and pointed to a chair. "You will have tea and something to eat while we wait for Papa?" She was courteous, an eager little hostess, though she couldn't be much beyond her teens yet, he thought.

"Yes, thank you." He took the seat. "You say you are Jewish? You do not appear to be—" He hesitated, surveying her blond hair and round full figure in the bright blue dress and white neat apron.

"Yes. My father and I—we are part Jewish. We are permitted to live here only because we inherited from my German mother, who died when I was quite small. When Father dies, I must go, however. Only the man inherits." She stifled a sigh, and went to the tiny efficient kitchen to prepare the tea.

Charlotte's heart was pounding hard, and she felt dizzy as she poured out the tea and dipped some hot soup into a bowl. She cut a lavish piece of bread to go with it and carried the neat tray back to the unexpected guest.

When she'd finished serving him, she sat down in her rocking chair and questioned Gideon politely but eagerly. To her, it was an adventure to have a guest in their house! Her father worked all the time, bringing much wealth from his innovations, but leaving his daughter alone in their home all the time. And she had no friends because few Germans and Austrians would risk their reputations to be seen entering the home of a Jew. "You have heard of my father, yes?"

"Yes, he was recommended to me for some work."

"Oh, you are in the mining and smelting work, then? It is in Frankfort or Munich?" She couldn't fathom his accent. He was certainly handsome, with his black pointed beard and straight-looking black eyes, and he seemed very congenial.

"No. In America, Fräulein. In a place called Copper Creek, in the Rocky Mountains."

Her eyes widened. "From America?" she gasped, "all the way across the ocean?"

He smiled charmingly. "Yes, Fräulein. It is a long distance to go in a sailing vessel to another world, the new world of

America. But it's a place where one can be free and happy, even when Jewish, and it is worth the long journey."

Nothing could have been said that would have been more entrancing to her. She stared at him, bemused. America. This man was from America! No wonder he walked with a swing in his long-legged gait and held his head high—though he was Jewish! This man walked mountains, he carried on business, he was a proud man, unafraid of danger or risk.

He talked easily and courteously to her. Her father arrived home and gaped to see his shy daughter eagerly talking to a complete stranger.

The two men met, clasped hands, and before long became rapid friends. Gideon presented his proposition. "Come to America? Live among wild Indians!" Theodoric Loffler cried, his gray-blond hair ruffled in agitation by long slim fingers. He was not dark like Gideon; he was as light as his daughter. But he was enough Jewish that he would never be accepted in the Old World.

He was wealthy, for he had earned much from his clever inventions, and he was in demand as an engineer and chemist. But he was not happy. His wife had died when Charlotte was ten. He had no close relatives; he was shunned in personal relations.

"And my Charlotte has no friends," he mourned. "My lovely daughter, she has no friends. I had to do all her schooling myself. It is a shame. Such a shame."

"Is it true the wild Indians take all one's hair?" Charlotte asked, worriedly touching her thick blond braids. "Must I live apart from Papa, back in the cities?"

Gideon smiled at her kindly. "No, Fräulein. My own wife has lived most of her life in the mountains. An Indian woman and her daughters do the laundry and help clean house. They are as kind and good as you could ever wish to meet. And some Indian men work in the mines. Yes, there are savages, but most of them are young bucks off the reservation."

The Lofflers did not understand all that Gideon said, but he managed to reassure them. When he told them a house was being built for a smelter operator who would be paid a large salary which would eventually help pay for the house, they were shocked and incredulous. "But what will your government say?" Charlotte asked.

"Nothing," Gideon said positively. "They have no say in matters of this import. You must only pay your taxes—that's as much as is demanded of citizens, no more."

"That is too difficult to believe," Loffler said, shaking his head and frowning.

"America is a different world. Ask my father, who came from a ghetto in Switzerland with his family thirty-five years ago. From poverty to wealth, he came," Gideon said. He told them about his grandparents' journey, his father's struggles.

They talked long that night. Before Gideon departed, he had one final comment. "You must have a care for your daughter, Mr. Loffler," he warned.

The man looked worried. "How is this, eh?"

"There are ten times as many men as women in Copper Creek. She will be married off before you know it! Most of the men are bachelors, and when they find she is as good as she is beautiful, and a fine housekeeper, well—you will lose her very quickly!"

"Ach! Now you jest!" Loffler said.

Charlotte looked bewildered. "But—are they Jewish men?" she questioned.

"Several are, including my brother Bart!"

When he had left, Charlotte and her father exchanged puzzled looks. "Can we believe all he says? Can it be true?" she whispered.

"He sounds a truthful man. But he talks like a madman when he speaks of America!"

"But if it is true—what then?" Oh, it sounded like paradise, she thought. Owning their own house! Living in the mountains, freely, with no shunning and no prejudice—and plenty of men to court! Incredible.

She lay awake much of the night, first disbelieving, then beginning to hope. She even planned what they could take with them—her mother's rocking chair, the small pianoforte, the little silver and pewter they owned, tablecloths of linen and lace, her father's desk—

Gideon came the next day, as persuasive as before. Before he realized it, Loffler gave notice to his employers and was helping his daughter pack their belongings in a dozen boxes and loading them in a wagon Gideon bought for them. He sold the apartment to a neighbor.

Within a month they were in a ship bound for the New World. Two months later, in late November, they landed in Philadelphia and went to stay with Jared and his family. Miriam Landau welcomed them serenely. She talked much to Charlotte and answered all her questions about life for a woman in the New World.

While the men talked business and visited smelters around New England, Miriam shopped with Charlotte for the household goods they would need in Copper Creek.

Charlotte bought copper and iron pots and pans, a fine stove in very modern fashion, beds and mattresses, a sofa, and cedar chairs with silk cushions. Tables and cupboards could be made out west, Miriam said.

Charlotte also bought lengths of fabric for dresses, and Miriam gave her a beautiful large sewing basket of wicker and lined with taffeta, furnished with all the needles, pins, thread, and thimble that a girl could wish.

She went to plays, and she learned some English from Miriam and Rosemary, who now taught children in school. Rosemary was a frail gentle girl who caught at her heart; she was often ill but had an indomitable spirit behind her pain. Hannah, the other sister, had recently married, but went on shopping expeditions with them. As a new bride, she had many practical suggestions for furnishing a house. It was Hannah who suggested a mirror, extra pillows and bedding for cold weather and for guests, and one of the new cookbooks being printed for ladies who had no servants. She also had plenty of fashion ideas. Hoops were being modified, but still in use, and she made sure that Charlotte had several dresses with the newest hoops.

Charlotte was in a daze of delight. She learned a tremendous amount from Jared Landau's children—including the youngest, David, who when he was home from school, would wildly amuse her and teach her some of the current language. Soon Charlotte had more of a slang vocabulary than proper English, Rosemary said, sighing.

David was like a brother to her, yet he would flirt outrageously with her, then laugh like a fool when his mother scolded him for his behavior. But Charlotte could not take him seriously, nor did he wish to be her beau; He knew she wouldn't be in the East for long. "Wait until you meet Bart," he said frequently, darkly. "You won't believe some of the tales he tells!"

She could not imagine anybody like Bart, a bachelor who was very smart, like his elder brother Gideon, yet not like Gideon.

The men finished their work, and Gideon accompanied them on the trains that now extended deeply into the West. They rode to Chicago, changed trains, and continued west to an ever-changing landscape. First the small towns became fewer in number, then they were replaced completely by desert. And one day, peering from the train window, Charlotte saw her first Indians, racing their horses wildly against the speeding train. Their heads were shaven except for one long lock, their faces were painted, and they shook their lances at the train.

Charlotte shrank back from the window. Gideon noticed. "They will not harm us," he said casually, then continued his conversation with her father. Charlotte continued to stare at the Indians, and two men caught sight of her. They stared at her, one riding close to the train, peering as curiously at her as she did at them. He grinned fiercely, and she wanted to run for cover.

Early in March, they rode by mule up the mountain passes on the last stage of their long journey. Charlotte was weary, but fascinated by the scenery. This would be her new home! As the snows caused her sure-footed mule a little trouble, she gasped at the valley below them, at the sheer cliffs over their heads. But when they came into the valley and saw the new town, she could only stare.

The scene reminded her of the Alps, with small and large cabins set at random in the mountains. Between them coursed a white clear-running stream of icy waters. A few of the two-story houses had window boxes, and a flowering plant sprawled its vines through the railings on the balconies.

A young man opened the door of a white-painted building and ran out to greet them. He was tall, slim, dark-haired, and had laughing dark eyes.

"Hello, Gideon, you were gone long enough to go around the world!" he yelled. Charlotte gazed down at him as he stared boldly at her.

"This is my brother, Bartholomew Landau," Gideon said, sliding off his mule with relief. "Bart, I brought with me Mr.

Theodoric Loffler and his daughter Charlotte—"

"So I see!" Bart cried, and boldly reached up to help Charlotte down. She felt his firm, hard hands about her waist, and her startled blue eyes seemed to melt under his curious gaze. He put her down on the dusty plank sidewalk and grinned at her. "Well—the prettiest girl I've seen in years!" he said frankly.

"Is their house ready?" Gideon asked, frowning.

"All ready, has been for months," Bart said. "You'll like it, Miss Charlotte! Eight rooms, lots of space, and your garden already beginning to shoot up."

"Ach—what is this?" she asked in German.

"Speak English! You're in America!" Bart commanded.

She blinked and laughed. "Ja, ja," she said, and noticed his strong chin and beautiful mouth, so much more like David's than Gideon's. But when Gideon spoke to his brother, Bart answered seriously, and she saw a likeness between them.

Bart began immediately reporting to his brother about what had been happening with Landau business in his absence. They walked with the mules to the foot of the trail leading up to the newly-built house. When they paused, several rough and bearded men who blushed when Charlotte glanced at them, appeared out of nowhere to take the reigns of the mules and start unloading them.

"She looks like an angel!" one cried. Bart overheard and grinned frankly at Charlotte, who was reddening.

"Are you an angel?" he whispered outrageously as they walked up the path to the house. She reddened, then gasped as she spotted the house above them.

It was a large boarded house, with sloping dormer roof, several bay windows, and some carving along the cornices. The windows were shuttered, and the arched front door was flanked by pilasters and side windows. Gideon had insisted on the best, and this was the latest fashion in architecture. There was less worry about building a heavy, fortress-like building, as they'd done when Vashti and Jared had first moved into Copper Creek. The Indians were more quiet, and the town larger, making it less vulnerable to Indian attacks. And the fact the home was set upon a hill, and close to town, meant it fell within the town's protective defenses.

Her father tried to look severe, but he too was overwhelmed by the house. He never expected anything so grand. The outside was painted powder-blue, and the interior was papered with French fleur-de-lis. Inside, room after room flowed in one after the other opened on one another, though French doors separated the parlor and library from the wide foyer. A staircase rose to a second landing and set of rooms, and another staircase rose to a third. "There's a cellar for wines and storage, if you ever decide to need it," boasted Bart, smiling. He gazed intently at Charlotte, still taking in the carved beams and pilasters framing the oak French door which led into the parlor. "You will need to fill this place—with a fine husband and many children!" he said exuberantly. Charlotte, broken from her concentration, blushed wildly.

Her father too overwhelmed by the house, could only mutter, "Such a fine house, such a big place."

Charlotte peered about and exclaimed as she noted where they would set the furniture. And indeed, with many willing hands, the new furniture was unpacked and put into place by nightfall. Bart came early the next morning with another man, and with swift efficiency he set up the stove in time for Charlotte to cook breakfast. They had plenty of food. Rachel Landau had stocked their cupboards with canned and bottled victuals. And Charlotte had leavened bread the night before, weary as she was. By morning her first loaf of bread, under this roof, was ready for breakfast. Grinning, Bart invited himself in, then praised her cooking lavishly.

"I'll come often for dinner—and for breakfast," he promised, giving her an impudent wink that set her blushing again. "I get mighty tired of my own and the Indians' cooking. They don't have a talent for light breads and pastries!"

She felt overwhelmed by him, by the men staring at her whenever she went out. She was just seventeen and had lived a very sheltered life in Salzburg. The thought that every single man here thought her beautiful and desirable was dizzying.

The Landaus taught her to dance the formal dances of the East and the country dances of the West. Miss Ruth came over daily to teach her to speak English better and gave her brisk advice about the ways of America. Winona, came padding around to the kitchen and quietly took over her education in cooking cornmeal and the strange foods of her new life.

And best of all, her father took to the work eagerly, beginning at once to draw and plan the smelter. They treated him with respect due to his genius, she thought, and that made her very happy. She loved and adored him, for she thought he was the smartest man in the world and she had winced and wept over the scorn heaped on him in Europe. He deserved so much better! And in America he was receiving his just rewards.

So it was with joy that the new family settled into life at Copper Creek.

Chapter 17

Gideon felt his plans were moving forward swiftly. The smelter would be completed in a few months, in spring of 1888, just as had been planned.

Rachel was brought to bed with another son in February, and young Thaddeus proved a delight. He was strong and sturdy, and he rarely cried though he was spoiled mercilessly by his father and his two older brothers. Tad would stir and yawn in his crib, and one of the little boys would run to find Rachel. "Baby is awake and hungry, Mama! Come to the baby!"

Gideon smiled proudly over his growing family. How lovely his wife! How sturdy his sons! How handsome were they all!

But he wanted more for them than a crude cabin in a mining town. He wanted education for his sons; the eldest, Simon, was already seven years old.

Gideon had gone east again in 1887 and visited New York, talked to builders and an architect, examined many fine houses. And he had hired an architect and approved plans, all in a few weeks. He kept the word quiet until he was ready, and he then sprang the news on his family. He wanted to move them to the East.

Rachel was dazed. "You mean—leave here? Move to New York City? What would I do in New York? You would come here? We would not see you?"

He shook his head, smiling at her anxiety. "No, my love. I would live in New York with you and only come west each summer on brief journeys. The trains make it a quick journey, not like the old days, when it took nearly a half year. And I want my sons well educated. You shall take your deserved place in society!"

"You tease me!" she cried, growing pale. "I—in society? They would laugh at me!"

"Never. You are lovely, gracious, intelligent. You shall have velvets and diamonds to wear. And to put it bluntly, we are now too wealthy to be laughed at! You shall take your place with the Astors, the Vanderbilts, and the Morgans!"

She did not believe this, but the notion thrilled her. Bart protested the most bitterly, and Gideon knew it was not because of the work. He did not want Rachel to depart.

But Gideon went on with his plans. Amaris Malchus's eldest son, young Peter, was put in charge of the bank, for he had been clerking there for several years. His younger brother Andrew assisted his father in supervising the Landau mining venture and answered to Bart, who would head the whole business.

"And before long," Gideon said to his dumbfounded brother, "David will come out to assist you. Father is pleased with his progress at MIT and his summer work in the smelters. One day he'll be a big help for us out here."

"So you go east to society and I work!" cried Bart bitterly.

"Until the day when you are weary of the work here and ready to take charge of the sales in the East, you'll have to remain, Bart," Gideon responded. "You're a Landau, and no one else can handle this work. I must go east to organize a fight against monopolizers, otherwise our new smelter means nothing."

"Father can do that," Bart cried, but he knew the big eastern concerns were merging to buy out and destroy others and that his father was getting too old to deploy an organized resistance.

"You know his age is making that an impossibility," Gideon said. "We must begin to take charge against the day he cannot work any longer. Last time I was east, I was shocked at how crippled he is with arthritis."

Horatio Dallmeyer thought about the move and decided to go with them. He was sixty-two and ready to retire. Aunt Ruth Dallmeyer also came, ready to try the new life, though she was regretful at having to leave her school and all the people she had grown to love.

Amaris took over her responsibilities, since her own children were grown—Peter was in the bank, Andrew in the mines, and Esther and young Judith were married to miners.

Meanwhile, Eden and Asher Landau were traveling back and forth between Copper Creek and Denver, where they had a townhouse and could spend their hard won profits on finery. Bart still went to see them when they were in town, though Gideon refused to accompany him; he felt contemptuous of their double life.

"I worry a little about Bart," Rachel said one evening, as she was packing the children's clothing.

"So?" Gideon asked warily. "I think he will see more of young Charlotte Loffler after we leave. They make a nice couple."

Rachel was gently perturbed. "He is older than she, and so much more . . . well—worldly."

"He will settle down one day," Gideon said gruffly. He too was worried and felt responsible for Charlotte. She was so young, naive, eager for life, he had half-hoped she would be drawn to young Andrew Malchus.

"Well, we cannot settle everybody's future happily for them," Rachel said soberly, "though I would wish I could! I wish everyone in the world could be as happy as I am!"

Gideon kissed her hard, holding her close to his lean body. She was so soft and pliant, so sweet in his arms, her warm hands on his cheeks as she raised her head for him to kiss.

"I adore you!" he whispered passionately. "You are so lovely, so good! I am the most fortunate man in the world!"

Rachel rubbed her cheek against his. "Gideon, the Lord has been very good to us. When I come to New York, I shall ask your wonderful mother for advice. I want to do charitable works there, as she does in Philadelphia. One must repay to the world the good that has been received."

"She will be happy to direct you, my dear," he said. "To think you have never met! And you are so much alike."

Except, he thought, he had never betrayed her, as Jared had betrayed his mother with Vashti Cohen. He still felt a deep anger for his father, though the fact that he had not left Miriam lessened it.

Later that week, the Landaus and Dallmeyers boarded the train for the East. They had left all their household goods behind

214

for young Peter Malchus and his new bride. They took only their clothes and favorite personal possessions; it would be enough to make a complete new start, Gideon insisted.

They went first to Philadelphia, to stay with Jared and Miriam and young Rosemary, who was unmarried. The visit brought Rachel and Miriam together for the first time, and the two women reveled in the chance to know each other.

Jared was furious when he learned of Gideon's plans. "You dared to do this without conferring with me—I am the head of this household!" he cried, remembering his brothers' treatment of their old father, Lemuel.

Gideon talked long and patiently to convince his father, and they argued for what felt like hours. Jared finally became silent. He looked up, a gleam of pride in his clear, dark eyes. Only a Landau could do this, he thought. "That's a tremendous burden, son," he said. "How do you propose accomplishing what you've set out to do?"

Gideon visibly relaxed, releasing a great sigh of relief. Then he described his ideas, which he'd been forging over the last few months. "We must go to Mexico too, Father," he said. "We must get there first, before other mining operators do. It may be too late, but we have our mining experience and now the smelter on our side. I've found that the Mexicans desperately need our knowledge. And we want their lead and silver."

"You go too fast," Jared fumed, but the idea settled him down. He might be bodily crippled with arthritis and in pain, but his agile mind wasn't affected. Secretly he was proud of his cool, far-thinking eldest son. How smart he was! They would all be multimillionaires!

Under Gideon's prodding, he and his family moved during September 1888 into a fine, huge home on Fifth Avenue only two blocks from the Vanderbilt mansions. Theirs was also made of fine gray stone and Vermont marble.

Rachel gasped, wide-eyed when she first stepped into the spacious hallway lined with white marble. Two statues flanked the stairway, one of Diana, the other of Apollo.

"Naked!" she gasped, her hand to her mouth. "They are naked, Gideon! It is some mistake, they must go!" And she modestly averted her dark eyes.

He smiled, but shook his head. "It is the style, Rachel. And they have the loincloths, see?"

Rachel found it difficult to glance again at them, even in

their brief coverings. And to her dying day she would glance away from the muscular, lean-thighed Apollo and the rounded Diana, who aimed her marble bow keenly at every visitor who entered the Landau mansion, while others eyed them in admiration.

Rachel furnished the rest of the mansion, assisted by a modish interior designer who, before their association was finished, bowed to her aesthetic tastes. "You're right, Mrs. Landau. I didn't see that, but the colors and style furniture would complete the rooms' architecture fully," he would say, slightly befuddled. He was a short, bald man, with spectacles but with a pleasant demeanor. And in the end his role narrowed to pinpointing fabric and furniture stores that sold the kinds of merchandise she had in mind.

For the three drawing rooms, Rachel chose comfortable dark walnut armchairs that complemented the velvet draperies she hung in the rooms. For the formal parlor, the chairs were upholstered in red velvet to match the draperies. And in the other two rooms, which were where the ladies withdrew after dinner, she chose blue velvet chairs laced in gold. She placed around the room, on the various coffee and end tables, Chinese porcelain vases and figurines. And over a central Oriental rug, she hung a chandelier of flowers made by Meissen of Germany.

Two other chandeliers, made of sparkling Austrian crystal, were hung in the hall; they chimed softly when touched by an upper air current. The dining room was spacious, matching the size of the ballroom on the other wing of the Fifth Avenue house. And the back of the house caught the sun from the enclosed patio which comprised the morning room, a dainty room of cheerful blue and yellow and white. The central table was circular and made of light oak. With the silver coffee and tea service and a bird cage with several yellow canaries singing set in a corner, it was a pleasant place to begin the day.

Just beyond the huge kitchens and pantries was the entrance to a conservatory, where the gardeners grew lush flowers year round—roses, lilies, exotic orchids, and small plants—to replant in the huge gardens in the spring. The gardens were centered around a fountain, a sculpture of Neptune and some cherubs.

Gideon had his large office at the back of the ground floor, where he could receive distinguished guests in private. They marveled at his large carved walnut desk, the walls covered with ruby velvet, the roomy armchairs, the Persian rugs on the floor woven with deep red and blue threads. But even more they wondered at the animal heads he had brought east: buffalo, panther, and puma. All were animals Gideon had shot in the Rockies or in Mexico.

Many a railroad or oil or banking magnate envied him his trophies, and some went west to try to collect their own. The collection was the talk of New York City that first winter.

After the first few tentative dinners, Rachel settled down and entertained lavishly, as Gideon wished. In winters, they decided to stay in New York, where Gideon could forge the business contacts he needed to find out about the conglomerate. Many of his friends were from among that elite pantheon of the wealthy—the magnates of Wall Street.

Rachel helped immensely—her quiet charm, beauty, intelligence, and refusal to indulge in the vicious gossip of some women all earned her respect. She always received their elegant guests in some marvelous gown and jewelry she had carefully chosen—whether of blue silk and diamonds or red velvet and rubies or yellow velvet with a trim of mink fur—and she always had a gracious ready smile. She danced beautifully and served wonderful meals, and before long the Landau house was brimming with Manhattan's best and brightest.

Jared, on occasional visits, watched and envied. After much thought, he hired Gideon's architect and ordered an even larger house, with more rooms, built a block away. Miriam protested in vain, saying her charities were in Philadelphia. Jared responded that she would find causes enough in New York, where her good works were much needed.

And why not, he said to himself. He and his sons were all multimillionaires, though much of the money was invested in mining claims, smelters, and a real estate business in New York. Jared would live in New York; Miriam deserved as fine a house as her son!

And besides, Sapphira was settled and married there; he could see her more often without arousing the suspicions of his wife. He was proud of his pretty daughter. She looked more and more like Vashti, though she was of gentler nature, more satisfied with life, and vastly proud of her two young children. Her husband was a fine man, a banker, and one day they might become high society types too.

So Jared built a house in New York and moved in the

following winter. Miriam, protesting, soon found the causes her husband promised would be there, and she and her daughter Rosemary and her daughter-in-law Rachel went about to the hospitals, and slum resident areas of newly arrived immigrants from Europe, and the churches. They found many who needed help in finding jobs, housing, and a new life.

Rachel had her own carriage, so Miriam must have one also, said Jared. Gideon had his own dashing carriage and black matching stallions. Jared got a larger carriage, driven by a uniformed coachman, and soon was dashing up and down Fifth Avenue on weekdays, in Central Park on a Sunday.

In Copper Creek, Bart was growing restless. Charlotte noticed it most, of course. She had fallen in love with Bart on her first day. But because it seemed a hopeless love, she had kept very quiet about it. How foolish to think such a handsome charming wealthy man could love her in return!

Yet there were few women there, so perhaps her chances were good. Her hopes went up and down again. Sometimes Bart would come over, teasing her, offering to help her solve a household problem, such as cleaning the chimney or stove or raking the garden.

He could be so sweet when he chose! Other times, he would ignore her for a week at a time. Then he would appear for a game of chess with her father or for a taste of Charlotte's good cooking.

When Ruth Dallmeyer left with the rest, Bart came over. "Would you like to continue English lessons with me?" he asked seriously. "You are doing so well. We could work on it a couple of evenings a week."

Her heart pounded with pleasure. She could not control her beaming smile. "Oh, I would like it so much!"

Rachel had left many of her books for her. Bart built a new bookcase so it would fit beside the mantel next to the wall. He worked on it every Saturday and Sunday for a month, smoothing the wood, carving some little flowers and leaves into the frame. She could scarcely believe he would take such care—for her!

Bart started coming over more and more often. With Gideon and Rachel gone and himself in charge, he seemed more grave and absorbed then usual. Often after a good meal prepared by Charlotte, he would linger for several hours talking business

218

with her father. They would range over the gamut of subjects—from the smelter and the mines to a new claim.

"He is grown-up now," her father approved one night after Bart had departed. "He was always smart, but he left too much to his brother! Now he has to take charge."

"He is a very intelligent man," Charlotte quavered, taking up her candle and lighting it, for the stairs leading to her bedroom was dark.

Her father studied her face keenly. "Yes, a good man, I think," he said slowly.

Bart came more often as the nights arrived early. He liked to come over as soon as he had bathed and changed from his dusty work clothes to freshly pressed slacks and shirt. Charlotte had always welcomed him and was always prepared now for one more guest. She strove to cook all his favorite dishes. She used the recipe book Rachel had left her, and she asked Winona for more dishes using his favorite, cornmeal, from mush to fried tomatoes to johnny-cakes. She served the latter with honey, and she sighed as he ate the last bites ravenously.

Charlotte had invited him for a big Sunday morning breakfast that day. Bart eyed her mischievously. "Charlotte, you are too good a cook to waste your talents on your father! He does not eat much; he does not appreciate you!"

Theodoric Loffler protested mildly. "Come now, I much appreciate my good daughter! She is a fine girl."

"You see? He thinks you are just a girl! I can see with my good eyes that you are a woman!" And Bart laughed, his black eyes flashing in his handsome face.

"What a tease!" Charlotte murmured, reddening as he took in her rounded figure. She tossed her hair, with the yellow braids wound up and fastened in a coronet. She had tried several things to look older, and this hairdo was the most successful.

He drew in a deep breath, and stood up. He grasped her hands before her father. "Charlotte, I am bold enough to ask you this question. I love you very much. I will try to be a good husband to you. Will you do me the great honor of marrying me?"

At first she thought it was one of his crazy jokes. She gulped, stared at him wide-eyed, and looked at her father with puzzled wonder. Her father stared back.

Bart gave her a sudden impatient shake, and she began to know it was true. "Won't you answer me, Charlotte? I want

219

to marry you!" he said imperiously.

Her father said, "He likes your cooking." He was giving her an out if she wanted one.

"You mean this?" she whispered to Bart. "Do you tease me? I am so silly, I think you might mean—"

He bent and kissed her, his lips warm and tender on hers. Her first kiss, and he was so gentle. Tears came to her blue eyes, and he kissed them away.

They were married two weeks later. Bart impetuously said there was no reason to wait. He was wildly pleased with himself, saying there was no need for her father to move out—there would be plenty of room until they had five children. Then he burst out laughing and counted the bedrooms aloud, "One, two for Father, three for the sons, four for the girls! Eh, enough!"

They were married in late November, and it was a joyous occasion at the camp. People found gifts somehow—a length of bleached cotton sewed into a beautiful tablecloth, a length of wool made into blankets with satin binders, candles hand-dipped and colored with green herbs or red berries, carved wood candlesticks made by a miner in his free time. The residents of Copper Creek gave generously of their own handiwork, and Charlotte was grateful to tears.

For her grand wedding in the little synagogue of Copper Creek, she wore her best gown, of a pale blue silk shot with silver. She had saved it for a grand occasion—her wedding. Her hair was worn up in a coronet and covered with a fine white lace veil.

Bart caught her breath when he presented her with a magnificent sapphire necklace and matching dangling earrings. Her engagement ring was a beautiful sapphire surrounded by diamonds. "But—where did you get them?" she cried out, gazing at the jewels, scarcely daring to touch them.

He laughed with pleasure at his surprise for her. "I bought them a year ago in Philadelphia."

"A year ago?"

"Yes," he said soberly. "I planned then to marry you." He said it and smiled tenderly at her. She melted against him. He planned it so long ago! She loved him with all her gentle heart.

He was good to her after their marriage. The wedding night was difficult, and she was hurt by his reckless ardent embrace. But he was sorry and murmured his pleas for forgiveness. "I wanted you so much—I'm sorry, love. Forgive me!"

She forgave him, as she always would. She lay and wept silently for the pain as he slept beside her.

But the next nights and the following weeks were better. He always came to her with ardor and enthusiasm and deep passion. She lay in his arms, glorying in his kisses, responding to them happily.

He could be so sweet and gentle. Sometimes he would kiss her mouth softly and play with her a long time before his passion overcame him and he took her wildly. She learned to respond to him, learned what kisses he liked. When he held her and lay over her, she put her hands on his back and stroked his spine, burying her fingers in his hair to kiss him with growing ardor. She forgot her shyness with him and kissed him as he wished.

So the first months of the marriage went by. He came home from work, tired and dirty. She had his hot bath ready, clean clothes prepared, his shirts ironed. He washed and splashed about, singing more and more merrily as he cleaned up. When he was hungry for his supper, she served him the hot, lavish meals he enjoyed—roast beef, lamb, or chicken, with side dishes of fresh or bottled vegetables and fruits, then pies or tarts or cakes, filled with bottled hot fruits. He especially liked apple pie and cherry pie, and she tried various combinations to please him.

Then Charlotte became pregnant with their first child. Bart was radiantly happy—until he found she was sick and weak for a time. When she could not lie with him in bed, he went to another room to sleep.

Around February 1889, Bart began coming home later from work. He was absent-minded, and he said, "Forgot the time," again and again. But his clothes smelled of perfume.

And one night he did not come home at all on Friday night. Charlotte waited for him, worried. Her father went to synagogue, and when he returned, Bart still had not come home. She begged her father to go out and find him, but Mr. Loffler evaded her pleas.

Then Charlotte realized her father knew where her husband was, and so did she. He did not come home for two days, and when he did, he was hung over with a violent headache that made him cross and ill. He lay in bed for another day, though Charlotte confined him to the guest bedroom.

She didn't utter a word of scorn after his recovery, even when Bart continued his wild affairs, which became the talk of Copper Creek.

Charlotte suffered in silence and kept her head up. Amaris said nothing, but the other women were not so kind. Behind her back they whispered that she couldn't keep her man, he went to other women—in the bawdy houses and to Indian women—to be satisfied.

Her first shy hopes for happiness, her first radiant joy, was crushed. Bart did not love her or he would not do this. She remembered the nights when he had wakened slowly in her arms, muttering the name of Rachel. She remembered the sly gossip of Eden Landau, the bright eyes watching for her re-action. She began to decline their dinner invitations, though Bart continued to go.

Her refusal infuriated him. "He is my uncle," Bart raged. "You will be polite to him!"

"I will be polite to him. I will not dine with them or greet them in my home," Charlotte said, with what he called her German obstinacy. "I do not like them, they do not like me, and I will not pretend!"

Bart was furious and would stomp off by himself for dinner with his relatives. Mr. Loffler would compress his mouth and say nothing to scold his daughter. He felt the same way about Asher and Eden Landau—they were sly pieces. Asher had even tried to pry secrets about the smelter from Mr. Loffler, and the scientist was outraged.

So Charlotte and her father had dinner together, the bright candles shining in vain for the master of the house. Again he did not return until after midnight, and his fumbling at the key and the door, his stumbling up the stairs, told its own story.

Charlotte put her hand protectively on her stomach, over the child they had made together in her love and his passion. Bart did not love her. He had wanted a comfortable house and a good housekeeper, and he'd gotten one, she thought bitterly.

It seemed she was always to serve without the rich reward of the love of a husband. Well, she had made a marriage bargain and she would keep it.

"If I were you, I would give him a boot to the head," gentle Amaris raged one day, after another two-day binge of Bart's.

"Nay, I cannot do that," Charlotte sighed. "Pray, say no

more of the matter. It is a shame to me that I cannot keep my man!"

"One day he will wake up and find what a good wife he has," Amaris prophesied, giving Charlotte a kindly pat on the hand. The motherless girl had found in Amaris a mother on her frequent visits and kindly advice. "Now, give me a length of cloth, and I will help you with the baby's clothes. Did I tell you my young Peter's wife expects just two months after you? Imagine that—two little babies in our Copper Creek."

Chapter 18

In June 1889, Jared went west on the train with his youngest son, David. Bart was overjoyed to see them. He wanted to put them up at his house, but Jared refused firmly.

"Your good wife shall not be troubled! She is about to have her child. How can you think of burdening her more?"

Jared had seen the careless way Bart treated Charlotte, and he visibly disapproved. "She is a good woman," he grumbled to Theodoric Loffler. "I am ashamed of my son! One day he will appreciate what a good wife he has!"

"I hope so," Loffler said crossly. He disapproved of the whole situation. Charlotte was so patient, so hard-working; why did her husband not remain home when he could and help her with the work? He did not even appreciate her good cooking now. It was as if he had won his wife and now he could take her for granted. She had to be patient and silent, never scolding him, or he would be angry and cross with her.

The men soon forgot domestic problems. They were intent on starting another smelter, and with David—who'd studied engineering at MIT—among them, they could begin planning the next smelter, which would be larger and have a far higher capacity than the one Loffler had just completed.

They would soon need this second smelter, for forces were combining back east to crush the Landaus, who dominated the exploitation of Colorado ore. The eastern smelter operators were refusing to buy ore, and it was now building up in vast piles against the blue Colorado skies.

The dissatisfied miners were threatening to strike again. They wanted more of a share of the profits, and some provision for injured men and families of those killed.

The Landau men, after long hours with their employees, coming home weary and troubled, had to discuss provisions that would be fair to their employees, while figuring out a financial settlement that would be fair to them.

Nothing had yet been resolved when Charlotte Landau went into labor in August 1889 and had a fine boy, whom they named Emil Jared. Jared, the Landau patriarch, was immensely pleased and visited Charlotte and the baby very often.

"What a fine boy! What a good mother!" he praised her, anxiously trying to make up for the behavior of Bart, who was delighted with the infant, but unrepentant about the recent past.

Bart handled the boy awkwardly at first, and Charlotte held her breath as she watched. She would not protest, however; she merely hovered over them to make sure Bart would not drop him!

But she didn't have to worry. Bart got the feel of it soon enough, and it was delightful to watch the two together.

Bart had never felt so proud. He had reproduced himself, he had a son, and he was as close as he would ever be to immortality. He could not articulate these feelings, but Charlotte understood.

He still treated Charlotte with a shameful neglect. He would say he would come home after work, then he would forget and remain to play cards and drink with the men in the saloon. He would go over to have dinner with Eden and Asher and not even tell Charlotte where he was going. When she protested gently, he growled, "But you do not like them!"

Gentle Theodoric Loffler went into a rage one day when Bart had been gone for two nights and returned with a hangover. All knew he had been with an Indian woman.

"I shall leave him! I shall not work with that fool! I shall take you east and find a fine job. How disgraceful! A man with a splendid son and wife, and he acts like this! No, I am ashamed!"

"Now, Papa!" Charlotte was distressed. She rocked little Emil in her arms and looked at her father over the infant's fuzz of black hair. "You must not speak so! Bart is a good man. He has his bad habits—"

"Bad habits!" her father snorted, shaking the weekly gazette with his long hands. "He is careless with his happiness. One day—"

"Father, I beg you, do not say these things to me. I . . . I love him deeply. He is my husband, the father of my son." Tears formed in her large blue eyes, but she blinked them back with determination.

"If I had thought, when Gideon came to me in Salzburg, that such trouble would come—"

"Oh, Papa, we had much trouble in Austria too," she rebuked softly. "This is much better, ja? We are free, we're in America—"

"I, yes, but not my daughter."

She sighed. "Do not think of it, I pray you, Father. Bart needs you, the Landaus need you, they have been good to you. And I love him—I pray you, do not think of leaving here."

Theodoric Loffler kept on grumbling. "When he insults you, he insults me! My only daughter—"

"So, so, so!" Charlotte chided, smiling with affection at his troubled face, the waves of gray-blond hair ruffled by his long fingers. "If I do not object, do not object for me, Papa! Come look at your only grandson, how fine he is!"

Her father's face softened as he took up the boy and rocked him for a time, singing an old German song to him. Charlotte rocked and sewed and mused about their situation. Surprisingly, she had calmed him down, and instead of leaving the Landaus, he worked all the harder with them.

David was a real help; for all his wildness, he worked hard and was very smart. He amused and worried them all that year. David could play such jokes! The visiting rabbi lost his Torah for a time, and when it was discovered that David had hidden it, he unleashed such wrath, the family was quite embarrassed.

There was the time he let his father sleep late, and when Jared awoke, David soothed him. "Sleep again, Papa, it is Sunday."

Hours later, Jared woke again to find it was Saturday, payday at the mines. David howled with laughter. Even Bart was angry with him, for the miners were enraged, only calmed when they learned it was another trick of that "wild boy."

"Besides, he needed the sleep," David said cheerfully to

Charlotte, who was the only one who would listen to his rationale. "Papa is not well, he tires easily. His back troubles him."

She shook her head at him, but could not resist his laughing black eyes. "And were you thinking of his health when you let him sleep late, my brother?"

He laughed. "No, I was thinking of the miners! How they grumble and growl, no matter how well we treat them, how much we pay! Let them worry about their paychecks for a time and worry about where the money comes from!"

In early December, David disappeared. The Landau patriarch came stomping through the snow to Bart's and Charlotte's home. "Is David here? He has not slept the night with me."

"No, he is not here," Bart said, frowning. "Come, eat with us, Papa. You should not tramp through that snow, it is too wet. And the wind blows cold."

He settled him tenderly in the armchair with a blanket about him. Charlotte put his overcoat out to dry before the stove, and Bart took hot coffee to him. How sweet he could be, Charlotte thought as she prepared a plate of hot food. He hovered over his father so anxiously. She knew there was much love in Bart, though he could at times be careless with it.

As for her, only the love of her son and her father's anxiety kept her going. Bart rarely slept with her, unless he felt hot passion, then he would steal away to her room late at night, waken her, and lie with her for a time, until she ached with his reckless excitement. Then he would go back to his own bed and sleep late the next day, while she rose to start the day's housework. She wondered at herself, that she accepted this, and even looked forward to his coming to her those nights.

David did not return for four days. The family were all sick with worry, the miners even offering to go hunt for him in the mountains. "Maybe an Injun got him," said one.

Charlotte cried out. "No, no, you must not say that!" She had nightmares of David lying in the snow, bleeding, with his soft black hair dangling from the roof pole of some Indian cabin.

And late one afternoon, two Indians were sighted, toiling up the winding road to the mining town, with huge bundles in the saddle before them. And behind their horses was David mounted on a little Indian pony similar to theirs. All the town turned out to gasp and call to him.

"Where you been, Mr. David?"

"What you got there?"

"Who's them bucks?"

The solemn Indian warriors, young and lean and wary, cast sullen looks back and forth between the black-bearded miners, and the wide-eyed women.

Charlotte ran out of the cabin, a black scarf about her shoulders, her yellow hair pulled back in braids that fell almost to her waist. "David, where have you been?" she cried.

He waved at her, his face creased in a wide bronzed grin. He looked as dark and dirty and wild as the Indians with him. He'd thrown a red blanket jauntily over his torn and dusty suit.

Bart emerged from the mine office wielding a pistol. The Indians scowled and grunted to each other.

"Where have you been, David?" Bart asked sternly. Jared limped behind him, shivering in the keen wind. "We have been worried sick! And who are these fellows?"

David's clear laugh rang out. "Oh, I thought we should have some fresh meat for the holidays!" he explained. "I went hunting and ran into these fellows. We had a slight disagreement over the bear meat!"

Now Charlotte realized that the pungent odor she had been conscious of for several minutes came from the huge sides of bear and deer hanging from the pony saddles. David had some on his saddle, but he hardly seemed to notice.

He slid down with the aid of a couple of miners, who also took command of the meat, though they were slightly repelled. Jared began to scold his son. They were all standing awkwardly in the cold wind.

"Papa, get inside," David scolded affectionately. "Do you want to catch your death of cold? The handsome youth hustled his father back into the mine office. The Indians waited outside, glaring uneasily at the town residents, who began to walk away.

David came back out alone. "They are staying for dinner," he said, and grinned at the incredulous looks he received from the few remaining town residents. He motioned to the men, then, turning to Charlotte, said, "Charlotte, can you fix us a good dinner fast?"

Charlotte swallowed hard and looked at her husband. He was stern and angry.

David stopped smiling. "They are just human beings," he said quietly. "They were out hunting because they are about to starve to death. They've been hiding from the army and won't go back to the reservation. They'd rather die."

Charlotte looked from his young face to the hardened bronzed visages of the Indians. Could she welcome such roughened men into her home? She nodded slowly. Trying to make herself understandable to the Indians, she spoke in halting, brief sentences, which sounded silly to her ears. "I fix dinner. All come in one hour. You come now."

They seemed to understand her, though they stared at her blankly.

David beamed. "I'll come with them; they ain't tamed yet."

Bart came also, obviously not trusting anyone. When the unlikely group stepped into the foyer of their spacious home, the rank smell of the two Indians and David seemed to fill the house, annoying everyone. Mr. Loffler particularly was horrified, though he held his tongue, uncertain of the situation.

Charlotte prepared the dinner without complaint. When it was ready—the brown and white meat tender, the garden yams and string beans steaming—the Indians refused to sit around the table with the Lofflers and Landaus. They peered about them instead, as though fearing some trap. David finally took the lead and led them to the back porch, where they could sit cross-legged and eat with their fingers from a tin tray. They ravenously devoured the delicious fare, and afterward they rolled up in the blankets, made sleepy by full stomachs, and went to sleep, except for one who kept a sloe-eyed vigilance over the others, leaning against a porch pillar.

This evening would go down in the lore of Copper Creek— the story about the crazy Landau youth who put up wild Indians at his house, no one knowing if the town and its residents would last the night.

David, red-eyed for lack of sleep, took a realistic assessment of the situation and sat up during the night with a rifle cradled in his arms, two blankets around him, sleeping with one eye open.

In the morning, he started a fire in the backyard. With curious children gathering about him, he and the Indians cooked some of the remaining bear meat and cut it into long strips to dry. By evening they'd made a hefty supply of dried beef, and after wrapping it up in their saddlebags, the Indians were ready to leave town, to the relief of everyone. David, forever an obliging host through the ordeal, had their ponies brought around the house, then rounded up some men to accompany their guests to the edge of Copper Creek. David waved his hand in farewell, a broad grin creasing his handsome, unnaturally dark features. "You go now. Maybe hunt again with you!"

The Indians nodded, but as they pulled out of town, they kept looking over their shoulders as though fearing someone would take a shot.

The miners grumbled that David had let them go. "They'll come back some night and scalp you for sure!" they growled.

"No, not them," David said. "Maybe some other ones, but not them." Then he went back to the house where he lived with Jared and slept for twenty-four hours. He had stayed awake the four days and nights since he had first stumbled on the Indians' trail.

Without the menacing presence of the Indians in town, the incident took on the proportions of an exciting adventure. They now had fresh meat to eat, and David's wild escapade to talk about, which cheered the miners immensely.

Those who worked for the eastern conglomerate went on strike for higher wages and better working conditions. But those who worked at the Landau concern found joining the mass effort unnecessary. They were offered better wages by the Landaus, who felt they could afford the pay hike since the second smelter was on the way.

Asher raged at them. "You are ruining us!" he cried. "You must not settle with those greedy wolves! We must all stick together and hold out against their demands!"

Bart laughed at him. He had recently cut back on the number of visits he had made to Asher's and Eden's house for dinners. Now that Jared was in town, he and Charlotte usually stayed at home for dinner, with Jared and David as their guests.

Charlotte listened in silence to Bart's conversation with Asher, who had come to the house that Sunday afternoon to persuade the family against the miners' demands. Jared had turned him down, though with regret since he didn't want to exclude a brother, no matter how distanced from his own immediate business concerns, from playing a decisive part in Landau matters.

"Father said you can come in with us if you leave the combine," Bart said. "That is the final offer. If you are not with us, you are against us."

"You forget our blood relationship," Asher raved.

"It is you who forgets it," Bart snapped. "Why did you insist on going in with the combine? You knew they wanted to drive us out of business! And they are greedy pigs. Look at how they treat their miners!"

Asher sulked, and failing to persuade Bart, he stomped away. Bart's black eyes flashed with anger.

Charlotte went over to him shyly and hugged him. Surprised, he stared down at her. She flushed, but managed to speak. "I am proud of you, Bart. It was right what you said."

She rested her head on his shoulder for a moment.

Bart hugged her quickly and, smiling, kissed her. "You think because I like his company and find him amusing at times that I cannot see through his greed? No, our miners will receive much better treatment with us than with the combine."

"Yes, Bart, you're right. They're hardly selfless people. Aunt Eden does everything she can to make me feel foolish with her," Charlotte confessed. "And I don't like the way they treat their own men. Their families suffer because Eden must have another diamond ring."

Bart frowned thoughtfully. "Yes, you are right, my little dove. And I think I will not go often to them. I do not like their manner with my lovely wife." Teasingly, he kissed her small nose. "You have my permission to turn up your sweet tiny nose at them!"

Charlotte laughed, and they were easier with each other than they had been in a long time. After dinner, Bart stayed in and rocked little Emil, talking to him absurdly as old Mr. Loffler read the paper, a contented look on his relaxed face.

"So my little son yawns at me?" cried Bart, looking down at the infant. "You blink at me, eh, little Emil? And your so-blue eyes! Never did a Landau have such eyes. They'll make the girls sigh at you, eh? Such a handsome boy, and you're growing so fast! Pretty soon you will be fighting me with your little fists—eh?" And he caught the little waving hand in his big one and kissed it gently.

Charlotte got out her sewing and sat down beside the blue lamp. She was making another shirt for Bart; he seemed to go through his so quickly because of the nature of his work. This was of blue checked wool and would keep him warm in the bitterly cold winter. She smiled at his foolish talk with Emil.

Her father laid down the gazette. "Tomorrow there is another meeting with the miners. What do we do if they strike, Bart?"

Bart turned serious. "Well, we have offers to present. Father says he will authorize a ten-percent increase in wages and a bonus to the men building the smelter if they finish by May. Also, any miner injured will receive half pay for the rest of his life, or his family will receive it if he dies in the mine. Can we be more generous?"

His voice rang out with his pride. Charlotte glanced toward her father hopefully. Surely he would see how much Bart was growing in good sense and seriousness.

"Ah, ja, well I hope they will accept this offer. I think it is generous. But some combine men go among them and make trouble with their talk."

"I know that. It is foolish talk, but the miners do not always realize that." Bart absently rocked his son, and Emil cooed up at him. He gazed down at the baby, and brushed his lips softly against his rosy cheek. "We must present our position well. I wish I had Gideon's gift of talk!"

He sounded bitter. Charlotte lowered her lashes and sewed slowly and carefully. Did he still resent it that Gideon had won Rachel for his wife? Perhaps so.

"You have the gift of talk, my son," Mr. Loffler said, and Charlotte caught the irony. She hoped Bart would not. "You must say what you mean sincerely and tell them of the future. I think they will listen to you and to your father. They believe in him, he has built up the region and brought us prosperity."

"I hope you are right. Perhaps I should write out a speech." He glanced uncertainly at Charlotte.

She knew he hated to write and that he would be no good reading the speech. She shook her head quickly. "No, the words will come to you as they always do, Bart. You know of what you speak. The words will come."

Seeing that the baby was asleep, Bart rose. "I will put him to bed," he said softly. "Come with me, Charlotte."

Blushing, she left the room with him, and they went up to put the baby in the crib. When the infant was settled, Bart turned and put his arms about her.

"I want you tonight," he said softly.

She wished he would say, "I love you," instead, but he talked in terms of passion and wanting, which was better than nothing, she supposed.

They went to bed in her large bed, and he made love to her with passion. She lay with him, feeling his taut, hard body pressed to her own soft one. He moved on her, groaning and cried out in his pleasure. Afterward, he sprawled over her, sleeping, and she managed to push him off so she could breathe.

She lay looking out the windows into the nights that came early this December. She could see the purple sky, the white snow on the peaks, the shadows of the pines. She curled her arm protectively about her husband, holding his head to her large breasts. "I love you so, I love you so. Why do you not love me? I would do anything for you!" But she never dared to confess this aloud. She had been trained to obey, and no good came of complaining.

The talk with the miners went well. Mr. Loffler returned home, beaming, with Bart at his side. They were both excited. Bart was raving about the session.

"They listened, they liked what I said. They even applauded! They promised not to switch allegiancies. Father raised their wages, promised them bonuses. It worked like a dream."

"And the pay to the injured?" urged Charlotte, who, having worked in the homes of the injured miners to help the families, knew of their plight.

"Yes, yes, that shall be done also. Father has promised. A fund has been set up; it will be in the bank. Money shall be set aside regularly to reimburse the miners for their doctor bills and food for their families. They shall not suffer. They will receive half pay also, as promised, as soon as it is determined they cannot work again."

"Oh, I am glad—and they are going back to work?"

Bart laughed exultantly. "Are they going back to work? Yes! Tomorrow. They return to work tomorrow, even though the mines of the combine remain closed! Father says he can raise the rates of the ore from the smelter, there will be such a demand. And the longer the combine remains shut down, the more our ore will cost!"

Charlotte guessed that would be good, her husband seemed so happy. She exchanged smiles with the men and relaxed.

"I will fix a good dinner tonight," she said. "Bart, you will invite your father and David?"

"Yes, yes, we must celebrate!" he laughed. He ruffled his hair and said to Mr. Loffler, "Come, let us go to the office and talk with Father! I have things to say—"

"Come back at six for dinner!" Charlotte called as they went out. "We will feast tonight!"

They waved back at her as they slid down the slippery icy path to the snow-covered street of the town. She shut the door and clasped her hands.

It was a celebration. She would take out the red candles, the wood candlesticks. She would prepare two chickens. And they'd have Johnny-cakes with honey. Bart always liked them. And a pie of cherries she had bottled herself, and another of dried apples.

She got busy. If there had been someone to send, she would have sent for one of Winona's daughters to help her. The baby cried, and she nursed him hastily, cooing to him, "Hurry up, sweetheart, I must fix the pies quickly—"

She laid him down in the basket near the kitchen table and watched him kick his legs as she worked. She covered the dining table with a fine white linen cloth, set out the best silver china, and put the wooden candlesticks at each end of the table, with the red candles in them.

When the food was safely cooking, her face was red with her efforts and her forehead damp, and Charlotte hastily went upstairs to change her dress.

She washed, and dressed in her blue and silver silk dress, fastening a lace bertha about her throat with her mother's cameo brooch. Her hair was brushed until the yellow tones shone in her golden hair, which she wound into a beautiful coronet on the top of her head.

Downstairs again, she glanced anxiously at the grandmother clock on the mantel. She had brought it from Salzburg, always drawn to the intricacy of the carvings which portrayed the Alps and a flower-enshrouded chalet. It reminded her of her former home, and of her home in the Rockies.

It was almost six. She set the snowy white linen napkins around the table, wondering how many guests would turn up. Just in case, on a side table she laid out extra dishes and silver, and she had enough food for a dozen people.

Six o'clock came around. Nobody had arrived. She went to the front window and made a hole in the ice that covered it. There was no one on the road, but she could just catch the sounds of merriment from down the street. Doors swung on their hinges at the saloon that flanked the bank.

She went to stir the soup again, and when she returned to her outpost, there was still no sign of the others. She waited and waited, dividing her time between looking out the window and checking on the food. Six-fifteen. Six-thirty. Six-forty-five passed. A small figure emerged from the saloon and started for the house. Charlotte identified it as her father. So—they were coming!

She dashed to the kitchen, set the soup pot on the fire again, then ran back to the door in time to open it for her father. She beamed at him, peering over his shoulder as he stamped his feet on the porch before entering.

"They come now?" she said quickly, shutting the door behind him.

"Nein, nein," he said, nodding his head.

"Nein?" she said, not believing her ears. "Why?"

They spoke in German, forgetting the English they had painfully nurtured.

"They do not come," he said painfully. "They drink in the saloon—"

He avoided her gaze. "But they will come, ja?" she asked, "He invited his father, his brother?"

She was wringing her red hands unconsciously. "He said yes, he will bring them?" she added, when he did not speak.

"They all drink—in the saloon. They do not come," he said definitely.

"But they say yes—"

"Nein. The . . . the girls, they bring food, they make sandwiches. They sing, they dance," he added hastily, not looking at her.

"Ach, ja," she said numbly. She tried to recover. "You are hungry, Father? We will eat now, and let them eat later?"

"Ja, we eat now."

He moved to the dining room hastily, as though to change the subject. He paused at the door, seeing the fine tablecloth, the red candles waiting to be lit. "Ach, so fine," he said slowly.

"Ja. Enough for a dozen," Charlotte said cheerfully. "Maybe Amaris and Peter come?"

He shook his head. "They go home to the young ones, they celebrate—that is, they eat together."

Charlotte pictured the cheerful noisy group of the Malchus family gathered in love and joy. She swallowed.

Her father sat at the table. "You have soup? I will just have soup and bread."

Charlotte nodded and went back to the kitchen. She took the chickens and the overbaked potatoes from the oven. Silently, she spooned out two bowls of soup, a small one for herself. She set the bread before her father, and a plate of cheese.

They did not bother to light the candles. Silently, they ate the soup, and her father went back to the living room to read a scientific magazine that Jared had brought him. He must have already read it a dozen times, she thought.

She spent hours, in a numb trance, putting away the food.

Her father went to bed at ten, and still she waited. The sounds of boisterous revelry reached her ears. There was laughter, singing, occasional yells, and revolver shots fired into the night.

Finally, at midnight, she rose wearily and blew out the parlor lamp. She went out to the kitchen one more time and cleared away the food she'd left out for any late-night arrivals. She made sure to wrap the bread in a damp cloth. Bart disliked stale bread.

She went up to bed and sat for a time on the mattress in her heavy white nightdress, her feet chilly. There was a lump in her throat, and tears blurred her vision as she looked out the window. Still, the mountains were there, white and snow-covered, eternal, unchanging. Only human beings changed, she thought. The mountains did not care who looked at them.

Part III

1890−1900

Chapter 19

By the spring of 1890, the Landaus had amassed wealth beyond belief. Jared spoke jubilantly as he related how much gold and silver occupied their bank vaults.

"If we can, we'll sell directly to the government, without middlemen. All we can dig and put through our smelters will be fully returned to us in cash!" he cried, rubbing his hands together, like a child.

Gideon had come west too. He was smiling at his father's joy. He patted the stooped shoulder. "And all your dreams have come true, Papa," he said gently. "All you wished to do when you came from the ghettoes of Europe so many years ago with Mama."

"Yes, yes, your dear mama," Jared murmured. "How happy she is, what a fine house she has, what a fine brood of sons and daughters! She has nothing left to wish for. We are the most fortunate of people!"

David glanced quickly around the little group. He saw the distress in Charlotte's open face. Bart had behaved openly jealous of Gideon since his brother's arrival because Gideon had a fine house in New York, he dined with wealthy bankers and railroad men, and he had Rachel. All the family knew about Bart's infatuation with Rachel.

Gideon saw Bart seething.

"One day you will also come east," he said. He turned to David. "Father has agreed that we will go to Mexico, David. I wish you to meet Porfirio Díaz, the ruler there, and his generals. I hope they will agree to turn over some of their mines to us, especially the silver mines. We will agree to build a smelter for them—"

"And you will remain there to oversee construction," Jared said, nodding to his youngest son. "David, you must not be so wild and thoughtless. I want you to settle down and work hard, or I will have to send Bart there."

Bart looked enraged. He jumped up. "Send Bart there! Send Bart!" he mimicked. "Have I done so poorly that I must be exiled to Mexico? What about Gideon? Why not send him there and keep him there in the East? What does he do in the East?"

Jared looked aghast. "Boys!" he said sternly, as though they were children once more. "I will have no quarreling! Each goes where he can work best! The family trust must be preserved, we must work for each other, not in isolated empires!"

Charlotte got up. "I must see to the baby," she said hurriedly, and went upstairs.

David's heart went out to her. He tried to smooth over the quarrel. "I look forward to my going to Mexico, Father. There is much good hunting there! Thank you for the new rifle."

Jared scarcely heard his youngest's words. He looked from Bart to the angry, stern Gideon. "I will have no fussing among you about who works hardest. All work hard for the good of the family. Gideon is needed in the East. He works hard, he travels from one place to another, he studies the latest reports on the smelters and the mining operations. He goes to Washington to talk to our congressmen and presses for bills that are for our benefit."

Bart set his mouth sullenly. "And his wife goes to balls, his sons go to the best schools—"

"Bart, your son will also go to a good school—when he is of that age!" Jared said evenly. "Gideon worked long in Copper Creek, now it is your turn to advance our interests here. And Mexico will not be a playground for David! He will work hard in the heat of the deserts and the freezing cold of the mountains. He'll be among bandits and feuding ranchers and obstinate Mexican officials—many of whom are corrupt. So don't feel so deprived, boy."

"Thank you, Father!" David laughed, ironically. "I look forward to my new playground!"

"You too may someday come to New York," Jared said soothingly, suddenly worrying over his youngest son's safety.

While Bart had been shamed to silence, David laughed aloud. "Oh, and I look forward to the life of a dandy in Manhattan," he said sarcastically. The truth was, he ached for the frontier and the wild adventures he would have—interspersed with his responsibilities, of course. He had savored the long hours he'd spent with Jared and Gideon in which they briefed him on conditions there—the character of the Mexican people, the officials he must please, the local people he would work with.

"They live in poverty," Gideon said. "The work will be a godsend to them. Make conditions good for them, make them comfortable, see to the wives and children, that they are fed and get good medical attention. If the familes are happy, the men will be content and all will go more smoothly."

David felt rather overburdened with all the advice by the time he and Gideon mounted up and set out for Mexico on two good horses. He had his new rifle, an older shotgun, two handguns of a good Colt revolver type. He and Gideon hunted their own meat on the trip, and he learned much from his quiet but solid older brother.

They lived as Gideon had lived on his first journey to Mexico, living off the desert land, or off the peasants who shared their beans and campfires. They avoided the bandits who eyed the fine horses greedily and their weapons even more jealously.

In Mexico City, they met with the dictator Díaz, and David was pleasantly surprised by the older man's dignity. He greeted Gideon as an old friend and embraced him warmly.

"Ah, so you did come back one day! I despaired of your return! What do you think now? You want only the mines, eh?"

"No, señor, we have now the knowledge to build and operate smelters. We hope to start one at once. I will help design it with my young brother, an expert on them!"

The Mexican and his aides looked with polite dismay at the young merry-eyed man, who seemed much too reckless and juvenile to handle weighty tasks. Gideon smiled behind his beard, his white teeth showing.

"He has his degree from MIT, gentlemen. Also he has assisted our smelter expert by helping to design and build a large smelter this past winter. He works well. We brought some plans with us." And Gideon unrolled the plans onto the wide table before them. "David, explain these, please."

David stepped forward, and having taken Spanish in university, which Gideon had made him exercise by speaking with the few Spanish miners in their employ, stifled his nervousness before the stern, decorated generals and the black-frocked businessmen with their cold distrustful eyes, and began to explain.

David knew the work, and before long his enthusiasm and pride took over. He explained, answered questions, talked of how their ideas would work.

The Mexicans questioned and questioned. "How will you train the miners to handle this? What of their families? Where will they live?"

David and Gideon had worked out the village plans, which they unrolled, and began expanding on. "The village will be built just a mile or less from the silver mine. The smelter can be on the edge of the town. If a town is already there, well and good. If not, we will build a church, a town hall, houses, all they need to live full lives."

"Ah, so that is how you plan! If the town is not there, you build it!" one man exclaimed, impressed. "A better life for our people! That is good! That is what we want!"

"Under the Spanish and then the French, they lived in more misery than they'd ever known," cried another. "Now we have a chance for the land of Mexico to belong to the Mexicans! We must work hard and struggle and make the revolution a success! It's for the good of the people!"

David was impressed by their seriousness. He had been aghast at the sheer poverty of the farmers and villagers, living in mud or clay huts, eating only beans and corn tortillas. Yet they had a dignity and a kindness that he found appealing.

Gideon explained they wanted to begin with a silver mine.

"There is one on the estate of Señor Alfonso Portola," one man said thoughtfully. "He is eager to have it exploited and has offered good terms for any company willing to do so. He is a good man, Spanish, yet part Mexican Indian. He worries over his people. And he will aid you much."

They talked over this location, which was on a desert plain with a border of rich grass for cattle. The mountain nearby was overrun by bandits, which was a big problem.

"They come down and rob and steal and Señor Portola is much put about to protect his people. They protect the bandits because they are threatened and have little enough to lose to them. So it is in our poor country," another man sighed.

"But the mine sounds good," Gideon replied thoughtfully. "You say it was worked only a time by the Spanish many years ago? And they closed it for lack of workers and its dangerous location?"

"Si. It is there, it is rich. And the mountains nearby are said to be lined with silver."

"We wish to have much silver. It is one product all the world wants," explained Díaz, who had been listening in silence. "If we have our silver to sell, we can buy the products our country badly needs. I say, let us start here." And his finger stabbed at the place on the map where Portola's rancho stood.

Díaz sent two men and a guard of half a dozen with the Landau brothers to the site of the rancho. Señor Alfonso Portola greeted Gideon and David with a blend of politeness, courtesy, and suspicion.

They negotiated for days. Gideon and David inspected the mine and the poor village nearby, which they thought perfect for a mining town. They upped their price, and Señor Portola accepted.

Gideon remained the rest of the summer, in the torrid heat and cold nights, to help David start the smelter. The mine was reopened, cleaned out of rubbish and old timbers, and several Americans were hired to help supervise.

A man named Jim Foster was put in charge. He had some mining experience, said he was an engineer. Gideon cautioned his brother: "I doubt he has much education, but any man with experience will be needed. Keep an eye on them all and fire any man who fools around with the native women. The Mexicans are quick-tempered and very proud, for all their poverty."

"Right you are."

David already had his eye on a Mexican woman—Anita Portola, the bright-eyed daughter of Señor Alfonso Portola. He had two grown sons, and a married daughter. The youngest child, the light of his eyes, was spirited, mischievous Anita, seventeen years old, much courted for her beauty and the dowry her father promised.

Anita was short, slim, and round of figure, with long crinkly brown hair, sparkling brown eyes, and a bit spoiled by her father and her many admirers. She had a laugh like a softly chiming bell, David thought. She could ride well, she sang and played the piano, and she was a devout Catholic, like all her family.

Difficulties, difficulties—David thrived on them. He went to the many fiestas the señor had for his people. Dressed in his finest suits and wide-brimmed cream-colored sombrero, he joined in their horse races and won some of them; he shot in sharpshooter contests to win prizes; he strutted and swaggered as the Spanish and Mexicans did—she seemed to see him not at all.

Señor Portola eyed the American brothers with much suspicion. They were handsome, one was married, the other a daredevil. And both were Jewish, wealthy beyond belief. The fact that one might be serious about his daughter never crossed his mind.

And Anita did not walk in the moonlight with any man, he informed David sternly when David dared to ask.

The smelter was begun, the village improved. Gideon helped, then left as the nights turned colder. He returned to Colorado alone, and he and Jared went back east on the train. He had his own work to do.

Under Gideon, the work had seemed like play. David asked his advice, consulted with him, but left him to make the hard decisions. Then Gideon left—and David was in complete charge.

It went slightly to his head. He made enemies before he realized what he was doing, then toned himself down. It was better to ask the American engineers and mining men for advice than to order them about.

He organized them. Jim Foster, one of the most experienced, was put in charge of the smelter project. They consulted often. Two other men were in charge of the mining, and they worked two shifts of miners. He used the three other Americans to manage the renovation of the Catholic church, the building of a town hall, and improvements to the town wells and even a park next to the town hall, where all might stroll in the evenings.

David had learned about the *paseo*. It was necessary in a Mexican town to have a park where all might sit or walk in the cool of the evening. There the young men walked in one direction, the young girls in the other, and there was much flirting, and swinging of skirts, and covert glances under the stern eyes of the duennas. Even Anita was allowed to stroll there one evening a week, her mother and aunt sitting on a bench at the edge of the park, their sewing on their laps. David took to the *paseo* and strolled there the nights that Anita did.

He tried to catch her sparkling eyes, the long lashes that fluttered on her cheeks, but she did not look at him. He kept at it, amused and intrigued by the "game" of courting.

He had more troubles than the work, however. Bandits from the mountains plagued their village and the rancho. Horses were stolen, cattle killed and carried off. A man was shot, badly injured.

David ordered his men to carry weapons. The Americans carried rifles and shotguns or pistols. The Mexicans always had their long curved machetes, and sometimes sharp daggers in their wide, studded belts.

Still the bandits stole in, usually around three or four in the morning, boldly wandering the dusty streets and roving at will in the tall grasses at the foot of the mountain. Señor Portola kept his horses guarded in a corral. But the cattle that roved away were killed or carried off.

David wakened one night sharply. Rising, he pulled on his pants and shirt and grabbed his rifle. He had heard something peculiar.

Cautiously he stepped to the second-floor window and peered into the dusty street outside. He saw two dark forms. One, bent over the other, grabbed something and ran to a nearby horse. He was up into the saddle and pounding down the street.

It was early Sunday morning. David raced to the hallway, peered into the room where another bachelor slept—Jim Foster was not there. His bunk was empty. David went back and pulled on his boots, cursing.

He ran down the stairs and into the street. By then men were gathering, drawn by some instinct into the streets.

"Who is it?" David barked.

"Jim Foster. Dead."

"Bring my horse!" David yelled to a sleepy stableboy who had wandered outside.

"Si, señor!"

Bending over the man, David felt like gagging. Nausea

overtook him. Jim lay in his own blood; his throat had been slit. His clothes were mussed—the money belt he kept about his waist was gone.

Jim had been seeing a woman at the side of town. He must have returned late. Reckless fool, to wander about this time of night! David cursed silently.

The horse came. A man protested, "Mr. Landau, you can't go out alone! Wait till morning, we'll form a posse—"

"Too late—the trail will be cold." David swung up into the saddle, made sure his water bottle was tied on securely, rushed headlong down the street before anyone else could protest.

The stableboy had had sense enough to bring David's own stallion, a big bay with a stalwart heart. David raced him at full speed out into the desert. A thin plume of dust rose above him, just visible against the night sky. A thin sliver of moon and a few brilliant stars were all that lit the sky.

Ahead loomed the Sierra Madres. The bandit would know every twist and turn—

David thundered on, hearing the faint sounds of horse's hooves pounding before him. He went on, paused a moment—the hooves still echoed in the vast desert and mountain lands. All else was silent, the small animals crouching in their burrows against this invasion of their night territory.

He went on, and all he had learned from Bart and their weekend expeditions hunting and chasing Indians came back to him. Bart had taught him well, and David had taken to this rough life like a duck to water.

The hoof beats ahead of him suddenly stopped. He pulled up the stallion at once and fastened him to a small Judas tree. The stallion panted for a time, then bent his head and began to graze at the sparse desert grasses.

David slid down, took the water bottle, his rifle, and the little pouch of bullets, and went off softly into the desert. He chose a spot about two dozen yards away and sat down in the sand under a couple of bushes to wait.

The horse was a tempting target on the flat plain. One could make out his stalwart form against the night sky. David sat still, listening, straining. His hard patience settled in as the hours went on.

It must be close to dawn, he thought. No sound of horses, no sound of small animals. Someone was near. No rabbits scurried, no little animal shrieked when caught by a roving hawk. All was still, a man was near.

Slithering—close to him—behind him—

He laid down his rifle cautiously and clenched his long knife between his upper and lower teeth. He braced himself—then a form launched itself at him out of the darkness.

David was ready. He rolled over and moved free of the hard sweaty body. The scent had given the man away. He smelled of urine, dust, and dirt. His rough clothes brushed against David. A hand came out, a hard muscular arm—

They fought in the darkness, in silence, life against life. David found himself beneath the man; he brought his knee up and struck the man in the groin. A groan and muttered curse sounded before something flashed toward David, who barely shifted in time. It was a machete which sliced harmlessly into the sand. The hand rose again. David lunged upward with his own knife. He found something soft, a belly, and ripped upward.

David was young and tough, but this man seemed tougher. Though he had to be bleeding from the vitals, he continued fighting—grunting with pain, but fighting fiercely. In the dim moonlight their limbs thrashed, and the stallion whinnied in fear. They rolled over and over in the sand, David found his knife hand free for a moment and struck at the man blindly.

The knife sank deeply into the man's throat, and he groaned and went limp. David yanked himself free and rolled away. He sprang up, his bloody knife poised for a long moment. Then he bent down and cautiously felt for any sign of life.

The man was dead.

David yawned and stretched, his body bruised and aching, appalled that he'd killed a man. It did not seem possible. He must be dreaming—

Dawn came soon, a pallid gray light that gave way to sunlight. David studied the face of the man, a bearded man with scars on his face and a line of blood from his throat to the ear. Looking around, David found the man's horse tied some hundred yards away. The man had stalked him for hours, slowly, in the sand, wriggling on his stomach. David traced the path carefully to learn something of the ways bandits fought in their own world.

He brought up the other horse and, after a struggle, tied the bandit across the saddle. The horse protested at the smell of blood but finally stood still long enough for David to take the reins into his own hands and vault into the saddle of his own stallion.

About eight in the morning on Sunday, he trotted into town. Men paused to gape, women to stare wide-eyed, children to cry out. "Look, Mama! Look at the man. Is he dead, Mama?"

"Hush, little one." They crossed themselves.

The Portola family were riding into town from the opposite direction, from the ranch, as David paused at the stable. A man came running, and another, and more. Two men cut the bandit loose, and he slid down into the dirt.

"It is Diego Garcia," one man muttered, and crossed himself, as did others. "A bad man, a wicked man!"

"He killed Jim Foster," David said, swinging down. "Rub the horse down, give him hay," he said to the stableboy. Wearily he turned toward the two-story frame house where he lived.

Señor Portola had swung down from his carriage. The womenfolk remained there, averting their faces from the dead man. Portola strode over to David, looking like a cross banty-rooster. He was a short and wide man, with a black sombrero as big as his body. But he had dignity, and a fierce pride, and his black eyes were coldly accusing.

"What is this? Have you killed a man, señor?"

David faced him, blood-covered, dusty, weary from the struggle to the death. "Si, señor. A bandit called Diego Garcia."

"What has he done? How do you know he is a bandit? Or do you recklessly kill our people?"

Out in the open, his antagonism and suspicion of all Americans was released.

"Last night," one man in the crowd said quickly, "he killed Jim Foster. See, his body lies in the stable, waiting for the priest!"

Señor Portola looked a little shaken. "But who knows this is the same man who killed Foster?" he said quickly. "What evidence is there?"

"I followed him," David said slowly.

"How can we know that?" David met the black eyes steadily.

He tossed a loaded money belt onto the sand between them. "The bandit carried this belt. It was stolen from Jim Foster."

Portola looked down at the belt and touched it gingerly with his booted toe. "And is this belt surely belonging to Foster? Who knows the belt?"

"I know it," a man in the crowd said, moving up. "I make it myself in my shop, Señor Portola. See the little designs with the studs? He asked me to put on the belt, 'Foster, American,' and a star. Right there." He turned over the belt, squatting in the dust, and showed them the design. All gazed down at it.

David felt haunted. Foster, American, a star. All that was left of a man. His hands on his hips, he stared down at the belt. When he raised his head, Portola looked at him with a twist of his lips. "I apologize, Señor Landau," he said very stiffly. "It seems your cause was just. I will speak with the alcalde."

Portola's words with the alcalde would save David the trouble of a trial, he realized. "I thank you, señor," he said politely. "It was necessary, you see. I cannot have bandits killing my men."

"But of course not, Señor Landau," Portola said. "I will speak with the mayor after church this morning." He bowed and moved back to his large carriage.

David looked after him thoughtfully. The three women in their carriage had their faces veiled by black mantillas. Only their eyes showed. But little Anita's sparkling eyes shone on David. She admired him. She was shocked, but admiring. The little devil, David thought. He gave her an extra bow, and her eyelashes fluttered at him.

"We will take care of this, señor," one of the men said.

David nodded his thanks and went back to his boarding-house. The woman there got a hot tub of water filled for him, and he soaked until he felt relaxed and sleepy. But he never forgot the day he first killed a man.

He had stalked Indians but never killed them. He admired them; they had a sad dignity, a fierce desire for freedom that appealed to him. But the bandits—paugh! They killed for money or a horse or a stolen woman—he could not like them any more than a rattlesnake.

The next morning he gathered the Americans in his office, and several Mexicans who headed various work troops. "We will all carry weapons from now on. Jim Foster was caught with only his pistol," he said brusquely. "And no visiting with women to all hours of the night. If you have a woman, stay all night, don't come home. And marry her, by heaven's sake!"

His words were repeated through all the village and the rancho. The priest used them as an occasion for a sermon on the evils of adultery. David roared with laughter when he heard. He, a Jew, giving rise to a Catholic sermon!

All he had meant was for his men to protect themselves from being killed!

David attended the festivities at the rancho for Christmas. In silent curiosity he attended the Christmas mass, the dinner, the dancing that followed. He danced correctly with the ladies. He was an excellent dancer, and they liked him, flirting at him with their fans.

He managed to get one dance with Anita Portola. "Señorita, you have the prettiest eyes I ever saw," he complimented.

She shrugged daintily. She had heard this before.

In a lower tone, he added, "And one day I will have you looking at me from the pillow beside me!"

"Señor!" she gasped. The sparkling brown eyes flashed at him. "You insult me!"

"How can a man insult his future wife?" he murmured. "I do but make you a promise!"

"You are mad! My father would never consent!"

"I am not going to ask him to marry me," David laughed, and flung back his head to laugh louder at her expression.

She frowned at him, aware everybody was staring. "You go too far, señor. My father does not approve of you. He says— he says you are too wild—and have too much money to spoil you!"

"And he says I am a Jew—one of those who killed Christ," said David keenly. "Right?"

She flushed and shook her head.

"Well, I am a Jew and proud of my religion. We endured much through the centuries, and we have survived! Yes, señorita. I am a survivor, and I am a man who must win! You will see that," he promised her.

She surveyed him very curiously as he nodded grimly. "A survivor," she murmured. "I think I like that . . ."

He grinned again, quickly moving from seriousness to laughter. "That is a good beginning, *querida!*"

"Oh, you wicked man!" she breathed. "A stranger, and you call me—such names!"

"I can think of more," he whispered boldly in her ear as

one of her brothers approached suspiciously. "Darling, love, dove, adored, beautiful one, *amante, enamorada*—" The brother reached them. David dropped the arm with which he had held her and said with solemn formality, though laughter flashed in his black eyes, "My deepest gratitude to your graciousness for the privilege of this dance," and he bowed from the waist.

Though outraged at his words, Anita could not resist smiling at his daring and quick change of character. Her eyes sparkled as she curtseyed low in her lovely Mexican dress of full white skirts and embroidered blouse. "You are most kind, señor. Welcome to our house on this occasion. May you have a splendid new year."

David bowed again, keeping the brother waiting. "Your graciousness is only exceeded by your kindness. May you also have the finest of years in the new year before us!" And his bold eyes added his silent message, reminding her of his words about marriage.

Then, satisfied, he crossed the room to the bowl of rum and fruit, and drank to everybody's health, especially that of his honored host!

Chapter 20

In January and February, the work progressed rapidly. Cold winds blew across the desert and plain, and on the mountains the snow fell in blizzards, sometimes halting their hauling work. In the valley, the work on the smelter progressed to the point they could begin processing.

David had another crew building in the village. The church had been repaired, and the priest was grateful and more friendly. He had been very suspicious of the Jew from their first meeting and had grumbled that the Americans should at least have sent a Christian. But a new bell tower and fresh stucco applied to the building made him feel more kindly to the Landau family.

The town hall was erected, and the alcalde was also grateful and strutted about more proudly. Did he not have a fine office of oak, with a large polished table and a picture of Díaz above his chair? He and his family moved into the apartments above the offices, and savored their new prosperity.

Before David started improving the houses of his workers, he decided to build a huge recreation building. The villagers watched him with curiosity and some disapproval. What was this? They lived in the patios of their homes, in the streets, in the park. What would a building be used for?

He soon showed them. There were long tables where food could be served on festive occasions, where men could play their card games. He ordered two billiard tables, and the Americans eagerly took to the sport. David was one of the best players, and he enjoyed relaxing evenings in this way.

Now the Americans also had somewhere to go, and they were more content. A bar was set up, and drinks served, from whisky to hot tea and cold fruit drinks—not providing competition for the saloons, but somewhere pleasant to drink. Some of the villagers began to come, some with wives and children, and no rowdiness was permitted.

David felt satisfied with the progress. Nothing went as fast as he wanted—all too often there were religious or state holidays, when all activity had to cease. But during the work days he kept the men busy steadily from six in the morning until noon, when the siesta took over their lives. Then they resumed from three until six in the evening. And with many projects in mind, David hired more men and oversaw their work.

The village was more prosperous than ever. Drifters came through, some Americans, some British, one man from Brazil. He hired them all, watched them work, promoted those who worked hard and expertly. Other Mexicans came, hearing that work was there to be had. The village grew, and by the end of February, the population had swollen by a third of what it was.

David rode down the steep, winding trail from the mine one late afternoon, his horse stepping cautiously to avoid the slippery pebbles and mud slides. He gazed proudly down at the village, which shone white in the sunlight. He could see the new church tower, make out the ranch of Señor Portola, see dusty plumes rising from the trail as horses trotted along the town roads. He gazed critically over "his" village and saw where new houses were springing up outside the old town. The men worked with a will, building their new homes.

The dusty plumes rose higher; the horses being driven faster. A shot rang out, echoing across the plains to the mountain side. His gaze returned sharply to the horses. He leaned forward, as though it could help him see.

Four horses—three men riding hard, following a woman in front of them—broke into a clearing. The black skirt rested across the horse as the woman rode sidesaddle, and beside her was a man, turning to shoot, then to fall, slowly, slowly. The woman rode on alone, riding toward the ranch. The men caught up with her.

"Damn!" David muttered. He touched his booted heel to his horse, and they started down the mountain trail recklessly. The horse flung up his head, startled, but kept going. They slithered on stones, but David kept the reins loose so the horse could find his own footing.

The men had caught up with the woman, and she was fighting them, striking with her whip. No, they had her, they were forcing the horse to turn about, they were riding toward the mountains . . .

Bandits—must be bandits. David could now see the huge black sombreros, the dark clothing, the bearded faces.

They came in his direction. David thought quickly. Down the trail there was a small grove of pines, and a dark ravine behind it. He rode rapidly, turning the horse in that direction, away from the trail. The horse reared, and he kept in the saddle. With difficulty he forced it on a new path, soothing with his hands and soft voice.

He slipped into the ravine behind some pines, just in time. The bandits passed on the trail, and he heard them laughing and jeering. "You come with us, sweetheart!" one said mockingly. "We treat you good."

"My father will kill you," he heard a voice say in Spanish.

It was Anita's voice, girlish, stiff. She must be terrified! And she had been out riding with only one guard! The reckless little fool! David set his mouth grimly. With hard patience he waited until they had ridden past, then slowly he followed.

They turned off the path to the mine about halfway up the mountain, turning off to cross a small ravine. They rode slowly, sure they were not being followed. One man held the reins of Anita's horse. David caught brief glimpses of them as they appeared on the trail ahead of him, until a curve in the mountain cut them from view. He rode steadily, cautiously, listening for the sounds of the horses.

Sunset came, a brief flare of crimson like blood. The snows gleamed, then gray dusk fell followed by black night, as swiftly as a stage curtain fell to shut off all view. He rode on by instinct, for he did not know these mountains. He depended on the sure feet of his stallion.

Then he stopped abruptly. Ahead of him was a valley and below him shone the orange glow of a small campfire. He walked the horse forward until he came to a clump of pines.

He got off, tied the horse to a pine securely, then crept

forward slowly to see what was there. His knife was between his clenched teeth, the loaded rifle in his hand, and he was silent as an Indian.

He crept about six hundred feet downhill, then paused where he could overlook the campfire. It was down in a grouping of boulders. If he had not been up on the trail overhead, he would not have seen it at all.

Anita sat before a rock, her feet tied. Her hands lay on her lap, probably tied also. Her sombrero was pushed back from her face, and her eyes glowed in defiance.

"My father will pay you well if you free me!" she said in her youthful voice, which quavered a little.

"Si, señorita! He will pay well in silver, again and again," one man laughed. He swaggered over to her, touched her face with his big hand. She flinched away from it. "But you will not return to him! Your place is with us—for a time!"

At the menace in his voice, David stiffened. They meant to make Señor Portola pay over and over—and in the end he would still not get his daughter back.

Anita's head was bent. The man returned to the fire and issued orders. "Pablo, you stand guard. Listen and wait."

"Si, Jacinto," the man said, and obeyed at once. He picked up his rifle and melted into the darkness behind the campfire. David watched carefully the direction he went, then shifted his attention to Anita.

How brave she was! She did not whimper or weep. He watched the other two bandits begin to prepare food. One made coffee, which soon steamed on the fire. And the other man rolled out tortillas from some cornmeal and water.

David laid the rifle under a tree, marking well where he put it. Setting his knife between his teeth, he crept around the campfire at a good distance, listening and moving very slowly.

It took David more than an hour to slip through the scant grass and shrubs to the dark trees where he knew the bandit stood guard. Finally, he spotted the man, leaning against a tree with his rifle in hand, gazing toward the trail from under his big sombrero.

David slowly maneuvered around to the man's back. The few birds singing in the dark had gone still, though the bandit probably expected nightfall to be the cause. He remained quiet.

Then David sprang on him, hooking his left arm around the man's head and silencing his startled grunt. With the long sharp knife in his right hand, he thrust upward into the man's throat.

The body slumped and slid down. David checked his pulse. Satisfied there was none, he wiped the knife clean on the grass beneath the tree, then found a perch from where he could watch the group around the campfire.

They were eating and drinking. One man gave Anita some hot coffee and a tortilla with beans on it. She ate in silence, awkwardly, with the food held between her tied hands.

Good girl, David thought. She had courage. She was waiting to see if there was a way she might escape or bargain for a price. It was in her eyes.

Presently the leader, Jacinto, grew restless. He kept glancing into the darkness. "Pablo," he said in a low voice.

No one answered. He kicked at the fire.

"He has gone to sleep out there!" he announced. "Sebastian, go and awake him and send him in to eat. We have much riding to do tomorrow."

"Si, Jacinto," the other man said submissively. Jacinto was evidently very much in charge. He was bigger and tougher than the rest.

"And if he sleeps, wake him with the *butt* of your rifle!" Jacinto called after him with a snarling laugh.

David did not wait. He was crawling around the campfire again, to where he had left Pablo's body.

The back of the second guard loomed above him unexpectedly. "Pablo—you there?" the man called softly. "Pablo?"

He ended with a grunt. David had come up behind him, one arm hooked quickly about the burly neck. The man cried out just as David's knife went into his throat.

The cry would bring the other bandits. David wiped his knife, crouched down, and waited.

Jacinto was more wary and tougher. A twig cracked. David turned but could see nothing in the dark. But he could smell the scents of fear and dust and filth. He waited in cold patience. And before long Jacinto appeared between two pines, crouched and wary as he neared the two bodies, still not seeing them. David, now able to plot a strategy, slipped around behind the man and waited. Just as Jacinto spotted the bodies and froze, David leapt from his hiding spot and thrust his knife toward the man's throat, but Jacinto ducked and David's arm swung helplessly over the man's head. Swinging around, David confronted the other's ferocious look as they closed in combat.

256

Jacinto was taller than David and tougher, but David was more wiry and quick.

They struggled silently across the sand and sparse grass, brushing against a shrub, falling against a pine. They fought over the ground, David on top, then Jacinto. The burly fist was raised, and a knife blade gleamed briefly.

David caught the hand that held it and kicked the man in the groin. Jacinto grunted and fell forward, David still holding his burly wrist. With his right hand he struck upward, and felt the war blood gushing over him. Jacinto fell slackly to the side.

David rose painfully and bent over him. Jacinto's eyes gleamed in the moonlight, and his stillness was unearthly. David felt for a pulse, but there was none.

He sighed and stood up. He was breathing so hard, his heart felt as if it would burst. He had killed three men in a couple of hours and he felt sick—but there was Anita to worry about.

He walked softly back to the campfire. Anita was staring into the darkness, a terrified look on her beautiful face. She saw him come out of the dark and gulped.

"David?" she whispered. "Those men . . . out there . . ."

"Dead," he said softly. He walked to untie her.

"You came . . . you came," she said, and began to cry softly.

"Don't break down now," he said roughly. "We aren't out of this yet. Other bandits could come—"

She nodded and made a visible effort to stop crying. He cut her hands loose and then her feet. She stood up, and stumbled against him. With an iron hand, he held her and listened. There were no sounds, but other bandits could come at any moment. The mountains were full of them, and the campfire might draw them in curiosity.

He stopped to have a quick cup of coffee, a tortilla and beans. Satisfied, he turned to Anita. "You want more?"

She shook her head. Her eyes were big in her pale face. He kicked out the fire and took her wrist in his hand.

"Let's go, then."

"We will ride back now?" she whispered. "To my home?"

"Can't tonight, dear. I don't know the path, and we could run into more bandits."

"What, then?"

"We hide out. Come along now."

He got her back to his horse, untied it, and found her horse among those of the bandits. He cut them loose and swatted them with his sombrero to send them galloping away.

She took the reins of her horse and followed him onto the trail. He was watching, looking, and finally found a good hiding place, a small ravine with a gap in the mountain just wide enough to admit their horses.

They slid inside. The ravine was dark and shadowy. David waited until his eyes grew accustomed to the dusk, then gazed around. There was a little stream, scant vegetation, and some pines but it was safe. He explored until he was sure there was no other entry but the way they had come in.

They tethered the horses to a stunted pine, then David motioned to Anita. He spread out a saddle blanket, and she sat down gingerly. His every joint ached.

"You will sleep?" she whispered.

"No, I'll stay awake and listen. You sleep, Anita."

"I am . . . afraid," she whispered. "Will someone . . . find us?"

"I'll find them first," he laughed.

"Oh, you are such—" she whispered, "such a crazy reckless man. I can't believe you followed us."

"Yes," he murmured. "I was up on the trail, coming back from the mine. Lucky, I guess."

She sniffed a little, but held back tears. "Lucky? You are what we call a fool!"

"Thanks, dear!" He grinned, then got up and went to the stream. He tested it, decided it had no strong metals in it, for it tasted pure and mountain fresh. He drank from it, then filled his bottle and a cup for Anita.

Then they settled down for the night. Anita lay down, but he thought she slept little. David sat in the entrance to the ravine and watched, alertly for any signs of movement.

Dawn finally broke, cold and gray. Anita was wrapped in the blanket, sleeping heavily. He touched her, then put his hand gently over her mouth so she would not cry out. She struggled awake, a brief fear in her dark eyes that disappeared as she recognized his familiar figure bending over her.

"Say nothing," he whispered. "I'll saddle up. Get a drink of water if you want."

She nodded and stood up shaking out her long black riding skirt, then moved stiffly from the chilly long night on the cold ground, to freshen up. He saddled the horses and helped her swing into the saddle.

"We'll go slowly. Do you know how to use a pistol?"

She nodded and took the Colt from him. He carried the loaded rifle on his arm, and they started out, David leading the way. He sensed a nervous anxiety in Anita, but his reassuring glance and a smile calmed her again. What a woman, he thought proudly.

From the trail, he sighted a couple of dark forms riding on horseback in the valley below. He pointed them out to Anita, who nodded. He could see fear in her face. They rode on slowly, trying not to stir the dust.

When they reached the foot of the mountains and had to come out into the desert, they knew immediately the figures were bandits who had spotted them as if sighting prey.

They preferred the dawn and evening hours—when it was difficult to see them against the desert and mountains—but David knew mid-morning would suit them just fine.

He cried out tersely, "Ride ahead of me and don't stop!"

She rode like the wind, her hair streaming out from beneath the sombrero that slipped down her neck. David rode after her, his rifle at the ready. They sped at a steady gallop across the desert, their horses so far not laboring. The bandits might have good stolen horses, but they took little care of them, and they couldn't last this pace.

In the distance ahead of them a cloud of dust rose in a ball. David peered ahead, his mouth grim. Such a large ball. It must be a number of men and horses—surely not so many bandits; they rarely rode in such numbers.

Then he relaxed and sighed. Anita was reining up, turning her anxious face to him.

"Go on!" he shouted. "It's your father!"

She smiled at him, her face lighting like the sunrise.

They sped on, the bandits behind them slowing reluctantly. Then they turned around and galloped back toward the mountains. Several of the Portola cowboys raced past them.

David pulled his horse to a dead stop. "Don't follow them into the mountains! They know too many ambushes!" he shouted to them.

But it was too late; they sped on. The remainder of the men pulled up, and Anita flew right toward her father. He grabbed her and buried his face in her hair.

David relaxed for the first time in more than fifteen hours and realized how weary he was. They rode on, Señor Portola was unable to speak. His mouth was tight, and there were worry lines in his face and around his dark eyes.

David pulled up to where the trails diverged. The others ranged around him, but he only spoke to Anita. "I'll go on. You're safe now."

She nodded, her eyes brimming with tears. She tried to blink them back. "Thanks to you, señor."

He grinned at her. "You're a brave lady! Don't have nightmares, now. That's an order!"

She gave him a quivering smile and nodded. "I will try not to. You will come soon, and let us thank you properly?"

"Yes, my pleasure."

"I will tell you then—" Señor Portola choked. Their eyes met. The father understood even better than she did what horrors had awaited his lovely daughter. "My gratitude—"

"Si, señor. I understand." He touched his hand to his sombrero and rode alone to the town. Two men followed him some distance back, respectfully. He guessed they would tell the alcalde what has happened.

The alcalde was outside his office, waiting as David rode up. His round face peered anxiously up at David. "Señor—what happened? Is Señorita Portola found?"

"Si, alive and well. There are three dead bandits in the mountains," he responded.

David rode on after his brief report to the mayor. On seeing him, his boardinghouse landlady registered shock. "Señor—your clothes—the blood! You are injured, yes?"

He glanced down at himself and grimaced. The blood of three men stained his trousers, his shirt, and coat. Even his hands were bloody, for he had washed carelessly in the stream. "I'm fine. If you'll bring up some hot water, señora—some hot coffee—"

"Si, si, Señor David!"

He stomped up the stairs wearily, and in his room, he sank in an armchair, closing his eyes. He felt sick now, and deathly tired.

It had been so close—so very close—and he had killed three men with his own knife and hands.

Nearly noiselessly, a man came in. David's eyes flew open. But it was only Bill Bartram, one of the new engineers—an American. "I heard," he said briefly. "Brought you some whisky. That is the best stuff for what you done." He offered the opened bottle and a glass. David smiled and accepted it. Draining the

260

first glass, he felt the raw whisky burn in his stomach.

Bill's glance flicked over the bloody clothing. "That's the first man you killed?" he asked.

David eyed him coldly. "No, the second, third, and fourth," he managed to say, the nausea rising in his throat.

"Huh. Have another," Bill said. "I'll tell the woman to bring up some hot food. And eat it up, then sleep." He strode out, shaking his graying head.

David bathed, and the woman took away his soiled clothes to wash them. He managed to eat some of the hot food she brought, then went to bed. But it was difficult to sleep; he wakened several times in a cold sweat despite the midday heat.

Over the following days David found a marked respect in the way he was treated by everybody. The men trod warily around him, treated every order as if it came from a divine oracle, did all he asked and more. The women treated him with awe and whispered behind his back. The children stared, and he heard one gang of small boys playing "Mr. Landau and the bandits," and shooting each other with wooden pistols.

On Saturday, he quit work early and went back to the house to wash up. He put on his best white linen suit and cream sombrero and went out to the Portola rancho.

Señor Portola came out to the porch to greet him. Many were gathered on the patio, and guests spilled over into the saddling yard and the paddocks, where the best horses were kept.

For once the ranchero was wearing a beaming smile. He held out his small, strong hand for David to grip firmly.

"Señor Landau, my house is yours! *Bienvenido! Esta es su casa!*"

"*Mil gracias,* señor. You are very kind. May I inquire, Señorita Anita is well?"

"Si, thanks to you! Come, you will see her yourself." And, urged by a friendly hand, David went into the patio. Anita, her cheeks dimpled in a smile and her skirts spinning about her slim form, came up to greet him.

She was so lovely! Her long dark curly hair was tied back with a red ribbon. "Señor David!" she cried, extending one of her slim hands.

He took it, and bent to kiss it. He heard an "Ooh" from the assembled ladies. He took his time over the soft hand, then stood erect. She was blushing.

In a low voice, so only she could hear, he said directly, "May I have your permission to ask your father for this hand—and your heart?"

The dark eyes went wide in shock, and she gasped. He was serious; did he mean it? Her eyes asked. He nodded.

"I love you, I adore you, and you will be safe forever once you are in my care!"

"Oh—David!" she gasped, a mischievous smile on her lips. "If Father consents—but he may not!"

He smiled, and tucked her hand in his hooked arm. They went about greeting her relatives and friends. Some of them eyed him with suspicion, others thanked him in simple or elaborate words. Men had been sent into the mountains to retrieve what was left of the bodies and to bury them. They had found he had killed all three, and the word had traveled swiftly.

What manner of man was this who could obliterate three ferocious bandits?

David later turned to Señor and asked to speak with him in his study privately. Señor Portola nodded.

In the study, the door closed, he said, "Ask what you will, señor. No sum is too great to thank you. You know what those beasts would have done to my—my precious girl."

David sat down on his invitation and looked at the man thoughtfully. "I will ask a tremendous reward, señor."

The man nodded. "It is worth any sum," he said with Spanish fatalism. "My silver mine? You have it, it is yours."

"No, señor, more than that. Your daughter Anita. I love her more than my life."

The man jerked upright, his face pale. His dark eyes studied David's face.

David straightened in his seat. "I do not jest, this is a serious matter. You think because I am a Jew, it is not possible. I do not ask her to give up her faith."

He paused. Señor Portola could not seem to summon words.

"I have thought a long time about this—I have loved her from first sight. Señor, I cannot give up my religion, it is deep in me, as is yours in you. However, there is a way. The priest has suggested it. I will sign papers that Anita will continue in her Catholic faith, and I will permit her to bring up our children in the Catholic faith. The priest will marry us in the church, if you consent."

Portola was still speechless. David went on, after a slight

hesitation, "Perhaps it would be best if I went away. But I deeply admire Anita, as well as love her. She has spirit, courage. I feel there is no other woman in the world whom I could ever cherish for a wife or wish to be the mother of my children."

Señor Portola gazed at David for a long time. David waited in silence.

The man heaved a great sigh. "I will ask my daughter, then—"

He had won.

The marriage was held soon after Easter, in early April of 1891. All the relatives and friends for hundreds of miles came to the fiesta and ceremony. Porfirio Díaz even sent two representatives from the government. The feast went on for many days, with David only wishing they would all go away and leave him with his bride.

Anita was a loving girl, but a fiery one. When he brought her to the boardinghouse to live with him, she was scandalized.

"What—no house of our own?" she cried, her hands set defiantly on her hips.

"Not until the other houses are complete," David responded calmly. "I have promised myself, our house will be done by the end of summer."

"What will I do? No servants to direct, no patio to sew on with my sister and aunts—"

"You might learn to cook," he suggested.

"To cook? I? That is servants' work!"

"Querida," he told her patiently, "we may live anywhere in the world. We may live one day in a mansion in New York or in a hut in Brazil. We will go where my work takes me, I will always work hard for you. But you must be prepared to be a true wife, to cook, sew, clean house—"

"Clean house!" she said incredulously. "Are you insane?"

"Possibly," David said, grinning. He kissed her swiftly, before she could strike out at him, and grabbed her wrist when she did swing. He held her still before him. *"Querida,* I think you will do very well!"

They fought more, he battling with his passion and affection until she gave in and agreed to take cooking lessons from the boardinghouse mistress and one of her aunts. Her relatives were scandalized, but David was persuasive. She must learn well, so she might travel everywhere with him and be a gracious hostess whether she ruled a hut or a mansion.

In bed, she pleased him with her quick responses and her fiery passion that matched his own. They lay a long time together in bed on weekends, going to a late mass so they might enjoy each other. He accompanied her to her services, listening respectfully to the prayers and sermons.

Anita learned to cook, and by the time their house was built, she enjoyed it so much she often did the cooking even after they had many servants. She took pride in her clean house, entertaining graciously. David lavished jewelry on her—set with turquoise stones, and a diamond necklace that Gideon sent him by a messenger from New York City.

They laughed and fought and learned to adjust to each other. Her father watched, troubled, but was reassured when he saw that she was obviously radiantly happy.

They constantly surprised one another. Sometimes, they rose in the middle of the night, to dress and stroll in the paseo park, to gaze at the shining white moon and the stars, and to talk. She rode with him and two other men into the mountains to overcome her fear of the bandits and her experience with them that still gave her nightmares.

He sent for dresses for her—all the latest eastern styles—and she proudly wore the slim lace and satin gowns with high necks and pearl chokers. She looked radiantly lovely in them, and every other girl in town envied her.

David took her to his office and explained the work to her and even taught her how to do bookkeeping.

Her father was aghast when he learned of it, but Anita exclaimed, "Father, I am so important to David!" Her father fell silent.

David also taught her English, so they could read the books that Rachel and Gideon sent together. And when the piano he ordered from Mexico City arrived in time for Christmas she went into raptures.

She sang for him, played for him, sewed his woolen shirts, prepared his meals, filled a tub of hot water for him when he was exhausted, taught him Mexican Spanish—did all she could to repay him for his generous love.

And he taught her more exciting ways of making love. She learned quickly, giggling with him in bed at night. She was radiant, and women envied her and men envied David.

Meanwhile, in the mines David was strict with his men. He insisted they go about in groups of not less than three and always carry weapons or have a guard. The bandits, so frustrated, found that the Landaus' mines were dangerous places, not worth the risk. Their threat over the lives of the citizens dwindled to nothing.

Another claim was purchased, another mine opened. David was busier than ever after the smelter was finished, and they sent the finished silver to Mexico City, by guarded wagon trains supplied by Porfirio Díaz. The ruler rewarded them lavishly—with contracts as the mines prospered.

So it always seemed to go, as prosperity became part of the Landau heritage.

Chapter 21

Bart walked wearily through the front door to the kitchen, where he found Charlotte cooking at the fireplace, her cheeks flushed and her blond hair escaping from the braid down her back.

Emil ran to his father. "Papa, Papa!" he cried, and held up his arms.

"I'm too dirty," Bart said ruefully, though he reached down and playfully filliped his son's nose.

"The hot water is ready, Bart," Charlotte said. She turned back to the huge pot that steamed on the fireplace crane. She lifted it off, her arms straining.

"Let me——" he said quickly, and took it from her, carefully keeping hold of the cloth. "You should not lift such loads, Charlotte."

She had lost a child last winter, and he blamed himself. She had been working so hard, silently, without complaining. She never complained. But shoveling the snow, lifting heavy pots and pans, and doing the housework that kept their home immaculate had wearied her, bringing on the premature birth. She had wept, and so had he, for her. It had brought them closer together.

About to move up the stairs with the heavy pot, Bart paused and gazed down at his blue-eyed son, who was staring up at him. "Who is this very dirty child?" he asked.

"Me!" Emil cried. "Me is Emil!"

"It can't be, you look like an Indian!" Bart teased.

Emil, like all young boys, hated baths. He pouted.

"Yes, you look like a wild Indian," Charlotte said, a smile in her tone.

Emil beamed. "Yes, wild Indian!" he echoed proudly. He pranced around the kitchen, racing his wild imaginary pony. "Bang, bang!"

"You come upstairs and have a bath with Papa," Bart commanded.

Emil began to protest when Charlotte scooped him up under her arm and carried him up the stairs behind Bart. After finishing his son and bathing himself, Bart stepped out of the tub, feeling relaxed and warm again. The cold air of the mountains was good, but sometimes it chilled him to the bone. He toweled himself roughly, gazing at Charlotte as she dressed their son. How tender she was, how good, how gentle. He was a lucky man.

If only he could forget Rachel—and his burning anger at Gideon for stealing Rachel from under his nose. How beautiful and dark and mysterious she was, with her mystical eyes, her enigmatic smile. She had laughed with him so readily, seemed to so enjoy him—

And now she and Gideon had a mansion, servants, and the best schools for their sons.

His brow darkened, he scowled, and kicked away his dirty clothes. Charlotte glanced up questioningly.

He sighed and gave her a weak smile as she dressed Emil in this thick cotton pajamas. Emil refused to wear a nightdress; it was girl's clothes, he said. Other little boys wore nightdresses; Emil would not. Emil had a strong mind of his own, even at four.

Charlotte's hair was thick and fine and soft. She washed it often, to get out the smell of grease and wood smoke. Bart kept her supplied with the lavender water she liked, and she used it in the final rinse, she said. She always smelled clean and girlish, and looked so young with her pink cheeks and wide blue eyes.

He bent and kissed her brow. She smiled at him, and he kissed her lips. "You are a sweet wife," he murmured, and she returned a grateful smile.

"And you are the best husband in the world," she said at once.

Whenever she said that, he felt guilty, because he was not. His father-in-law scolded him bitterly that he neglected Charlotte. When he was depressed he stayed away and visited the saloon where he had a favorite girl. And Charlotte knew, she could not help but know. Never a word of reproach to him—though she lay still in bed at times, not responding to him.

"Come along, son," Bart said briskly. He picked up Emil, tickled him to make him squeal, and jogged with him down the steps.

Charlotte had the table set for them all, and Bart set Emil in the highchair and helped Charlotte bring in the platters of roast turkey, sweet potatoes, and fresh baked bread. She set the platters of corn and beans and baked apples beside her own plate to serve them.

"Father? We are ready, if you will come." Charlotte spoke softly to her father in the living room, reading.

Theodoric Loffler set down his paper and came into the dining room. He smiled vaguely. "All is well today," he said with satisfaction.

He and Bart had struggled for days to repair the smelter, which they believed had been sabotaged. It was working today, at last, and the piles of ore could start being processed once more.

"Yes. I can't help thinking—" Hesitating, Bart glanced quickly at his wide-eyed son. "It may have been caused by . . . you know who."

A frown marred his father-in-law's fine features. "I fear so. Only someone knowing how the smelter works could have damaged it so cleverly. It was not the work of dissatisfied miners."

There was a silence at the table as Bart served the meat and potatoes.

"You will report to your father?" Theodoric asked finally.

Bart nodded. "My letter should reach him in two months. If the mails go through as they promise, he should get it in January or February—though I expect he won't come until spring, to avoid the snow."

"Yes—well—we must all be on our guard."

"I've already warned Peter to set up double guards at night, and never the same two nights running."

268

"Bribes?" Theodoric asked hesitantly.

Bart nodded. "Some toughs hanging about."

After dinner, Charlotte took a protesting Emil up to bed. But by the time she reached his room, he was already falling asleep on her shoulder. She gently patted his back. "There, there, no fussing. Your toys will be there waiting for you in the morning, my angel."

Bart and Theodoric exchanged a smile. "Only a mother could call him angel," Bart said warily.

"He has some mischief in him," his father-in-law admitted.

"I fear he takes after his father. His mother has no mischief in her," Bart said tenderly.

"Aye, that is so," the older man responded.

They dropped the subject and went to the living room to continue their earlier discussion.

"That conglomerate is making trouble with reason," Theodoric Loffler said, lighting his pipe. "They want us to join them or sell out."

"That is why I want Father to come out west. If he means to sell out, he'll have to make the decision," Bart said. "I myself have no wish to work under Martindale or Campbell! Godrich isn't so bad, but he is a bit weasely."

"I would trust none of them," Loffler said flatly. "I find they use questionable methods."

"Such as?" Bart asked, settling himself comfortably in his own big armchair. "I know I suspect them, but it is a feeling deep inside me. What do you know?"

"Know? What is there to know?" Loffler grumbled in German. Then he changed to English once more. "I have been here long enough to know the value of our silver and copper. And I know that when a smelter quotes a lower value, they're not being honest."

Bart considered this silently. He respected his father-in-law's scientific mind, and his shrewd evaluation of ores. The older man could look at a chunk of ore and tell from which mine and from which state it came. And he could assay with no more than a look, the value confirmed by a later detailed laboratory analysis.

"So what is their intention? They talk so smoothly, I do not trust them one iota."

"Nor do I. But I suggest you do not encourage them."

Bart grimaced. "God knows I don't. But they keep coming

back with more favorable offers. And I would like to move east. Charlotte deserves a better life than this."

"Do I hear my name?" Charlotte asked as she came down the stairs.

Bart looked up at her. She looked lovely in her long chemise robe. "I said you deserve a better life," he repeated, more strongly. "You work so hard—and Rachel has servants and goes to balls and wears jewels dangling from her as if she were a Christmas tree."

He saw Charlotte catch her breath, move a quick hand to her breast. Then before he could take his words back, she picked up a candle from the table and held it to her blond hair. "You wish me to look like a Christmas tree?" she asked gaily. "How do I look, eh?"

Both men laughed.

Bart relaxed. He knew he had pained her with his thoughtless words. "But one day Emil must go to a good school," he said as Charlotte began to clear the table.

"So—so—one day he will do so," Charlotte said soothingly. "Until then we can teach him. I will teach him the sums, and you will teach him good English, eh? And the reading and writing. We can do, eh?"

When her accent grew thicker, he knew she was distressed, though her face would not show it. He rose and went to her, draping his arm around her shoulders.

"You are a good wife," he said again. "We shall manage between us, won't we?" And he kissed her warm flushed cheek.

She lifted her mouth to his, and he kissed her warmly while Theodoric looked on, visibly approving. Bart hugged her, then went back to his chair to finish his talk with his father-in-law. Charlotte retrieved her knitting and joined them as they talked into the night.

In early spring of 1894, more Landaus—Jared, Gideon, and Gideon's eldest, Simon—rode out to Copper Creek. They were worried about the smelter concern which, having become more powerful, had bought out most of the Landaus' rivals. Asher and Eden Landau had so far held out against the conglomerate's enticing offer, but Jared wanted to make sure his brother kept resisting.

His grandson Simon was a fine lad of thirteen, eager and wide-eyed to see and do everything his father did. He trotted around after the men, silent, but observing everything.

Gideon was the only Landau who refused to see Asher. He had never liked Asher and Eden. But Bart thought it was odd that his brother would not even go to talk business with them.

Bart and his father sat at table with Asher and Eden and listened to Asher talk. "But it is a fine offer!" Asher cried. "We could all go back east and live in luxury! In luxury!" he emphasized. "It is no mean offer. They will send us money from time to time, and we need do nothing!"

"It was my thought at first," Bart admitted slowly, "but I no longer trust them. How do we know they would not cheat us? They could send us any amount they wanted and we could never challenge unless we came back to check again and again. We might as well remain here and do the work ourselves."

Jared was listening keenly, his aged body, sunken into the tall chair, but his eyes as sharp as ever.

Asher slammed a fist on the table. "Why should they cheat us? They have plenty!"

Jared looked at Bart, indicating that he respond.

"A man who is wealthy does not suddenly become generous to his rivals. He only wants more money," Bart said, sensing the underlying irony, since Asher was like that. The more he and Eden had, the more they wanted—and they spent money as if it grew on trees. Eden dripped in diamonds.

"I must meet these men," Jared cried suddenly. The conversation ended until they could resolve this new family schism face-to-face with their antagonists.

Bart set up the meeting in his office for the next day. Gideon and Simon, Asher and Eden, Theodoric Loffler, Peter Malchus, and the men from the conglomerate were there. Mr. Martindale was the senior and most powerful official, Mr. Campbell and Mr. Godrich seemed equal in their holdings. Bart wondered how much they actually had—how it compared to the Landau holdings. They were anxious to have the Landau mines and smelters; it was in their faces.

"We need your smelters," Mr. Martindale said, chewing on his unlit cigar. "If we do not have them, we must build more in Denver. It would be damn convenient to have them here." His hard black eyes flashed at Jared.

Jared listened in silence, considering. Gideon conducted the negotiations, with the sophisticated charm of a New York board member.

Bart envied him. His older brother had a smoothness that in contrast made him feel brash and crude. If only he could go east, have those meetings with men like Morgan and Astor...

Gideon was scribbling on a notepad. "You would wish to buy our smelters, and the sum would be about eight million dollars—"

"Six," Mr. Martindale murmured with a pained smile.

"At least eight, if not nine," Gideon corrected. "They earn over a million a year. That means, if we consider the earnings over a ten-year period, which is the projected earning capacity of some of our older mines—"

Oh, Gideon, you are clever, Bart thought. He would make the men pay through the nose. And those smooth tones, that suave approach, the thoughtful pose with the pad, when Gideon knew damn well that when their holdings were divided between all the Landaus, the produced income would be much less...

"And what about the mines?" Gideon was asking thoughtfully. He cocked his head to one side and smiled at Mr. Martindale. "Do we understand that you do not wish to buy them, but lease them? You would operate them for us?"

"Actually, we would be pleased if we jointly operated them with you. We don't want Uncle Sam to think we own them all," Mr. Godrich said, smoothing his long hands over each other. "I mean, with all that fool talk about trusts and such— idiots that they are. Congress does not understand businessmen. Best you keep them in your control, and we shall meet sometimes to talk of events and pricing that will be to the advantage of all of us."

"Ah, I can see that," Gideon said brightly.

Simon was staring at his father, a blank look on his face, though his eyes sparkled.

Bart stiffened in anticipation.

Gideon glance toward his own father. Jared gave a short sharp shake of his head. Gideon looked at Bart. He too shook his head.

So Gideon gave them the answer. "I am afraid, gentlemen, that we must decline your offer. We wish to keep control of our own mines and smelters, and we see no advantage to running them for your profit. And if we join in pricing with you and conduct negotiations, then the government will be rightly concerned that we are acting in collusion."

The men reddened. Godrich could not contain his fury.

"How dare you—" he sputtered. "It is just business. To suggest we will be criminal—"

"Did I suggest that?" Gideon asked thoughtfully. "Yes, I must have. You may run what risks you wish, gentlemen. We prefer to keep our hands clean."

That was the end of it. After the Landau men had gone back east, Bart was pestered by the smelter men, and by Asher and Eden. His uncle was particularly irritable.

"Why should they not accept the offer?" he asked again and again. "Talk to your father, he is an obstinate old man! He cannot know his own mind—doesn't he want to get rich?"

Bart did not conceal his grin. Asher knew Jared was a millionaire many times over. "You are mighty concerned about Jared!" he exclaimed.

Asher's jaw hardened. "Yes I am. He can throw away millions! Talk to him, write to him, that's a good lad, Bart!"

Bart at first laughed him off. Then when his uncle persisted, his anger grew. "Let me alone, Asher. Father knows his business, and Gideon is a smart businessman. They know better than to get in trouble with the government, and you should also!"

"Who says there would be trouble with the government? And what does the government care about us out here, anyway? I'll go in with them, whether Jared consents or not!"

It was an empty threat. Asher depended on Jared's generous rates at the smelter. And if he went behind Jared's back to join with the smelter men, Jared would wash his hands of his brother. So Bart thought. He felt he could relax, if only for the moment.

Early in 1895, Charlotte expected their next child. Bart was very worried about her. She had dragged about heavily the last months and had a weary air about her that upset him. Her father hovered about her protectively while Bart tried to take more care of Emil.

Charlotte finally went into labor in late February. A heavy blizzard had set upon them, and the wind howled ferociously. Bart sent for Winona, but the messenger never got through. He gave up and sat out the storm in the saloon.

He and his father-in-law delivered the child. Bart had never felt so terrified in his life. The hours dragged out. Charlotte moaned at first, then cried out, then fell into a dead faint. Mr. Loffler was white with anguish. Bart had to do something. He brought cold water and wrung out a cloth, wiping Charlotte's hot face. He sat beside her, held her hand, let her clench at his arms as the child neared delivery. Toward the end, he would have wrenched the child from her to save Charlotte from the anguish of the last moments. But then the baby's head appeared and before long he held the soft tiny body in his hands. He felt such a wrenching in his breast, he knew he would never forget this moment.

Charlotte was moaning incoherently in German.

"It is over, darling. We have another son. Gently, my darling," urged Bart. He wrapped the baby in a blanket, and Mr. Loffler took it in his care, gently wiped the eyes and ears and nose as Bart turned his attention to Charlotte. Afterwards, she blushed with shame when she realized two men had attended her, though they felt no such emotions. All had been too urgent for niceties.

Bart brought her some hot tea, soothed her with a cool cloth on her face. Then he grinned down at her proudly. "Well, we did it, Charlotte!"

In spite of the pain and drowsiness, she had to smile. "Yes— we—did."

Winona came the next day and took over with one of her daughters. But Bart never forgot how he had helped bring his own son into the world. They named him Theodore for his grandfather, and Mr. Loffler, too, was inordinately proud of him.

They paid much attention to the baby, and soon Emil became jealous. Bart was horrified when little Emil struck the baby one day in the chest. Teddy gasped, then began to scream, and Bart spanked the older boy.

Charlotte came running from the kitchen. "What is it, what is it?" she cried.

"He struck the baby," Bart said grimly, and he took Emil upstairs and shut him in his bedroom.

When he came down, Charlotte was rocking the baby. She looked at Bart in troubled fashion.

"He is not even six," she said finally.

"Old enough to know better!"

"And very jealous of his brother," Charlotte said. "I have given Ted too much attention. I must spend more time with Emil, read to him, and so on. It is hard to explain to a child that he is loved as much as his brother."

"He is old enough to know a baby needs attention. He should not be jealous!" Bart said sternly.

She smiled faintly. "Jealousy knows no age," she said simply. "I have often been jealous of—of Rachel."

Bart stared at her. Her head was bent as she caressed the baby, her cheeks pink. And he had been so jealous of Gideon; Charlotte must know that.

"Well—" he stumbled. "Each has his own talents. Emil must learn that he is a fine lad, that we love him, that we do not love the baby more than him."

"Yes, he must learn that. Bart—could you spend more time with him? He grows fast, he longs to follow you about."

"I could do that," Bart said. "And read to him of an evening, while you settle the baby down. That shall be our time together."

He did so, and pondered at the same time the strong jealousy he had felt for Gideon. Why? Had it been the attentions his father had given to Gideon? For many years as a boy he had been so jealous—it had begun long before either had met Rachel.

From then on, he took Emil to the mines occasionally, teaching the boy about safety, about lead and silver, about bookkeeping. He set up a little book for Emil in which he could keep an account of a small portion of a mine. Emil struggled over the sums and was never so proud as when his father told him he had come out exactly correct for the month. It was an excellent way of teaching him sums, and the boy learned quickly.

Bart took him on his horse when he went out riding in town. He was careful with the boy, for Emil had a reckless spirit like his own. He was firm with him, but not rough; he did not want to crush his spirit. Charlotte also spent afternoons with Emil, to show him no child was preferred over another.

Bart was so absorbed in his work and his family, he was annoyed when Asher practically forced him home to dinner with him one evening. Bart finally sent a message to Charlotte and resigned himself to having to spend an evening with his uncle and Eden.

The two Landaus used the occasion to urge Bart to join the conglomerate behind his father's back. "You could fix it all up and take the money before Jared finds out," Eden urged feverishly.

"Well, I'll be damned," Bart said fiercely. "You'll have me

cheat my own father and brothers? That is your opinion of me?"

"Well, Gideon stole Rachel from you, didn't he?" Eden cried. Asher was licking his lips, watching Bart's face.

Bart felt so stunned, he didn't know what to say. Then he found his tongue.

"Stole Rachel? She was not mine," he said. "She chose Gideon, and they have a fine marriage. And so is my marriage good—after all, Charlotte is the prettiest and sweetest woman in Copper Creek!" and he grinned fiendishly at the pout on Eden's face.

"You said I was the prettiest woman!" Eden said angrily.

"You used to be. But then Charlotte came along!" Bart said deliberately. "My, what a lucky man I am! Such a beautiful wife, such fine sons! Two wonderful sons to follow in my footsteps!"

That did rub it in. Asher turned dull red. The two had never been selfless enough to have children.

Bart left the house in anger and would not return.

Asher tried again to urge Bart to fall in with his plans at the office. "They will pay me well—they will pay us all well," he almost wept.

"No, never! You are an old thief! Haven't you gone through enough money, you and your wife? If you want to sell out, fine, but don't come crying to us when they cheat you."

"They made promises—they would not deceive me—and we will have good contracts—"

"No! And do not ask me to dinner again—and do not let Eden come to my house! Charlotte was most disturbed by her visit the other day! I will not have her upset!"

"She meant well! Your wife took offense!"

"My wife is smart. She does not take offense when none is meant. Tell Eden she is not welcome in my home! Nor are you!" Bart growled, for he had been most disturbed. Charlotte had wept, and she did not usually weep like that. Oh, a few tears when he was drunk and late. But not like this, a storm of sobbing that would not cease for a time. "What did your bitch of a wife say to her?"

Asher shifted his gaze. "Who knows? Women are strange." He shrugged. "That does not need to come between us. We are old friends, eh? Come to dinner tonight. Show my wife that all is again well between us."

"No more, this has gone too deep," Bart said. "You want me to cheat my father. Your wife insults my wife. Forget us. Go to Denver. Don't hang around me—and stay away from my mines!"

"You would have me forget all my friends!" Asher cried, trembling. "Why should I not go to the mines?"

"Because you stir up trouble constantly!"

Asher took offense then, and the conversation ended in a deadlock. Later Bart told the mine managers to refuse Asher's entrance to the mines.

"He is a troublemaker," he grumbled to Charlotte later. "The older he gets, the worse he is. He should look after his own mines, they need his care. But let him stay away from me and mine. What did Eden say to you?"

He blurted it out fast, hoping to take Charlotte off guard.

Charlotte shook her head. "It is over and done with, Bart. But I am glad you will not go to them again," she said gently.

"Tell me."

"Oh, it was some insult," she said vaguely. "Forget. Forget. She is jealous of me, I think, that I have such a fine husband and two wonderful sons. Yes, she hates me because I am so fortunate." She smiled up at Bart, and her blue eyes twinkled.

He swooped down on her, clasped her in his arms, and pressed his warm mouth on hers. She yielded to him, her rounded form willing in his arms. She felt so good against his body.

He brushed his lips against her pink cheek, down to her soft smooth throat. "You are so lovely—so good—so sweet to me, my Charlotte!"

"I love you," she said.

He had said that to her, but not really meant it. The shadow of Rachel had hovered between them. He sighed a little, kissed her again, and held her close. How obstinate a man could be, against his will. He wanted to love her completely, forgetting all others. But he could not.

Two months later, officials of the U.S. government came west, prying and poking around, as Asher claimed resentfully. They were investigating the possibility of the smelter operators having formed a trust.

"Thank God our hands are clean," Theodoric Loffler said worriedly. "What questions did they ask again today?"

"I showed them the books," Bart said. "I am also glad that

our hands are clean. They know their accounting—they ask shrewd questions. We have Father and Gideon to thank as well as God. Only two years, and they are already coming to peer down our throats."

There was a fire at Asher's house within a week, and all his accounts were burned up. The government men were very suspicious, but after all, what man would deliberately burn all his accounts? Asher wept and wrung his hands convincingly, and Eden scolded him and sympathized with him all the time. It was a good act, and Bart wondered if his suspicions were wrong.

After all, Asher had also burned up records of what money was due him. He would have to depend on the smelter operators to pay him what was owed. His miners had been paid the Saturday before, which was fortunate.

"Ah well, not my concern," Bart said to Charlotte. "But I am glad I did not hear Asher's advice when he gave it to me! Gideon was right—"

"He was right, and also you, Bart," Charlotte said firmly. "It was your decision to remain out."

Bart was pleased with her words, but tried to brush them off modestly. "No, no, it was my father and Gideon—" It did not sting so much to say Gideon's name like that.

"It was your advice to them," Loffler said, puffing at his pipe. "It is you who are here on the ground, so to speak. It is you who run the mines and observe what goes on in Copper Creek and Denver. Without your words and counsel, Mr. Landau would not have been so quick to make a decision. And he might have given in to their flattering words and good terms. They offered much."

Bart did not answer, but he was happy with their praise. He thought they both meant it, that they were not trying to make him feel less envious of Gideon.

He picked up his son Emil, who was listening curiously to all that was said. "Well, my fine big boy, how about going to the mine with me tomorrow? We will check the silver, all right?"

Emil's eyes, so like his mother's, lit up. "All right, Papa! Me help—I mean, I will help—" he said more slowly. "Emil helps Papa much!"

Charlotte groaned. "He is not speaking English right," she worried.

"He'll learn," Bart consoled. "He is a smart boy." He hugged the boy to him, enjoying his smell. "I'll bet he learns to ride his pony very quickly!"

Emil drew back and stared. Then with a cry he threw his small arms about Bart's neck. "My pony—my pony—" he yelped. "Papa, my pony!"

Bart laughed. "Yes, you shall have him day after tomorrow! Ace found one that is just your size!"

"Emil ride good!"

Bart lectured him gently. "You mean to say I will ride well. Say it, I will ride well."

"I will—ride—well," the boy said clearly.

Bart's dark laughing eyes met those of his wife, who sat opposite him, and they smiled at each other. Charlotte nodded slowly, making a gesture as though to say she was leaving the boy in his father's hands.

Chapter 22

David Landau rode north late in 1898. He brought with him a saddlebag of ore samples.

Bart hugged him fiercely. "Why haven't you come more often?" he demanded, happy to see his wild young brother. "What are you up to in that hot country?"

David laughed at them all, beaming his wide happy smile. "Up to? I have four children!" he grinned. "You should see my growing family!"

"Oh, I wish they could have come," Charlotte cried. "Tell us about them and your wife Anita."

He grimaced. "I cannot stop talking once I start," he said proudly. "Let me have a hot bath with lots of water and a huge meal of your fine cooking, Charlotte. Then I'll talk until I cannot speak!"

He had a slight Spanish accent, and Bart teased him about that. "Yes, I learned to speak Spanish, and now I rarely speak English! I'm going east for a quick visit, to buy some gowns and jewels for my beautiful wife!" He groaned and laughed all at once. "Father won't half scold me. He never lost his German accent, and now I have a Spanish one!"

By the time David had washed up and donned clean clothes Mr. Loffler had returned from his assay office and was examining the silver samples keenly.

"Um, these could be a problem for you," he mused, turning them in his long fingers. "Too much lead combined with the silver. How do you handle it?"

"I don't, that's the trouble," David said bluntly. He brushed back his dark wet hair with his bronzed hand and nodded at the samples spread on the newspapers on the parlor table. "Our smelters are running full speed, and I have about decided to start a third one. We cannot handle any more ore, yet we have opened three more mines farther west. I put one engineer in charge of them, and they are producing well. Yet—our smelters cannot get all the silver from the ore."

"I don't wonder, it will take—um," Mr. Loffler paused and shook his head. "I don't know. I will have to work on this. You say you cannot get all the silver out—um—that means another method—um—" He was intrigued by the problem and sat silent during dinner.

David was weary from the long journey. Charlotte made up a bed in the guest room for him, and he retired early. But after sleeping until noon the next day, he seemed ready for work again.

When he learned that Bart was not running the smelters at night, he nodded happily. "Just as well, Bart. We can use that capacity. I came north to ask whether you can process our Mexican ores. I talked to the authorities, and they agreed reluctantly. You see, our smelters are running twenty-four hours a day, six days a week. Even if I build another one—which I am planning to do—we have a lack of skilled help. I want Father to try to find me more engineers willing to work in Mexico."

"You have such mines?" Mr. Loffler asked.

David turned to him. "You would not believe the wealth there is in Mexico," he said enthusiastically. His dark eyes glowed and looked distant. "Now that we have worked successfully these years and helped the economy of Mexico, other men are offering the mines on their property in other parts of Mexico. We just cannot handle it all. Other firms will come down eventually, but some of them cannot endure the heat and cold, the difficult housing, and food problems. I think they are too soft!" and he laughed heartily.

"Yes, not everybody is equipped to handle the living conditions," Bart said thoughtfully. "Not everyone can live in rude

281

cabins and eat the local foods, or fight off Indians and bandits—"

"It takes a special breed of men—and women," David said
to Charlotte, and gave her a gallant bow. She acknowledged
it with a smile.

"And you will tell us of Anita?" she prodded gently. "She
is well, and your children also?"

He settled himself to talk enthusiastically about his lovely
wife and four children. "My Anita managed well in the old
little house, but now that we have a big hacienda—well, how
she does me proud! Such a beautiful hostess, so gracious, she
still prepares some foods with her own hands! Everyone loves
to come and visit us. And her proud papa—at last I think he
is reconciled to our marriage!"

"I should think so!" Bart exclaimed. "You are wealthy, you
have four children, three sons and a daughter. What more does
he want?"

David grimaced. "A Catholic husband," he explained. "However, the children are being raised Catholic, and I have almost
forgotten my religion." His eyes darkened, but he shrugged,
hands up.

Bart was shocked, but tried not to show it. David had forgotten his religion! No wonder—there was nobody else in his
town of the Jewish faith, no rabbi, no synagogue. Bart realized
he was fortunate, that he had all those here in Copper Creek,
and a wife who was Jewish as well. He had more than David!

David was telling them about his children, his eyes sparkling. He reached out and hugged Emil, as though missing his
own sons.

"There is my son Juan, who is six, and what a fine lad like
this one," and he pressed Emil's shoulder. "He is already riding
his pony, and trying to follow me to the mines. And my beautiful daughter Maria Anna! How lovely she is, the picture of
her mother! And little Cesar, what a charmer he is! How he
flatters his grandfather, until the old man will give him the
earth! And the baby, Francesco—ah, he is so dark of eyes, so
sturdy, you would not believe!"

Three-year-old Ted was listening gravely, leaning on Bart's
knee. Bart laughed a little. "Yes, we would believe! Our Emil
and our Ted are true Landaus too!"

David grinned across to his older brother. "How glad I am
for you," he said simply. His eyes were satisfied as he studied

the two boys and Charlotte Landau sitting next to Bart on the sofa. Then he burst out laughing. "I was thinking what a trick Anita played on me," he said happily. "I was at the mines in Taxco when I received a message from Anita to come quickly! I had been gone three months—you can imagine my concern! I rode my horse to a lather. Then—" he boomed with laughter, and his face creased with glee.

"What happened? It was some trouble?" Charlotte asked, puzzled.

"Ah! My Anita told me that she was to have a child! However, she was not sure if I was the father! You can imagine how I burned with rage! She kept me in suspense for days, for a week! She was cool to me, my Anita! She teased me, she went out riding without me, she flirted with one man and another, until her father rebuked her!"

He rocked with laughter. Bart was silent, thinking how he would feel if Charlotte played such a trick on him. He would have been infuriated.

"Then finally she admitted she was teasing, she had been angry that I was gone so long! It was my child, but I had best stay at home more often or she would be unfaithful to me, she swore!"

There was a proud look on his face, it was not fury. David was proud his wife loved him enough to do such a thing because she wanted him home!

"These modern women," Mr. Loffler sighed, shaking his head.

David smiled fondly. "Ah, she will always be a wild strong one, my wife! It was that which attracted me to her. What courage! What independence! What intelligence! What spirit!"

The next days, Mr. Loffler and Bart worked in the smelter office, testing the silver to weed out its components, David watching on.

"You see the problem?" David said, watching the ore crumble to nothing. When he talked of the smelters, the mines, his eyes glowed. "We must come up with some other formula or much of the silver will be lost. Then it must be processed again and yet again, which wastes time and money."

"It will take some work to figure out which chemicals will deposit all the silver out of the ore," Loffler said. He too was excited by the prospects. "The ore is rich with silver, the mines are good. It would be a pity to have to give up on these."

"Give up!" Bart said. "Of course not! Why should we give up? Start sending us the ores, David, by mules or by wagons, if they will cross the mountains. We'll take care of all the ore you can send, but it may be a while before we can convert one of the smelters to this ore."

"How will you come?" Mr. Loffler asked, but he was already lost in mixing another formula to test on the ore which was piled to the side of the long work table. He had surrounded himself with glass vials and bottles of chemicals, some of which remained uncapped, and a pad on which he did his mathematics.

David and Bart meanwhile studied the maps given them by the Mexican government.

"I think it would be best," David said finally, tracing the routes with his bronzed finger, "if we load the ore on a railroad train in Mexico. We could build a spur twenty-six miles from my headquarters to the main rail line, then put the ore from my wagons onto railroad cars, send it north, where the rail lines stop. We'll set up a headquarters there and put the ore onto wagons to be sent to you."

"But that means running the wagons over mountains." Bart frowned. "Hum. If we have to convert a smelter or build a new one, it might be best to build a smelter nearer to the border."

They discussed the possibilities back and forth and decided that Jared and Gideon would have to give approval for building a new smelter in Colorado or down in Mexico. A Mexican one would present a problem, since David had no more engineers to spare. For now, he would send the ore to Bart in Copper Creek, in smaller quantities than he would have wished, and plan for the future when more ore could be sent north.

David left them to return home, and for a time they missed his sunny and charming personality. The children kept asking when Uncle David would come back.

Mr. Loffler worked hard to discover the right formula for processing the Mexican silver ore. He and Bart worked long hours in the laboratory that Mr. Loffler had built behind the assay office.

Inevitably, Asher Landau found out what they were doing. He freely roamed the mines and the offices, though Bart had tried to keep him out. He knew Jared would never condone barring his own brother from the family business. Asher picked up the piece of silver ore on the table in the lab and studied it.

"Hey, this isn't our Colorado stuff!" His keen dark eyes were alert. "Where did you get this?"

Bart sighed. "From Mexico, Uncle Asher. Now let it alone."

Asher could not let anything alone that smacked of money. He nosed around, talked, teased Bart, until he found out what was going on. And eventually the conglomerate also found out what was going on: that David Landau was sending ore north from Mexico. By the time the wagons began to roll in, all Copper Creek knew, and finally all of Colorado.

Mr. Loffler had worked long, so had Bart, and one of the smelters had been successfully rigged to work with the Mexican ores. But the smelters were becoming overloaded. Rumors started as the local ores piled up outside the factories awaiting processing.

The manager of the Landau concerns, Peter Malchus, was visibly shaken. "The miners are uneasy, Bart," he said quietly. "And, I have to admit, so am I. Does this mean you'll be mining less here and smelting the Mexican ores instead? The miners worry they may soon be out of jobs."

"For God's sake! Of course not. Where did they get such a crazy notion?" Bart was cross and tired for lack of sleep. He and Loffler had been working into the night on the design for a huge new smelter, after Jared Landau accepted the idea that another had to be built.

"The Mexican ores are pouring in. Someone said you are going to have more sent up by railroad. And our ores are piling up, untreated."

Bart calmed down. He explained carefully to his manager what was going on. Peter seemed relieved, if still doubtful. But later he fumed to Charlotte. "All that gossip! A lot of old ladies! Do they think we will shut down our own mines after all our battles to keep them operating, and by Landaus?"

"It could happen, Bart," she said slowly, worry lighting her blue eyes. "You said much wealth is in the Mexican mines. What if ours play out, as Asher has suggested? The miners here would be out of work. And the Mexican workers can come in and mine for much less pay. I think they are right to be disturbed."

285

It was one of the few times she had contradicted him. His surprise and anger flared. "Now, Charlotte! Don't say such things! It is nonsense!"

"You have already told others in town many times how much you wish we could go back east—close down the mines and let someone else operate the smelters. They repeat that talk now, Bart."

He mused silently, frowning, then turned back to her and spoke more quietly. "It is true I do wish we could go east, Charlotte. But it is as much for your sake as mine. You have worked so hard, and this is an uncomfortable, hard place to live. Why should others—others—have comforts and luxuries and my wife work so hard her hands are always red and worn?" He took her hands in his firmly.

"Bart, I do not care about that!" she protested.

He held her firmly. "And the boys should have a good education. I have little time with Emil now, and he neglects his sums."

"That does not matter—" she tried to say, but he shook his head.

He bent and kissed her lips gently, his mouth lingering on hers. "One day you shall have the life you deserve! And it shall include servants for you, my girl!"

She tried to smile. "And who would cook your Johnny-cakes?"

He laughed and pinched her cheek. "You shall, darling! I cannot imagine you neglecting my wants!" And he laughed at her blush as he patted her hips.

By spring, Loffler and Bart had conquered the chemical formula that would smelt the Mexican ores. The piles outside the smelters began to diminish until David sent up another train load, and then the ore stood in cones against the blue Colorado sky.

The rumors started again, worse than ever.

Peter Malchus came to his boss once again. "They talk," he said stolidly, standing with feet apart in the laboratory.

"What about?" Bart asked.

Loffler looked up from his desk.

"About the Mexican ore. They say that you will shut down the Copper Creek mines, you will convert the other smelter to Mexican ores. They say you will fire them and keep the Mexican workers, for they ask for much less in wages."

"Damn it to hell! That isn't true!" Bart yelled. He pounded his fist on the table. "We have no intention of closing our silver mines here! The silver is too good and the demand too high! Congress is firmly set on using silver! Damnit, can't they understand that?"

"Four miners were fired yesterday," Peter said stubbornly.

"For trying to sneak out silver in their pockets!" Bart said angrily. "Damnit, Peter, you know that! We can't have stealing!"

"I know it, but the men are saying—"

"Well, you'll just have to tell them the truth! I know I didn't want it advertised that men are sneaking silver in their pockets, but tell the truth to them—it is more important for them to know that we are not closing the mines! Hire four more miners to take their place if you have to—but settle the situation, now!"

Peter bent his head, relief on his honest face. "Okay, Bart, I'll send out word we are hiring four to take the places of the others. That should help."

Bart went home that night feeling frustrated and angry. The miners wanted jobs, wanted security, but four men had stolen from him, had been stealing for some time. Damnit, what did a man have to do for his employees? Give them a license to steal?

He ate his dinner in silence, frowning. Charlotte shushed Emil, who wanted his father to talk to him.

After dinner, Bart sank down into his big chair. Ted sat at the parlor table, his tongue curling around in his mouth as he tried to write some letters on a page. Emil worked in silence also, his dark curly hair ruffled as he jotted again and again in his little red book, doing sums. Loffler was going over some formulas, deeply absorbed. Charlotte was doing dishes, trying to muffle the sound as she bent over the sink. Her men were working; she would be quiet.

Ted's head drooped over the work. His head went down briefly on the table, and he yawned widely. Charlotte was drying her hands in the kitchen, moving to put away the cold food on the porch in the cold box.

Bart rose and picked up Ted. "Bed for you, young man. Tomorrow is coming fast."

"I'm not sleepy, Daddy!" Ted said, yawning widely again. Bart laughed down at him tenderly. He called to Charlotte as she came back into the kitchen. "I'll put this young man into bed, darling!"

"Oh, Bart, I will. I didn't realize he was sleepy—"

"No, go on with the kitchen and be done with it. You are tired also." He surveyed her weary face with troubled eyes. She did seem so exhausted. Was she pregnant again? He would enjoy another baby, but he did not want Charlotte to be sick again. In fact, when David had described his beautiful little daughter, Bart had found himself thinking how sweet it would be to have a little girl. Yet he kept remembering Ted's birth, how Charlotte had screamed with the pain.

He put Ted into his bed, told him a quick bedtime story about a pony that got lost, and then as the boy's eyelids slid shut, he tiptoed out of the room. As he came down the stairs, he caught Emil's reproachful look, the blue eyes sad.

Bart sank onto the couch again. "Let me see your ledger, Emil," he said in businesslike tone. "How is your mine earning?"

Emil brightened and came around the table to him. He handed over the book, and stood like a worker expecting criticism, his blue eyes shining.

"Hum. Sit down, my lad!"

Emil sat down beside him.

"What is this?" Bart pointed to an entry.

"That's the extra bonus pay for the week, Papa. Four miners worked longer to make up for the ones fired."

"Um, yes, I had forgotten. Good work. Hum," he said, and turned over another page. He talked further to Emil about the book, then nodded and put it down with satisfaction. "Fine work, Emil. Your accounts are kept as well as our office's. Did you show Mr. Malchus?"

"Yes, Papa. He said to check it with you, then turn it in for the month." The young face so like his, yet with an echo of Charlotte's, was turned up to Bart. Anxious for praise, yet diffident. "Did—did I do it right, Papa?"

"You did it exactly right, Emil. If your mother agrees, you shall come to the mine with me tomorrow and help hand out paychecks."

Emil loved to do this. He knew every miner by name, as well as his work record. The small face glowed.

"I'm about ten, Papa," he said anxiously. "When can I be a regular worker?"

"Hum." Bart exchanged looks with Charlotte. She shook her head slightly. "Well, Gideon worked only part-time from the time he was twelve," he said solemnly. "Rachel worked part-time from fourteen to eighteen, then she began to work full-time. Hum. You are starting early, you began at six. I would say you should go to school and learn your lessons for at least five or six more years. But if your mother agrees, you could come to the office with me every Saturday."

Emil looked anxiously at Charlotte, and she smiled. He went up to bed happily, calling down, "Don't forget me in the morning, Papa!"

"He learns so fast," Theodoric Loffler said complacently. "Such a smart boy!"

"Look who he has for grandparents," Bart teased. "You and my father!"

Mr. Loffler laughed aloud, pleased. He went up to bed soon thereafter.

Charlotte came over at Bart's beckoning. "Damnit, Charlotte, that boy ought to go to a good eastern school."

Charlotte did not try to answer. Emil would be ten in August.

"I'm not still jealous," he said unwillingly. "I am thinking of my sons, not Gideon's. They deserve a good education. Emil is a very smart lad, and it seems Ted will be also. If Jared does not agree to let us move back east—" He paused, unwilling to go ahead with that threat.

"What are you thinking, Bart? That I should let the boys go east without us?"

He sighed and drew her into his arm. "I am needed out here, and I keep remembering what a tough lot David has, without uttering a word of complaint. He treats the difficulties as a joke. Yet he, like me, wants the easier life for his wife and children."

"It would be—difficult to let Emil go east without us—" she murmured. "Yet, if he must—"

"He could probably go to some school with Franklin and Thaddeus—"

"And perhaps David's boys will one day also go—"

"It will be more difficult for them, they speak only Spanish now."

Charlotte looked visibly shaken. "Perhaps his boys could come here when they are a little older and spend the summer with us. I could teach them English—"

289

"That would be very fine, Charlotte," and he kissed her, moved by her generosity. She looked fatigued. He would insist that Winona's daughters come more often, in spite of Charlotte's protests that she could handle all the work. They could at least do the heavy laundry and scrubbing.

Her mind was still busy on her previous proposition. "I would enjoy knowing them, and perhaps Anita could come for a little while. She should know her relatives. David should bring her with him when he travels," Charlotte said firmly. "He told me she is afraid of us! Imagine. Her father has filled her with fears, that we are all wealthy gringos." She laughed.

Bart was silent. He had not thought about his brother's words for a while. David was shut off from them most of the time. But Anita and the children should come on a visit to Copper Creek, and go to New York. Jared would want to get to know them all. Bart would suggest it tactfully, in a letter to David, and one to his father. He smiled to think of himself as the intermediary between them. A new role for him! Perhaps he himself had changed over the years.

"And you should come east with me next time I go," he said finally. "Yes, Charlotte. My mother should get to know you better, and my sisters as well."

"I should like that," Charlotte said quietly. "I think perhaps your father will come west this summer, though. He will want to decide about the new smelters, I believe."

"Yes. This summer he will probably come. And I hope he can lay the rumors to rest..."

Landaus liked work, not the speculations about it. And Bart knew the Landau mines were rich enough to last decades.

Chapter 23

But the miners wouldn't be appeased. Peter Malchus complained to Bart again. "They talk of striking, we have to do something."

Bart ran his hands through his thick black hair. "Why the hell do they want to strike? We pay them better than any other outfit. We take all the ore they mine. What's on their minds?"

But he already knew the familiar refrain.

"They want higher pay for digging deeper in the shafts. It is more dangerous, and they worry about injuries. Also—they want guarantees they won't be laid off. They say the Mexicans work more cheaply, which is why you are bringing the Mexican ore up here. They fear losing their jobs because you will close the Colorado mines."

"That's patent nonsense!" Bart cried.

But the workers remained unconvinced when they were told.

"It must be those smelter men," Charlotte mused aloud one evening. "They want you to sell out and go back east, and if they succeed in making the miners strike, your father might close the mines. He does not really need them, you know."

"Of course he does, and so do we, Charlotte!" Bart said impatiently, staring at her in surprise.

"Well—I've heard talk," she pressed. "It made sense to me. You can get much richer ore in Mexico."

"Is that what they say?"

She nodded.

"Well, if a sensible woman like you believes it, then the others will also," he sighed.

She flushed at his words and brightened. "Then it is not true?"

"No. We are *enlarging* our operations. And if there are any rich claims, we'll buy them. We're already planning to expand on the smelting side of things."

She shook her head. "I guess I'm gullible, after all. Why aren't you satisfied with what you have?"

He gave her a wry smile. Mr. Loffler, sitting over his journals, raised his head.

"Frankly, darling, if Father had had more sons, he would have sent the next one to Chile for nitrates. Or to Alaska for minerals, or—as rumors have had it—to western Canada for gold. And California too is rife with adventures, though many men have been lost going there. And Africa—"

Her blue eyes widened in disbelief. "Bart! You would go to all those countries?"

"If we had the men, the trained engineers..." He softened his voice, smiling. "And when our sons are grown, darling, I think my brothers and I will train them for places we cannot even envision yet. Just think, by the early nineteen hundreds, Simon, Franklin, Thaddeus, our Emil and Ted, and David's three sons will all be men. Think how many places in the world Landaus can go!"

"Gott in Himmel!" Loffler gasped.

Charlotte was speechless.

"We must have patience until our sons are older," Bart said mischievously, and laughed at their expressions. "No, I do jest, but only a little. Father has had many plans. He has men bring him reports from all over the world, places we may survey and study...we are one of the few firms in the world capable of surveying, mining, and smelting, all in one company. Perhaps one day there will be many such firms. But today, we're among three or four."

Loffler seemed baffled. "But—but this would mean such big operations! Canada—Chile—Mexico—where next?"

"Wherever we can turn a profit," Bart said simply.

When Gideon Landau arrived with his son Simon the following month, he confirmed Bart's words. "Oh yes," he said as though surprised by their wonder. "We shall expand, we are already doing so. I have hired a Canadian to work for us there, and he is sending back encouraging reports from western Canada. If only I could find more good trained men—but so many want company stock in return. Father is unalterably opposed, he insists the shares be kept in the family."

Gideon had brought his eldest son, eighteen-year-old Simon. He was a strapping, dark, and handsome youth—less severe in bearing than his father, but definitely a Landau. His eyes too sparkled, like a Landau's, at everything around him. "I want Simon to work with Mr. Loffler this summer," Gideon said. "He goes to MIT this fall. Within four years, he shall be in charge of these mines."

Everyone froze.

"Bart, you will be going east, to help handle some overall operations. Your headquarters will be in New York. But you may be asked to travel anywhere in the world to explore promising new prospects. Father said to tell you that he'll explain more later when he arrives this summer . . ."

Gideon grinned broadly at their surprise.

Bart was speechless. It was all he had ever wanted. He turned to his wife. "We shall move, Charlotte. Did you hear that? We shall move to New York, and you will reign in New York society!"

"Oh no, Bart!" she cried out, and put her hands to her face.

"You can manage. Rachel has done beautifully," Gideon said, smiling warmly at her. "And she has asked if you would let Emil come east with me this year. He will go to a good boys' school with our sons; it's become a Landau tradition."

He was quite serious, Charlotte realized. She felt crestfallen, at a loss for words, then visibly upset.

Bart tried to calm her. "My dear, you can manage. You have all the graces and beauty, and we won't stint on money! We shall begin at once to plan a beautiful mansion, with servants and—"

"Oh, Bart, this cannot be! Not for me!"

"Yes, my love!" He was firm, holding her rough red hands. "Four more years, then we shall go east! It is what I have always wanted for us, for us—"

She bit her lips. He wondered if she worried still about his love for Rachel. Well, Rachel was out of his reach, and Charlotte was a good woman, a fine wife and mother.

"Do you think you can manage? Rachel did—and she too was a native of this rough land. Gideon says she does well, and only waits to help you. And Mother will be there—dear Mother—you know how she is, how she loves you."

"She is so good. But, Bart—I am not the kind—I am not—you will be ashamed of me—" she whispered.

"Never! Charlotte, listen to me. Even if society shirks you, do you think I would cease to love you? No, that does not matter. It is you, my wife, the mother of my children, who is important. You have never failed me a moment..."

She raised a glowing face to him. "You mean this," she breathed.

He had meant to reassure her firmly, but he found he meant it as well. "Yes, I do," he said.

Charlotte glowed for days afterward. She hostessed the miners' wives, serving them tea and biscuits in the afternoon, or visited their homes to explain the situation. "The Landaus are not retreating," she would say. "They're expanding. They are planning to build four more smelters—two in Mexico, two in Colorado—and they're only waiting to hire more men! You will see—"

But the miners were still bitter and resentful. The fact Bart was leaving only added kindling to the rumors. "We have heard talk from sources very close to you," one contingency complained to the Landau brothers in the mine office the following Tuesday. "They say you are lying, that you will turn over all your smelters to the Mexicans' ore. They say you are firing men from your own mines—"

"Only those who steal," Gideon replied, angrily. "We have fired nine men now—and we hope it will put an end to the stealing. But we do not fire from a design to tailor down the work force. If anything, we are searching for more men to hire."

The men seemed to calm down for a while. But soon the rumors were rife again. Who was sabotaging the Landaus?

Gideon was puzzled and pensive. "I wish Father would come," he said one afternoon. "I think he could get to the bottom of this—the rumors are growing, not ceasing."

"How could he, though?" Bart said fretfully. If the miners struck for better contracts, his father would reject them. They had already been given one of the best contracts in the region. "What can he say, what can he do, that we have not done?

294

You talked as if Father worked miracles!"

Gideon shrugged his broad shoulders. "I think it is a problem only he can solve this time. He comes in two weeks. We'll hold out—by our thumb nails—till then."

Charlotte's pretty face creased with worry when she noticed Bart's pensiveness. When he became aware, he tried to soothe her. They stayed awake talking into the night or stayed downstairs on the sofa after everyone else had gone to bed.

One night he got up wearily to blow out the table lamp. "I'll go and see if Emil's pony is as restless as he sounds. It was a lean winter for the wolves."

"Oh, don't go out alone, Bart!" Charlotte jumped up, her hands clasped together in anguish. She'd had an eerie feeling of late, something she couldn't express in words. "Wait until morning—or let me go with you if you must."

Bart waved his brown arm, his shirtsleeve rolled to his muscular elbow. "No, love. Be still. Go on upstairs. I'll be up as soon as I check out the back."

He caressed her cheek, then picked up his rifle and checked the loading chamber. It was full. They kept the guns out of reach of the children, but before long he would have to teach Emil how to shoot.

As Bart stepped outside, he heard a stir near the small back corral where they kept his stallion and Emil's high-strung pony. He went around to them, moving quietly. If there was a wolf, it was best to shoot it. They were pests—

A gunshot blasted out of the darkness, and fire seeped into his shoulder. It was his left shoulder. He dropped to the ground with a groan. God, who was it shooting at him—or had it been accidental?

There had been a brief sharp pain. Then it was gone, replaced by a numbness. He felt his shoulder, shocked that blood was flowing from it. He found it difficult to lift his rifle again, but despite the resistance his muscles were putting up, he managed to pull the rifle to him, and squinted into the dark. It must be Indians, surely. He had to move, get into the house, shoot—

But he could not put forth the thrust needed to rise to his feet. Suddenly, the sound of the house door clapping shut sliced through the night air. Had the Indians gotten inside? Oh, Charlotte was there—he had to get to Charlotte. But his head swam, and he heard another bullet from a rifle crack in the night.

A second bullet? He raised his head—and before he could

think, it began to throb. He'd been grazed.

The next thing he remembered was seeing Charlotte kneeling at his side. He saw her dimly, but heard her whisper clearly. "Bart, oh Bart—"

"Charlotte," he managed to say. "Get out of here."

She pressed her lips together. "Yes, give me the rifle first—" Before he could resist, she was taking it from his arms. She stood and fired into the pitch darkness. There was only silence at first, then the sounds of men retreating, their faint cries of distress broken by cracking twigs and underbrush.

Bart looked up at her, amazed. She'd chased the Indians off, singlehandedly. His timid Charlotte. "Help me—into the house—" he managed to say.

With little help from him, Charlotte grasped the rifle in one hand, and wrapped his arm around her shoulders with the other. In a half-drag, she got him back to the house, up the porch steps, and into the kitchen. He dropped to the floor, gasping, the blood from his shoulder spilling over his clothing. But even as he held his hand to the wound, Charlotte was racing around the house for a sheet from which to tear bandages. Just then, Mr. Loffler walked into the kitchen, looking disheveled and bewildered. He was wearing his cotton robe tied loosely over his pajamas, and with his hair in disarray, he looked like a mad scientist. When the scene before him registered, his eyes widened in shock. "My God, what has happened here?" he cried to his daughter, just then returning with a bedsheet.

"Some shooting father," she said hurriedly, not looking up as she began tearing the sheet into strips. She folded some of them into a thick pad. "Father please get me fresh water while I bandage Bart."

Mr. Loffler, glad to be of use, jumped toward the bucket and rushed out the screen door to the well.

"It's a clean wound, Bart," Charlotte spoke to him softly as she applied a thick pad to his shoulder and wound a strip over it to fix the pad in place. Bart already knew, but the conversation helped calm him. After finishing with the shoulder, Charlotte turned to his graze wound, wiping away the blood and cleansing it with the water her father brought in. Then she wrapped a bandage around his head. All the while Bart gritted his teeth against the pain, and balled his good hand into a fist. But he was beginning to come out of his stunned state, and asked Charlotte to loosen the bandage on his upper arm. It was too tight. She did, though the bleeding started again, this time less forcefully.

He felt so tired, so exhausted. He knew the blood, as well as the shock of the shooting, was draining his strength.

Charlotte whispered, "I'll make up a bed on the floor down here. It'll be easier than getting you upstairs."

He nodded and whispered, "Yes."

She went up for a mattress, dragged it down, then retrieved some more sheets and blankets for him. Even though it was June, the night air could be cold in the mountains. She set him near the fireplace in the living room, and he let her spread the blankets over him.

"Best get some rest," he muttered.

"I'll watch," she said steadily. "Papa, you get some rest now."

"It's best I stay," her father said worriedly.

"Not now. I'll stay up for a time, then you replace me in the morning—"

Bart's eyes closed even as they argued softly. Finally her father went upstairs, leaving Charlotte to her silent watch at the windows. She moved from one window to another, and Bart was vaguely aware of her vigil. If only he did not feel so sick and dizzy—but he could barely lift his head without feeling nauseous.

Toward dawn he awakened. Charlotte was silhouetted at the window. She was tense, and he heard some sound.

"What is it?" he asked.

"Hush," she said tautly.

He was silent, straining to hear. Both heard the rustle of a bush just outside their window. Charlotte bent as she watched from behind the curtains.

Then she fired. The window was open, and he realized she had opened it. The crack of the rifle echoed, then again—she had fired a second time.

They both heard a stifled cry, then sounds as someone crashed through the bushes and ran down the lane that led up to the house.

"What happened?" Bart cried. He felt so helpless, lying there, but he could not move.

"I shot a man," Charlotte said, her voice strained. "He was inching to the window. I saw him—his face. It was that man called Ferd—"

297

"Ferd—and probably Hank," Bart said. "Two bums. Damn them."

Charlotte was silent. She finally closed and locked the window as her father came down.

"I heard shots—" he said.

"I fired at two men—and hit one," Charlotte said.

"My poor girl!" her father cried, alarmed. He crossed over to her, and held her as she set the rifle down.

She did not cry. Bart cursed his own helplessness.

Mr. Loffler was gentle. "You go up to bed, I'll watch now. It is about four in the morning—"

"Yes—"

"Come here, Charlotte," Bart said. "There is room for two on this mattress."

He did not want her away upstairs. He wanted her there. She came over and dropped down beside him.

"How are your injuries, Bart?" she asked anxiously.

"All right. Come and rest." He tried to make his voice sound strong.

Her hand gently brushed over his face in the darkness. She must have felt the heat. "In the morning," she murmured, "I'll get the doctor right away. Oh, darling, I'm sorry. If only I could get him tonight—"

"Don't you think you have done enough, going outside to drag me in?" he tried to joke. "You stay quiet, my love."

She lay down beside him, and he felt his heart going out to her, his brave wife. She was naturally timid, but she had made herself go outside—

No, he thought as she lay quietly beside him. She had not forced herself to rescue him. It had been a completely natural act. She had just run outside when she knew he was hurt, when the rifle had cracked twice.

And she had found the strength to drag him inside all by herself. What a woman, what a wife!

As soon as it was full daylight, his father-in-law went for the doctor, then for his flesh and blood, Gideon and Simon. They came at once. Gideon was quietly enraged.

"If I had known this would be attempted," he muttered.

"Who could have known it?" Bart said, puzzled. "I mean, those two bums attacking me. They must have been drunk—"

Gideon shook his head and watched somberly as the doctor

298

cleaned the wounds, leaving instructions with Charlotte for Bart's care.

He and Simon dragged down one of the beds and set up the mattress and bedding on it. "But we'll stay and guard, for the rest of the time we are here," Gideon said firmly.

"Whatever for?" Bart burst out irritably. He hurt, he ached all over from the fever. "Get somebody to arrest those stinking bums and put them in jail."

"They have left town," the doctor said, shaking his head. "I understand one of them was wounded in the chest."

"Good riddance to him." Bart cried. "If they come back, I'll shoot them!"

"I don't want Bart downstairs," Charlotte said. "I want him upstairs and out of danger!"

"They cannot stay here all day and all night," Bart said crossly. "Let me alone, Charlotte. I'll guard today. Those stupid idiots have left town—"

Charlotte and Gideon exchanged looks.

Bart did not understand them. "What's up?" he snapped. "Why do you think there is any further danger?"

"There were more than two men out there," Charlotte said reluctantly. "Gideon found the tracks of four or five men. And two of them wore miner's boots."

Bart was silent, aghast. Did they mean some miners had conspired to kill him? That meant much more than a drunken attack for some fancied slight.

Chapter 24

Jared Landau arrived ten days later. Though the patriarch was sixty-nine years of age and stooped, his black eyes were as alert as ever. He had endured the long journey well, for the railroads now reached within two hundred miles of town.

He was furious when he found Bart lying weakened from gunshot wounds.

"Now, Papa, I'm getting along fine," Bart said. "Charlotte won't let me up yet," and he exchanged smiles with his wife.

Jared was glad to see good relations between them, and he observed how much more tender Bart appeared with Charlotte. She had certainly deserved it, she had always loved him deeply and silently.

He sat beside Bart's bed and talked with him about the mines, the impending strike, the miners' hostility, the shooting. Jared's suspicions grew as Bart told him everything that had transpired.

"And Charlotte reassures the wives—and you told them of our plans—and still they grumble?" Jared asked. His still black eyebrows lifted in surprise.

"Yes, Papa. Gideon has promised that you will settle things when you come. What do you plan to say to them?"

"I'll get to the bottom of this," Jared promised, and he went to talk to Gideon.

"So you have the same suspicions that I do," Gideon said when they had talked.

"Yes. If Asher is at the fountainhead of this mischief, I shall have done with him! My dear son shot up, lying wounded. He could have been killed! And more men are prowling around at night, so Charlotte says. Five of them! And she had to shoot one! She turns green when she speaks of it! What a thing for a good woman to be forced to do!"

"A good woman, and a strong one—" Gideon said.

"Ah, Bart is a fortunate man, so I told him! And he agrees with me."

Gideon Landau nodded. His son Simon was listening avidly, ears and eyes opened to all that was passing. Jared gave him a grim smile. "You know how to keep your mouth shut, boy? Do so. If Bart learns that Asher is behind the attack on him, he will go wild and kill my brother! I shall not have a bloodletting in the family, not if I can help it. We keep this to ourselves. But first I must speak with my brother. It may be I wrong him."

"He was always full of mischief," Gideon muttered to himself.

"I will not speak, Grandfather," Simon said softly.

Jared rode around the areas of all the mines on horseback and muleback for several days, asking questions; then he accepted an invitation from Asher and Eden Landau for dinner.

They dined well, but he could not force himself to be cordial and happy. Asher was uneasy with him.

"So—" He set down his coffee cup and went with them into the parlor—Vashti's parlor, how many memories it held. But how Eden had changed it—purple drapes, red cushions, Tiffany lamps, and china figurines that he kept knocking off with his elbow. Damn uncomfortable for a man to walk in.

"Sit, sit," Asher said, hospitably. "Will you have brandy, cognac, sherry?"

"No, thank you. But help yourself."

He watched in silence as Eden signaled no to her husband, and reluctantly Asher sat down without a glass in his hand. So—they were wary of him.

"You know Bart has been injured?"

"Yes, too bad!" Asher said nervously. "Some bums shot him, eh?"

"You have not gone to inquire?" asked Jared, though he knew better.

Furtive glances flitted between the couple. "Bart has not been much to see us of late," Eden said. "His wife turned him against us. Oh, the pity of it, such a shame."

"Good woman, she is," Jared murmured, mostly to himself. "So—you know of the shooting. Thank God my son was not killed."

"Killed! No, God forbid," Asher said hurriedly.

Jared narrowed his eyes. "Maybe they did not mean to kill."

"No, no, probably to make him realize they are serious. The miners are very unhappy, they say they have poor contracts," Asher said, leaning back. "I keep mine happy with good pay, good contracts. And they know we will stay!"

"So will we," Jared said. "We bought two more claims last week, one silver, one gold. Loffler is to build a new smelter for us in Denver."

He leaned back to watch their reaction. "But you are not wise to remain!" Asher cried. "The miners do not like the Landau Company. They are suspicious of such a big outfit! Bart has not handled their grievances well, and Gideon is too cold for them!"

"Cold? Cold? What does coldness have to do with a miner's pay envelope? They trust him, it is enough." Jared said solemnly. "Gideon is my right hand. And my sons Bart and young David are as close to that as possible!"

He was quick to observe the twitch in Asher's face, now creased with age. Asher still bore the handsome Landau features, though they'd gone soft and puffy from his overindulgent life. Eden, who had aged more gracefully, was pouting.

"So, Asher, I will be honest. I think you are behind these rumors of our closing," Jared said, stretching now to his full, lean height, like a panther crouching for the kill.

The tension was palpable.

Eden finally answered for her stunned husband. "How can you say such a thing to your brother, Jared? Asher has always loved you!"

"Love?" For a moment Jared was thrown off the track. Then he regained his composure. "Asher, I've asked you straight—as one brother to another. Did you start those rumors?"

Asher squirmed in his seat while Eden tried to cover for him. But Jared knew her words were evasions, and he pressed

302

on remorselessly, until he'd tripped them up on their own words. Yes, they grudgingly admitted, they were behind the rumors, because they had believed them. Asher swore that when he saw the piles of Mexican ore he could not believe Jared would keep the mines open much longer.

"God help you when Bartholomew finds out you were behind the attack on him—" Jared said.

But his brother tried to protest. "I swear, those men were just supposed to frighten Bart, and no more—"

"And possibly spur on the momentum to chase the Landaus out of town," Jared said.

Asher hung his head in silence. Eden was silent, looking desperately from one man to the other as if she wanted to say something, but managed to refrain from doing so, as if knowing it would be better to restrain herself.

Jared broke the heavy silence. "My son will go crazy when he hears. He has a quick, volatile temper. I can't promise to restrain him. You will have to sell out, my brother Asher, and go back east."

"How can you say that?" Asher cried, though he already looked defeated. "You have no right to tell us to leave!"

"You want my son to kill you?"

"You cannot make us leave!" Eden wailed. She looked ugly when angry. How could Jared have ever thought she was as beautiful as Vashti? Vashti had been good and generous, she'd never stooped to vile behavior.

"It is my last word. I will arrange to buy your poor mines. They are almost exhausted anyway." Jared said, as somber as they.

Asher's cunning eyes flashed. "Poor mines? How can you suggest such a thing?" He exchanged looks with Eden. "You will have to pay high if you buy them, Jared. Maybe I will exchange them for your two new claims—"

"Why should I? I have looked at your mines and they're nearly clean out. You have only four mines left to work. Best to sell now, Asher. The money I give you will help finance your journey and your life in Philadelphia or New York—or wherever you choose to live."

"You will give us some business to carry on," Asher prompted desperately. "How can we live on so little?"

They bargained into the night. Jared knew his brother didn't want to face a dissatisfied Eden. But when no deal had been struck by two o'clock in the morning, Jared left them. He knew they would eventually relent.

Bart got out of his bed, walked for a short time, then began to work again, impatiently. It was too soon, Charlotte protested, but Bart said he felt better in the open air.

He accompanied Gideon to one of the new silver mines to examine their operations. Two men had begun shoring up the mine entrance with timber. Simon had trailed along with his father and uncle, absorbing the practical information exchanged as they examined the site.

When they left, Gideon was carrying his rifle loosely in his left hand, casting a critical look about the landscape, wary as always. He was the first to spot the glint of sunlight on a rifle barrel.

"Down!" he shouted, and with a powerful hand he shoved Bart to the ground. Simon hit the dirt behind them. A bullet whined over Bart's head.

The three men wriggled over the dirt ground to the cover of some low bushes.

"Who is it?" Bart panted, sweating. His wounds hurt him, and he had scraped his forehead on the dirt.

"Don't know yet. Probably those bums," Gideon responded shortly. His dark eyes glinted. "They've been hanging around. Someone saw Ferd two days ago."

Bart scowled. He had heard sounds in the night, but he had not wanted to awaken Charlotte. She worked so hard, she slept out of exhaustion. But he had heard the sound of men creeping around the house, and twice he had risen to gaze down at forms moving around the small corral.

"I wish they would clear out. I'll kill them if they don't," he muttered. If they harmed Charlotte or his sons, he would kill them! And what did they want? He knew two of them were miners who'd been fired for stealing silver. Surely they did not imagine he would hire them back!

Gideon was silent. His narrowed eyes searched the brush and thick grove of trees beyond the mine entrance. The hot midday sun beat down on them from overhead. It was a Sunday afternoon; the mines were silent, so was the town below. They were perched high on a hillside about ten miles outside Copper Creek.

Simon checked the load of his rifle and settled down again.

Bart frowned at him, but the lad seemed as cool as his father. The same breed, he thought proudly. The Landaus had never cringed from danger.

Gideon lifted his rifle, aimed, and fired. In the brush, a man cried out, then he sagged down over a bush in their sight, arms flung out. The rifle fell from his hands.

Gideon checked his load again.

Bart watched alertly. He had sensed a movement out of the corner of his eye to the left. He stared in that direction until he felt his eyeballs burning with the strain. Then he saw it again, just a slight waving of a branch, and he fired.

A man fell out of the underbrush, sprawling. Bart caught a glimpse of an unshaven face, black hat—

He fired again as the other rifle went off. The man sagged. It was Ferd, whom Charlotte had shot. Bart could see the dirty bandage across his bare chest as the shirttails flapped in a slight wind.

"We're goin', we're goin'!" a man cried, and he crashed through the underbrush away from them.

"Never come back!" Gideon yelled after them. "You'll be killed for sure!"

They waited until the sounds receded. After a time, they got up cautiously and strode over to the bodies. Both men were dead.

"This one is Ferd and this one is Hank—don't know their last names," Bart said, swallowing his nausea at seeing the blood spilling from Ferd. "They are just bums; they never worked in the mines."

Gideon poked around the bushes and squatted to examine some marks on the ground. Simon imitated his father, watched, and listened.

"Miners' boots," Gideon said. "Two of them. The other one had run-down high heels, probably some drifter. Well, if they come about, they'll join their friends," and his head jerked to indicate the two bodies.

They went back to Bart. Bart was feeling dizzy now; his forehead burned, and blood trickled down into his eyes.

"Can you ride, Bart?" his brother asked gently.

Bart nodded. They got him on his horse. He gritted his teeth, but hung on. "I'll ride beside you," Gideon said anxiously. "Simon, you ride ahead and watch for signs. If you see anything at all, find cover as soon as possible and signal us!"

"Right, Dad," the tall, lanky youth said. Bart thought he looked a lot like Gideon, the same hard jaw, dark cold eyes, alert and shrewd.

They rode slowly back to Copper Creek. To Bart, it felt as though the journey took all day. He swayed dizzily in the saddle, jolted with pain at every step of the mule's. Finally Gideon put his muscular arm about Bart's frame and held him, forcing the mules to walk side by side. In a daze, Bart felt grateful toward his tough, dependable brother. Gideon would never let him down. Gideon was the kind you rode with in a tough situation.

At the house, Gideon slid down first, then helped Bart slide from the saddle. Charlotte flung open the door and flew out to Bart.

"Hey, sweetheart. I'm okay, just a little dizzy," he said.

She looked pale. "What happened?" she demanded. Jared followed her from the house, and Loffler had come after him.

"Those bums again," Gideon said briefly. "We killed two of them. I'll send the sheriff up with a couple of men to help bury them."

"Damnit to hell," Jared cried furiously. "I thought that was all settled!"

They helped Bart into the house. Simon went for the doctor. When he came, he said Bart had reopened some of the wounds. He would have to lie quiet for a few days.

"Charlotte, don't fret," Bart chided gently when the doctor had left. "It's just an excuse for me to lie quiet and let you wait on me!" And he pulled her down to give her a swift kiss.

It did Jared's heart good to see them together. Charlotte did not care if they lived in a rough cabin, if her hands were rough and reddened from long hours of housework.

And Bart—he had come to appreciate his wife, to love her. About time, Jared thought. Those two fine boys she had given him! And all the years of uncomplaining labor. Such a smart woman. Yes, Bart was a fortunate man.

Charlotte took some soup to Bart, and they murmured for a time upstairs. When she came down, she had an empty cup and plate.

"He sleeps now. I think he's resting well," she said, frowning. She sat down with them. They had coffee and fresh biscuits hot from the oven, and slices of hot apple pie.

After supper, Jared looked serious. "I think I'll go talk to

Asher. I have a little business with him."

Charlotte nodded and took the dishes to the kitchen. Gideon gazed at his father, a question in his dark eyes. "Want me to come with you?" he asked.

"No, no, you don't get along with Asher, and this I must handle alone," Jared sighed.

"Not alone," Simon spoke up unexpectedly. "Those scoundrels might be around. I'll come with you, I shoot well."

Jared nodded. "You come, my grandson. We can talk together, eh?" And he patted the lanky boyish arm. Simon had stuck a loaded revolver in his belt.

It was just dusk when they walked over to Asher and Eden's house. The pair were on the porch.

"Come in, come in, brother!" Asher greeted jovially. "And there is Simon, such a tall fine boy!"

"We have dinner ready," Eden said. "You'll stay!"

"No, I've eaten already. I'll just sit a minute," Jared said heavily, and eased himself into a straight chair. Simon leaned near him against a porch post, the rifle crooked in his arm.

"You come as if you're looking for bear!" Asher's accent was strong, a sure sign he was agitated, though his face was wreathed with smiles.

"Yes," Jared said. "My two sons and my fine grandson shot at this afternoon, what a shame!"

"No!" Asher cried. "That can't be! No. Those bums went away, didn't they?"

"Now they've gone away," Jared said. "Two shot dead, the others scared off."

A silence yawned between them.

"Two shot dead?" Eden asked, twisting her hands in agitation.

"Ya. I think you best take my offer and go east," Jared said. "It's my last offer."

"But I have to live," Asher said, plaintively. "You buy me a business, Jared. Some nice store in Philadelphia, yes?"

"No, you buy your own," Jared said. "I'm offering sixty thousand for the mines, ten thousand five hundred for the house and store. You go east and buy your own store. If it's still not enough, maybe you should sell the diamonds. She's got plenty, plenty," he added, nodding to Eden.

They fussed more. But when Eden got hysterical, Jared rose to leave. Asher hastily accepted his offer.

307

"All right, but go quickly," Jared instructed. "You can hire wagons to take what you want from the house. But be on the train in three days." At the bottom of the porch steps, Jared turned. "And don't mess around any more with my family, Asher. My patience has worn thin. You are no more my brother after today."

He left with Simon. On the way back, the boy looked puzzled. "They hired those bums, Grandpa?"

"Yes," Jared said briefly. "Bart is not to know, nor Charlotte. He has a quick temper, and I don't want any more hurt than is necessary."

Simon, in the darkness, grunted. "Grandpa, you are the greatest man I know besides my father!"

Jared was deeply touched. Respect. That was a good feeling granted by a grandson to a grandfather. He said gruffly, "You are a fine lad. You grow up well. Learn, son, never forget you owe your parents much respect. They trained you well. Be straight and honest and smart, and always keep important matters in the family."

"Yes, I will, Grandpa!" The boy had shortened his long strides to stay beside Jared's hobbling step. He clutched at the lad's offered arm and found comfort in its lean muscled hardness.

Simon listened with attention to what talk there was in the next weeks. Asher and Eden Landau left, and Jared turned over the house and its contents to Winona's second daughter and her new husband. They would run the store and take care of Winona in her old age. Vashti had liked the woman very much, had taught her English and been a friend to her. She deserved to inherit Vashti's house.

Jared fought with his anger at what Asher and Eden had done. They had lied, cheated, tried to kill his son. It was a stench in his nostrils.

But Bart was soon on his feet again; he was a tough man who loved the outdoors and hated confinement. Jared wondered if he would like New York; he had a hunch his rugged son would detest it. But Charlotte would keep their home going, and their boys would go to school. Bart would travel around the world enough to satisfy his craving for the outdoors and for adventure.

They had already begun to discuss their future plans, Loffler adding his ideas, Gideon his shrewdness and long-range vision.

Simon listened, absorbing all this eagerly. And Bart most of all was enthusiastic, his dark eyes shining all the time.

His sons, Emil and Ted, sat on the floor and listened to it all. Emil was drawing pictures of mines and horses and mountains. Ted played with a wooden horse and small cowboys that Simon had carved for him.

"Africa," Jared said. "The report from Africa cannot be read without catching our breaths. Such riches! Silver and gold, platinum, and even diamonds! Diamonds on the ground, for just scooping up. Why, the possibilities are limitless!"

"The railroads will need metals as they expand," Gideon interjected. "And if those new automobiles catch on for public use, they too will require our resources. Men invent more machines all the time. I predict within two more generations the amount of metals needed for all the machines men are inventing will be unimaginable. And that petroleum they are finding—what is the report we heard?"

"Much in Texas, some in Ohio," Jared responded. "But I like metals, not that oily stuff. We'll stick to metals."

It was an order, gently given. His sons nodded.

"Alaska," Jared said. "And Utah had copper, much copper. We'll go after that next."

Gideon and Bart began to discuss the possibilities eagerly. Simon sat down next to Jared on the couch.

"Grandpa, what do you think made you so successful?" he asked seriously. "One of my friends at school asked me to ask you."

Jared thought. He remembered the days in Switzerland, those incredible long-ago days when it had been enough just to stay alive and out of jail. Then they had come to America for freedom, and had seized all their opportunities.

But Jared knew there'd been costs.

The family had drifted apart: Malachi, an old man now, uselessly dreamed away his days in the grocery store, dreaming about the gold he had never discovered. Naomi had a house, with grown sons, satisfied in her placid existence. Enoch was a family man, neglecting his work for his wife and children, who were mercilessly spoiled. Isaac ran the family's store in Philadelphia. And Asher, that wicked mischievous man—where was his pride? He had caused the deepest rift in the family. What an evil man.

But Asher had been a mischief as a child, then a mischief

309

as a man. It showed he had never grown.

But Jared's own family! His three sons were nothing but joys to him: they were hard working, enterprising, ever more eager to shoulder their responsibilities in the Landau empire. And dear Rosemary, working with her mother in the fine charities they supported and encouraged. And Hannah, with her children, a fine sensible woman, so good, so respected. Hers was a happy lot, a good marriage of like minds.

"It is the family," Jared murmured to himself.

Simon perked up. Everyone else was engaged in heated conversation. "Family, Grandpa?"

"Yes, my boy," Jared said, smiling. "The secret of a man's success is his family—no matter what their personal disagreements, they should always stick together. Look at us. We are both a family *and* a company. If I had worked alone, what would I have been? A millionaire, yes, probably, but without sons helping me, planning with me, my line would have come to a quick, uncelebrated end."

He paused. Bart and Gideon and the others had ceased their talk to listen to him. He smiled at them affectionately.

"Yes, my family stuck together," he repeated. "And together we are stronger than any one alone. Together we are like a bundle of sticks which cannot be broken. Alone, each stick can be twisted and bent or snapped apart. But together we are stronger for it!"

Simon patted the lean arm next to his. "I'll have a family like that, Grandpa," he promised, his dark eyes shining. "Just like yours! We will build together, and nobody can tear us apart!"

Jared leaned back, a little tired. He was getting old, all this talk wore him out, and the excitement of it. When he got back home to New York, he would himself fall into Miriam's capable hands. He would let her persuade him not to go west again. The boys could take charge, and soon his grandsons. Yes, he would gradually turn over the day-to-day operations to Gideon and Bart, and to David in Mexico.

He was almost seventy; he and Miriam had made a long journey from those dark days in Switzerland. He had built an empire of metals, and he rejoiced in his achievements. Now he was ready to turn over that empire to his sons, and they would one day make it bigger and stronger and grander than the one he had ever dreamed of. And their sons would continue it, and theirs.

They had built something of splendor, and it would shine to all future generations, of what they too could reach out for, and claim as their own.